the book of
BLOOD
AND
ROSES

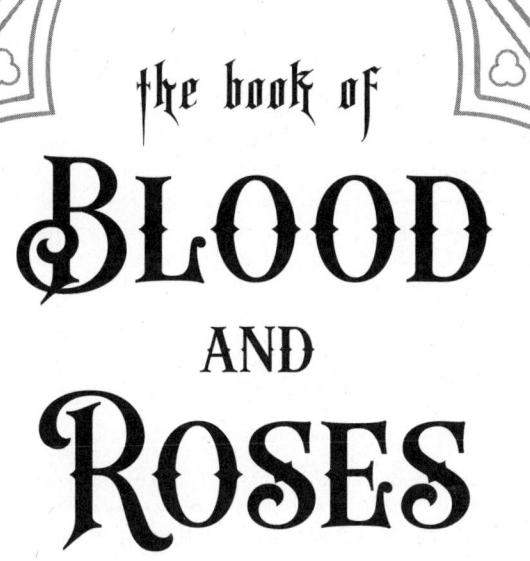

the book of
Blood
and
Roses

book one of the
Callisto Chronicles

Annie Summerlee

NEW YORK

Del Rey
An imprint of Random House
A division of Penguin Random House LLC
1745 Broadway, New York, NY 10019

Copyright © 2026 by Ana Gil Boyle

Penguin Random House values and supports copyright. Copyright fuels creativity, encourages diverse voices, promotes free speech, and creates a vibrant culture. Thank you for buying an authorized edition of this book and for complying with copyright laws by not reproducing, scanning, or distributing any part of it in any form without permission. You are supporting writers and allowing Penguin Random House to continue to publish books for every reader. Please note that no part of this book may be used or reproduced in any manner for the purpose of training artificial intelligence technologies or systems.

DEL REY and the CIRCLE colophon are registered trademarks of Penguin Random House LLC.

ISBN 979-8-89242-751-7

Printed in the United States of America

BOOK TEAM: Production editor: Robert Siek • Managing editor: Paul Gilbert • Production manager: Angela McNally • Copy editor: Madeline Hopkins • Proofreaders: Robin Slutzky, Susan Gutentag, and Karina Jha

Endsheet illustration by Adam Burke

Adobe Stock illustrations: mirskaya (title-page roses), paprika (chapter opening illustration), Gizele (space break ornament)

To Ade, for bringing vampires back

the book of
BLOOD
AND
ROSES

prologue

A bouquet of roses, lying upon a mahogany coffin, hides the stench of death. Tall, misshapen candles decorate every corner of the room. I stare at their flames, white and blue, while the vampire rummages through an old chest of drawers.

She turns to lock her crimson eyes with mine. "Don't move yet, darling," she says.

"I won't." My voice is listless. Entranced. Her red eyes give her the ability to twist a human's will however she pleases. When she first saw me at the party downstairs and caught my scent, she wasted no time in making me follow her, as though she was in a rush. As though she won't live forever.

Her room's décor is the opposite of the downstairs club's. Dame Danger is an industrial mess, all pipes and neon lights. But here the room has thick velvet curtains, a red Persian rug over a wooden floor. She doesn't hide her vanity: Framed portraits of herself fill every wall. Her striking features, chestnut hair, and thick red lips, unchanged through centuries, appear on each canvas. "Ah!" she says. "Finally." She draws out a dagger. A golden blade with a crystal hilt embedded with flowers. "Now we can begin."

I stare at the weapon, my heart pounding.

"Begin what?" I whisper.

My back is pressed against the wall. I stand exactly where she told me to—in the very same spot, I imagine, as all her past victims. She closes the distance between us and places the cold crystal in my hands, drawing my fingers tight around the hilt. Then she leans down, presses her nose into the crook of my neck, and inhales. "Delicious," she whispers.

My blood, Type-S, is extremely rare, only one in ten thousand humans are said to have it. And with its scent alone, it can make a satiated vampire thirsty again.

My fingers tremble around the dagger. I know what comes next. I know what happened to her previous victims. She leans back just enough for her red eyes to meet mine again, and they glow bright before she commands: "Slit your throat."

I lift the blade to my neck, and her pupils dilate. Her lips part. She has fangs, razor sharp, but she doesn't want to use them. Perhaps this is her MO: Instead of biting and sucking from small puncture wounds, as most vampires do, this one wants me to slit my own throat and provide her with a heavy flow of blood so she can gorge without tiring herself.

Police sirens fill the street below. They're too far away. No one will hear me if I scream.

Luckily enough, I don't need to.

"I'd rather not," I say.

She's frozen, bent to drink from the wound I've yet to open. She stares up at me, confused. "What?"

"But thanks for the dagger," I say, my trembling hands relaxing. I slice just beneath her chin and the blade hits bone. She clasps her neck, speechless as blood sprays from the gash. I kick her, and the same smile she used on me when she assumed I was easy prey appears on my lips now.

If she was a Heritage vampire, the kind of vampire who is born instead of made, her open neck might heal in a matter of minutes. But as a Convert, someone who used to be human, it'll take days.

At a first glance it can be hard to tell what kind of vampire you're facing, because they look identical except for the fact that all Heritage vampires stop aging when they turn thirty, while Converts are frozen at whatever age they were sired. Dame Danger here doesn't look a day over twenty.

"Callisto sends its regards," I say, before sliding out the weapon hidden in the bustier of my dress. A slit throat won't kill a vampire, but a stake most certainly will. I slam it through her chest, hearing ribs crack before it pierces her rotten heart.

Like all vampires, she leaves no corpse behind. Just smoke and dust.

I stretch my arms above my head. A low buzz fills my right ear after I tap on my silver earring. "You really expect me to believe *she* was dangerous?" I say.

"Just get out of there," Penny, my supervisor, replies.

I blow out the candles and pull open the velvet curtains. A full moon hangs above London's jagged skyline. The window opens with a creak as the old Victorian building protests at my strength. Wind blows my short black hair, and I jump out. "Seriously, these missions are getting too easy," I say. I know I shouldn't complain. But hopefully Penny will get the hint. Understand that I'm ready.

Ready for her to tell me the truth.

A black car comes to a halt beside me. Penny rolls down the window. Her red hair is in a tight bun, a grey scarf wrapped around her neck. "Hurry up," she says. I climb in beside her, twirling my new dagger between my fingers. "And I told you not to take anything from the crime scene."

I roll my eyes. "It was a *gift*," I say, slouching back onto the leather seat. "It would be pretty heartless of me to throw it away after killing her, don't you think?"

Penny doesn't deign to respond.

PENNY'S BASE IS in an abandoned convent an hour west of the city, halfway up a hill and hidden by a forest. From the outside, there appears to be nothing here but ruins: stones with dried-up weeds hiding what centuries ago was a holy site. She parks in the driveway and waits for the base's security system to recognise her car. A single lamppost flickers on through the fog, signalling it's safe to get out.

We make our way across the cloister, a well at its centre, half hidden by a coat of ivy. Most of the convent got blown to rubble during the Second World War, though it had been lying empty for centuries at that point. Luckily, the refectory, as well as three narrow bedrooms, survived the blast. Callisto uses it as a satellite base, big enough for five hunters, at most, but it's just the two of us out here.

"Did the rescue team save anyone from the party?" I ask. I work alone, and my job is to kill, not save. But Penny has promised me there is always a rescue team from Callisto to get the human survivors out of each blood party I dismantle.

"That's none of your business, Rebecca," Penny says, putting down her pen. She can't have a meeting with me without writing my every word down in a leather-bound notebook.

"You don't have to give me an exact number," I add.

Her cold eyes pause on mine. "We've talked about this."

We have. I breathe out between my teeth. There are so many things I need to know but Penny never tells me. How many humans survived the blood party. How the surviving humans can go back to their ordinary lives after crossing paths with creatures that shouldn't exist.

Who killed my parents.

I still remember sitting in this very office, four years ago, when she made her promise. *Work for us, and I'll tell you who did it.*

But not yet. Only when I'm ready.

"When's my next mission?" I ask, tapping on the chair. Penny tugs at her scarf, loosening it slightly, though not enough to reveal the bare skin of her neck. I know she's been hunting since she was sixteen, shortly after she and her sister were kidnapped for a blood party. Penny made it out alive. Her sister did not. I've never seen her without her scarf, but I can imagine that if I ever see her neck, it will be riddled with bite marks.

She shuts her notebook and pulls out a folder. I have never seen Penny smile, except on the day I agreed to join Callisto. Tonight, her expression is more guarded than usual. Instead of replying, Penny flicks through the folder until she lifts out a photograph. She hands it to me, and I study the image. "Cassie Smith," Penny says. "Heiress to an Edinburgh-based textile-distribution company."

I stare at the girl. Large, gold-framed glasses and long red hair, the colour of blood. There's something eerily familiar about her, and it's only when I focus on her eyes that it hits me. "She looks like me, doesn't she?"

"She *is* you," Penny says, leaning back. "Cassie is your new identity."

I gawk at her, then back down at the picture, which I only now realise must have been photoshopped. "Identity for what?"

"You didn't go to university, did you, Rebecca?"

"Bit busy hunting vampires," I say.

"Well, congratulations," she says, taking a black envelope out of the folder and pushing it across the mahogany desk. "Cassie Smith just got accepted into Tynahine University."

I tighten my grip on the chair, not looking at the envelope, focusing only on Penny. *Tynahine.* My heart skips a beat. "Who am I going to kill?" I ask. I've never been allowed anywhere near the kind of vampires that go to Tynahine.

"No one," she says. "There are only treaties-abiding vampires at Tynahine. You know that."

"The *treaties* don't mean shit," I hiss, ignoring the fact that she said I'm not killing anyone. Killing is the only thing I'm good at. Before I can ask *why* I'm going there, Penny rises and walks to the bookcase by the door, a silver sword hanging above it. The weapon belonged to Catherine Lovelace, founder of Callisto. The greatest vampire hunter to have ever lived.

She runs her fingers down a leather-bound spine, and then turns to face me. "You're going to find a book," she says.

"A *book?*"

"*The Book of Blood and Roses,*" she says, leaning against her collection. "An ancient compendium of every vampiric weakness we haven't discovered." There's a gleam in her eyes now. Still, she doesn't smile. "This book is the key to finally rid the earth of all leeches."

"But how did a *human* get into a *vampire* university?" I glance at the black envelope. For some reason I'm scared to open it.

"For the first time in Tynahine's history, they're accepting human students."

A chill runs up my spine. "What?"

"The Council's new initiative," she says, walking back to her desk. A medieval tapestry, depicting Michael slaying a serpent, hangs behind her chair. "To encourage integration with humans who are already *in the know*."

"Bullshit."

"There's no one better suited for the job than you," she adds.

"I don't want to go back to Scotland," I say. I know these words show my weakness. But it's true. I haven't gone back since my parents died.

I still remember being eighteen, standing on the damp and grey platform of Glasgow Central. My hands trembling on my dad's old suitcase. The sky was heavy, rain pattering on the grimy roof of the station. That was my last day in Scotland, and I can't imagine going back now.

"If you find the book, I will make sure you get promoted."

I gawk at her, not quite believing what I just heard. I missed my chance last year and have been stuck in Callisto's lowest rank, Cross, for four years. "To Hymn?"

"To Stake," she says. That's Penny's rank. While I try to process this, she adds: "And I'll tell you everything."

My breath catches. "You'll tell me who killed my parents?"

"Everything," she promises.

I take a shallow breath. For a moment the room disappears, and I'm back to the eighteen-year-old who'd just lost her parents to vampires. Back to the girl I was before Penny took my grief and twisted it into a stake.

"I'll find your book," I say.

chapter ONE

The girl in Penny's photograph comes to life in the mirror. I run my fingers through the red extensions that fall to my waist. My mother was a hairdresser, so I wonder what she'd say if she saw me like this. She would have been excited to see me finally skirting away from black—and no bangs, too. I hate it already.

The metal door rattles as the train takes a bend, and I steady myself on the sink.

My new glasses dig into my nose. Cassie Smith. Rich girl, spoiled rotten. I've practised saying her name a hundred times already until I nearly believe it's my own, because if there's one strength a vampire has that I'm not immune to, it's the ability to tell when someone is lying.

At least I'm not going *home*. The train is going nowhere near Wishaw, where my remaining family live. They believe I'm now living in the States. Occasionally, I get messages from them, asking when I'm coming over to visit. Sometimes they'll even remember my birthday.

But there is no *home* when vampires tear through your world.

I walk back through the first-class cabin. The seats have plenty of legroom, and my table is set with coffee in a porcelain cup and a buttered scone. I settle in my seat and wipe my glasses with the sleeve of my cashmere jumper. The landscape takes on a once-familiar shape, dark hills with low clouds, bog fields, and sheep. My heart pounds as fast as it did during my earliest missions. I never thought I'd come back.

The dreary streets of Inverness are damp. Seagulls perch on every roof. When I step outside the small station, a black car waits in the drop-off car park. A golden statuette of a crow with wings outstretched ornaments the hood. The tinted windows are framed in the same gold. Penny promised someone was going to pick me up, but she warned me in advance that it wouldn't be a fellow vampire hunter.

I catch my breath. As soon as I set foot in that car, I will be someone else: Cassie Smith, who does not mind the company of vampires.

"Miss Smith?" The driver gets out, offering me a curt wave. He's in a simple cream suit, with a white turtleneck beneath a linen blazer. A human, with mortality colouring his features, and a body that won't turn to dust when its heart stops beating. He's young, probably just a few years older than I am.

"Cassie's fine," I reply, hoisting my suitcase into the open boot, not waiting for him to help. "Does Tynahine pick up all of its students?"

He chuckles, though the sound isn't entirely natural. He disappears into the front of the car, and I join him, fastening my seatbelt. "Most of our students fly here. We do have a small landing strip, should you wish to bring your private jet next time."

I study his neck for bite marks. "I'll keep that in mind," I say.

"You will have to adjust your sleeping schedule starting tomorrow," he says, eyes on the road. We leave the Highland capital behind, picking up speed on the motorway, heading south.

"Do you know what kind of place Tynahine is?" I ask. The murky waters of the loch appear to our right, and vanish just as tall trees envelop the road, moss-ridden trunks heavy with brown leaves.

"My master is a professor there," he says. "So, yes, I know quite a lot about Tynahine."

My skin crawls at the admission.

"You're a Familiar?" I try to sound curious and not disturbed. "What made you choose that line of work?"

"I want to control my own destiny," says the servant. My lips twitch, and I focus my attention outside. "I take it that you don't wish to become immortal?"

I'd rather die, I think.

"Immortality is not my cup of tea," I say, trying to keep my voice light. "Plus, I'm not sure if I'd be able to live without seeing the sun." It's the most inoffensive answer I can muster, and given the Familiar's short sigh, he seems to have bought it.

The woods become dense, and the tar road turns into a dirt track.

"You'll have a fairly quiet day today," he says, breaking the silence. "Just a welcome lecture with the Deans of Day and Night. After that, your time is yours."

"You said I'll have to adjust my sleep schedule," I say.

"It would be a good idea. Your Integration lessons take place during sunlight, with human professors. That's where you'll learn everything you need to know to live in Vampiredom. All your other classes"—he steals a glance at me—"will be at night, with vampires."

I shudder. The road darkens as the trees form an archway, blocking out all but a few sparse rays of sun. "We've had the odd human student before," he says. "So don't worry, your presence won't be too shocking."

"Why the sudden interest in admitting humans?" I ask. *Other than having walking blood bags at hand, of course.* "I mean, I'm glad that you are. But I'm curious."

"At Tynahine we believe knowledge should not be kept behind locked doors," he says. The words sound rehearsed. With yearly tuition being higher than what my parents ever had in their bank accounts, vampires certainly have a narrow concept of which humans are worthy of their *knowledge.*

The dirt road becomes smooth again, and I rest my head on the glass. A redbrick road climbs up to a towering gate of wrought iron, a tall fence at either side covered with ivy.

It'll be a quick mission, I tell myself. Steal a book and get back out. Tynahine officially has eight libraries, but according to Penny there is a ninth, hidden one. Somewhere deep in the passageways beneath campus, a secret collection of books, banned for centuries, collecting dust. And amongst them, *The Book of Blood and Roses.*

I catch a glimpse of four words that decorate the gate. *We Invite You In.* They open with a groan, shovelling fallen leaves out of the way.

They have no idea who they're inviting in.

STONE HOUSES START to appear through the trees. I spot a grey bridge in the distance, running over what I'm assuming is Tynahine's river. "That's the Raven River," the Familiar says. "But Tynahine was founded long before the river had a name. They used to call this place *an taigh ri taobh na h-aibhne*. 'The house by the river.' They then shortened that to *Taigh na h-Aibhne,* before it was anglicized to the name we have today."

"Why would they call it 'the house'?" I ask as the buildings start to double in size. By the size of their bricks and the darkness of the groves between them, I can tell they're all centuries old. Some have great twisted columns, others are blanketed entirely in ivy, leaves crisping in a gradient from salmon to dark purple.

"The original scholars were probably referring to the old hunting lodge across the river." He slows the car as the cobbled streets between each building begin to narrow. I spot a wide square with a fountain in the middle, fringed by a willow grove, its branches almost bare. He doesn't point me to the hunting lodge. Instead, he hands me a paper map and a rusty old key. "You're in room 904, Tynarrich Hall."

I get out of the car, crisp air biting at my cheeks. Fallen leaves crunch beneath my new boots, and I hoist my case out of the back.

"Straight up that hill, through the pine grove," he adds.

The Familiar is gone before I can thank him.

THE DAMP AIR is so fresh it stings my nostrils. After four years in London, I know I should welcome the sweet scent, but I'm not here to clear my lungs of smog.

My acceptance letter, inside the black envelope that Penny gave me after my last mission, was filled with pictures of the campus, but none of them do it justice. Most of the buildings are clustered in the deepest point of the valley, except for Tynarrich. I spot the towering shape of my hall of residence in the far left, separated by a sloping pine grove, just as the Familiar promised. It's one of the oldest buildings, an austere fortress of sandstone and small windows.

I trek through the grove and stop just outside the wooden doors. A sign on the stone archway spells out *Taigh nan Nathraichean,* and below, in English, *Tynarrich Hall.* Inside, I find Tynarrich's reception hall still and quiet. Not a single vampire in sight. A fireplace burns next to a cluster of bookcases. I stare at the vaulted ceiling, chandeliers falling from each archway. The small windows all have shutters and heavy curtains, which do not let in a single ray of daylight.

The wheels of my case are caked with mud, dirtying an otherwise immaculate carpet. I stop in front of a spiralling staircase with a golden banister and look up at the walls, lined with portraits of old aristocrats. My room, 904, is on the ninth floor. I stare at the staircase, measuring it. *Definitely not.*

I turn back towards the cosy library and find a lift between two bookcases. I play with my suitcase handle as the lift climbs up the old building. How many leeches will I be sharing this hall with? I swallow hard and try to calm my breathing. The lift's floor is black, dark enough for vampire-corpse dust to blend in, if I were to accidentally kill someone in here. *Oh, I wish.*

The ninth floor has a low ceiling, painted dark green. Lanterns flank the walls with warm light. I turn two corners before I finally find it: 904. I draw out the old key the Familiar handed me, with a snake curling around the bow, and slot it through the equally old keyhole. The lock clicks, and I push it open.

I feel the wall for a light switch and flip it on, then rest my back against the door and breathe. I'm safe in here.

The room is old but cosy. There's a single bed, with an ornate frame and red velvet curtains with golden tassels. Just like downstairs, there's a chandelier with crystals and cobwebs. I cringe at the sight. There's something inherently *vampiric* about the décor, even though vampires don't sleep in beds. A wooden desk faces a shuttered window, with a narrow wardrobe at the side. The right wall is shrouded in black curtains. *Interesting choice,* I think.

I undo the buckles of my suitcase and take out my clothes—or rather *Cassie Smith's* clothes. Cassie wears corduroy skirts and flowy blouses, as opposed to my all-black uniform. Next, I pull out the books. *The History of the Modern Vampire* by Into Antilla and *An Introduction to the Treaties of 1912* by Andrea Ceretti. But beneath the ordinary possessions of a twenty-two-year-old postgraduate student is a black wooden panel. And under that false bottom, a sheet of translucent fabric called *zia,* which conceals silver from X-ray machines and metal detectors. I lift the zia, and my racing heart calms when I see them.

A folded bow and twenty silver-tipped arrows. Three wooden stakes. A gun and a dozen silver bullets. A white mask. Two crosses. A watch with a silver blade inside it. My name, Rebecca Charity, is etched into the stakes.

Just as I fasten the watch to my wrist, I spot a jar of supplements in the corner of the case—the supplements that I should have taken last night. The pills contain an extremely high concentration of allicin, the main compound in garlic. My heart skips a beat. *Shit.* If a single leech gets a whiff of my blood, it'll be over. I'll be an immediate target for every hungry monster lurking in the shadows.

I dry-swallow two, just to be on the safe side. It'll take an hour for them to come into effect, but I should be fine. Leeches sleep during the day, after all.

I spot a poster on the wall next to my desk, displaying a list of forbidden items.

At the very top is garlic. Funnily enough, stakes are not listed, but I'm assuming Tynahine isn't expecting to have a hunter in their midst. I glance down at the watch. My rank, Cross, is embedded in the leather. Usually the sight of it makes me grimace, but not anymore. I'll be leaving the lowest rank of Callisto behind as soon as I've completed this mission.

How exactly Penny will be able to get me into the highest echelons of our organisation, I have no idea. It usually takes a hunter a year or two to rise from Cross to Hymn. Hymn-ranked hunters are allowed to live in Callisto's headquarters, instead of the satellite base I live in, and are given more advanced training. Then they take another four or five years to reach Silver. Silver hunters have full access to Callisto's weaponry and the first three levels of the archives. The other four levels are available only to Stakes. Stakes are also allowed to form their own teams, choose their own missions. Take on subordinates, like Penny did with me.

My phone chimes before I can explore the rest of the room. The welcome lecture is in just ten minutes, and the humanities building is at the other end of campus. "Fuck's sake," I say, rummaging through my weapons. I settle on the stake, dropping it into my leather satchel. I zip up the case and shove it under the bed.

I rush down the pine grove, my feet aching in the brown leather boots Penny bought for me, knee-high with deep green laces. Every item in Cassie's wardrobe, from her buttons to her nightgowns, was chosen by Penny. And just like my regular black uniform, each garment has plenty of secret pockets for me to hide a weapon or two. The boots in question have sheaths hidden behind the laces, ideal for a pair of long daggers.

The humanities faculty building rises on the riverbank. Columns fringe the outside, cracks running up their sides. Vines and moss fill their gaps. The large arched windows are boarded up to protect the monsters lurking inside, and I allow myself a shallow breath before pulling the heavy wooden door open, which is as thick as a tree trunk. Inside, I find the same candle-lit glow that filled Tynarrich.

The Familiar had said the Deans of Day and Night would give this first lecture. One of them will be a vampire. I hesitate outside the entrance to the largest lecture hall and swallow hard. There's a chance that I will walk in here and find myself surrounded by leeches. And considering the garlic hasn't come into effect yet, I may have to kill my classmates sooner than I hoped. But the Familiar assured me that day classes were human-only.

I step inside, and my eyes widen. The domed ceiling is bloodred, and a replica of the solar system hangs from its centre, every planet gilded gold, orbiting around the sun. All the planets' moons are there as well. Amongst them is Callisto, which Catherine Lovelace chose as the name of our organisation. Why she picked a lesser-known hunter, instead of Artemis, I'm not sure.

I can't see any wires holding the spheres in place, and the university, sensing my questions, offers me an answer: A small plaque by the door describes the moving sculpture as an amalgamation of iron, gold, and a variety of magnets.

I hurry down the stairs to one of the curved benches, throwing my satchel on the space beside me, and my coat on the other side. Luckily enough, no one says anything to me, so in turn, I keep my mouth shut, slowly surveying my fellow students. Penny told me that two hundred humans had been accepted during this first round of admissions, though they're hoping to double that number in the next few years.

A human has one of two viable (legal) roles in Vampiredom. A Familiar or a Council ambassador. Both are essentially lapdogs for bloodsuckers. I can't tell, at first glance, what my classmates want to be. When Penny first introduced me to "Cassie," she told me that if anyone asks, I should say I want to work in the Council's ethics department. I'm not sure how a master's in Modern Vampire Studies is going to get me there.

I still remember getting my acceptance into Strathclyde, four years ago. I was going to be the first in my family to go to university. I was going to be a doctor. I'd tried for Glasgow and Edinburgh but didn't make the cut. Strathclyde was good enough for me, though. Mum and Dad took me out for dinner to celebrate.

A month later, they were both dead.

Two figures walk into the lecture hall from a bottom entrance. Only now do I look at what's down on the platform. A large emerald blackboard, with the words *Fàilte gu Oilthigh Taigh na h-Aibhne* written on it, takes up half of the space. Considering my knowledge of Gaelic starts and ends with *fàilte* and *slàinte,* I really hope the lecture is in English. But my thoughts snap back into focus when I notice the man dressed all in black. The Night Dean, I presume.

A vampire.

He's tall with coal-black hair slicked away from a pale and conventionally attractive face. His shoulders are broad, legs a little too long. An untrained eye might think he's in his late twenties, but there's something about his demeanor that makes me suspect he's a good deal older.

None of the humans around me seem too disturbed by his presence. The Day Dean, a woman roughly Penny's age, dressed in white, breaks through the murmurs that had filled the lecture hall.

"I think we can get started," she says, turning to the bloodsucker, who offers her a flourish of his ghostly, sun deprived hand. I can't stare at him. *Act normal.* "I am delighted to welcome you all to Tynahine University! Your arrival has been a passion project that our wonderful Night Dean, Faust Nocth, has been working on for—how long?"

"A hundred and five years, I think?" His rich voice has an accent. Continental, but I can't quite place it.

"We had to ensure the utmost safety for human and vampire students alike," the woman continues. "And I'm so glad to say that you have all been chosen as the first class, of hopefully many, who will prove that our species can live and, most important, *study* together."

Safety, she said. I think of the weapons beneath my bed. The stake in my bag. The blade in my watch. *I'm* safe, that's for sure.

"I would like to encourage you all to befriend Tynahine's vampire students. You will find that they are not too dissimilar from yourselves. Driven, just as you all are, by a quest for knowledge. They share your appreciation for the arts, music, even cinema! The only exception you'll find, of course, is food."

At this, a chuckle travels through the crowd. I force a smile, playing with my pen.

"Speaking of," the vampire Faust Nocth jumps in. "All our students abide by the Treaties of 1912. We drink synthetic blood." He brings out a bottle filled with a thick crimson liquid. My stomach turns at the sight. "We do ask, just as we have asked our immortal students, that you refrain from doing anything that may harm each other. There is a full list of vampire weaknesses in your rooms, but as a rule, try to avoid wearing crosses around campus or saying prayers in front of vampires. And I'm afraid that those of you who enjoy garlic will find it lacking in our kitchens."

If the students here really do drink synthetic blood, they won't have to worry about the chemical currently flowing through my veins. Faust Nocth rattles on about what other things should be avoided. I'll have to ask Penny what she knows about him later today.

The self-aggrandising speech finally comes to an end, and two seats from me, a student drops a thick notebook. He swears in French, and I reach down to pick it up for him. He's quite striking, with his large eyes, light brown skin, and a five o'clock shadow. His thick hair smells of ylang-ylang, and when he stares back at me, there's a moment's hesitation, as though he's measuring me.

"Thank you," he says, taking the notebook from me. I nod, and before I can get away, he says, "I'm Stephan."

"Cassie." I don't have time for friends. But glancing around, I notice the other students have started to flock into small groups. If I'm a lone wolf, I may draw more attention to myself.

"Is this your first time at Tynahine?" he asks, following me out of the bench row. I glance down at the deans, both deep in conversation. If they harbour any suspicions of a vampire hunter infiltrating their dear university, they haven't shown it. At least not yet.

"Isn't it everyone's?" I reply.

"I've come to visit a couple of times," he says. "My girlfriend is a student here."

My jaw tenses as I take in those words. "You have a"—I clear my throat—"a vampire girlfriend?"

His eyes narrow. I wonder if my disgust is obvious. "Do you have an issue with that?"

"No," I say quickly. "Of course not. I mean, if you love each other, that's all that matters, right?" I want to be sick. But this is the sort of nonsense Cassie Smith believes.

He grins, slapping my back. We leave the auditorium, and I glance at the other humans. The wide hall, with an arched ceiling, is incredibly noisy. This place might have looked like an ordinary university if it weren't for the shuttered windows blocking out the sun. "Ife, my girlfriend, is in the library," Stephan says. "Do you want to meet her?"

Over an hour has passed since I took my supplements. And even though I'd rather do anything but *meet* a leech, the scent of my blood must have dulled by now. "Sure," I say. "Which library?"

"Kinsnet," he says. We step out into the park surrounding the building, the grey sky threatening rain. I suppose the Night Dean uses the underground tunnels to move about.

"Isn't she up a bit early for a vampire?" I ask. The damp air slips under the collar of my coat.

"We compromise," he says. "Plus, vampires don't sleep as long as we do. Four hours is enough for them."

The other buildings must be crawling with leeches by now. We make our way through the cobbled roads of the campus village, past cafés and pubs, which only recently started selling something other than blood.

Stephan is twenty-one, a year younger than me, and studying physics. Until last year, he was at la Sorbonne, but as soon as Ife told him Tynahine was accepting human students, he jumped at the chance. "I still can't believe I got accepted," he says, stopping in front of a bike rental to check out the prices. "I've got the black envelope framed above my bed. I even considered getting it tattooed."

"Wow," I say, though I didn't mean to say it out loud. He doesn't take offense, laughing instead. He seems decent, which is a pity.

"Why are *you* here?" he asks. He stops again, this time to grab a takeaway coffee. To make the university's so-called Integration easier, half a dozen human establishments have opened in the campus village. He orders himself an espresso, and after I nod, he gets me one, too.

"My folks have worked with vampires for centuries," I say. "I've always been interested in their world. And it'll be interesting to hear what vampires have to say about history."

He downs his coffee in a single gulp and then proceeds to study the paper cup it came in, dark brown with the university emblem printed on it. A rose and a book, encased inside a blood drop, with three Gaelic words between them. *Lorg is Meòmhraich.* "There are entire fields of knowledge only vampires have access to," he says. "Scientists who have lived for centuries, who uncovered truths long before humans did, but their works have been kept in the dark. And artists, too," he continues, still analysing the cup. "There are masterpieces hanging on the walls of this university which would otherwise be in the busiest halls of the Louvre."

I try my hardest to feign interest, but I care little about Vampiredom's so-called masterpieces. I follow Stephan through the campus village until we come to the largest of the eight libraries. Kinsnet Library is a giant vaulted building, with a bell tower and statues by the thick wooden doors. He tells me, as we stare up at it, that it got its name from Harriet Kinsnettle, one of Tynahine's founders. The damp wind blows rain against my back, and I breathe, forcing myself to remain calm.

Stephan must have noticed my unease, because he squeezes my shoulders. "Whatever kind of vampires you're familiar with, Tynahine's students are much better," he says.

Stephan opens the library door, and I run my fingers over the leather strap of my watch. The moment I look up, my budding fear vanishes. Five floors of books fill the space, golden railings, spiralling staircases, and wooden ladders climbing up to the ceiling. The vaulted wall is blue, with a golden constellation painted over it, cherubs holding the stars. The main hall has a hundred tables, all of them full of students with their noses deep in books, and for a second, I forget that they're not human.

"Ah, there she is," he whispers, gazing across the wide hall. Warmth colours his cheeks. I follow his gaze and spot her. Her dreadlocks are gathered up in a pink hair wrap, a few framing her round face. She's wearing what looks like a hand-knitted jumper, pastel pink and green, over a denim skirt. When she comes to stop in front of us, her eyes don't turn crimson, which is a first. The garlic is most definitely working.

I touch my watch strap and force a smile. Stephan swings an arm around her shoulders, kisses her temple, and then turns back to me. "Cassie, meet Ife. Ife, meet Cassie."

"You certainly didn't waste time making friends," the vampire says, showing me her fangs as she smiles. Her voice is sweet, and she's painfully gorgeous. But the pretty ones are often the most dangerous.

Ife glances at Stephan's now-empty paper cup and stares at the university's emblem. "*Lorg is Meòmhraich,*" she says. "Seek and reflect. Quite funny considering vampires don't have reflections, don't you think?"

"Tynahine's founders must have had a sense of humor," I say, glancing up at the ceiling. Those two words are engraved into an arch. The students surrounding us are all glancing in my direction, though they mainly seem curious, instead of thirsty. "I think I'll do some exploring," I say, my cheeks hurting as I keep a smile in place. "I'll catch you both later?"

"Have dinner with us tomorrow," Ife says, before I can run off. "I promise I won't bite."

I can do this.

"Sure," I say. When I finally get away from them, I take the first staircase I find. They probably noticed my discomfort, or the quickening of my heart. I can't shake off my disgust. Stephan could have had any life he had chosen. Anyone who can afford to go to Tynahine can.

Instead, he's throwing it all away for a vampire.

I'm not sure where to start. The history section, on the fourth floor, is incredibly busy. I search for books on Tynahine's founders, hoping to find some kind of map of the tunnels beneath the campus, but I get distracted. Kinsnet has manuscripts that were supposedly burnt in the fire of Alexandria, their scrolls whole and intact. Even Sappho's poetry is here, tomes full of it, a fountain of lost literature.

I spend far too long staring at the spines, pulling out volume after volume, until I almost forget where I am. I lean over the banister at the very top of the five floors. Ife is not the only leech in the library. My muscles tense, my body remembering my natural form. Night has fallen.

I've been in large crowds of vampires before. A hundred or more, with my wrists bound, playing the victim. I always got out alive. Tynahine has a student body of two hundred newly admitted humans, and three thousand vampires. And all three thousand, according to Stephan, are *well behaved*.

"Don't—" a voice moans. My hands tense on the golden railing.

I stare back at the labyrinth of bookcases, trying to pinpoint the source of the voice.

"—bite me!"

My heart races. They wouldn't dare. Not in public. I pull at the toggle on my watch, touching the cold metal of the chain inside. I'm outnumbered. I knew that already. But I'm *always* outnumbered. And no vampire who's faced me has lived to tell the tale.

"Faster!" the same voice cries as I slip between two rows of bookcases. I hear a sound now, a scuffling of sorts, and something wet. My brows knit together before I realise what I'm hearing. "Fuck!" the airy voice moans. "Bite me, damn it!"

I tug at my watch, pulling out the silver chain and whipping it until it hardens into a blade. Vampires won't—*can't*—drink from someone without consent. But consent doesn't mean shit if they can compel their victims.

"My turn," the same voice says, just as I slip into a row behind them, silver blade at the ready. "Can I bite you?"

"No," a lower, breathless voice replies. "You'll stain my shirt."

Two vampires, I realise, staring at the books. *What the fuck.* I can only vaguely make out their shadows, pressed against the case, their breathing uneven.

"Plus, we've got company," that same low voice replies.

Shit.

My heart is beating far too fast. Only then do I realise that I'm standing too close to them, well within the five-metre radius in which a vampire can hear a human's heart. I need to get away from them, fast.

I make my way down the stairs, avoiding eye contact. No one got hurt. So it's fine. It could have been worse. I could have seen their faces. They could have seen mine. If I hadn't taken my garlic, the scent of my blood would have certainly left an impression.

I glance around the ground floor. Stephan and Ife are gone, but to my surprise, some of the students seated at the tables are human. A few even send me sympathetic smiles. As though they, too, have just eavesdropped on two leeches fucking.

And I don't know why I do it, but I look up.

My mind tells me I just want a last glance of the painted vault, the golden strings of stars carried by cherubs. But that's not where my gaze lands. I look at the banister on the fifth floor, and someone is standing at the exact spot where I had been.

She's dressed in black from head to toe, so her white hair, short and windswept, stands out even more. She's striking. Unlike any vampire I've ever seen, with warm skin and black eyes that somehow see right through me. And despite being this far away, I can see the smirk tugging on her bloodstained lips.

I walk back to Tynarrich Hall in a daze. That leech's face is engraved in my mind already, and I want to scrub it out. I want Penny to call me, but I can't show signs of weakness on my first night. That's not the kind of hunter she trained. I can't fail when promotion is almost within my grasp.

I already miss my narrow room back in our satellite base, a stone cell once inhabited by a nun, next to the refectory. But when I find my door, 904, my muscles start to relax. At least I'll be safe here. I hit the light switch, letting out a sigh that's instantly interrupted by what I see in front of me.

My room, which had an abundance of curtains, has doubled in size. The right wall, which when I last saw it was adorned with black drapes, is missing.

I remain still, air gone from my lungs.

It can't be, I think. But my eyes aren't tricking me.

On the right side of my room, opposite my bed, is a coffin.

chapter TWO

It's a beautiful coffin. Long, elegant, built upon a cabinet. A golden moon, surrounded by a ring of thorned vines, decorates the lid.

I squeeze my eyes shut, certain that it'll be gone when I open them again. But it remains there.

Where there's a coffin, there's a vampire.

I rush back outside. The number etched into the wood is 904. *Jesus Christ.*

I take a deep breath. I'll head to the registration office. Contact the human dean, if necessary. *There's been a mistake,* I'll say. I clench my hands to keep them from shaking, and step further in. If I'd explored the room in its entirety before the welcome lecture, I would have seen it.

I don't blink as I stare at the coffin. After a moment's hesitation, I tug at my watch strap, pulling out the silver chain. I can kill the leech now. But it's dark outside. Meaning my *roommate* is probably up already, and on its way to class.

I slide the chain back into my watch and explore the bathroom. It has a large old-fashioned tub and a walk-in shower. All the appliances look old but are impeccably clean. There are two sinks, one with a mirror, the other with a screen and a camera. I press a button, and the screen comes to life. The creature's sink has a toothbrush balanced on top of a blue bottle of mouthwash. I can always drop one of my supplements into the liquid. A quick and easy kill.

I take off my glasses and splash my face with water. The cold helps. As much as I don't want it to be true, my roommate is a vampire.

I BARELY GET any sleep during my first night at Tynahine. I try to keep my eyes open, waiting for the leech to arrive, but soon, the usual nightmares start to invade me.

I've had this dream before: I'm at my parents' funeral, but instead of the closed-casket service my aunt organised in real life, in my dream their coffins are wide open, revealing their mangled bodies. My extended family don't show any horror at the sight. Instead, they ask me when the reception is starting, and if blood will be available.

Someone, a cousin, asks me what happened to my parents, and I try my best to explain, all while my cousin sharpens their fangs, not too interested in what I say. Instead, they point at the coffins, where my parents have started to stir, their skin knitting back together as fangs stretch out between their lips.

"It's your turn, Rebecca," my father says, before the nightmare ends.

Even when I wake, the images are stuck in my mind. My parents weren't attacked by *ordinary* vampires. They weren't compelled to offer their veins, nor were they taken to a blood party. Instead, they were killed by *parched* vampires. A vampire becomes parched if they spend seven days without drinking blood. They transform into monsters stripped of all human features, with bloated bodies, elongated limbs, and razor-sharp teeth.

And even though the monsters that killed my parents were completely feral, their death wasn't a random accident. Someone had calculated it: My parents had won a trip down to London, to dine in a nice restaurant and stay in a fancy hotel. At three A.M., their corpses were found in a car without a license plate, drained of blood and torn to shreds.

I went down to London to identify the bodies. It was my first time in the city, my first time out of Scotland. And in the mortuary, instead of a police officer, I found Penny. She was the one who lifted the sheet covering their faces. She told me what kind of monster did it. Then, after the funeral in Saint Ignatius, she offered me a train ticket and a chance at revenge, and I seized it as if it was my last breath.

I should sleep, I think, turning. If I don't, I'll be far too tired come tomorrow. I pull the sheets up to my neck, closing my eyes, just before a soft beeping sound comes from the front door. Instinctively, I reach for the stake hidden under my pillow. The warm wood slows my racing heart, and I remain still as the front door clicks open.

They're finally here.

The footsteps that follow are quiet, careful, as though my roommate doesn't want to wake me. My throat tightens. Maybe they've got a syringe with them, and will steal some of my blood that way, thinking I won't notice. I'll let them. The garlic in my blood won't kill them quite as fast as a stake to the heart will, but that kind of death will be far more painful.

I breathe as quietly as I can, waiting for them to open the canopy. Instead, their steps turn to our shared bathroom. Seconds later, I hear the shower. My heart is racing, and they can probably hear it, can't they? I hold the stake so tight my palm aches. I know I can't kill them, but the weapon still calms my nerves.

Minutes pass and the shower stops. I hear the rustling of clothes, and I sit, waiting. I glance at my watch.

Just when I was wondering if three A.M. is a bit early for a vampire to go to bed, I hear the front door open once again, then slam shut. My breath slips through the gap between my front teeth, and I lift the curtains. The room is empty. The vampire's side of the room is exactly as it was before I went to bed. Messy but deserted. The only difference is the bathroom, steam-filled, with a damp towel hanging from the heated towel rack.

I go back to bed, every muscle in my body tense. Adrenaline still rushes through my veins and, beneath that, the frustration of an unfinished mission, an enemy escaping unscathed.

Unsurprisingly, the next morning I am exhausted. The black curtains that separate the room are shut, just as they were when I arrived. Red hair dye runs down the drain as I shower, and when I get back out, I realise the vampire's toothbrush has moved. Yesterday it was at a ninety-degree angle over the mouthwash. Now it's at an eighty-degree angle. They must have come in here again after I fell asleep. Their towel is gone, the floor is clean, and there are no traces of blood.

I open the curtains that separate our room. On the right wall is a false window with a picture of the Highlands drenched in sunlight. Above it is a shelf full of books, thick tomes on different painters, some I've heard of, like Frida Kahlo, Gentileschi, and Van Gogh, followed by a dozen more with names that, based on the books' opulent bindings, I imagine are vampire artists.

Just as I pick up one of these books, I picture the leech doing what I'm doing now. What if it has already rummaged through all my things? Before my thoughts spiral, I tug the curtains shut.

I really can't do this.

I can't stay here. Now that I've calmed down, now that I'm thinking clearly, I know there's no way I can share a room with a vampire. I won't be able to sleep, I won't be able to focus. I skim over the campus map, looking for the registration office. Surely, if I ask for a new room, they'll say yes?

Regardless of what I think is the best course of action, I have to tell Penny first. I leave the room and head to the end of the hallway, where there's a small common area. A bunch of bookcases and three green velvet armchairs. I stand next to a small and blacked-out window, from where I have a perfect view of the hallway.

I dial her number, and she picks up after a minute. Even before she speaks, I can sense her bad mood. "I told you *I* would contact *you*," she says, and I force myself to ignore her, clearing my throat. I look up, studying the cross vaults of the ceiling, and wait. "What is it?"

"I have a roommate," I say, stepping over to the window. The shutters don't budge when I try to open them. I thought Penny would have snapped at me immediately, told me that *of course* I have a roommate, and that I shouldn't be complaining. But instead, she hesitates.

"You're not supposed to have one," she says. I try to picture her in her office, in the run-down convent, scribbling this conversation into her black notebook.

"And it's a vampire," I add. A heartbeat later, I say: "I'm going to ask for a new room."

"No," she says. "Any other student would be glad to have a vampire roommate. Jealous, even. Who are they?"

"I don't know," I say.

I hear a familiar sigh, somewhere between irritation and exhaustion. "As soon as you know who they are, tell me. But be careful," Penny says. "Some vampires can be deceivingly *friendly*."

"Don't be ridiculous." Frustration builds up inside me. But once she hangs up, I force myself to calm down. If Penny says I can't ask for a new room, I won't. I won't disappoint her.

According to Penny, the hidden library is somewhere in the depths of the campus's underbelly. A web of tunnels, centuries old, built for vampires to cross the campus during the summer. I can imagine the new human arrivals are not welcome down there.

I pull out Penny's compass as I eat breakfast. It's a clunky thing from the 1850s that's supposed to help me make my way through the tunnels. While I'd been hoping for something a little more modern, Penny said it was all I'd need.

The white needles are supposedly made of vampire dust, and the black background is a mix of cobalt, blood, and silver. Penny herself used it eleven years ago, when she broke out three hunters from a Council prison. They'd been kept in a dungeon, hidden deep beneath a labyrinth, and after she got them back to headquarters, she became the youngest hunter to ever be promoted to Stake. She hasn't told me about any of her missions after that one.

I stare at the compass, knowing it will also lead me to a promotion.

The fireplace in Tynarrich's dining hall warms my legs. I'm already getting used to the smell of ashes and old books that clings to every corner of the hall.

Breakfast is warm porridge, with a sprinkle of salt and cold semi-skimmed milk. Back in the convent, breakfast was usually coffee and protein bars. And before that, when my parents were alive, toast and runny eggs. The tables around me fill with groups of fellow humans talking excitedly about their new classes and lecturers. I search for Stephan amongst them, but he's probably still asleep.

I'm not changing my sleep schedule. I'm going to find *The Book of Blood and Roses* and get out of here before my first week is over.

The first tunnel I come across is directly beneath Tynarrich, with deep brown bricks and a low ceiling. Lanterns cast an amber glow on the dark stones. I draw out Penny's compass and shine my torch on it. The white needle is ticking back and forth like a metronome, but after I glare at it for half a minute, it settles on north.

"Here we go," I whisper. The hall curves and then forks into three separate tunnels. I pull out my notebook and sketch the first lines of what will hopefully become a coherent map.

There are two types of tunnels. I'll call group one the *modern* kind, although they could very well be like the leeches who built them, ancient but well-preserved. Their walls are made of grey bricks, smooth cement filling each joint. Vintage-looking gas lamps line the walls, just two feet apart, all fitted with LED bulbs. These tunnels, the modern ones, have signs pointing to different buildings. *Ambrose Hall. Palau Collection. Traquair Hall. Union Hall B.*

Then there are the old tunnels, serpentine, dark, following no rhyme or reason, some ceilings too low, others too high. Dead ends, broken stairways, puddles, and white weeds. They're on a constant incline, ramps or steps, sometimes so steep I'm forced to hang onto the wall. And while the modern tunnels are bright, here you're lucky if you find a single lamp. If I had to guess, the secret library will be at the end of one of these old tunnels. But after an hour mapping the network, I have a feeling I've only scratched the surface.

I REACH THE first Integration lecture three minutes late, and spot Stephan all the way down on the second row. He sees me just as I walk in, motioning at the empty space he's saved for me. Luckily enough, I'm not the only one late; Professor Clemence, a human in his late fifties, tells us he got a little lost on his way here.

After projecting a syllabus and a reading list, he lets us know, in a matter-of-fact way, that anyone who fails Integration will be expelled. Apparently, there are hundreds of equally motivated students waiting to take our place if we don't exceed his expectations.

"The Old Council," Clemence says, walking across his wooden platform with a piece of snapped chalk between his fingers. His hair is shaved, and he's wearing a Steve Jobs–like turtleneck. "Unlike modern vampires, the Old Council were very much in favour of using humans as a source of food, with no regard to their well-being."

My knuckles whiten. Did the *modern* vampires who killed my family care for their well-being?

"However, after the massacres of 1781, and the Coup of the Heirs, which we will delve into during your second semester, nine of the ten families that comprise the Council went through an *enlightenment*. It is around this period that we find the first attempts to create synthetic blood. And during those attempts, the rights of human feeders grow."

I roll my eyes, and his gaze, his naïve and brainwashed gaze, falls on mine just in that unfortunate moment. "Anything you'd like to add, Miss . . . ?"

"Cassie Smith," I say. I clear my throat, and heads turn, necks craning in my direction. So much for not drawing attention to myself. "The president of the New Council, Ares Astra, governed the old one for over a thousand years, didn't he? Even if the rest of the board is different, if the one calling the shots has been in power for so long, how can we be sure things have really changed?" I ask, trying to sound curious instead of insolent.

"Great question," he says, twirling the chalk stick between his fingers. "Ares Astra is still in charge because unlike the other family heads, he was able to adapt. He also wasn't killed by his offspring, like his peers. Though his actions in the past may have been dubious, he is very much a reformed man."

Does his boot taste nice? I want to ask. But I've already drawn too much attention to myself. Clemence moves on, stopping on the invention of synthetic blood in 1908. "We'll see this in the second semester," he says. The ramifications of the invention, the subsequent splintering of vampire society, and then the victory of the New Council over its dissidents.

"That was brave," Stephan whispers, and I sigh. "You're having dinner with us, aren't you?"

"Do I have a choice?"

"Of course not," he says.

At dinner, around the time most vampires are probably starting to wake, Stephan and I make our way to one of the dining halls. "Tynarrich is too busy," he says, already an expert. "Plus, Ambrose Hall is *much* better." We enter a large building in the campus village, and I stop in my tracks when I see what's inside. An illusion decorates the walls, projecting an image of trees, identical to those outside, with branches arching over the ceiling. The light from the projection that shines on my face feels natural and warm. I gawk up at the clouds, trying to figure out how it works, all while Stephan walks ahead, heading towards one of a dozen food stalls.

Ambrose Hall has been set up to resemble a food festival. Bunting hangs between tree branches, along with strings of fairy lights that will become brighter as the false sky darkens. There's a bandstand in the corner, currently empty, but a few instrument cases are set up against the wall, waiting for their owners. The place is huge, with countless tables stretching across the hall and queues forming between them.

There's one stall in particular that makes my stomach turn. A large sign on top of it reads *BLOOD BLOOD BLOOD*. My heart starts racing as I look around. I must get used to them. I grab a wrap from a Greek food stall, and when I spot Stephan again, he's already found a table. I suck a breath in through my teeth.

I knew Ife would be here. But she's not alone.

I walk over, steadying my trembling hand. The feeling of being watched from every corner crawls across my skin, and I try my best to ignore it. The garlic supplements are hiding my scent. No one will try to attack me, even if this place is ridden with leeches. "Mind if I join you?" I ask upon reaching the old wooden table, a stained checkered cloth covering it.

"I *knew* you'd come," Ife says as I place my tray on the table. She's wearing cherry blossom earrings, and a fang peeks out between her full lips. There's only mild curiosity in her large brown eyes. It's strange. I'm not used to vampires looking at me as anything but a walking meal.

"This is Julia," Stephan says, nodding at the second vampire he forgot to mention would be joining us for dinner.

Where Ife is warm and deep, Julia is a white canvas. Her eyes are pale blue, fringed by white lashes, and her hair is long and fair, almost as white as the hair of the vampire I saw at the library. I spot several paint splatters on her milky skin, and she pulls her sleeves down to hide them.

"I'm a painter," Julia says.

"Cool," I say, and I'm glad that Julia doesn't smile, because I don't want to force one, either. A painter, she said. I think of my roommate's books. What if *she* is my roommate? I look about the table, taking them both in. Two vampires. *I can do this.* I've done small talk with vampires before. It always ended with them turning to dust, that's true, but if anything, this should be easier. I just have to think of them as human.

"And what about you?" Ife asks. When she looks at me, I don't get the feeling she's trying to get through obligatory small talk. Her attention is genuine.

"I'm— My parents work in logistics. They want me to take over the company, but I'd rather work in the Council."

"Which department?" Julia asks, still busy with her sketch. I glance over to see she's drawing a train cabin, shadowy silhouettes filling every seat.

"Ethics," I say.

"I assume you'll be looking at a lot of Familiar contracts then," Ife says. "Making sure everything is aboveboard, and that sort of thing?"

"And that no one is sired against their will," I add, though I highly doubt the *ethics* department of the Vampiric Council does anything whatsoever. I watch the two vampires, trying to figure out their impression of me. I've told a few lies in the last minute, but neither Ife nor Julia seems to have noticed.

"You're staying in Iolairean Hall, right?" Iolairean Hall, or *Taigh nan Iolairean,* as it's labelled on the campus map, is on the edge of the campus village, built on the riverbank.

"No, Tynarrich," I say. Her mouth makes an *o,* and I furrow my brows. "Is that strange?"

"I didn't know they'd let humans into Tynarrich. I thought you were all in Iolairean."

Why, exactly, am I not in the human hall of residence? I pause, try to hide the panic rising inside me, residue of when I saw that bloody coffin. "I guess that explains why my roommate is a vampire."

Julia's pencil, which had been busy scratching the corner of her page, stills. Ife's eyes widen. "No way," Stephan says.

"Aye," I say, frowning at the three of them. "You don't have a vampire roommate?" I ask Stephan.

"I *wish*," he says. "But it's already a miracle that Tynahine's managed to get Heritages and Converts to coexist."

"Why?" I ask. Despite knowing there are two types of vampires, I never stopped to think about how they see each other.

"*Heritage* vampires usually think they're superior," Julia says. "Ife is an exception to this rule, of course." She smiles at her friend, who in turn grins back.

"So you're—"

"A Convert," Julia says, her dry voice telling me she isn't interested in sharing anything else about herself.

"There're only a couple hundred Heritage vampires here," Ife says. "The Council doesn't have a single Convert on their board, even though their population far outnumbers ours. So you can imagine why there's some tension between us."

"Seems a bit unfair," I say, and Ife nods.

"Definitely. I have a classmate who was persecuted by the Spanish Inquisition back in the day, and I'm always telling him that he should apply to be on the board. He'd be fantastic."

"You have a classmate who survived the *Spanish Inquisition*?" I ask.

"When he was human. Five hundred years ago."

"Why—" I lean back. "Why the fuck is there a five-hundred-year-old in your class?"

Stephan laughs, and Ife shakes her head, as though I'm an ignorant child.

"Vampire and human education are not the same, Cassie."

"How so?"

"Well, when a human studies, unless they want to stay in academia their entire lives, it's mainly to get a job, isn't it?"

I think I know where this is going. I nod anyway.

"A human life, a mortal one, is *linear*. Structured, too. It's not the same for vampires. Our interests change every century. My brother was a famous opera singer before he became a doctor. And I'm not sure if you've gone through Tynahine's website, but we have an undergraduate degree—philosophy, I think—that lasts sixty-two years."

"Wow," I whisper. "How many decades have you been here?"

"Oh, only four years," she says. "But I'm pretty sure the Night Dean told us the average age of Tynahine's students is eighty-nine. Plus, some of our faculty have been here since the university first opened its doors in the thirteenth century."

I try to picture someone working the same job for eight hundred years. Ife walks off to get another round of blood, and as Stephan chats away with Julia, I feel myself growing awkward.

"So," Ife says, putting down two steaming glasses of blood. "You were telling us you have a vampire roommate?"

"I haven't met them yet," I say. I bite into my wrap, lettuce, spinach, and crispy Halloumi filling my mouth. I glance towards the edge of Ambrose Hall just as a new crowd appears.

A dozen girls, all with an ethereal vampiric beauty.

One stands out amongst them. Tall, hair short and white. The same girl I saw up on the fifth floor of the library. The fifth floor was near-empty when I ran away, so I'm pretty sure it was her voice I heard, either begging to be bitten or saying, *We've got company.*

"Not her, right?" Ife asks, noticing who I was just staring at.

"Uh . . ." I clear my throat. "I don't know."

"As if Aliz Astra would share a room," Stephan scoffs. Every muscle in my body tenses when I hear the name. *Astra?*

"Never mind live in a hall," Julia says, looking up from her paper to stare at the white-haired vampire. "Doesn't she own the hunting lodge?"

"More like hunting *palace*," Stephan says.

"You're right. She does own it," Ife says, pouting. "Damn it."

"Astra?" I whisper the name, still not believing it. "*The* Astras?" I ask. Ife nods, amused by my reaction. The vampire in question, Aliz Astra, joins the queue to the blood stall, while the girls around her fight for her attention. The Astras are the most powerful vampires in Europe. And I was bad-mouthing her father in our last class.

Before I look away, Aliz Astra turns, and our eyes meet from afar. Just like last night, something tightens inside me, as though there's a chain drawing me towards her.

She cocks her head slightly, her cool features broken by a sly grin. My heart skips a beat.

"Why is she looking at us?" Ife asks, drawing my attention away from Astra.

"I—" Why indeed? "Well, I may have accidentally overheard her last night."

"Saying what?" Ife asks in a hushed voice, eyes wide with excitement.

"More than saying, it was *doing*," I say, and for some stupid reason, my cheeks burn.

"Shocking," says Julia, rolling her eyes. Astra must have a reputation, then. I look back over at the crowd. She's no longer looking at me, and air flows easier into my lungs now that her attention is gone. I wish I knew which of the girls flocking around her was the one I heard her with in the library.

I also wish I could get her out of my head.

"Most of the vampires here are serious about their education," Ife says, playing with her straw. "And if I remember correctly, Astra was, too, at the start. I had a few classes with her during my first year here. Then she started failing."

"Failing?" I ask, glancing back at the white-haired vampire.

"She may come from the most powerful family in Europe, but she is surprisingly stupid."

"She's had to retake the same classes four years in a row," Julia says, her slender neck elongating as she turns to stare at Astra. "Vampiredom is truly doomed if *she* is going to become the next leader of the Council."

"So, humans can be expelled for failing Integration, but Aliz Astra gets to stay here for as long as she likes?" I ask, and Ife nods.

"She treats Tynahine like a playground," Julia says. Her pale eyes meet mine, and for a second, I forget that she, too, is a vampire. "So, you better hope she doesn't decide you're her next *plaything*."

chapter
THREE

The compass makes an odd whirring sound as I walk, but when I draw it out, nothing seems to be off.

Unfortunately, night has already fallen, so I don't have the tunnels to myself. But the reactions of Tynahine's alumni are not what I'm used to. There are no heads snapping around. No deep inhales or noses pressing to my neck, breathing me in. No whispers of *Is that Type-S?* Only one in ten thousand have it, which means we're incredibly high demand. Perfect prey—or a perfect trap.

I've never been near a vampire without being in danger.

But here, they barely even notice me.

I need to map as many of these tunnels as I can. I make my way out of the crowd, scribbling the name of each tunnel into a notebook. Most of them are simply numbers, others don't have names at all. I find one of the old ones, narrow but dreadfully long, with a sign on the bricks that reads *Cat's Tail*. And as I walk along it, counting my steps and following the compass, the line I draw in my notebook does in a way resemble a feline's tail.

I pull out my phone, glancing at my schedule. Two more classes before I'm done for the night. My options for the first hour are: the Vampire Tradition in Music; Ethics and Immortality; or Gaelic Dialects of the Supernatural.

That word *supernatural* stops me in my tracks. I wonder if there are other beasts out there that I've not faced before. Kelpies, selkies. Maybe even witches. But something about those monsters feels too otherworldly when compared to vampires. Plus, Penny would have told me if there were other creatures lurking in the shadows, right?

As I try to make my way back to the modern halls, I notice Penny's compass twitching, and it twitches faster when I take stairs, of which there are too many. Staircases shoot out in every direction, some leading to bricked-up tunnels, others to empty classrooms and laboratories.

I come across dusty jars filled with murky green liquid, hiding what I suppose one might call a *collection*. Severed fingers, fetuses, eyeballs, all labelled with neat handwriting that looks centuries old.

One abandoned classroom is filled with paintings, packed frame to frame, without leaving an inch of wall visible. Their golden frames carry inscriptions dating the paintings back to the fifteenth century. The ceiling here is higher than in other classrooms, painted with frescoes of moonlit landscapes. And at the centre, slightly out of place, a large table surrounded by a dozen chairs. Something about the gallery doesn't quite make sense until I lean on the mahogany table.

The canvases and frames are covered in dust, thick paint cracked. There's even pale mould crawling over the faces of some old vampires, filling the air with a stuffiness that's thicker than that of the rest of the tunnels. But the table feels like silk beneath my fingers, not even a speck of dirt on it.

I flash my torch over it, taking in the ornamental engravings running across the side. The chairs, upholstered with red velvet, are also clean. As are the candles in the centre, slightly tilted upon a golden, seven-armed candelabra. Someone has used this room recently.

For what? Near the end of the table, on the floor, a sheet of yellowing paper reads: *Minutes of the Red Ribbon Society*. I pick it up, tucking it into my satchel. I've never heard of the Red Ribbon Society.

I glance back at the wall of paintings, and one catches my eye.

It's the smallest, yet at the same time, the most detailed. A woman with white hair wearing a lace ruffle collar above a black velvet dress.

For a split second, I think it's Aliz Astra. But her skin is too pale, and her eyes, instead of black, are piercing blue. The inscription reads: *Ada, Dreamwalker of Rome. 1582.* The Astras are Hungarian. So, the resemblance must be purely coincidental.

When I look at the compass, the needle is spinning. My own hands are steady, but just to be sure, I place it on the ground, waiting. But it doesn't stop. "For fuck's sake," I hiss under my breath. I shake the compass, as though that will somehow make it stop. I'm going to have to find a different way to avoid getting lost. Like Ariadne and her golden thread. Maybe if there was a monster for me to kill in these tunnels, I wouldn't find the search quite so frustrating.

As I walk down another staircase, I hear it.

Low, somber string music echoes off the tunnel walls. I look back the way I came, at the darkness and silence.

The sound isn't a full orchestra. It's a single instrument, a cello. I follow the sound along the damp tunnel. It's the sort of music you'd have your casket lowered into your grave to. Penny listens to a lot of classical music, but during our long drives to and from vampire clubs, I've never heard anything like this.

The plain walls of the tunnel widen, and the ceiling gets higher as stained-glass windows puncture old rock. The dim glow of candles within is barely enough to illuminate the roses which decorate the panes.

Strange place for a church, I think, but I soon realise there's nothing sacred about the underground structure. The code *U-34* is painted above the wooden doorframe, and I recognise it as the code for one of the electives on my syllabus: the Vampire Tradition in Music.

I'm five minutes late, but since I'm already here, I might as well go inside. I strain my eyes against the stained glass and spot long tables, identical to those in Integration, with pew-like benches behind them. At the very front, up on a platform, is a figure with a cello between their knees.

Drawn-out notes snake beneath the old solid wood doors. I squeeze my eyes shut, hoping the door won't creak when I push it inwards.

The door jolts and I find the already-damp air weighed down even further by burning wax and incense. I step in as quietly as I can, just as the cello music staggers to a halt. For a moment I expect the cellist to shout, or maybe hiss, considering they're most likely a leech. But they don't seem to have noticed me.

"Over here," a familiar voice whispers. Two rows behind the door, at the very back, is Ife. I shouldn't be relieved to see her, yet her kind eyes are a welcome sight in the dim lecture hall. She pats the free space next to her on the bench. I take a careful breath and nod, trying to be quiet as I drop my bag on the tiled floor.

A few of the neighbouring students, all vampires, shoot me furtive glares. I'm not sure if it's because I'm late or because I'm human. My eyes slowly adjust to the chapel-like room, with its high-vaulted ceilings ornamented with crumbling frescoes of mythological figures. And then I finally focus on the cellist. The candles on the desk behind him give him a golden aura.

His fair hair falls in soft waves, just below his chin. He's pale, with milky skin even lighter than his white shirt, and it must be because of that snowy complexion that I can make out his green eyes. His white shirt is cut by a pair of red suspenders, and I see a blazer hanging on top of his cello case.

I swallow. I can't tear my eyes from him.

And then he speaks, as if he was waiting for me to sit.

"Is anyone familiar with that piece?" the professor asks, cutting through the silence in class. Despite the deep anguished notes he was playing a minute ago, the professor's voice is surprisingly warm.

Only one student lifts their arm in our full classroom. The professor glances in our direction, and after a brief nod, Ife answers.

"If I'm not mistaken, that was the third movement of Concerto

Number Seven, *The Final Dawn*." She clears her throat, before adding: "It's one of your own compositions, sir."

A somewhat bashful smile appears on the professor's features, and he nods. "You're not mistaken." The students around us scribble what Ife said, while he continues. "You all might find it quite vain of me to start the semester with one of my own pieces—though our kind are not particularly known for our humility, are we?"

A few chuckles travel across the candlelit hall. I stare down at my own notebook, the scribbles of what I've drawn so far staring back at me like an unravelling spiderweb. I feel like tearing out the page, crumpling it up, and throwing it away, but instead, I move to another sheet.

"Regardless, I thought it would be an ideal piece to introduce our semester. During your first four months we'll be looking at how conversion affects composition. What you just listened to was the first thing I composed as a vampire, just three days after I was sired." He brushes his pale blond hair away from his eyes. He has high cheekbones and full lips, though he's maybe a little too thin. In an odd way, he reminds me of Julia.

I glance down at my schedule. The Vampire Tradition in Music is taught by Dr Sven Gustavsson.

He proceeds to narrate the story of how he was sired. He was a well-established cellist in Stockholm at the age of twenty. Gustavsson began playing for aristocrats and was invited one night to play for a mysterious countess, who wouldn't share her name and hid in the shadows. He expected she'd offer her patronage and sponsor him, like many other aristocrats did, but instead she simply followed him. Every concert, every salon, he'd see her lurking at the back. Sometimes he'd even dream of her. But she always kept her distance.

"It was the most frightening and exhilarating year of my life," he says. "Finally, one night I received a letter. She asked me to compose something inspired by her, and promised that if it pleased her, she would give me a gift that no other patron would ever be able to match." He sits down, carefully lifting his cello. "This next piece is the one that convinced her to gift me with immortality."

His story creeps under my skin. I'm far too tense, and I can't help fearing that the woman who sired him is lurking somewhere behind us, waiting to strike again. There are too many vampires, and I appear to be the only human in the room. Gustavsson's music doesn't alleviate the feeling. It's raw, awful, as though he knew his end was coming when he first wrote it. Once it finishes, the room is too quiet. Professor Gustavsson remains seated, eyes shut as if he's praying.

And then he's up again, striding across his platform to tell us about another composer, Caroline Campbell. "Only three of her compositions survived," he says. "She was famous for not writing anything down, and her melodies were so complex that even if you tried to memorise them, you could never capture the original sound. Campbell played for royalty, human and vampire alike, though most of her repertoire is now as lost as *The Book of Blood and Roses*."

I'm rummaging through my bag for another pen, too caught up in the movement to fully react to the name of the book. Gustavsson drops his gramophone's needle onto a record, a crackling piano filling the lecture hall. I grasp my pen, tight, and stare down at the blank paper. I didn't imagine that.

He said it.

The Book of Blood and Roses.

I bite down a smile. *Finally.* I watch those around me. No one appears to be confused by the title.

"What's *The Book of Blood and Roses*?" I whisper to Ife, as Professor Gustavsson bobs his head to the piano piece.

"You've never heard of it?" she asks, disbelief widening her eyes.

"I don't think so."

"A compendium of lost knowledge," Ife says, leaning closer. "Though it's been missing for centuries. No one knows who the author is, but people say it took them until their last breath to write the last word."

"What sort of knowledge?" I ask. I need to know everything, yet I have a feeling I'm about to hit a wall, like another dead end in the meandering tunnels that run beneath this godforsaken campus.

"Methods," Ife says slowly, "to kill vampires."

A thrill runs through me. It is just as Penny said.

"And where is it?" I ask, trying to keep excitement out of my voice.

Ife frowns at me for a split second, with what I think is suspicion, but then shakes her head. "It's lost," she says. "And let's hope it stays that way."

I focus on the professor as he moves between one piece and the next, occasionally picking up his cello. The lecture drags on, two whole hours that feel like ten, before giving us three topics to choose from for our first essay.

"Human," someone whispers in front of us as I pack my satchel. I glance ahead, surprised to find an unfamiliar vampire staring right at me. "Professor Gustavsson wants a word," he says.

Ife furrows her brows, first at the vampire, and then at me. "She has a name," Ife hisses.

"Well, I don't know it," the vampire counters. I shrug and tell her to leave without me.

The stench of incense grows stronger as I walk down the aisle between the tables, my boots echoing on the ancient tiles. Gustavsson is erasing his blackboard, filled with names of several obscure vampire composers. He then sets about fixing his tie before finally looking down at me.

"Ah, you must be"—he glances over at a list on his desk, and then at me again, with a frown—"Cassie Smith?"

"Yes," I say. The wooden door slams shut, lifting a momentary breeze that snuffs out a few candles. The already-dim classroom becomes even darker. And now, we're alone. "Sorry for being late," I start, because I imagine that's why he wants a word. "I took a few wrong turns in the tunnels," I say, hiding my clenched fists behind my back. "But it won't happen again, Professor."

"Oh, don't be sorry," he says quickly. "I imagine studying in a university like this must be a shock for a human."

He keeps his distance, somewhat awkwardly. "I suppose so," I reply. The echo of our voices fills the room, and I wait for someone passing by to open the door and peek inside, but even the tunnels seem to have quietened now. "But I've been looking forward to coming here."

"Me, too," he says. "It's Tynahine's first year opening its gates to humans, and also its first year allowing a wretched soul like me in, to share my so-called wisdom."

"It's your first year teaching here?" I ask.

"I was here two centuries ago, but as a student," he says. "That's not why I wanted to talk, however. You are my only human student, Cassie, so I just want to make it clear that if you are ever in any sort of"—he pauses, looking for the word—"*trouble,* then you can come to me. My office is a safe space for humans. As confident as Faust Nocth is in his little project, there is still danger. So, should you ever feel threatened, you'll find my door is always open."

"Thanks," I say. My muscles are stiff. His words come across as genuine, but the thought of running to a *vampire's* office when I'm in danger is a little disturbing. "Earlier you mentioned Campbell's compositions are as lost as *The Book of Blood and Roses,* and that made me wonder . . ." I pause, hoping he'll answer without me having to probe too much. "What exactly is that book?"

He considers me and starts folding paper, so meticulously that I think he's going to ignore my question. "A book of secrets," he finally says. "It's best known for its instructions on how to kill a vampire. But it contains much more. Remedies for curses, spells from forbidden grimoires, and a list of every vampiric weakness ever observed in the West," he says. "It's both a history and a collection of theories—some even say it contained a cure for vampirism. A way to reverse our *disease.*"

He blows out the candles on his desk, so that the only source of light now is the stained-glass windows, glowing in the dim of the tunnels. "Though I wouldn't concern yourself with books as dangerous as that one, Cassie Smith," he says, hoisting up his cello behind his back. "Someone might mistake your curiosity for something a little more . . . sinister."

chapter FOUR

Professor Gustavsson's warning has left me with a layer of sweat that doesn't dry, even as the tunnels around me cool down.

Is he onto me? I was too bold, wasn't I?

"Doesn't matter." My whisper echoes off a winding tunnel, riddled with puddles, white weeds growing beneath the lanterns.

But at least I now know *The Book of Blood and Roses* is not a secret.

Which means that I should be able to find more information about it in Kinsnet. Just as long as I don't have to see *her* again.

The air is damp, moss clinging to the stones. I hear water dripping somewhere in the distance. It's an old passageway. The air is too close, the ceiling low. The more I walk, the older and darker the tunnels become, stones larger, with candles illuminating the arched ceilings instead of electricity. And each new tunnel, I realise, is stranger than the last, some with crumbling mosaics on the floors, and others with long poems etched into the walls, in English, Latin, or Gaelic. Just as I run my fingers along one of these words, the sound of high heels clicking on stone reaches my ears.

A chill runs through me as I make out her silhouette through the shadows, lanterns flickering on as she walks, following her steps.

Something about her presence, even in the distance, makes every instinct I've been trained to pay attention to come to life. My eyes adjust to the dark hallway, and I take in her entrancing features. A cascade of chestnut hair falls to her waist. Her eyes are a twilight blue, her full lips stained dark red. A perfume of blood and rosewater prickles my nostrils. I expect to see her lips dripping crimson. But the blood is on her hands. Small puncture wounds litter her palms and fingers.

"Lost?" she asks. Her sweet voice is instantly familiar. She's the one I heard up on the fifth floor of Kinsnet, begging to be bitten. My cheeks are aflame as I try to push the image of her and Aliz Astra out of my mind. But my imagination works against me, and I fill in the blanks of what I heard last night. Aliz Astra pinning her to a bookcase, deadly fangs puncturing her neck. The sounds she made echo in my mind.

She arches a perfectly groomed brow, waiting for me to reply.

My mouth is dry, and my voice comes out in a croak.

"I think so." The more I look at her, the more I understand why Astra would choose her. Though the word Julia used, *plaything*, doesn't suit her in the slightest.

"These tunnels were carved for vampires to avoid the sun." Her voice is suddenly too sharp. "There's no reason for you to be down here."

"Some classrooms are underground," I counter. Her gaze sweeps down my body, stopping on my watch.

"Where were you going before you got lost?" she asks.

"Kinsnet."

The tunnels are completely silent but for the sound of my own breathing. Her gaze burns through me, and I fight the urge to back away from her.

"You're in luck," she finally says. "I was just heading there myself."

Despite her staggeringly high heels, she's already five metres ahead of me before I even start walking after her. "Thanks," I say.

She reminds me of some of the vampires I've killed during my missions. The old ones with centuries of blood stolen through their fangs.

"What happened to your hands?" I ask. When she stretches her fingers, the wounds are gone. She looks at her skin, furrowing her brows.

"My hands?"

"You had cuts on them," I say, and she seems amused.

"No, I didn't," she says lightly. All vampires heal quicker than humans do. But the speed at which they do so is usually determined by whether they are Heritages or Converts, and by the type of blood they've been drinking. Given the speed with which her wounds vanished, I wouldn't be surprised if she has been drinking fresh blood.

Before I can ask another question, the tunnel comes to an end, and a sign over an archway reads *Kinsnet Library*. She walks up a stone staircase and glances back down at me. "See you around," she says, smile not reaching her eyes.

THE RELIEF OF finally being out of those dark, narrow tunnels loosens my every nerve. And being left alone certainly helps.

I make my way up to the fourth floor of the library. I notice new details in the blue dome, a bunch of words in Latin fringing the paintings. The fourth floor has two dozen tables, with six chairs each, and they're just as busy as the tables on the ground floor.

Even though existence of *The Book of Blood and Roses* seems to be common knowledge amongst the vampires, I can't find any books about it. Had I asked Professor Gustavsson for more information, he might have pointed me in the right direction. Or reported me to the dean. So, I start with a broad search; *Vampire Myths and Legends,* along with some other books that will hopefully help me locate the secret library: *The Complete History of Tynahine, The Architects of Tynahine,* and *Vampires in XIII Century Scotland,* amongst others.

I spot a table right by the balcony, which is yet to be claimed by any other students. I open my notebook, placing it on my left side, and work my way through the glossary of the first volume, searching for the book's odd title.

The chair diagonally across from mine squeaks as someone pulls it back.

While good manners dictate that I should look up and exchange hushed pleasantries, I keep my attention focused on my book. Only when I hear the rustling of a page, do I glance up at my tablemate. Instantly, I wish I hadn't. My heart lurches, breath stuck in my throat. It's as if the entire library became invisible, because all I can see is her.

Aliz Astra is focused on the book she just opened, with a blunt pencil dangling between her long fingers. She holds a single page up, and her lean frame, her broad shoulders and long neck, all angle towards that piece of paper. Her white hair is a tousled mess, and she runs her fingers through it, keeping it away from her eyes. The top buttons of her cream shirt are unbuttoned. I force my expression into a mask of neutrality, waiting for her to notice me.

My blood burns, shame colouring my cheeks. *What the fuck am I thinking?* And more important, what is she doing *here*? Aliz Astra isn't supposed to *study*. The library is of no use to her, except as a spot to mess around with her girls. And out of all the tables, why did she have to sit at mine?

While my mind rushes, the heiress draws a flask from her bag, the scent of hot blood reaching my nostrils. She slips a metal straw between her lips, not glancing in my direction. As though she doesn't know I'm here. But she sat here on purpose, didn't she? All because I looked at her.

I try to look away, but I can't. She's still focused on her book, rubbing the page mindlessly. Her white hair has a pine needle stuck in it, and when I allow myself a deeper breath, I find she smells like moss and rain.

She takes another sip of blood before wiping her lips, staining her index finger crimson. Aliz Astra runs her tongue over the blood on her finger, and her gaze locks with mine.

Her eyes, surrounded by white lashes, are black, not red. But all the same, it's like being compelled. As though she's invaded my mind in a way no vampire has been able to since my recruitment. Time slows, and the whispers of the surrounding tables quieten to the thudding of my own heart, harnessed entirely by her attention.

I hear her again, against the bookcase. I see the girl from the tunnel, with those small cuts on her hands, pressed against her, moaning, and Aliz Astra's lips in the crook of her neck, her fangs piercing her skin, *my* skin, my blood, rushing to her tongue.

And as this vile desire sears through me, she takes another sip, her eyes not leaving mine, as though my every thought is filtering straight into her mind.

Her lips curve.

I look down at the book open in front of me, the words upon it a scrambled mess. That's the third time she's smiled at me, and the third time I looked away. I won't let it happen again.

It's not unusual for a hunter to be entranced by a vampire.

We can't be compelled, we've been trained not to be, but we're still human. I don't know what it is about her. Maybe it isn't even *her*, maybe it's just this fucking place.

When I see Penny's number light up my phone, my anxiety only seems to increase. "What is it?" I ask, phone pressed to my ear.

"Hello to you, too," Penny says. "How is the search going?"

I stare up at a streetlamp, a few moths braving the damp air to fly towards its light. "I've covered forty tunnels, but I have a feeling that I've only scratched the surface."

"Send me your progress," she says.

"I will," I say. "But I need more information. Where did you first hear about *The Book of Blood and Roses*?"

"In one of Callisto's libraries," she says. In the headquarters. Which I'll finally be able to access once I get my promotion.

I make my way along the narrow streets of the campus village, glancing up at the bars, all of them advertising blood. "I have another job for you," Penny says. "Something unexpected has come up."

"But I've just arrived," I say, stopping in my tracks. She can't make me leave. Not yet.

"A girl was found half drained in Inverness last Thursday," Penny says, and my racing heart slows.

"Can't you send someone else?" I ask.

"This should be easy. I just need some intel."

"Fine," I say. I spot a group of vampires walking along the campus village's main street. Despite the cold, they're in thin blazers and white shirts. But what makes me look at them, perhaps longer than I should, are the red ribbons tied around their necks. "Send me the details," I say after a shallow breath.

chapter FIVE

I spent my first week at Tynahine mainly in the tunnels and taking my meals with my new *friends*. During my classes, instead of paying attention, I made lists of the different tunnels and staircases. Luckily enough, I only saw Astra from afar, entering Ambrose Hall surrounded by her flock, with an arm around a different girl every day. But every single day, just for a split second, she'd look across the hall at our table and lock her eyes with mine.

"The Red Ribbons?" Ife whispers Thursday afternoon, after I ask her about them. A few times, I've wandered down to the stuffy gallery where I assume they hold their meetings, and though I've not had a run-in with any of the Ribbons, the chairs have changed position each time I go. Both Ife and Julia stiffen at the mention of the group, though Stephan is as oblivious as I am. "Did they say anything to you?" she asks, looking around Ambrose Hall, afraid we might be overheard. I shake my head.

"Who are they?"

"Vampire supremacists," Julia whispers.

"*Convert* supremacists," Ife adds. "We knew they were some sort of student club, but we didn't know what kind until they tried to recruit Julia last year, after the Integration was announced."

"I said no," Julia adds in a matter-of-fact way.

Vampire supremacists. So much for Tynahine being safe for humans.

THAT NIGHT, I grab a bike from the rental shop on the edge of campus and make my way through the woods. When I reach the gate, I double-check that I've got my weapons. It's already dark out, and the small Highland roads are sparsely lit, but I remember the route the Familiar took from the city when I first got here. Once I find the motorway, it takes me just twenty minutes to reach Inverness.

I'm going to a pub called Silverbirch, next to a warehouse where several girls have been found with just enough blood to keep them alive, and no memory of how they lost the rest. Each attack has happened on a Thursday night, and Penny is convinced that the vampire behind the attacks must either be doing night shifts in the pub or is a regular customer.

River Ness glitters with the reflection of streetlamps, a thin mist rising from its surface. It feels good to be out of campus, even if it's just for the night. The crisp air bites my ears, and I find a line of bike racks, right across from the bridge leading to the river islands.

I chain my bike, and a bloated seagull lands on the handlebars, watching me with yellow eyes. "Shoo," I say, and it lifts into flight.

It starts to drizzle, and I make my way across the first Victorian footbridge. I follow the path amongst the woods, illuminated by old-fashioned lampposts. The trees, firs and red cedars, are staggeringly tall, some so wide they must be centuries old. There are seagulls here, too, perched on branches.

SILVERBIRCH IS SMALL, with a carpet that smells of sweat and spilled beer. The music is loud, and the staff all look human.

I order a plate of chips and an Irn-Bru and scan the premises. There's a hen-do taking up four tables, all the women wearing tiaras, while one has a cheap white veil sticking out from hers. They're noisy, singing over the music, but no one seems particularly bothered by them. Closer to me is a table of three, parents with a daughter in her late teens. Roughly the age I was when my parents died.

All three of them are alive, bickering over meaningless things.

The last time I went out for dinner with my parents was shortly after prom. Prom night had been a blur, even though I'm pretty sure I didn't drink. My girlfriend at the time, Vicki, broke up with me after the party. She said I cheated on her, but I have no recollection of it. *She's not worth it, hen,* my dad had said. I wish I'd agreed with him.

I wish I'd thanked them for bringing me out for dinner, instead of sulking the whole night. If I'd known it was going to be our last time going out together, I would have enjoyed it. I would have told them that there was something fishy about a prize for a competition they had no memory of entering. I would have told them not to go to London, and they'd still be alive.

And maybe we'd be sitting here as a family, just as those other three are.

My gaze shifts over to the bar, and I spot him, holding a glass of water and smiling at the waitress. She's mousy, her uniform ill-fitting, and I wonder, based on the glint in the man's eye, if her blood is like mine. Type-S.

I keep my head down but continue watching him. Then he does it. His eyes glow red, and the waitress's flustered expression slackens. No one in the pub notices. Humans never do. It's only once you've faced them, once you've felt it, that you sense their power. His thin lips move, uttering an order. He gets up, dusting down a black blazer. His long fingers glide across his phone. A second later he heads out the main entrance.

"Going for a smoke," the waitress says, loud and clear. I don't waste time. I've studied the layout of the Silverbirch in advance, so I know where I'm going.

I slip my mask on once I reach the narrow stairs leading to the roof and pull up my hood. The wind hits me as I take in my surroundings. The roof is riddled with rusty pipes, and a flock of seagulls perches on the ledge, watching me.

The warehouse is in complete darkness. I remember Penny's intel. A Thursday night, just like this one, and a girl with amnesia caused either by alcohol or compulsion. The waitress is not drunk. And if she survives, I'm sure the leech will compel her to forget everything. I tighten my boot laces, that familiar giddiness spreading through me. I stretch, breathing in the greasy air.

The waitress steps out, walking straight to the entrance of the warehouse. The door creaks open, and she disappears inside. I don't waste another second, leaping across the street and landing silently on the roof.

The gabled roof has a dozen windows. The back of the warehouse looks like an old train station, with a glass ceiling overlooking a dark hall. I'm twenty metres above the ground, so I hook a wire to a pole, tugging it to make sure it's sturdy. When I look back down, the waitress enters the hall. And across from her, half a dozen vampires.

Fuck.

This isn't what Penny told me to expect. Quickly, I snap a picture of them, sending it her way. She wanted intel, that's all. But even though saving people is none of my business, I can't let them hurt that girl. I find the window sash and give it a small push. It opens just enough for me to hear their voices.

"That's all?" a woman asks.

"She's the only one with passable blood," another vampire, the one who compelled her, replies.

"Blood?" the victim asks. A small part of her is still lucid, despite her eerie, doll-like stillness.

The vampire's eyes flash red again. "You will forget that you ever saw us. When someone asks where you went during the following hour, tell them you walked to the river and then came back."

They're keeping her alive.

The girl nods. I try to open the window all the way, but find it jammed. And I'm too slow. One vampire holds the girl, keeping her upright, while the one who compelled her drags a dagger across her clavicle. My heart drops. The girl doesn't make a sound, shocked as blood spouts around her.

I smash the window, leaping in.

"Hunter!" one of the vampires shouts.

A thin fog fills the warehouse as they turn into bats, all before I can even show them a cross. They fly out the same window I jumped through. The girl collapses. "Get back here!" I scream, just before I realise that one, the vampire who compelled her, has stayed behind. He leaps on me, knocking the gun out of my hand as his eyes flash red.

"What is Callisto doing here?"

I draw a knife from my sleeve while he clasps his hands tight around my neck. I stab his hand, and blood sprays the side of my mask, dripping onto my clothes as I try to wrestle my way out of his grip. His cold blood sticks to my jacket. This is why hunters always wear black.

Despite the wound in his hand, he tightens his grip, pinning me to the ground. "Take a bite and I'll tell you," I choke out through my mask, lifting my left wrist to his lips. The leech smirks, not thinking twice before sinking his fangs into my skin. Pain sears through my nerves, but it's worth it. He swallows, and his grip around my neck loosens.

His eyes widen as he chokes, and I pull out a wooden stake. I slam it into his chest, and I wish he'd take a little longer to die. But once his heart is pierced, his rotten soul slips out of his body in an instant. His corpse turns into a cloud of smoke, leaving nothing but a pile of dust behind.

The girl's glasses are tangled in her hair. Soon her co-workers will realise she's missing. I press my hand to her neck, feeling a faint pulse, and use her phone to call an ambulance. I tell them there's an unconscious girl in the street behind Silverbirch and that they should be quick. Luckily enough, I always carry a small but basic first aid kit on my body. I cover the wound on her clavicle with gauze and a large plaster. Hopefully it's enough to stop the bleeding.

I leave her slumped against the wall of the pub, her pulse dangerously slow. I need to get out of here before the ambulance arrives. Why did they run away? Surely six vampires would at the very least *think* they'd be able to take on a hunter?

More important, why are they sparing their victims? If it was just one vampire, I would understand keeping their targets alive to ration their blood and avoid the attention that a string of murders or disappearances would bring to a small city like Inverness. But there were six of them. And there was something almost clinical in the way they stood around her. Measuring her.

For what? A blood party?

I stash my bloodied mask under my jacket and run back to the Ness Islands. By the time I'm crossing the old metal bridges, the wound on my wrist is burning. I locate my bike, and the seagull I saw earlier this night is perched on the handlebars once again. "Fuck off," I tell it. I need to get out of Inverness. The other vampires might be following me in bat form. They'll be able to smell the blood on me if they fly close enough. I cycle into a residential area before joining the motorway. I don't see any bats following me.

But that doesn't change the fact that my clothes are soaked in vampire blood.

TYNARRICH HALL HAS a laundromat on the first floor, and luckily enough, it's deserted. I dump my uniform in the washing machine and look at the time. It's already four A.M. If anyone asks why I'm up this late, I can tell a half truth. I wanted to hit the town. The fact that I killed a vampire is irrelevant.

My bedroom is quiet and empty, no signs of my roommate. I take my bag into the bathroom, scrubbing my mask of any extra blood before stepping into a scalding hot shower. Crimson runs down my body, blood and hair dye mixing on the porcelain shower tray, while I rest against the cold glass.

I'll have to lie low for the next few weeks. Five vampires got away, and now they're probably looking for me.

I glance at the moon-shaped wound on my left wrist. I turn the tap, water running cold, and think of the girl. Will she truly not remember anything that happened?

I wrap a towel around myself, another around my hair, and brush my teeth.

And it's while I do this, as the bathroom becomes quiet, that I hear it.

Slurp.

I stop brushing for a second, wondering if I just imagined the sound, before it resumes, another long slurp. My roommate is here. I take a deep breath and continue brushing, taking my time. I think of all the art books they have lined up on the wall and try to picture what my roommate looks like.

I towel-dry my hair and realise I didn't bring a nightgown in with me. *Shit.* Then there's my wound. I glance at the puncture marks, next to the slight indent caused by his other teeth. How am I supposed to explain this? I rummage through my bag; the first aid kit doesn't have any plasters left.

I just have to keep it hidden. I make sure my towel is wrapped and tucked tightly, and after a deep breath, I unlock the bathroom door.

The window is wide open, the crescent moon gleaming through clouds.

She's sitting on the coffin, facing me. Her white hair is messy, and a metal straw is stuck in her mouth. There's a paper cup in one hand, and a book in the other. I blink, certain that I'm seeing things.

But I'm not. She's really here.

"Why are you in my room?"

It's her.

Aliz Astra.

She doesn't seem surprised to see me. Her dark eyes sweep down my body. "*Your* room?" Her voice is low, and she lifts a brow. "I've been living here for five years."

"What?" I ask, breathless, and she jumps down from her coffin. *No.* Aliz Astra owns the hunting lodge. Why would she be *here*? I tighten the grip on my towel. *This isn't happening.* She's not my roommate.

She can't be.

She walks towards me, and she's somehow even taller than I thought. I take a step back, hitting the bathroom door. Her gaze trails down my neck. I don't have a weapon on me. "What are you doing?" I ask.

Her black eyes narrow as she smiles.

She steps closer, and I grip my towel even tighter, until my knuckles turn white. Something truly demonic flashes across her eyes when she whispers: "Having dinner."

chapter SIX

My gun's in my bag; everything else is under the bed. But I can take her. Even without a weapon—I just have to let her bite me.

My muscles tense, and I'm about to pounce on her when she takes a step back. "Just kidding," Astra says. She holds up her hands, spreading out her fingers, and has the nerve to grin. I can't hold my towel tighter than I already am. A layer of sweat mixes with shower droplets. Slowly, my short-lived fear is replaced with rage.

"Kidding?" I ask, my voice sharp. "What is *wrong* with you? You're a *vampire*," I say, itching to grab a weapon.

We stand in silence, staring at each other, until my damp hair causes me to sneeze.

"So are most students here," she finally says. She turns and grabs a cardigan hanging by her coffin. Before I can escape, she's wrapping it around me. "Why come to Tynahine if you're afraid of vampires?"

"I'm *not*," I say. Her fingers brush my shoulder as she lets go of the cardigan. It smells of pine and moss. I don't want to touch anything that's hers, much less wear it.

Then she has the nerve to smirk. "Sure."

This can't be happening.

Just as I thought I was getting her out of my head, she's here. She's been here, all this time. *No.* I take off her cardigan, and pull a nightgown over my head, only letting my towel drop once the skirt has fallen to my mid thighs.

"Did you know I was your roommate?" I ask.

"What do you mean?"

"I've seen you looking at me."

"I've seen *you* looking at *me,*" she says, crossing her arms.

"Pretty hard not to," I say.

"Oh, I know," she says with a sigh and runs her fingers through her hair. I realise then, horrified, that she thinks I'm complimenting her.

"Because you're a fucking exhibitionist," I snap, and Astra's expression drops, colour rushing to her cheeks.

"What? No, I'm not. You were the one spying on me."

"You were having sex in the library!" I hiss at her.

"Yeah," she smirks. "You should try it sometime. It's exhilarating."

"Why didn't you tell me we were roommates?" I ask, ignoring what she just said, and the way she looked at me. My heart's beating too fast. *I can't do this.* I take a deep breath, and instead of handing her back her cardigan, I put it on, shivering. My hair is still damp.

Astra narrows her eyes at me, sitting on her coffin again. "You're not exactly the most approachable person in the world, are you? Every time you look at me, I think you want to kill me," she says.

"Well, you're right about that," I say. Astra glares at me.

"I don't know your name," she says.

"Cassie," I say, and her frown stays exactly where it is, measuring me.

"I'm Aliz," she says.

"Yeah, I know," I say a little too quickly.

"Well, Cassie." She crosses her legs. "I've got good news for you. There's a room in Iolairean Hall that you can move into tomorrow morning. I'll even help move your stuff, and we can act like this never happened." Adrenaline slowly leaves my system as I steel myself. She wants me to leave? "Your new room is bigger than this one, *and* I'm positive your new human roommate is lovely."

I take her in. Every time I've set eyes on her, Astra's been wearing a perfectly tailored three-piece suit. Tonight, she's in a billowy cotton shirt, with a matching pair of white shorts, which just about cover her toned thighs.

"Should I help you pack?" she adds. Every new word of her privately educated English adds to my building frustration. Who does she think she is?

"Why should I be the one to go?" I ask.

Her smile, which didn't seem entirely genuine, tenses. "I've stayed in this room for half a decade. I'm not sharing it with a human."

"You own the hunting lodge. Why aren't you sleeping there?"

She falters. After clearing her throat, she says: "That's none of your business."

I've always been the first to look away. Aliz Astra has made me feel weak again and again. There's no chance I'm stepping aside this time. "Well, I like my room," I say, running my hand down the curtains protecting my bed. I feel her cardigan, so soft and warm, getting wet as my hair sits against its fibres.

"But you're scared of me," she says.

I snort. I'm a little too sleep-deprived to be thinking straight. I may feel a myriad of emotions towards her. But *fear*? "Definitely not."

"You were freaking out just a second ago."

"You threatened to bite me," I say.

"That was a friendly vampiric greeting," she says, swirling her paper cup. "And it wasn't a lie, I *am* having dinner." She takes a loud slurp through her straw, the synthetically red liquid vanishing down her throat.

"I'm not leaving." I wanted to leave from the moment I saw her coffin. But I will *never* take orders from a vampire. Much less *her*.

"You can't stand me," she says, exasperated.

"We've been able to avoid each other until now," I remind her, crossing my arms. The bite wound stings against the cardigan. Something doesn't quite make sense. Astra has been living here for five years, yet Ife said she lived in the hunting lodge. "Why does no one know you live in Tynarrich?" I ask.

"Because I have the ninth floor to myself," she says. "And no one ever takes the maintenance stairs. But like I said, the ninth floor is *mine*."

"If you really want me to leave, why not compel me?"

Exasperation turns to shock. "And spend a century in jail?"

I scoff. "Oh, I'm *sure* the Council will care about their princess breaking the rules."

"Don't call me that," she growls. Her face is red. I've struck a nerve. *Good*.

"You're probably used to getting everything you want because you're an Astra," I say in the softest voice I can muster. I step towards her. The open window allows a breeze in, the cold biting my cheeks. "But you're not stepping over me, *princess*."

"You know nothing about my family," she says, hand tightening around her paper cup. "So, watch your words, Cassie."

"Or what?"

The woods rustle outside the hall, the highest branches brushing against the windowsill. A few droplets of rain hit our desks. Her face, red with rage, remains tight. I don't think I've ever seen a vampire this angry before. As soon as they realise what I am, their expression shifts to terror. I wouldn't mind seeing that fear on Astra's features.

"Give me back my cardigan," she finally says. Her voice is small and dry. I peel it off and toss it at her.

"I never asked for it in the first place."

Her expression changes, and too late, I realise she's spotted the wound on my arm. "What is that?"

I clasp a hand over the puncture marks. "None of your business," I say.

She glares at me, jaw tense. Even when she's angry, she's beautiful. She opens her mouth to say something but, instead, just sighs. She takes the straw out of her cup, removes the lid, and tips it to her lips, letting the last few drops of blood touch her tongue. My breath hitches at the sight, and I swallow hard. "Don't get too comfortable," she finally whispers, before grabbing the black curtains that split our room and pulling them shut.

chapter SEVEN

Local newspapers don't seem to know anything about last night's incident, and when I call Penny, she doesn't pick up.

Astra's cardigan is lying over my chair.

I still remember the feeling of her hand, cold, as she wrapped the garment around my shoulders. My heart races in a way it shouldn't. It's not my fault that she's gorgeous. Who *wouldn't* be attracted to her? But I try my best to remember our conversation. The ease with which she thought she could get rid of me.

I glare at the curtains hiding her coffin and whisper, "In your dreams."

SITTING ON THE steps leading down to the Cat's Tail, I go over everything I've mapped so far. It's far too messy, but hopefully, once I transfer the scribbles to a larger sheet of paper, it'll make sense. Working down in the tunnels may not be the best idea. They're cold, damp, and I can hear the sound of my own breath. But I can't bear the thought of staying in my room, where I might see her again.

I have my own symbols on the paper. An arrow, pointing up or down for slope, a zigzag for stairs, and a happy face, which I use only once, for flat ground. In less than an hour, I've filled three more pages, and my legs ache. It's harder to breathe down here. At least all this discomfort is keeping me from thinking about her. Until I *am* thinking about her, and my skin crawls at the memory.

Astra already knew we were roommates. Meaning that at some point, she must have pulled my bed curtains open. She's been spying on me.

I kick a wall, frustration bubbling in my veins.

Something isn't right. *Why* are we roommates? Who put us together? I feel a chill in the back of my neck and swallow hard. No one knows what I am. No one in their right mind would pair the Astra heir with a vampire hunter. Yet I can't shake the feeling that we've been forced together on purpose.

By the time I'm sitting in the Integration lecture hall, I'm on my fourth coffee, this one with two shots. Every muscle in my body aches, reminding me of what I got up to in Inverness. The bite mark itches under a plaster. Stephan frowns at me, but we both keep quiet as Clemence talks us through the composition of synthetic blood and all its benefits, as opposed to human blood.

"Can anyone name any of the adverse effects?" Clemence asks, and without thinking, I raise my hand.

"Synthetic blood does not allow them to transform into bats," I say, picturing the monsters I faced in Inverness. "They're also weaker when they drink synthetic blood."

"But they're still able to compel us," another student chimes in.

When Penny first told me about treaties-abiding vampires, who drink synthetic blood instead of human blood, I didn't believe her. Every mission I've ever been on has revolved around a vampire's thirst, their bloodlust, and not once has a single monster shown any remorse towards their victims. The thought that there were vampires out there who would forsake the taste of human blood, forsake their innate powers, just to abide by the treaties, was inconceivable.

And yet I'm now surrounded by those very vampires.

"You look tired," Ife says later, once we meet in Ambrose Hall.

"Had a bit of a long night," I say, and at this she meets my gaze, raising a brow.

"Doing what? Found yourself a boyfriend?"

"I'm a lesbian," I say, and at this, Julia looks at me, blinking with surprise. I narrow my eyes. "Does that bother you?" I ask.

"No," Julia says, and despite being a vampire, blood rushes to her cheeks. "So am I."

I look away just as Astra walks into the canteen, wearing a brown suit that matches the screens of Ambrose Hall, which are currently showing an autumnal forest. I watch as she looks up at the sky, shielding her eyes as though the sun is real. Her arm is linked through the arm of a girl with long chestnut hair. The one I saw deep in the tunnels, with cuts on her hands. The girl she fucked in the library.

"Astra is also a lesbian," Ife says, noticing who I was just gawking at. "But maybe a tad out of your league."

"I'm not—"

"And even if she took a liking to you, it would be bad news, Cassie."

"I'm not interested in her," I say, but my cheeks are burning.

"Maybe she *has* taken a liking to Cassie," Stephan says, picking up a piece of sashimi. "She's looking at you again."

I glance over, unable to help myself, and this time, when our eyes meet, Astra *hisses*. As in, a vampire's hiss. Like a fucking animal. The kind of hiss that summons their venom, signalling either fear or aggression. I gawk at her, wide-eyed. *What is wrong with her?*

"Uh," Ife says, and soon I realise that quite a few tables have turned their attention towards us. "Did she just hiss at us?"

"You're seeing things," I say quickly. Why. Why would she do that?

"Wait," Ife says. "Is *she* what you were doing last night?"

"For fuck's sake," I say. "Of course not."

"Why did she look at you again, then?" Stephan asks.

I let out a short sigh. "Well, I was hoping no one would find out, but"—I lower my voice—"she's my roommate."

"You're joking," Ife says.

"I wish." I look back over at Astra. A few of the girls surrounding her are still staring at me, but the white-haired vampire is focusing on her *plaything*, arm around the other vampire's shoulders as she bends down to kiss her.

"But why is she staying in Tynarrich?" asks Julia, who as usual is keeping her hands busy with her sketchbook.

"No idea," I say.

"Has she tried to bite you?" Stephan asks, and Ife makes an affronted sound.

"She wouldn't be standing there if she had," I say, a little too quickly.

"I don't think you have to worry, Cassie," Ife says. "Your blood smells—I wouldn't say *bad*, just not interesting enough for someone to risk a century in prison. No offense," she says.

"None taken," I reply.

I shouldn't feel comfortable sitting next to two vampires. But Ife's words have finally illuminated *why*. Without the scent of my S-Type blood, I'm not a rare delicacy. I'm just an ordinary person, not defined by the crimson inside me.

I CAN'T HELP but feel distracted during the rest of my classes, dreading going back to my room in case I see her again. During Gustavsson's class, the students in front of me turn, whispering amongst themselves. One of the vampires who glares at me, perhaps even more intensely than the rest, is a girl with short black hair. And as I stare back, I realise she's wearing a red ribbon around her throat. What if the Red Ribbons were involved with what happened in Inverness?

On my way to my next class, I walk straight into a hard chest, and my books tumble to the floor.

"Oh dear," a man says in a smooth baritone. He picks up my books, and when our eyes meet, I get the feeling I've seen his face before, glacial blue eyes and jet-black hair. His tweed suit matches his briefcase. I *have* seen him. He's the Night Dean, Faust Nocth. He presses the books back into my hands, taking a cursory glance at them. "Do forgive me, Miss Smith," he says. I consider following him. Asking him why I have a vampire roommate when no one else does. And why said roommate is Aliz Astra, of all people. But I'm not in any position to make myself look suspicious.

THE NEXT DAY I take lunch in the candlelit dining room of Tynarrich. As I dip a slice of fresh sourdough into a bowl of Cullen skink, I think of our prisoners. Callisto always leaves a vampire alive when dismantling a blood party, but only to take them back to HQ and gather intelligence.

And after they've answered all our questions, we use them to train against compulsion, as well as venom immunity. Most of our prisoners are Convert vampires, but Callisto never acknowledges their past humanity. The moment you decide to participate in a blood party, your humanity becomes null and void. I stir my soup and think of Julia, wondering how long she's been a vampire. Does she even remember what it was like to be human?

And although I'd rather do anything else but study, I actually have to pass my Integration subjects, which means handing in assignments on time. Such as writing an essay called "The First Hours of a Newly Sired Vampire."

I stick to my room. Astra, who never studies, nevertheless keeps her desk in a state of perpetual chaos. A dozen books are sprawled over the mahogany surface, and I'm pretty sure they are just there as décor.

I've barely written a page when I hear the clicking of the door, hinges creaking as it opens. As fast as I can, I pull my headphones on, hoping she'll ignore me.

"I can tell you're not listening to music," she says.

I turn, clenching my jaw. The vampire in my room glares right back at me from the door, her arms folded over her brown waistcoat.

"They're noise-canceling headphones," I say curtly.

"They're not very good if you can still hear what I'm saying," she retorts, a stupid smirk curling her lips. I grit my teeth. I've never wanted to drive a stake through someone's heart more than I do hers. I keep the headphones on, taking a deep breath to focus on the words on the pages in front of me.

As death settles, the blood of the sire ties the new vampire to its host. The vampiric germ will first latch on to the corpse's sinus, followed by—

"Early siring symptoms?"

She rests one hand on the back of my chair, and the other on the page. Her slender fingers are spread out, nails clipped short. On her index is a ring with a small emblem. I don't want to look up. But she's intent on annoying me. I crane my neck, and Astra fixes me with her insufferable gaze.

"What?" I ask sharply.

"Are you considering converting?" she asks, her voice too sweet.

"I would rather die," I say, and I offer her the tightest smile I can manage.

I expect her to back off. Instead, her left hand leaves the back of my chair and yanks down my headphones. "Dying is usually part of the equation," she whispers, breath against my ear.

My heart thuds painfully against my ribs. For her own safety, she should run. She should hope I never see her again. But the spoiled princess remains put, far too close to me, to the extent that I can smell the moss and rain fragrance she carries with her everywhere. The hand that pulled down my headphones is now on my shoulder, a finger drawing a line over my jumper. *Too fucking close.*

I grab her hand, crushing her cool fingers between mine. "If you even *think* about siring me, you'll live to regret it, Astra."

I let go of her hand, and she stares back at me in a stupor.

"As if I'd ever bite you," she says. "I'd rather become *parched.*"

"You'd do us both a favour."

"Or maybe I'll change my mind." She steps closer. Her skin is flushed. "So maybe you should find a new room, before it's too late."

"Make me," I say. *Fight me already.* I just need an excuse. Anything to wipe the smug look off her face.

"Don't worry," she says icily. "Sooner or later, I will."

chapter EIGHT

"Have you found the library?" Penny asks as soon as she picks up the phone.

"Not yet. I'm still working on my map." I look up at an overly ornate lamppost, possibly a few centuries old, painted black with golden embellishments. I give her a rundown of everything that happened in Inverness. "Five vampires *did* get away, but at least we now know Highland leeches like working together."

"Could they have been students?" she asks.

"I'm not sure," I say, looking around. The campus village is quiet, cobbled road blanketed with fallen leaves. "Though I'd like you to do some digging for me. Have you heard of the Red Ribbon Society? They're Convert supremacists. Maybe they're involved."

"Red Ribbon," Penny says slowly, drawing out each syllable. "It doesn't ring any bells."

"I can get some intel on them, too, if you're interested."

"No," she says. "Stay out of their way and focus on your mission. We can't have anyone finding out what you are."

"All right," I say, even though I know my curiosity won't let me keep far from the Red Ribbons' gallery for long.

"Have you met your roommate yet?"

I take a careful breath. "Yes," I say. "She's an Astra," I say her surname, breathing it out, and hear Penny's silence on the other end. She isn't one to hesitate, so the fact that she doesn't say anything strikes me as odd. "You there?" I ask.

"An Astra?" She whispers the name, as though it's poisonous. "At Tynahine?"

"Aye," I say, trying to keep my voice light. Penny says something, voice low, but I can't make it out. "Do you still want me to stay in that room?"

"I should have known this would happen," she says, and I swear I hear panic in her voice. "But yes. You have to stay there. Who is it, exactly? Is she from the main branch?"

"It's Aliz Astra," I say, lowering my voice, afraid she's lurking in the shadows, eavesdropping. "The heir."

Another long silence. I try to picture Penny. She's probably pacing from one bookcase to another. The moon is most likely shining through the stained-glass window of her office in the abandoned convent.

"Has she done anything to you?" she finally asks.

"As if," I say.

"You must be careful," Penny says. "You have no idea how dangerous that family is, Rebecca. Especially the heir. Their powers go far beyond that of a regular vampire."

I'm used to hearing Penny being in control. She sounds nothing like herself.

"Don't underestimate me," I say.

Aliz Astra may not be a regular vampire.

But I'm not a regular human, either.

Penny told me to not make myself known to the Red Ribbons. But if there's a chance they were involved with what happened in Inverness, I must do *something*. So, I get up earlier than I should, just after I hear Astra lowering the lid of her coffin. The narrow hallways of

Tynarrich Hall are dark, lanterns low, chandeliers lacking their usual glow. I know that if I go outside, all I'll find is an overcast sky. Wind and rain.

And even though I'd like some fresh air, I go down to the tunnels. This time I'm not looking for the secret library. I head straight to the gallery, hoping once again that the Red Ribbons may have left something behind. I take a meandering staircase, and just as I reach the hallway where the little gallery is hidden, I hear them.

Voices.

I stay back, waiting. They can't belong to vampires. Not this early. I peer out from the staircase; the hallway is empty, and the low drone of voices comes from behind the wooden door. I keep my cheek pressed to the stone wall, slightly damp. I can't make out a word they're saying. The staircase beneath me is still and silent. Slowly, I step out into the hallway, keeping each step as light as I can.

The door to the gallery is shut. But I can finally make out what the voices inside are saying.

"This would mean breaking the treaties," a husky baritone says. I glance through a thin slit in the side of the door.

The gallery inside is busy. Ten—maybe twelve—vampires, all in white shirts with red ribbons around their necks, leaning or sitting around the large table, drinking blood from ornamental glass goblets. The liquid is half a shade lighter than the synthetic stuff the university provides them with. I could recognise human blood anywhere. They all have those strange and frozen features of a Convert vampire. The table has a dozen candles, wax dripping onto metal dishes, while they all pass around books and leaflets.

"The treaties get broken all the time," a girl with short black hair, seated at the top of the table, says. She's the one I saw in Gustavsson's class. "I met an Avignon who kept a collection of vampire hunters in his dungeon just to drink fresh blood."

"Hunters don't count," another voice says as I suppress a shiver. *Avignon.* One of the Council's board members. The vampire speaking now seems to be a boy, no older than fifteen, though by the cut of his clothes, I can imagine he's been around for at least a century. "I say we send them a message. Drain a few humans, enough to spook them." I swallow hard.

"No," another voice interjects. "We should compel one of them to kill a vampire. Preferably someone with ties to the Council. They'll put Faust Nocth in jail and keep our campus free of roaches."

"Who, then?" the teenage boy asks.

"Aliz Astra," a voice says, and gasps travel around the table.

"No," the girl at the head of the table says, her voice tight.

"She fucked you once, three years ago," another vampire drawls. "Get over her, Jannet."

"If we get caught killing an Astra, the Council will make us sunbathe. Choose someone else."

A pause. "How about Elia Tamarit?"

No one complains at this suggestion. Who's *Elia*?

"And which human?" Jannet asks.

"Stephan Lazaar, the one with the vampire girlfriend."

A gasp escapes me, and although a human would definitely not have heard it, the vampires beyond the old wooden door most certainly did; Jannet looks straight through the gap, meeting my eye. I'm not sure if she sees me, but that doesn't matter. I run, and I'm only three steps away when I hear the door swing open, and a vampire shouts, "Get her!"

Vampires are fast. But I'm faster. I leap down the staircase. They didn't see my face. And I'm hopefully not the only human with red hair. I can hear them behind me, swearing. I know I could take them out. I feel for the stake in my satchel. But that would make a mess, wouldn't it? I take three tunnels, until I find one leading to the humanities building, still empty. I don't stop running until I find an exit. Only when the rain hits my forehead, do I start to calm down, grasping my knees and getting my breath back.

My boots sink into the mud, and as much as I want to look back, I'm afraid they're watching me. A part of me is disappointed. I shouldn't have run away. I should have stayed and fought.

But at least I know what they're planning.

The ice-cold drizzle starts to lighten by the time I reach campus security, located in a low building with a thatched roof, right next to the other hall of residence. *Taigh nan Iolairean,* or Iolairean Hall, is the slightly more modern building that Stephan—and most of the other newly arrived human students—are residing in. And had Penny not told me to remain in Astra's room, I would be living there, too.

I stop next to a willow tree, not yet going inside, and press the dial button on Stephan's contact. I don't know what I'm going to say. The dial tone rings out five times before he finally picks up, voice croaking as he says: "Cassie?"

"Are you awake?"

"No, I'm sleep talking," he grumbles. I hear a mattress creaking. "It's nine o'clock."

"I—" *You're being targeted by the vampire supremacist cult.* I can't seem to get the words out. "I need to talk to you. All three of you. Meet me in Tynarrich's dining hall in half an hour."

I hang up before he can protest.

I see a light switching on in one of the hall's rooms and make my way into the headquarters of campus security. A bell rings when I step in, and there's only one person here. It's the man who picked me up from the train station. The Familiar. He's taking notes, phone attached to his ear as he listens to what the person on the other end of the line says. He glances up at me, and then tells whoever he's speaking to that he'll call them back.

"Miss Smith," he says, as I close the door behind me. His office is quite bare. There are a dozen posters on the wall, most of them related to the dangers of spiked blood, but there is no sign of any weapons that would protect a human from a vampire, which is what I imagined the office existed for. "You're up early."

"Still working on changing my sleep schedule," I say. If he's a Familiar, why does he also work here? Does his *master* not pay him a living wage?

"How can I help you?"

He doesn't offer me a seat, despite the cushioned chair at the other side of his desk. I swallow, the adrenaline from the chase down in the tunnels slowly leaving my system. "Have you heard of the Red Ribbon Society?" I ask. His phone rings again, and he declines the call.

"I have not." A frown creases his brow as he stares at me. "You're from Edinburgh, aren't you?" he asks.

"Aye," I say. "The Red Ribbons are—"

"I'm not really getting Edinburgh from your accent," he says. A clock ticks from the wall, and for a moment it's the only sound in the office, louder than the drizzle outside.

Shit.

"I've moved about," I say. I did ask Penny, after she gave me a rundown of Cassie Smith's fictitious past, how I was going to convince people I was from Edinburgh when I don't have the accent. All Scottish people must sound the same to her, because she didn't think it would be an issue.

His phone rings a third time, and he lets it ring out as he stares me down.

"As I was saying," I start again, trying to ignore the tension in the room. "There's a group of vampires, the Red Ribbon Society, who're planning on framing a human for murder."

My hands feel numb. Until now, all my confrontations have been with vampires. But there's something about this man that sets all my nerves on edge. *Does he know?*

"Who are these vampires?" he asks. My mouth is dry. Before I can think of what to say, he continues, "You should know that Tynahine takes these kinds of allegations seriously, Miss Smith. If you're reporting someone due to your own prejudices, there will be consequences."

My face burns. "I have to answer this," he adds. "If you don't mind waiting."

Useless bastard, I think, and walk out, swallowing hard. Why did I expect him to help me in the first place? Campus security is clearly here for vampires only. I rush back to Tynarrich, taking off my glasses as the wind blows rain onto the lenses.

By the time I reach Tynarrich's dining hall, Ife and Stephan are already there. "It's too early," Ife complains. The cosy dining hall is quiet, most vampires still asleep. "You better have a good reason for waking us all up."

It's for your own sake. I bite my tongue and look down at my satchel. "Depends on your definition of 'good,'" I say. "I went for a walk this morning. Through the tunnels under the campus."

"As one does," Stephan says, while Ife yawns into the billowing sleeve of her jumper. Julia appears, slightly out of breath, and takes the empty armchair next to mine.

"Why are we here?" Julia asks, her eyes red with sleep.

"Cassie is telling us about her adventures in the tunnels," Stephan says.

"Aye. Well, I had a run-in with the Red Ribbons."

Ife is suddenly wide awake. Julia leans forward, gawking at me. "What happened?" Julia asks.

"They didn't see me. At least I don't think they did." I leave out the chase and my narrow escape. "But they have a plan to get humans kicked out of Tynahine."

All three of them stare at me, stunned.

"Well, go on," Ife urges.

"They want to compel a human to kill a vampire." And that human is Stephan.

"What?" Ife says, eyes wide as she looks around the dining hall. "Have you told the Night Dean?"

"No," I say. Perhaps I should have. But considering how I was treated by campus security, it would have been a waste of time. "And I won't. Do you really think they'll believe a newly arrived human over vampires who may have been here for decades, if not *centuries*?" No one says anything. "But *you* could tell them," I say carefully. "If it comes from a vampire..."

Ife rubs her eyes, drawing out a flask from her bag. She takes a swig and clears her throat. "I'll need names," she says. "If you see any of them, point them out to me."

"You'll have to be careful," I add. I glance at Stephan, ignoring the guilt that's made a home in my chest. *I have to warn him.* "Anyone could be a target."

"You should also be careful, then," Julia says, narrowing her eyes at me. "Perhaps going on walks down in the tunnels by yourself is a bad idea."

"Definitely," I say, before looking away from her. The worst thing that could happen if I cross paths with a Red Ribbon is they get staked. Bad idea, indeed.

I STRUGGLE TO fall asleep, dread tightening my stomach. I saw Jannet again, in Gustavsson's class, but she didn't spare me a glance. They don't know it was me. After two miserable hours of sleep, I wake to the sound of slurping. I grit my teeth. Why must she wake me? I push my bedsheets off my skin, far too warm, and take a long and careful breath.

The slurping has stopped. Maybe she's retreated to her coffin already. I sit up and bleary eyed, I peek through the gap in the curtains. The black drapes splitting our room in half are wide open.

Astra is on top of her coffin, lying flat on her back, with one leg dangling over the edge. In one hand she has a book, and in the other, a paper cup, presumably empty. I wish I could stop staring at her.

"You do realise how creepy you're being, don't you?" she asks.

I'm still hidden behind the curtains, staring through the sliver of open fabric. She tilts her head to the side, catching my gaze.

"I can hear you mouth-breathing. It's quite unsettling."

"Forgive me for being alive," I say, pulling the curtains open. I'm not wearing my glasses. I feel strangely naked without them. Astra's dark gaze trails down my body. I know why she's staring. My low-cut nightgown leaves very little to the imagination.

I'm used to vampires salivating over me, but Astra seems nothing except amused by my getup, pressing her lips together to hold back laughter. She looks back at her book, still smiling. If my blood wasn't laced with garlic, she wouldn't be so composed.

"Could you drink a little quieter, please?" I say, not hiding the acid in my voice.

"Where's this politeness coming from?" she says, feigning surprise.

"I'm trying to sleep," I say.

"I'd tell you to move to another room, but we both know you'd miss me."

"Piss off," I say.

"I know you're obsessed with me, Cassie," she says, and I scoff. She doesn't bother looking at me again when she continues speaking. "I have a feeling you don't quite understand how vampire senses work. Perhaps they haven't taught you this in Integration yet, but they're, how should I put this?" She closes her book, staring up at the ceiling. "Heightened."

"How so?" I ask. I already know the answer, but maybe if I listen to more of her arrogance I'll stop finding her so bloody attractive.

"It's in our nature," she says. "Vampires are predators. Humans, *you*, Cassie, are our perfect prey."

I fight the urge to laugh. A few too many vampires have made the mistake of assuming that. And now they're smoke and dust.

"Are you threatening me?" I ask, crossing my legs.

"Of course not!" she says, sitting up. "I just want you to understand that my senses are much more refined than yours. I can hear, see, *feel*, far better than you can. If you spy on me, I'll know. If you lie to me, I'll know that, too." She taps her fingers on the coffin. "I can prove it. Let's try with a simple yes-or-no question."

"I don't want to prove anything to you," I say.

The wind rattles our window, the highest branches hitting the pane. She's opened the heavy shutters, and the moon is almost full, perched upon silver clouds.

"Here's a fun one," she says, leaning back slightly. Her eyes meet mine when she asks: "Are you hiding something?"

Is she onto me?

"Everyone is hiding something," I say, and she purses her lips, disappointed.

"Sure." She seems to think for a moment, furrowing her brows before asking again. "Why come to Tynahine if you hate vampires?"

"I have vampire—"

"Friends?" she interrupts, scoffing. "Only for appearances," she says. "I'm pretty sure you can't stand them."

She's wrong. I can't believe that the thought crosses my mind, but I don't, in fact, hate Ife and Julia. I should, considering they're vampires. But there's nothing unsettling about their company. Unlike hers.

"Has it not occurred to you that perhaps the only vampire I dislike is *you,* Your Highness?" Humor slips from her face, hardening at the last two words I said. "I suppose that innate *superiority* of yours is only good at . . ." I pause, narrowing my eyes. "Are you good at anything, aside from sleeping around?"

"Be careful, Cassie," she says, a growl in her throat. One more push, and she'll lash out. She'll show her true colours and we'll put an end to this charade.

But instead, Aliz Astra pulls the black curtains shut. "How boring," I whisper, knowing she'll hear me.

Before I fall asleep, a plan starts to materialise in my mind. Once I have Penny's book and my revenge is secured, I'll stop taking my garlic supplements. I'll stay undercover just a few days longer than I'm supposed to, and I'll put Aliz Astra through hell. I'll stay just long enough to see the look on her face.

Maybe I'll bleed for her. Then she'll be the one *obsessed.* I'll have her on her knees, I'll let her have a taste. She'll lick blood from my fingers, and she'll plead for more. I'll make her break the treaties; I'll drive her insane. And then I'll go, and she'll spend the rest of her wretched eternity dying to taste me again.

chapter NINE

I wake the next morning with a cool dampness between my legs and pain shooting up my back. I already know, before I move, before looking down, what that pain is. Penny prepared me for this. She said to use either tampons or a cup, no pads, and I won't draw attention to myself. Cramps squeeze at my lower back, making my legs ache, and I wish that I could tear out my ovaries.

The one thing she *didn't* prepare me for, was disposal. Because I didn't think I'd have a vampire roommate. I find tampons to be the most comfortable, but I can't imagine having to go outside every time I change a tampon. Even if my blood smells bad, the thought of a vampire rummaging through the bins makes me nauseous. I fish through my things for the silicone cup, brand new, still in its box. I've never worn one before, but it can't be too difficult, right?

I hear Astra in her coffin, mumbling nonsense in her sleep. I focus on the instructions of the cup. I have to sterilise it before putting it in, and luckily enough, the microwave will do the trick.

But using the microwave means crossing into her side of the room. If she can use it in the middle of the night without waking me, then

I should be able to do the same. I make a makeshift pad with toilet paper, and I tiptoe over, tugging at the curtains.

Just before the microwave beeps, I hear a creaking sound behind me. Her coffin lid has moved up an inch, and although I can't see her eyes through the dark, I know she's watching me. I remain still.

What if she attacks me?

What if the garlic in my blood isn't enough to keep her away?

"Something smells weird," she croaks, voice like sandpaper.

"I got my period," I say, calm, before pulling out the bowl in which I'm sterilising the cup. She drops the lid of her coffin again, not saying another word, our room falling into silence. I head to the shower, my stomach clenching. I'm not sure if it's because I'm hungry or because I want to throw up. Probably both.

When I step back out into the room, the light is on, the curtains separating our sides of the room drawn open. The false window behind her coffin shows a caramel sunrise, half hidden by clouds. Astra stands next to her coffin, wearing a surgical mask the same shade as her hair, spraying down the walls with some kind of air freshener.

"I told you my senses are stronger," she says, voice muffled by the mask. "This is why I didn't want a human as my roommate."

I should probably be offended. But my cramps keep my temper in check. "Go back to bed," I say.

"Do you need painkillers?" she asks, pressing her mask tighter. "I think there is a pharmacy just outside Ambrose Hall."

Is she being *nice*? That's even more unsettling than her taunting. "No," I say again, and Astra narrows her eyes.

"I'm so disappointed, Cassie," she says, pulling her mask down. She sniffs the air, making a face. "I don't know what perfume you were wearing the day you arrived, but it smelled *amazing*." My heart skips a beat as she talks. I know I was late taking my garlic supplements, but I didn't think she would have picked up on the scent. "I did think that if that was what my human roommate was going to smell like, maybe it wouldn't be so bad, after all."

"Is that so," I say, trying to not let my temper show on my face.

"But *this* . . ." She points in my general direction, scrunching her nose. "Too metallic."

"Thanks," I say. If this is how she's planning on getting under my skin, it most certainly won't work.

"When are you going to wear that perfume again?" she asks, leaning on the wall.

"Maybe the day you move out of my room," I say.

She smiles, and it doesn't reach her eyes.

The full moon is hidden behind a curtain of rain clouds. I need to focus. The sooner I finish my mission, the sooner I'll get away from her.

I pointed Jannet out to Ife in Gustavsson's class, and she said we needed more names, more faces. If we only report Jannet and tell administration where the Red Ribbons are holding their meetings, they'll simply find a new spot, and a new name. "At least three," Ife said. But there's no way I'm risking another visit down to the gallery, not so soon.

I spend a good half hour amongst the history books of the fourth floor of Kinsnet. Professor Gustavsson mentioned that *The Book of Blood and Roses* may also contain spells from old grimoires, so it won't hurt to start looking in that area.

After searching every floor for anything resembling a witch's manual, I make my way to the front desk and try to appear normal as I mutter the word *grimoire*. The vampire librarian, a girl who looks no older than sixteen, types into an old computer. "The archive," she says with a melodic Inverness accent. "Over there."

She gestures to a collection of bookcases, all pretty bare, and between them, a white door with the words *Tasglann Kinsnet* above it. I glance back at the librarian, and she nods.

The metal door groans, revealing nothing but shadows. I step down onto a metal staircase, and a fluorescent light flickers on above me.

The archive is a fraction of the size of the library. It has metal pipes along the ceiling and far too many bookcases. They're all on wheels, with red turnstiles, most of them clustered together. Long lists are printed above and below the turnstiles. The stairs have a thick coat of dust, and I cough as I make my way down. More lights switch on as I cross the room, and by the time the last light switches on, filling the room with a buzzing sound, it's far too bright.

I should have looked down here ages ago, but there's something eerie about the archive. It's too cold, though it's missing the damp of the tunnels. There's something clinical, hospital-like, to the place. I breathe out, trying to remind myself that I'm a mere staircase from Kinsnet's grandiose hall. Halfway through the archive, I finally find a list with the word *Grimoires* printed on it, followed by a series of numbers that I'm sure will make sense once I get in.

The bookcases are pressed together, so to access it, I turn the turnstiles three rows away, slowly making my way back. As soon as the aisle opens, the stench of mould and dust hits my nostrils. The last turnstile squeaks, not used in years, if not decades. I give myself a shoulder's width of space, take another glance at the list, and step into the narrow aisle.

The tomes in here are *ancient.* Some are wrapped in plastic, with signs of *do not touch* stuck on their spines. Others are like works of art, miniature engravings on dark leather. They all have strange titles. *The Book of Lions, The Frog Catcher,* or, rather ominous, *Read This and Perish.* For a split second I think I'll find *The Book of Blood and Roses* tucked in beside them. I grab the first two, carefully placing them on the floor, before taking another one, called *Beiteag's Book of Spells.*

I open the latter, and before I can make out the first word, the lights die with a sudden clang.

"Great," I say. These three books should be enough. I can't see anything, but I can still feel the books beside me. Just as I shove them into my satchel, I hear it.

The turnstile turning, the wheels of the bookcase in front of me squeaking, getting closer.

I look towards the end of the aisle, pitch dark.

There's something there. Breathing. And then, flickering on like an old lightbulb, a pair of deadly red eyes.

chapter
TEN

The bookcases get closer, pressing against my shoulders. *Stay calm.* I run my hands over a shelf, grabbing the tallest book I can find. I shove it on the floor, just in time to stop the cases from crushing me.

The vampire doesn't move, but the red glow of her eyes helps mine adjust to the dark.

"This is a bad idea," I say slowly. The turnstile continues its squeaking, but the book beneath me seems to be sturdy enough. For now.

"You little roach." The vampire finally speaks, and I know I've heard her voice before. Jannet. *Don't get involved with the Red Ribbons,* Penny had said. I'd thought they hadn't recognised me. But I was wrong. "It wasn't enough for you to invade our campus," she hisses. "You just had to stick your nose where it ought not to be, didn't you?"

"I don't know what you're talking about," I say. The turnstile, which had for a second gone quiet, starts squeaking again. But this time in the opposite direction, giving me breathing room. "Listen, I don't want trouble."

"A little too late for that."

I hear footsteps at the other end of the aisle.

I draw out the chain from my watch.

"Jannet," a voice says behind me, weaker, trembling. "This is a bad idea."

"I told you to not join us if you can't handle the dirty work, Stella," Jannet says, voice sharp. She stalks towards me, entering the narrow aisle.

Her red eyes bore into mine, and I feel the back of my head prickle, then grow numb as she attempts to compel me. "You're going to kill Elia Tamarit," she says, putting a hand on my neck, forcing me to look into her deadly eyes. Her nails are sharp, strangely damp. "And then you're going to kill yourself."

"But I don't know who that is," I say. *Bite me*, I think. Instead, Jannet stabs her nail into my neck, tearing the skin. Pain shoots through me, my knees suddenly weak.

"Look for her, and then—"

Before she can finish, I tighten my grip on my blade and slice upwards. The silver melts through her face, and she screams. Burning flesh hides the stench of her venom. Stella cries out behind me and starts running. But just like last time, I'm faster. I grab her long hair and shove her against the cold metal wall. She whimpers, while behind us, Jannet is clasping her face, making a gargling sound. I hold the blade under Stella's neck, and she sobs. I hear it sizzling against her pale skin. "You won't tell anyone about this, will you?" I ask in a low voice.

She shakes her head.

I should kill them both. Shove their dust under a bookcase, and hope no one comes back down into the archive. But they're not working alone. *Shit. Shit. Shit.*

What would Penny do? She's always in control. Jannet crawls out from between the aisles, holding her bloodied face, and when her wide eyes meet mine, she's terrified. Stella is still clasping her neck, trembling. Maybe they'll keep quiet.

And when questions come, I'll say I was defending myself.

The excuse might not last long. But it'll have to do.

Gritting my teeth, I turn on my heel and run through the dark.

The pain in my neck deepens. She must have licked her nail before stabbing me with it.

A few heads turn to stare as I race out of Kinsnet, and my head is pounding once I stumble out into the cold night. The wound is burning, mixing with the ache in my head. Then there are my period cramps, still twisting my insides. Pain continues to spread, my sight blurring. Does that leech even know her venom could kill a human?

I reach Tynarrich, hand clasped over the shallow cut on my neck. I slump against the cool wall of the lift, doors closing before it starts to climb up to the ninth floor. My head is swimming, cold sweat covers my forehead, red hair sticks to my skin in damp strands.

My room is empty. Penny told me to stay away. Focus on my mission. Why didn't I listen to her?

I struggle out of my coat, and then grimace when I see the bloodstain on my shirt. I take it off, and hope Astra doesn't walk in now. My period cup is full, so I empty and rinse it. My cold sweat turns into a shiver. A bath wouldn't do me any harm, I think, turning the hot tap until steaming water pours from the faucet. Astra has a selection of bath salts. I consider pouring them all in just to piss her off, but I'm too dizzy to do anything except climb into the scalding water.

She probably won't be back for several hours. She's probably in some semi-public corner of campus, fucking another vampire. The cut on my neck burns as Jannet's venom sinks into my blood. I stare up at the ceiling. How am I going to explain my way out of this? But before anxiety can distract me from the pain in my neck, the white steam clouds my vision, pulling me under.

"Cassie?"

Her voice is distant, yet somehow near at the same time.

"Go away," I manage to say. The bath has gone cold, but I can't move, my bones heavy, melting into the porcelain shell of the tub.

"Please." Astra's voice is tight, much closer now. I can feel her breath on me. "Cassie, please wake up."

I do, blinking as I find her leaning over me, face too close to mine, metallic breath against my lips. I'm not in the bath, but in my bed.

"Must have been a very low concentration," Astra says, one hand on my cheek, her skin cool and smooth.

"Low?" I croak, and I don't sound like myself.

"Vampire venom is deadly," she says. "And quick."

When I was first recruited, I spent months poisoning myself. One small dosage at a time, my own personal attempt at mithridatism. But clearly all that work was for nothing, because the venom has taken a real toll on my body, weighing down my muscles. My period cramps just add an extra layer to the pain.

"If it had been a higher dosage, you wouldn't have made it home."

That word, *home,* is so incredibly strange. So out of place.

"It's too hot," I whisper, head thumping. The curtains of my bed are open already, but she pulls them further apart. Then she unlocks the shutters and opens the window wide. Wind blows in, making a mess of Astra's short and carefully styled hair. Why is she here?

"I have to cure you now, before it's too late, all right?" she says, and I blink, staring at her.

"Cure me?" A panic the likes of which I've not felt in years seizes ahold of me. "If you bite me I—"

"I'm not going to bite you," she says, dumbfounded. She vanishes for a moment and reappears with a dagger. "I'm going to pour a few droplets of my blood onto the wound," she says.

The wound burns, and I stare at her, my eyes wide. "No, you're not."

"My blood has healing properties," she says, aggravated. She puts the dagger down. It's close enough for me to grab it. I can still defend myself. "It's an antidote for practically every wound and poison you can imagine."

"I'm *not* being turned into a vampire," I snarl, and my hand is close, so close to the dagger.

Astra sighs again, shaking her head. "I— You do realise you would have to die first for that to happen, right? I'm trying to stop that from happening!" She twists the hem of her shirt. She's nervous.

"Why?" I ask.

"What?"

"Why do you want to help me?"

"Because it's the right thing to do?" she says. "Just because you think I'm a monster, doesn't mean I actually am one."

I think I'll recover naturally—but what if I'm wrong?

"Please, Cassie," she says, leaning over me again, her brows knotted tight, as though glaring will somehow convince me.

I have to say no.

Just the thought of her blood mingling with mine makes me want to throw up.

"Are you sure it won't kill me?"

"It won't," she whispers.

Clouds clear, revealing a full moon. A crow flies past our window, joining the murder that lives on the branches below. "All right, then," I finally say. The moon's silver glow shines on my bed, covering us both.

She breathes out, relieved, and lifts the dagger. "Look away if you don't want to see my blood," she says, holding her palm out.

I watch. I've seen plenty of vampires bleed before. She winces as she draws the blade across her skin, the dark liquid instantly pooling in her cupped hand. "You won't feel a thing," she assures me.

She presses her blood-soaked hand to my neck, and just as she promised, I don't feel anything. Nothing but my own pulse, loud, beating against her skin. A strange feeling rushes through me as her blood seeps into the wound, warmth slowly eating away at the pain.

Her frown relaxes, and she smiles. "There. It's gone."

The pain, as she promised, vanishes. Even my period cramps. Slowly, I sit up. I'm in my nightgown, although I have no memory of putting it on. Her shirtsleeves are wet. It's only now, as the pain recedes, that I realise she must have gotten me out of the bath. She's seen me naked.

I touch my neck. The wound has healed completely; all that's left is the sticky residue of her blood. The feeling makes me want to vomit, but I keep that to myself. I can't believe I let her heal me. "Thank you," I say.

Aliz gawks at me, shocked by the words. She clears her throat, and I could swear she looks embarrassed. "You should rest," she says, mattress creaking as she gets up. "But now I need to have a word with whoever did this to you," she says, darkness slipping into her voice.

"Did what?" I ask, reaching for my water bottle. Astra crouches down, picking something up from the floor. My white shirt with a couple of spots of blood on the collar. I sigh. "Some girls," I say.

"What did they look like?"

"Vampires."

She narrows her eyes at me. "Very funny. At least try to describe them."

"A vampire's beauty is impossible to describe," I say. Strength slowly returns to my muscles.

"Was it the Red Ribbons?" she asks. I bite my tongue, keeping my expression neutral. *Shit.* I see her rummaging through her bag for something. A makeup wipe of some sort. Before I can ask what she's doing, she sits next to me again and rubs it against my neck, cleaning the blood. I clench my teeth, trying to ignore our proximity. "I knew they were plotting something, so if—"

"How did you know?" I ask, not breaking eye contact. She's so close. The scent of her blood, of my own, mingle with the mossy fragrance she carries everywhere. "Are you a member?" I already know she isn't, but I like seeing her frown.

"Don't be ridiculous."

"Just last night you told me you were superior."

"No, I said my senses were more refined. And I was only trying to annoy you," she says. "Please, Cassie. Just tell me."

"I don't remember them," I say. "It all happened very quickly, all right?"

"I'm trying to help you."

"You already did," I say. "The wound is gone."

"Fine," she says, exasperated. "But I'm going to find whoever did this to you, whether you like it or not."

I wait until she's out of the room before picking up my phone. *Did you know that Astra blood is magical?*

I type this, almost hit send, but I stop. If I tell Penny about Aliz's blood, I'll have to tell her about my encounter with the Red Ribbons, after she explicitly told me to stay away. The feeling that I might have disappointed her aches almost as much as the wound in my neck did.

That odd warmth that slipped beneath my skin when Aliz healed me hasn't left yet.

I stare out at the moon one last time before shutting the window. When I close my eyes, I can still feel her hand, pressed to my neck, and her breath against my lips.

chapter ELEVEN

My neck is itchy. I start scratching before I'm even fully awake, pulling at my skin as though there's something stuck inside. I open my eyes, and search through my bedsheets for my phone.

It's already eleven. If Jannet and Stella told anyone about last night, campus security would have barged into my room by now. The black curtains that separate our room are wide open, and for the first time, I'm not perturbed by the sight of her coffin.

Why would she help me? I let out a shaky breath, trying to get her out of my mind. Until now all she's wanted was to get me out of here. And yet last night, for some reason, she helped me.

I scratch my neck again, my blunt nails not alleviating the feeling. I wonder if this itch is some kind of side effect of her blood. Either way, I don't have time to sit around pondering. I rush into the bathroom, fighting with the demonic silicone cup. And I almost, *almost,* don't see my reflection. But I look up for just a second as I brush my teeth and see it.

At first, I think it might be some kind of spot, or maybe a scar.

But then I peer closer.

The place that Jannet stabbed, and Aliz healed, is tattooed with a small black moon, two thorny vines surrounding it. It's beautiful. And I'm sure I've seen it somewhere before.

Still holding my toothbrush, I step out into the room, turning on the light. I walk over and stare, without a word, at the design that decorates her coffin. Hers is gold, mine is black. But it's the same. A crescent moon, surrounded by a tangle of thorns.

I take a step back, nausea almost knocking me off my feet. I put my toothbrush down on the desk, swallow the toothpaste, and knock on her coffin, trying to remain calm. There must be an explanation for this. Whatever *this* is.

"Go away," she groans from inside, and I hear her turning.

There's an empty paper cup on her desk, stained red, next to a large book about colour theory. A pile of notes, some of them crumpled up. I find the handle on her coffin, and I pull it open.

Despite being a vampire hunter, I've never seen the inside of a vampire's coffin before. It actually looks comfy, although far too narrow to be able to sleep in. The sides are padded with velvet. But the only thing I can look at is her, her bare legs kicking off her black silk sheets, her toned arms trying to hide her face from the light.

"Aliz?" I say, keeping my voice calm.

"No," she says, trying to pull the lid back down.

"Aliz," I repeat, keeping the coffin open, light flooding into it. She hisses, showing her fangs. "Look at me!"

"Go away," she croaks, her voice low and hoarse.

I grab her arms, pulling them away from her face, and she finally looks at me, glaring. It takes a few seconds, but she sees it.

"When'd you get the tattoo?" she asks, sitting up, and I feel like screaming.

"What is this?"

She rubs her eyes and looks at my neck again. She reaches out to touch it, and with the contact, the unbearable itch subsides. Her skin is like a cooling balm, and I breathe out an involuntary sigh of relief. I almost step closer to her, but then she speaks. "It's my family crest," she says in a small voice.

I swat her hand away and the itch returns. "Your family crest?"

"Well..." She clears her throat then yawns. "A moon bound in thorns. That's the Astra crest." My heart thuds against my ears, and she grabs my arm without a care in the world, pulling me closer to get a better look at it. She touches it again, lips ajar. My breathing hitches, but for once, she doesn't react.

Focus, I tell myself, prying my arm free from her grip. "What the fuck is this?"

"Uh..." Her expression is lost, inching towards panic. "I don't know."

"But you did it!"

"No, I didn't," she protests. "You think I can draw? I would be an art major if I could."

"Aliz, this is where the cut was. The one you healed with your blood."

She blinks. Her white brows settle into a frown, and she narrows her eyes. "That happened," she says. "And you still haven't told me who attacked you."

"What happened to the last human you healed?" I ask, my heart thudding.

She rubs her eyes, still half asleep. "I've never healed a human before," she says.

"What?"

"You're the first human I've given my blood to."

"You better be joking," I say, anger coiling inside me.

"I was trying to save you!" she says. "You would have died."

"Fine," I snap. "But I want to know what this mark is."

"I don't know," she says, exasperated.

"Well, figure it out," I say. My teeth grit as frustration continues to bubble within me. "I've got class, but by lunch you better know how to get rid of it." I scratch it, and Aliz simply stares at me, bewildered. I have a terrible feeling about this. But she nods.

"I will," she says.

I grab a tartan scarf to wrap around my turtleneck, just for good measure, and hope that whatever this mark is, it'll be gone before I see her again.

Between each class, I stop in a toilet, hiding in a cubicle, using my phone to look at my neck. It's still there.

The itch in my neck starts to subside around dinnertime. I've been jumpy all day, waiting to see Jannet and Stella step out of the shadows, but they don't. When I spot Stephan and Julia at our usual table, playing cards, I finally feel a little normal again. "Where's Ife?" I ask, and when I sit, Julia's shoulders tense. She stares at me, lips ajar.

"I like your scarf, it's very fashionable," Stephan says. He places a queen down on the table, and Julia picks it up.

"Thanks," I say. I steal a glance at Julia, who doesn't say anything. Why did she look at me like that?

"Did you-know-who bite you?" he asks, resting his chin on his hand.

"You know they're not allowed to do that."

"Sure, but maybe the heir to the most powerful family in Europe can get away with things an ordinary vampire can't," he counters.

"Well, she didn't," I say. Instead, she gave me her blood. The more I think about it, the worse it sounds.

"What's your dissertation on, Cassie?" Julia asks, changing the subject.

"I'm not sure yet," I say. "Maybe Ravel's post-conversion pieces."

"Ravel?" Julia says. "Nice."

"Have you met him?" I ask, and Stephan, who was shuffling cards, starts laughing.

"Uh, how old do you think I am, Cassie?" Julia asks, leaning one arm on the table.

I look at her. Truth be told, she looks my age. Younger, even. Converts, like Julia, are frozen forever at the age they were bitten. So, although she looks like she's in her late teens, she could easily be thousands of years old.

"Sixty," I say, which seems a fairly reasonable number.

"I'm twenty-two," she says. "Got bitten four years ago. I was an ordinary human until I was eighteen."

The word *ordinary* catches me off guard.

"We're the same age," I whisper. I could have been in Julia's shoes.

Four years ago, our lives were identical. Four years ago, vampires changed everything. I feel as though she wants to say more, and for once I want to hear it. But instead, her gaze drops to my neck, eyes narrowing. I touch my scarf. It's still in place.

Aliz enters the canteen. I don't see her, so I have no idea how I know that she's here, but when I look up, she's cutting her way through the crowd, ignoring her flock as she heads straight to the blood stall. The itch returns to my neck, and I scratch it through the scarf. She doesn't look over at our table.

Ife joins us shortly after sunset, pressing a kiss on both Stephan's and Julia's cheeks.

"By the way," Ife says, leaning on the table. "I spoke to the Night Dean last night. I know we only had one name, but he says he's been looking into the Red Ribbons. And he won't let any harm come to his dear human students."

Considering I was almost crushed to death and poisoned, he's not doing a particularly good job. I play with the fabric of my scarf, forcing myself to stay calm.

"For some reason, they all stopped wearing their ribbons, but he told me he's caught a few of them already. Even if they don't give him names, the rest will chicken out."

"Right." What if it's Jannet and Stella? If he *caught* them last night, their silver-inflicted wounds would still have been visible. And what would stop them, at that point, from telling him I was the one who wounded them? Panic rises from my stomach, and I bite my lip. It's all right. I haven't been called to his office yet. He doesn't know what I am.

When I look up, Aliz is staring in my direction. She makes a short gesture with her head, nodding towards a back entrance of Ambrose Hall. I let out a sigh of relief. She's figured out what the mark is, hasn't she? And she'll know how to get rid of it. "I'll see you later," I say, and they watch me, not without suspicion, as I rush off.

I spot her in one of the wider tunnels, connecting Ambrose Hall to the history department. She's waiting in front of a painting, and before I can reach it, she pulls it open and steps inside. *A secret tunnel.* The painting depicts a canopy of white flowers and a sky free of clouds, the sort of landscape that a vampire will never see in person. I tug at the painting's ornate frame, finding a door behind it.

The dark tunnel smells damp. It's cold, with puddles reflecting the dim lanterns that fringe the old stone walls. Aliz is under one of those lanterns, hair dyed orange by the light. An odd warmth spreads through me as I get closer to her, and the itch in my neck slowly starts to fade again.

"So," I say, hands on my waist. "Do you know what the mark is?"

She hesitates, and only when I see her expression do I realise that something is wrong. Her eyes are wide, jaw tense. She's got her hands clasped together, rubbing them without pause. "I— Yes." She takes a deep breath, not looking me in the eye. "We fucked up."

"What do you mean, *we*?"

"We'll go to Kinsnet," she says, ignoring my question. "I'm sure we'll find a cure for it."

"Cure?" The itch in my neck increases. "But didn't you *cure* me last night?"

"I should have realised it when I saw it. But you woke me at that unthinkable hour, and well—"

"Yes?"

"It's a Familiar's mark." She looks away, her lips pursed tightly together. "I've never given my blood to a human before, so, you know—I didn't think that would happen, but why don't we head to the library? The sooner we get to work, the sooner you'll be rid of it."

I breathe in, trying to stay calm. "You're joking, right?" I say. I laugh, waiting for her to laugh, too. But her face remains frozen in a picture of guilt.

"I'm afraid not," she whispers, biting her lower lip.

"No," I say in a small voice. Familiars are the lowest scum in the vampire world. Humans who exchange their freedom for a chance to be sired, for a promise of immortality. They do a vampire's dirty work. Luring other humans into blood parties, just to please their masters. "I'm not your Familiar."

"Well," Aliz says, scratching the back of her neck. "According to that mark, you are."

I hear Penny on the phone, warning me about the Astra power. My throat tightens, and I run my fingers across the mark. A Familiar's mark.

"You knew this would happen, didn't you?" My voice, sharp, echoes on the curved walls of the tunnel. "That's why you were so friendly last night. Because I didn't move. Because you didn't get what *you* wanted."

Hurt flashes across her eyes. My mouth dries as I wait for her to say something. Tell me I'm right. But instead, her breath trembles, and she looks at the ground. If I didn't know better, I'd think she was on the verge of tears. The sound of dripping echoes in the distance, and I hear my own laboured breathing. I have to stop myself from hyperventilating. This isn't happening. "You don't have to believe me," Aliz whispers after a pause. "But I had no idea this would happen." *Bullshit.* "I'll fix this," she says. "We must have accidentally performed some kind of blood contract last night." Her voice trembles. "There was a full moon, wasn't there?"

"Blood contract?"

"I'm sorry," she whispers.

"How," I start, my voice low, "do I get rid of it?"

"I don't know," she replies. "We'll figure something out, all right?"

I should kill her right now, right here. I agreed to her giving me her blood, but I did not agree to *this*. "There is no *we*," I hiss, trying to keep my trembling hand from slipping into my bag and grabbing a stake.

It still hasn't hit me. I can't be.

A *vampire hunter* cannot, under any circumstances, be a vampire's *Familiar.*

chapter TWELVE

I leave Aliz in the tunnel. Well, my exact words to her were *follow me and I'll pull your fangs out*. I don't need her help. I will *never* work with her. But I rush to scour Kinsnet for some kind of cure. It must have one.

A Familiar may be a leech's lapdog, but they are a *willing* lapdog. Which I am not. So undoing the blood contract should be simple enough. Maybe I have to pour my own blood into an open wound on Aliz's neck. My garlic will kill her. What a pity.

Books about Familiars are located on the fifth floor. Most students must know that Aliz uses it as a hookup spot, so it's understandably empty. My neck itches again, and I dig my nails through the scarf. Why is it itchy? Just as I grab a hefty volume on the history of Familiars, the book behind it is pulled down, creating a window in the bookcase.

And through that window, Aliz's eyes, black holes beneath snowy brows, stare back at me.

"We'll find a cure if we work together," she says. Her voice is too calm.

"Piss off."

"Cassie," she says, exasperated. She pulls another book down, widening the gap. "I get that you're angry, but—"

"Angry?" I whisper. I get up on my tiptoes, but even then I'm still not quite at eye level with her. "Angry?" I repeat, letting her hear the ice on my tongue. "Ask me one more time to work with you, and I will pray so loud and clear that your beautiful little ears will bleed."

Aliz Astra presses her lips together, before shoving the books that created the window back into place. I hear her storm off, hopefully for the last time.

If I ever have to work with someone, it will be Penny. I grip the bookshelf, pressing my forehead against it. I should tell her. She'll know how to fix this. But maybe she'll kick me out of Callisto. Because no hunter in their right mind would let a vampire heal them. What was I thinking?

Before I can slam my forehead against the shelf in frustration, I continue my search for the cure. And after leafing through two dozen books, I finally find something in a crimson, leather-bound book. I run my fingers down the page, stopping on a passage.

Blood Familiars, those bound by blood contracts, are expected to serve their masters for a minimum of ten years before they are converted.

Ten years of service? I keep reading, certain that I'll find a way to annul the contract. But instead, I find something far worse. *Blood Familiars are bound to their master's word and will do whatever is asked of them.* I pause, my eyes widening. Suddenly, as I read what comes next, I'm certain I'm going to throw up. *Just as if they are being compelled.*

It can't be. It took months of training, but I'm immune. She can't compel me. What if the mark has changed that? What if her word alone can bend my will? A shiver runs through me, and I'm forced to sit, hands trembling as I picture this twisted future, scurrying after her, obeying her every wish and whim.

No.

There must be another way.

I squeeze my eyes shut, taking a deep breath, before I continue reading. And my racing heart, my dread, my fear, all of it vanishes when I see the next sentence.

Should either party die, the mark will vanish.

I STARE AT the ceiling, wide awake. An hour ago, I heard her coffin creak shut. I wipe cold sweat from my forehead, and open the curtains that shield my mattress from view, letting the cool air touch my skin.

Books are splayed open on her desk, and when I check my watch, it's already six.

Becoming a vampire's Familiar is a fate far worse than death. I reach for my burgundy satchel. As quietly as I can, I pull out my wooden stake and slow my breathing. I've done this a hundred times. And this time, it's not someone else's life that's on the line. It's mine. My freedom.

I step over, making it through the curtains. My eyes adjust to the dark, and just as I did yesterday, I slot my fingers under the handle of her coffin. It lets out a small squeak before I pull it open.

I can't hesitate.

She'll wake now, so before she does, I have to plunge the stake through her heart. It was on purpose. How could the heir to the Astra family not know what she was doing? She said she'd find a way to make me leave. This was all part of her plan.

But why am I trying to find excuses to kill a vampire? I've been able to do it without thinking for the last four years.

Inside the coffin, Aliz lies completely still but for the slow rise and fall of her chest. She's fast asleep, wearing a cotton vest and underwear. Her long legs have kicked off her covers. My hands tremble as I grip the stake, and very carefully position it over her chest. She doesn't even flinch when the wooden tip rests above her heart.

chapter
THIRTEEN

I keep the stake there. I must do it. I've spent four years giving my life, risking all I have for Callisto, slaying the same enemy, over and over. Penny would be able to do it. But Penny wouldn't have ended up in this position in the first place. I take a deep breath. Aliz's eyelids tremble, and her silver lashes flutter. "Cassie," she mumbles. My fingers numb as I stare at her, feeling my resolution crumble.

I can't.

As soon as I pull my weapon away, relief floods through me, as though it was my own heart I'd been about to pierce. As quietly as I can, I lower the lid of her coffin and wait, expecting to hear her stir. But Aliz remains asleep, unaware of the monster in her room.

I shove the stake back in my bag. Then I lean against the bed, sitting with a tight grip on my knees, folded, trying to breathe.

I can't hurt her.

THREE WHOLE DAYS pass during which I manage to avoid her, never looking her way when she walks into Ambrose Hall. I haven't seen

Jannet in Gustavsson's class, but I can't shake the feeling that it's only a matter of time before the Night Dean calls me to his office. So I have to finish my mission as fast as I can.

I split my day into three blocks. The main one, finding *The Book of Blood and Roses,* gets six hours, early in the morning, when I know I won't run into any leeches in the tunnels. And although I haven't found it yet, the map in my notebook has started to take shape, a great tangled labyrinth of a thousand tunnels, with as many as six floors digging beneath the earth.

I split another five hours between Integration and my *normal* classes. And what's left, I spend in Kinsnet, gathering books from the archive, searching for the words *blood contract.* Vampires walk past my cluttered table on the fourth floor, filled with empty coffee cups and a dozen books. Occasionally, they stop to stare at the subject of my research, but none of them say anything. So far, the only cure I've found is death.

I know I should try again, before it's too late.

On the fourth day, Aliz Astra finally decides to crack through the wall I built between us. I find her sitting on my desk, early in the morning, just after I finish showering. The mark aches against my neck, becoming itchier with each passing second. I know that if Aliz touches it, the discomfort will vanish, just as it did the morning I found the mark.

"I got you this," she says, lifting a long white box. I stare at her, not daring to step closer. "It's a topical cream, with aloe vera and"—she squints at the box—"chemicals. It's for rashes and bites, and hopefully—"

"Why?" I ask, folding my arms.

"I know you don't believe me, but it wasn't on purpose." She rushes, seemingly afraid I'll interrupt her. "I didn't know. I swear it."

I want to tell her that her words don't mean shit. But something stops me.

She pulls a tube from the box and holds it out like an olive branch. I grit my teeth, but finally walk over and take it from her. "You've been looking for a cure?" I ask.

"Of course," she says, gaze locked with mine. "I've searched through five libraries already." I blink. She's covered more ground than I have. I unscrew the tube and squeeze a pea-sized drop of gel onto my fingers. I rub it against the mark, and for a few seconds, the itch vanishes.

"I'm assuming you've found the full list of *qualities* a Blood Familiar has," I say, spreading a little more. Aliz gives a small nod, swallowing hard.

"Cassie, I didn't mean for this to happen."

I want to tell her to fuck off. But when I look at her, I get the sense that she's telling the truth. I've never seen her so fragile. I keep my lips pressed tight before letting out a sigh. "Sure, you didn't," I say. "We should test it."

"What?"

I step closer. "We need to know if it's true. If your *word* alone can compel me."

"I can't do that," she says, panic-stricken. "We'd be breaking the treaties!"

"I'm pretty sure we already have," I say.

We haven't.

If I was an ordinary human, then yes, I imagine that forming a blood contract without the human's knowledge is punishable with a century in prison. Fortunately for Aliz, however, vampire hunters are an exception. We are not protected by those laws. "We need to know how much damage this has done," I say, pointing at my neck. "So, hurry."

"But what—" She takes a deep breath, and you would think that Aliz was the one branded with a Familiar's mark. "What do I say?"

"I don't know," I say. "Just give me an order. Tell me to clap my hands or something."

She takes another deep breath and closes her eyes. "All right," she whispers and finally looks at me with an odd resolution. "Twirl," she says.

My body remains firmly in place. I don't feel anything, but Aliz's expression is twisted with worry.

"I didn't do it, did I?" I ask.

"No," Aliz says, and she lets out a long breath. "So, it's not working."

I lean against one of my bedposts, exhaling. *I'm not under her control.* But my relief is short-lived.

"Don't be so quick to celebrate," I say. "We don't know enough about the mark. Maybe it hasn't come into effect yet." My neck itches again just as I say this, and I dig my short nails into my skin, unable to get rid of the feeling. Her little gift only worked for a few seconds. "Can you touch my neck?" I ask without thinking.

"What?"

"When you last touched it, the itch went away," I say, and I start thinking it may have been a bad idea to ask for this proximity, until her skin touches mine. Her fingers are cool against my neck, instantly soothing the itch. I let out a short breath, closing my eyes. I almost thank her.

"I promise we'll find a way out of this," she whispers. We stay like this, closer than a human and a vampire should ever be. I swore to myself that I wouldn't work with her, but as her finger draws a circle around the black moon on my neck, I cave in.

"Where will we look next?" I ask, looking up. Aliz's expression brightens, lips parting as she realises what I just said. What I agreed to. I must be going mad.

"I still haven't looked in the Palau Collection," she whispers. The Palau Collection is the second largest library, adjacent to the history department, opened by a Catalan alchemist of the same name, in the fourteenth century. When she draws her fingers from my neck, the itch creeps up again, though nowhere near as bad as it was before. Almost as if the mark wanted me to stop avoiding her.

We leave our room, heading down into one of the tunnels to the campus village. Aliz stops at the top of a winding staircase to catch her breath, and glances down at me. "If we don't find anything in the Palau Collection, we could also try the secret library."

I gawk at her, and too late, I forget to hide my reaction.

"You've heard of it?" she asks, all while my pulse picks up. *This is it*. I'm finally going to finish my mission. Aliz, of all people, knows where the secret library is.

I suppose it's a good thing I haven't killed her yet.

"I have," I say, and she stares at me a little too long. Maybe I should have said no. But she would have known I was lying. "I mean, I didn't know if it was real or not. I did some research on Tynahine before coming here." Penny did all the research. I just leeched off her hard work. "Where is it?" I ask in the most casual voice I can muster.

"Somewhere deep in these tunnels." She leans against the stone wall. "But no one has ever found it."

I hide my disappointment. My throat tightens, but I nod. "Right," I whisper. Aliz knowing it exists is already a step in the right direction.

"Let's go," she says, suddenly grabbing my hand and pulling me along. I glance down at her fingers, cool against my own. I should tear my hand free. But just as I couldn't slam the stake through her chest, I can't seem to tug myself away from her now, either.

We reach the Palau Collection in a few minutes, a small building with a low roof. It's roughly the size of Kinsnet's archive, and the volumes are, to say the least, eclectic. Half of them cover transmutation, which is fitting, considering who compiled them. The librarian is an old woman, amongst the scarce human staff, and she stares at us with suspicion. Even if she's new, she must be aware of Aliz's reputation.

"Any books on blood contracts?" Aliz asks, and the librarian doesn't appear to think much about the question. She types into an old-fashioned computer and tells us to head to the seventh aisle.

We're the only students here, and as soon as we find the aisle in question, Aliz's expression changes, black eyes studying the books with the same intense expression I've seen on vampires scenting my blood. The bookcases in the Palau Collection are all mismatched, some hundreds of years old, while others are made of glass and metal.

"Here," she whispers, reaching for a book. Her other hand brushes mine, and this time, her fingers linger, not pulling back. I feel her thumb drawing a line against my palm, her touch incredibly light. I open my mouth, but I can't find words. I could easily draw my hand away, but I don't want to.

The contact vanishes, and she searches through the pages of her book. I inhale, squeezing my hand, trying to get rid of the lingering sensation.

"Blood contracts between vampires," she whispers.

"I'm human," I say, crossing my arms, keeping my hands away from where she can accidentally touch them.

"I know," Aliz says and continues reading. "Blood contracts with humans," she finally says, leaning against the wall of books. Her brows knot into a frown. "Ah, this won't do. A lot of killing."

"We're looking for Familiars," I whisper, ignoring the last word she said. I reach for another book, getting up on my tiptoes to grab it, trying to slide my fingers between the pages to nudge it out. Aliz pushes my hand aside and grabs it easily. I wait for a quip of sorts, but she hands it to me without a word.

"How many can we check out?" I ask.

"Five each," she says, standing too close.

And for the third time today, her hand finds mine. Her fingers brush down my palm, between my fingers, as though she doesn't know if she should take it or not.

I step away from her. "Maybe we should go," I say, grabbing another book.

"Good idea," Aliz replies. We end up borrowing nine books, and the librarian doesn't raise an eyebrow at the subject matter. I wonder if it's normal for vampires and humans to read about this sort of thing.

"You take the tunnel," I say, as I surveil outside the library. The history department is quiet. "I'll go through the pine grove."

"Why?" she asks, gazing down at me.

"People might think it's weird if we're suddenly best friends," I say. "You did hiss at me two weeks ago."

"That was my way of saying hello," she quips. I roll my eyes.

"Sure. And threatening to have me for dinner is a vampiric greeting."

She looks like she's about to argue, her jaw tight, but finally nods.

Once I step out into the October chill, a light drizzle speckling my jacket, I feel myself cooling down. But dread continues to twist inside me. No. It's not dread. I know what it is, but I can't admit it.

The ghost of her touch still lingers on my skin. Wanting her was so much easier when I only looked at her from afar.

I CLIMB UP the nine floors of Tynarrich Hall, hoping the exertion will somehow calm me, return me to my previously sensible self. I stare at the paintings on the wall and realise that I still don't know how old she is. For all I know, Aliz could be over a hundred years old. Over a thousand. I wait for her features to appear upon one of the canvases, but they don't.

Fortunately, when I get to our room, Aliz seems completely normal again.

"Can you pass me my phone?" She's sitting by her desk, five books in front of her, one of them open already. Her legs are crossed, and the top of her shirt is unbuttoned. I try my hardest not to look at her bare skin, her sharp clavicles and delicate neck. "It's on the coffin," she adds. "Is it still light outside?"

"It's not even lunchtime," I say. "You got up at a very *human* time, Astra."

"Well, I had no intention of waking you while you were sleeping," she says, and I could swear her cheeks gain colour. "I can't wait for winter."

"Maybe you should move to the North Pole," I say, tossing her phone towards her. She catches it with one hand, barely looking back. "You'd get six months of pure night up there."

"I like Tynahine," she says. "Even though I have to spend summer stuck indoors."

"You stay here during summer?" I ask, not hiding my shock. Aliz's cheeks redden. I imagined that at the very least she would travel back to Hungary, where the Astras are based.

"You don't know what it's like to be a vampire," she says, looking back down at a book. Despite her words, there's no sharpness in her voice. And she's right. I don't.

"Have you found anything yet?" I ask, sitting next to her.

"A load of nonsense," Aliz replies, flicking through pages. "There's nothing on blood contracts for Familiars, and the *cures* are not great."

"Maybe they're worth a try," I say.

"I'm not enamored by the idea of chopping off two fingers and killing a cat. Especially when it might not work." She turns the page. "Plus, these are for witches' Familiars."

"Witches?" I say, my eyes widening. "Are witches a thing?" Considering I almost got killed while looking for grimoires, I shouldn't be surprised.

"Palau must think so. She's the one who wrote this nonsense." She scratches her cheek, a small smile tugging her lips. "I really hope they do exist. And werewolves. I wouldn't mind finding myself a werewolf girlfriend; we'd be like Romeo and Juliet. Or Juliet and Juliet, in this case," she adds, nodding to herself as some bizarre fantasy fills her head. "Very sexy."

I gawk at her, trying to wrap my head around the heir of the Astra empire saying something so . . . *stupid*.

The afternoon flies by, and after lunch, the tension that had built up between us in the library fades, as though that strange proximity never happened in the first place. My neck, in turn, becomes itchier, but I focus on reading, flipping through moth-eaten pages, hoping that the cure for the mark will suddenly appear before me.

The sun's almost setting when I pick up another book, a drawing of a violet on the cover. There are some illustrations in the first half, naked women sinking their teeth into victims, some trying to escape, others accepting the bite. Heat rushes through me, and I continue to turn the pages, until I stop, eyes widening. " 'Nullifying blood contracts between vampires and humans,' " I read out.

"That must be it!" she says, and she pushes her chair towards me, wheels squeaking.

I nod, before I start reading. " 'Once both parties are in agreement that the contract ought to be nullified, a kiss must be placed upon the spot where the contract was first sealed.'" I stop reading, staring at the words to make sure I didn't imagine them. "Seems a little too easy, doesn't it?"

"Uh . . ." Aliz is staring at me, face frozen with panic. "Yeah. It doesn't really make sense." She laughs nervously. "Half of what Palau writes is utter nonsense, so maybe we should just—"

"It's still worth a try," I say, swiveling my chair until I'm facing her.

"What?"

"It's just a kiss," I say, trying my hardest to not think about what I'm asking her to do.

"Cassie, there's *no way* that a kiss is going to fix it."

"If there's a small chance it might work, we should at least *try*." I pull off my scarf, and Aliz's eyes widen. "What?" I ask.

"The mark is bigger," she says, blinking.

"Bigger?"

"The vines have spread," she says, panicking. She holds up her phone, switching the front camera so I can see my neck. And just as she said, the lines have grown, slipping further down.

"What the fuck," I say, touching my skin. Aliz pulls her phone away as panic seizes my throat. For a second I can't breathe. Why is it growing? "Was this meant to happen?" I ask.

"I don't know," Aliz says, not looking me in the eye.

"We need to try it," I say.

"Try what?"

I point at the book, trying to scrub my reflection, and those curling vines, out of my mind.

"But you're *human*," Aliz finally squeezes out, and I sigh.

"You can wipe your lips afterwards," I say. "It's just a peck." I know I can't compare myself to her vampire conquests, but she shouldn't make me feel hideous, either. Not after looking at me the way she did in the library. "Or we can look for other cures," I finally say. "And if nothing else works—"

"No, it's all right," Aliz says, getting up from her chair. "Let's just get it over with."

I'm about to stand, but she puts her hands on my shoulders, keeping me fixed in place. Then she swivels my chair until she's behind me. She *really* doesn't want to kiss a human. I let out a frustrated sigh, and she pulls my hair aside. Cool air touches my neck, and just as I grow impatient, her lips, cold and soft, press against the mark.

My skin burns, all while a shiver rushes through me. Aliz pulls back, letting out a short breath.

"Thank you," I say, a slight tremor in my voice. *Jesus, what's wrong with me?* "I'll check if it's gone," I say, jumping up from my chair, freeing myself from the hands on my shoulders. I know I can just ask her if it's gone, but I can't look at her now when my heart is beating too fast. I can't look at her when I want more, and she doesn't.

I walk over to my bathroom mirror, taking a deep breath. My cheeks are red, and the stupid mark is still there.

All that for nothing.

My grey jumper feels too heavy, so I pull it off and fix my eyes upon the mark. The twisted vines vanish beneath the white collar of my shirt. I undo the top three buttons. I have to see how far it goes. I undo another, the top of my black bra coming into view. The vines stop just above my left breast. I swallow hard. There was nothing in any of the books about the mark growing. Then again, we still have a lot of material to read through.

"Fuck," I whisper, tracing my finger along one of the thorned vines, goosebumps raising in the process. This isn't good. Penny may have taught me a lot, but everything I learned was focused entirely on one thing: killing vampires. Nothing about blood contracts.

I tug at the top of my bra, pulling it down, just to make sure there are no hidden lines.

Suddenly I feel something behind me. Hands gripping my shoulders. "What—" I start, my eyes widening. I can't see her. Her reflection is missing. But Aliz is behind me. Before I can turn, she tightens her grip.

"Don't look at me," she says, her voice low. I take a sharp breath. I still can't make sense of what I'm seeing in the mirror. My own features are flushed. And the space where I know she is, where I can feel her, is completely vacant. "Please," she adds, with a hint of desperation. There's something else. *Thirst.* Her eyes must be red, too. If I look at her, she might try to compel me.

"What is it?" I ask. Her grip on my shoulders loosens, only for her to wrap her arms around me. *What is she doing?* I should pull myself free, but instead, I sink into her, her arms strong and cold.

"We should try again," she whispers, directly against my ear. Her cool breath makes me shiver. One arm lets go, and the picture in front of me becomes all the more absurd when I feel her finger tracing a line up my neck, caressing the mark, but I see only my skin reddening beneath her invisible touch.

"Again?" I ask. And I wish she'd just go ahead and help herself, because I don't want to admit I want this. She's a vampire. I *can't* want her.

I hear her swallow. "Well—" she says, trying to sound composed. "Clearly the first kiss didn't work. So, you should let me try again."

"I thought you didn't want to kiss a human," I say, hoping to somehow get under her skin the way she does with me. I turn my head, trying to catch a glimpse of her, but the hand on my neck grabs my chin, forcing me to look forward.

"I know," she says, lips practically touching my ear as she speaks. "But I just want to help you, Cassie."

I hate that I can't see her. I feel incredibly exposed, even more so with the mark on display. My shirt is still unbuttoned, the top of my bra visible. I feel each line of the mark individually burning into my blood. "Do it, then," I say, and I fix my gaze on the invisible spot where I imagine she is.

"Fuck," Aliz says, and she's trembling, tightening her grip. "No," she says, her voice low. "You should tell me to let go."

"Why?" I ask.

"Because this is wrong," she whispers. "You know that, don't you?"

"Yes," I say, my breath hitching. I know it, and I know we're playing with fire. Every inch of reason left in my mind is telling me to push her away. But something else within me, far more visceral, can't stand the thought of her letting go.

"And you're scared of me," she says, short nails running over the moon etched on my skin.

"I'm not." I want to see her. I have to see how she's looking at me and know if her need is anything like my own.

"You should be," she says, and I feel her lips, soft at first, replacing her fingers against the sensitive skin of my neck. Every nerve in my body comes to life, and I inhale sharply, biting down my reaction. "Tell me to stop," she says, before tugging at my shirt. Her lips meet my shoulder, and I can barely think straight, but I do know that I don't want her to stop.

"Why?" I ask, digging my nails into her arm.

"Because I want you," she says, and I gasp when I feel her tongue running up my neck. I bite down on my lip. I want her, too. I've wanted her since I first saw her. Her lips are still on my skin when one restless hand slips inside my shirt, and the other tugs my hair, forcing me to see my reflection. "Look at yourself," she says, breathless, pressing her thigh between my legs.

I choke out a moan, and feel the sharp points of her fangs, tentative on my shoulder. I want it. My blood, my skin, everything, craves the wound and the ecstasy it will bring. My lips part, and I'm about to tell her to do it, take a bite, but instead all I manage is, "Christ."

And it's that word which breaks the spell.

She stumbles back. "Fuck," she hisses.

Cold air brushes against my skin, and slowly I feel my sanity slipping back. I see my reflection, shirt practically off, and in a rush, I pull it back on before turning to look at her. She's covering her ears, and her eyes, which are usually black, are glowing bright red. I step back, hitting the sink, and she recognises the fear in my features.

"Shit," she says, sitting on the floor, covering her eyes. "I'm sorry."

Any ordinary human would run away. Instead, I take a step forward. There's something about her expression, the guilt, that I want to wash away. Despite my better judgment, I crouch down in front of her, slowly peeling her hands off her face. "Hey," I say, and she looks at me, her expression that of someone who's lost. Her eyes have darkened to burgundy. "You're all right."

She stares at me, wide-eyed. "Why are you not scared?" she asks. I don't let go of her hands.

Because you can't hurt me.

"I don't know," I say.

"I got carried away," she says, squeezing her eyes shut again.

"So did I." I let go of her hands, taking a deep breath. I don't know what possessed me. I don't know how she got under my skin so easily, but I can't let it happen again.

chapter FOURTEEN

I do up the last button of my shirt. The feeling lingers. Less than a minute ago, Aliz was tugging at my bra, her lips were on my neck. I shouldn't have enjoyed it. She's a *vampire*. I stare at my grey jumper and sigh, tossing it on my bed. My skin is still too warm to put it on. Only now, when we're back in the room, do I realise how close I came to killing her.

Had I let her bite me, she would be dead. I stare at her, and she's still rubbing her ears.

"Was it really that sore?" I ask. I know, from my missions, the effect that hearing prayers or holy words can have on vampires, but the word *Christ* seems to have affected Aliz more than I thought it would.

"Yes," she says. "It's like a really loud horn that's also punching you in the face." Her cheeks are red, and she doesn't look me in the eye.

I swallow hard, trying to focus. "Sounds pleasant," I say, sitting on the edge of my bed. She stays at a safe distance. I'm pretty sure Aliz won't struggle to forget what just happened between us. She'll probably have another girl in her arms tonight, anyway. Meanwhile, I'll relive it in my mind, over and over. "What else are you allergic to?" I ask, trying to keep my thoughts in check.

Aliz stares at me warily. "Haven't you covered that in Integration?" she asks.

"I wasn't paying attention."

I already know what her weaknesses are. But I want to know how a vampire explains those seemingly random curses.

"The main one is garlic," she says. Garlic, which is flowing through my veins. Which she almost drank. "It clogs our lungs. Not a very pleasant death."

"Why?" I ask, scrunching my brows. I take off my glasses, cleaning them.

"Well, allicin, the main compound in garlic, is a natural antibiotic. In legends, our blood is considered a disease, so whenever we come into contact with it, it tries to *cure* us."

"But your blood healed me," I say. She gives me a pointed look. I touch my neck, wincing. At a cost. "I don't really get it," I say.

"Yeah." She jumps up onto her coffin, crossing her legs. "It's pretty hard to explain, but to put it simply, we are bound by the legends of the land where we were born." She leans forward, muscles on her shoulders tensing. "I was born in Hungary, where people's idea of a vampire is, well"—she cocks her head—"not *me*, but someone with my weaknesses. Silver, garlic, crosses."

"Wait," I say. "Your weaknesses are *psychological*?"

Aliz scoffs. "I wish." Her expression sours, and I sense I've hit a nerve. "We're monsters. Monsters adapt to flame the fears of those around them. But just as it took humans millions of years to evolve, we're also rather slow in getting rid of those curses." She leans back, thinking. "But it all depends on where you were born, or where you were converted. My mother, for example, is a jiangshi. A hopping vampire."

My eyes widen, and Aliz stretches her arms out in front of her, mimicking a zombie. "She can't go out during the day, just like us. But she isn't affected by crosses or Christian prayers. Instead, she'll hiss at a bagua, and her skin will burn if it touches the blood of a black dog. Different culture, different legends," Aliz says with a grin.

"Right." While Penny has told me a little about vampires from around the world, my training revolved entirely around the Western vampire. "Why do you sleep in a coffin?" I ask next. "I guess it makes sense for Converts, considering they're technically dead—but *you* were *born*."

"Father told me the original vampire was a Convert, so technically, we're still their descendants. Either way, we struggle to fall asleep anywhere else. Something to do with our blood being too restless if we're not in a wooden box."

"I see."

"What else do you want to know?"

"Silver," I say, suddenly standing, my eyes wide.

"Well, as I said—"

"No," I say. "Maybe silver will get rid of it." I'm about to pull the chain out of my watch. But I can't, not when she's here.

"And where are you going to get that?" she asks, jumping down from her coffin.

"I don't know. A charity shop?"

"Right," she says. She walks over to her fridge and pulls out a flask of blood.

"Are you hungry already?" I almost ask if it's because of me. Because of what she was doing, a few minutes ago. But I keep my words to myself and watch as she sticks the blood into the microwave.

"I last fed at one, so of course I'm hungry." She leans against the microwave as it whirs, looking at me with an unreadable expression. "You might be on to something. But what if the silver burns you?"

"Why would it burn *me*?"

"That mark," she says. "If it's vampiric in nature, it might react the same way my skin does to silver. Burning and whatnot."

It hadn't occurred to me that a part of me, a layer of my skin, could have been infected because of her. "So be it," I say.

"I guess we could give it a shot," she says. The microwave chimes, and her hands are shaking as she reaches for her meal. All the tension

I hadn't even noticed was in her shoulders eases as soon as she takes her first sip. She turns away from me, still leaning on the wall as she slurps.

"A shot?"

"I've actually got some silver," she says, and I gawk at her, my frown vanishing.

"You've—what?"

She takes the lid off her cup, gulping it down, before tossing it in the bin. "Yeah." She reaches under her coffin, and I walk over to her. Why on earth would a vampire have silver? She pulls out a case, and in an instant, I recognise the translucent material that covers it.

Zia.

She pulls the zia aside, and unzips the case; inside, a pair of gloves and a long silver sword. Engraved on the hilt is the same crest that's tattooed on my neck.

"I don't understand," I say, getting on my knees next to the sword. It's a hunter's weapon. So why—

"You think the Astras became the most powerful family in Europe by being friends with other vampires?" she asks, carefully picking up the gloves. I notice that they, too, are covered in zia. She puts them on and lifts the blade. "My family once had a dedicated team of assassins." She holds the sword up in front of her, silver almost touching her nose. "We called them Blood of Callisto."

I stare at the sword. The words reach me, but they don't make sense.

"Callisto?" I never thought I'd say that word in here, in front of her.

"I take you've heard of the hunters," she says, a grin stretching her lips. She jumps up, swinging the sword around without a care in the world. "Well, guess what. They were originally our bodyguards!"

Penny told me Callisto was formed to *stop* vampires. To protect humanity from them.

Sensing my confusion, Aliz continues. "My father was a bit of an astronomer during the fifteenth century. Even though their discovery was attributed to Galileo, my father was the first to identify Jupiter's four largest moons. And he named four factions of his staff after them. Blood of Io were the servants, Europa the gardeners, Ganymede his cupholders, and Callisto his hunters."

I listen to this, stunned. It can't be. "And your father saw himself as Jupiter?" I ask, and Aliz winces.

"I guess so," she says.

"What happened then?" I ask. "To Callisto."

"A falling-out," Aliz says, leaning against the false window, the night's first stars glittering behind her. "My sister was going to take over the family—she was destined to be the new head. Her plans differed from Blood of Callisto's. So, they killed her."

"Callisto killed your sister?"

I remember that phone call with Penny. The tension in her voice. Does she know the truth about Callisto's origins? I rub my head. It doesn't make sense. According to her, Callisto was founded by Catherine Lovelace roughly two hundred years ago. But according to Aliz, we date back to the fifteenth century.

"They drugged her and took her out into the sun," Aliz says, drawing me out of my thoughts.

"I'm sorry," I say.

"Don't be," she replies, resting the silver sword atop her coffin. "I wasn't born yet."

"When *were* you born?" I ask.

"How old do you think I am?" she counters.

I take a step closer; she takes one back, surprised.

"Hm..." I reach up to touch her face, turning it to see her features a little clearer. "Two thousand?"

She blinks. "Not bad," she says, and grasps my hand, her cool fingers keeping it pressed to her cheek. "You're off by just a few."

I gawk at her, "A few?"

"I'm twenty-four."

"Twenty-four!"

"Are you a parrot?" she asks, leaning down. I finally snatch my hand free from hers, taking a step back. "I've still got another six years of aging left. Then I'll be stuck looking like this for eternity."

"Wow," I whisper. "I was wrong."

She snorts. "Yeah. And you?"

"Twenty-two," I say.

"All right, let's see if you're allergic to silver," she says.

She lifts the sword again, and I feel the blade beneath my chin, tilting my head up.

"I don't get it," she says in a low voice. "You get all flustered when I hold your hand, but now, with a fucking sword at your throat, you've got no reaction?"

"Maybe it's because you're scarier?" I reply.

"Sure," she says. "Ready?"

I close my eyes, prepared for the cold metal to burn against the mark, but then Aliz's phone starts ringing. "Shit," she says, and draws the weapon away. I notice, just by the way she holds it, that she must know how to use it. She grabs her phone and whispers, "Fuck."

"Who is it?" I ask.

"Faust," she says. *The Night Dean?* She answers the call, and another language pours from her lips, fast, her voice slightly higher. Her native Hungarian, I realise. She glances over at me and my neck, and then shouts something into the phone. The only word I make out is *nem,* which she says several times, and I'm guessing, based on her expression, that it means *no.*

Finally, she hangs up, lips pursed.

"What is it?" I ask.

"He wants to see us."

"*Us?*" I say. "Why? Have you *told* him?"

"Of course not!" she says. "But Faust has eyes everywhere. It's all right." She paces around the room, still holding her sword. "Even if he knows, he's not going to tell my dad. I mean . . ." She looks at my neck again. Aliz is so nervous that when she bites her lip, she draws blood. Her wound heals instantly. "We'll be fine!" She doesn't sound convinced.

"He won't be able to tell your father anything if the mark is gone," I say, gesturing at the blade hanging at her side. Aliz jolts, as though she's only now remembering it's there.

"All right," she says.

"And try to avoid beheading me."

"I don't usually behead people," Aliz replies, face serious. I lean against her coffin, and she stands just a little too close. She raises the blade carefully, and I squeeze my eyes shut, waiting for the metal to burn me when it touches my skin. Instead, it's like a sheet of ice.

"Did that hurt?" she whispers. I breathe out slowly and meet her gaze again.

"It didn't," I say. "Is the mark gone?"

Aliz leaves the sword on the coffin and runs a finger over my neck. "No," she says, voice grave. I swat her hand away, trying to not think about how good her touch felt.

"Let's go, then." I find my tartan scarf and wrap it tightly around my neck.

"Right."

Dread prickles my stomach once we leave our room. What if the dean has finally discovered what happened with the Red Ribbons? And now he'll expose me in front of Aliz. *No,* I tell myself. He wouldn't have left me alone with her if he suspected me of being anything but an ordinary human.

It's dark out, so we're able to walk through the woods separating Tynarrich from the main campus buildings. Old lampposts, black and gold, fringe the narrow path that snakes through the woods. I realise, as we skid down a slope, that it's my first time seeing her outside. She walks fast, her brogues sinking into the fallen pine needles, and I run after her. "If the Night Dean knows, what'll happen to us?" I ask.

"I guess we're about to find out," she says.

We head into one of the largest buildings in Tynahine, the first floor made up of colossal lecture halls, and the second a row of offices. At the very end of the hallway, Aliz stops. I stare at the sign. *Dr Faust*

Nocth. There's more writing beneath the name, but Aliz doesn't give me time to read it, banging on the door.

A smooth baritone rises from inside. "Come in."

Aliz takes a deep breath. Which doesn't help me feel calm. "All right," she whispers.

She walks through, and I follow. The room is a simple office, walls lined with bookcases. A large glass desk sits before a boarded-up window, an old tapestry hanging over it.

"Hello, girls," Faust Nocth says. He smiles up at us from behind his desk, and a chill runs down my spine. His black hair is long, falling just past his ears, his cheekbones are high and sculpted. I'd been hoping to stay away from Tynahine's administration as much as possible. And yet here I am.

"Dean," says Aliz. She says a couple of words in Hungarian, and then remembers I'm here. "You wanted to see us?"

"I don't usually pay attention to what my students take out from the library. But three days in a row of borrowing books about blood contracts, and well, I've grown rather concerned," he says, his smile revealing his deadly fangs. I swallow hard. Well, at least he hasn't figured out I'm a hunter. "Can you take off that scarf, Miss Smith?"

There's no helping it. Aliz makes a sound of protest, but I ignore her, pulling it down. I just hope she hasn't left me with a hickey.

"I can explain," Aliz says, her cheeks bright red.

"Please do," says Nocth, leaning back in his leather chair. Silence falls in the office, and he focuses his attention on my neck. "You've had that for a few days, haven't you?"

Aliz shifts uncomfortably next to me and clears her throat. "It was an accident," she says. "And it wasn't Cassie's fault. So, if anyone is going to be expelled—"

"No one needs to be expelled," he says, smiling at her. "We simply have some rules that ought to be followed. Especially when it comes to Familiars." My hands twist into fists, but I keep my words bottled down. I can't say, *I'm not a Familiar*, not with this glaring mark on my skin.

"What are those rules?"

"Well..." He gets up. "Nowadays, when we talk about Familiars, we usually think of those who submit to their masters through written contracts. A vampire will promise that after five or ten years of service, the human will be converted."

"But we didn't do that," she says, and he nods.

"Yes, I'm aware of that. In the past, it was different. Instead of a document, the contract would be signed with blood."

"But how—" I feel my blood boiling, my throat tightening. "How can something be a contract when neither of us knew—" I look at Aliz, and she has the same expression as I do. "We didn't choose this."

"It's difficult for this mark to appear by accident," the dean says. "But let me guess: For whatever reason, Miss Astra gave you her blood."

We both nod, and a grimace of disgust momentarily flashes across his chiselled features.

"And for some reason, this blood was gifted beneath the glow of a full moon," he says. "Was it?"

I see it. The window, wide open, the silvery glow of the moon filling our bedroom. Aliz is thinking the same thing, her eyes wide with disbelief.

"I really didn't know," Aliz says, her voice tight, after the office falls silent.

"How do we get rid of it?" I ask. "Can we?"

"I'm sure you have noticed that it hasn't fully come into effect," he says. "You're not bound to Miss Astra's will just yet. But once the next full moon reaches the highest point in the sky, the contract will be sealed."

Those words, said so casually, stun us both. The room is spinning, my hands sweating as I gawk at him. *No.* "How do I get rid of it?" I ask again, trying to focus on the bright side. I'm still free. At least until the next full moon. "There has to be a cure."

"There might be," he says.

"Why didn't you start with that!" Aliz exclaims, shoulders slouching with relief.

"Because I don't know where it is."

We stare at him, and Nocth's blue eyes meet mine.

"What do you mean?" I ask slowly.

"You've both heard of *The Book of Blood and Roses,* haven't you?"

Yes. I hesitate to nod. "But isn't *The Book of Blood and Roses* impossible to find?" Aliz asks.

"Did you know, Aliz, that it was written by Ada Astra?" Aliz gawks at him and leans forward. "But the only copy that remains is hidden in her library."

"I'll go to Hungary, then," Aliz says quickly.

"No," Nocth says, shaking his head. "Her secret library here, in Tynahine. But no one, not even I, knows where it is."

The secret library belongs to an Astra?

The name *Ada* is familiar. I think back to the tiny portrait in the gallery where the Red Ribbons held their meetings. *Dreamwalker of Rome.*

"Can't you ask her where it is?" I ask.

"She has been dead for over two hundred years, Miss Smith," Nocth says. "Demanding answers from the dead is no easy feat."

A moment later, Aliz looks at me. "Ada was my sister. The one I was telling you about earlier." The one murdered by Callisto. She turns back to Nocth. "So, if we find the library—"

"You will find *The Book of Blood and Roses.*"

"But you don't know where the library is?" I press, and he shakes his head. "Well, if *you* don't know, surely Ares Astra will?"

"I know this place far better than he does," the dean says sharply, while I feel Aliz tense beside me at the mention of her father. "And if I knew where it was, I would have brought it to you already," he says. "Can you imagine the scandal that will spread amongst vampiredom if they hear that the Astra heir has chosen a Familiar before even deciding on a husband?"

"We'll find it," Aliz says. She seems completely unfazed by those last words. With everything that's happened in the last few days, I hadn't looked beyond myself to consider the implications of Aliz choosing a Familiar. Of course it's a big deal. But the panic that had filled her voice since we first came in here seems to have dissipated. I don't know how she can be so optimistic.

But now we know there *is* a cure.

Somewhere, deep in the labyrinth of Tynahine, lies my freedom. Both from the mark and from my mission.

"You can go," Nocth says. I turn to leave with Aliz, but Nocth clears his throat. "You stay, Miss Smith."

Aliz narrows her eyes at him, her mouth open. "Why?" she asks.

"I must speak to her alone."

"Right," she says. But she stops, looking at me. I shrug. After another hesitation, Aliz shuts the door behind her, and when I turn back to Nocth, his gaze is far more intense than it was seconds ago. Discomfort brews in my stomach. I ignore it.

"Take a seat," he says, pointing at the chair opposite his desk. I do as he says, tugging my skirt a little lower. Perhaps he's going to go into more detail about the symptoms of the mark. He looks towards his bookcase just as it slides open, and someone, a young man, steps in. He's in the same cream linen suit he was wearing when I saw him in the campus security office, where he decided my concerns about the Red Ribbons were not worth listening to. The Familiar.

He doesn't say anything, resting against the tapestry behind Nocth. Something tightens in my chest.

When I look at Nocth, I'm expecting answers. Instead, the Night Dean asks me a question. "Can I bite you, Miss Smith?" I blink, the words not fully resonating. And too late, I feel that familiar numbness at the back of my head, pins and needles. His eyes are bright red, glowing as he compels me.

As he tries to.

I don't move. I can't say yes.

"Impressive," he says, the glow leaving his eyes. "It's a pleasure to finally meet you"—his fangs catch the golden glow of the desk lamp—"Rebecca Charity."

chapter FIFTEEN

He says my name as if he's announcing the winner of a prize. And now it hangs in the air, rippling through the silence.

How?

It must have been Jannet and Stella.

He saw their wounds, asked the right questions, and they led him to me. But they didn't know my name.

"Who's Rebecca?" I ask, feeling at my watch for the chain.

The Night Dean opens a drawer in his desk and draws out a manila folder. He flicks through it before pulling out a document. "*Rebecca Charity,*" he says again. The old-fashioned lamp on his desk shines through the paper, illuminating what's printed on the other side. A picture of me, at eighteen. A form, writing too small for me to make out. But I recognise it. Penny made me fill it in when I agreed to join Callisto.

"Born on the seventeenth of March, in Wishaw, Lanarkshire. Daughter of Simon and Mairi Charity. Recruited in July, four years ago. Current ranking: Cross." Slowly, he puts the form down on his desk. Cold sweat dampens my shirt.

Shit.

"Oh, and Type-S blood," he adds, glancing at the form again. "I'm guessing you're hiding that with garlic."

I should run. I'll fail my mission, but that's all right. Penny will be disappointed, but she'll find something else for me to do.

And if I can't get out, I won't go down without a fight.

"Where did you get that?" I ask. My voice comes out low and calm. "The Red Ribbons?"

"Do you really think they'd be able to get their hands on your recruitment form?" He waves the paper at me. I see Penny's signature at the bottom, in blood-red ink.

He found Penny. My heart quickens. "What did you do to her?"

"To Penelope?" he asks, raising a brow. He utters her full name far too comfortably. "Nothing."

"Then how—"

"Who do you think told her about the vampires in Inverness?" he asks, leaning back. I want to slash the smug smile off his face.

I take in his words. He told her about the Silverbirch vampires? "How do you know her?" I ask.

"She infiltrated the university, just as you did. Eight years ago."

"You're lying," I say.

Penny would have told me.

"It wasn't official," he says. "Only twelve human students. I was testing the waters. Penelope was sent here to kill me, but soon she realised having me as an ally was far more beneficial."

"Bullshit," I say. My voice is tight. *No.* Penny wouldn't.

She loathes vampires. Even more than I do.

"And as you can imagine, having a mole in Callisto is also advantageous for the Council."

Every nerve in my body feels like a string about to snap. It can't be.

"No," I whisper again. He's fucking with me. There's no way.

He pushes a small glass dish across the desk. "Have some shortbread," he says. "You look like you're about to pass out."

"Why am I here?" I finally ask, ignoring his offer.

"When I announced the number of open slots for human students, I knew Callisto would inevitably try to slip someone through the cracks," he says. "To gather intel, to protect the other students—regardless, it's better for me to know who that hunter is from the get-go." He pauses, staring at me too intently. "I'm assuming Penelope told you your mission was something far more exciting, of course. She probably said your parents' killer is here."

"Do you know who—"

"No," he interjects, with a wave of his hand. His Familiar reaches across the desk, grabbing a piece of shortbread, swallowing it whole. Nocth hasn't mentioned my real mission.

"You're wrong," I say, getting my nerves back in order. "It doesn't make sense, *Dean*. Why would you put your vampire students at risk by letting someone like me in?"

"Because you'll prove useful soon enough, Rebecca," he says. He glances at his Familiar, clears his throat, and says, "Marcus." His Familiar, *Marcus,* goes to a little fridge hidden next to a bookcase and draws out a bottle of blood. He leaves, and I hear a microwave whirring next door. "You've already proved useful, in fact. Uncovering the Red Ribbons was quite helpful." Marcus hands him a wineglass filled halfway with blood. The glass is ornamented with vines, its stem too long. "Though you should have been a little more cautious. I had Gustavsson find the rest of them; they're currently awaiting trial in London's Council base."

I think of the last few weeks. Being scared of the dean finding out who I am. And he knew all along. Penny fucking *told* him.

I take a shaky breath as another question rushes through me. "Why am I Aliz's roommate?"

"Oh, I couldn't help myself," he says. "Knowing Callisto's origins—"

"If the Astras find out about this, they'll kill you."

"I *am* an Astra," he says before taking a short sip of blood. "Aliz Astra is my cousin, though I'm five centuries her elder. And considering what's happened . . ." He gestures at my neck.

"I could kill her," I say in a cool voice. The words don't ring true. I can feel the first prickle of a headache pressing against my temple.

"If you were going to, you would have done so already." He glances at Marcus again. "Get Miss Charity some water."

Penny wouldn't do this to me. She wouldn't send me here without warning me first. She isn't a Council mole. She can't be.

Marcus hands me a small glass of water. I want to throw it at him, but instead I take a sip, trying to stay calm.

She wouldn't lie. She wouldn't hide something this big. *No.*

I want to scream.

"Does Aliz know what I am?" I ask, chest tight.

"Of course not." He finishes his blood, and Marcus takes the glass away. "The heir is blissfully unaware of most things happening around her." He says this, but now I can't be sure. If Penny has been lying to me for four years, why on earth would I trust someone I've known for weeks?

Someone I was practically making out with before he called us.

God, what have I done?

"I would stop taking the garlic if I were you," he says. "If you do end up killing the Astra heir, you would be in serious trouble."

"Why would I stop taking it?" I ask. "She's not going to bite me."

"You can't be sure of that. The effects of the unsealed contract won't be limited just to you. She will also experience them."

"Effects?"

"Haven't you noticed any changes in her behaviour? Is she more erratic?"

Erratic. I remember her lips on my neck. Her fangs, grazing my skin.

"I don't know her well enough to notice *changes*. We both said it isn't going to happen. Plus, I can't be compelled."

"I know. But I don't think you fully understand what that mark will do to you," he says, crossing his arms. "She won't *need* to compel you. You will ask for it."

Something tightens inside me, but I don't let him sense it. He looks away from me, back at the door. "I told you she would start acting erratically," he says in a lower voice. "She's coming back for you."

I look at the door, unable to shake the panic creeping through me. Aliz might try to bite me.

And I might let her.

"Go," he says. "And keep me updated on your search for Ada's library."

I get up. Does he know that was my mission? He would have mentioned it. So maybe, *hopefully,* Penny is holding her cards closer than he thinks.

"Don't give me orders," I say, leaning on the desk. I slide the chain out of my watch, shake it, and hold the blade to his neck. Marcus doesn't move, as though he already knows I'm not going to kill his master. "And don't forget what I am."

"Don't worry," Nocth whispers, placing his hands upon the silver. His skin turns red before a dozen tiny blisters form around the metal. I draw it back just as they burst, and a second later, his skin heals itself. "I wouldn't dream of it."

Aliz and I walk back in silence. My expression is enough to keep her from asking what happened. I don't look at her. I need to be alone. Talk to Penny. Scream at her. But the angrier I get, the worse the itch on my neck becomes.

Aliz guides us up Tynarrich's maintenance staircase, accessed through a small door in the back of the stone building. The wooden staircase creaks with each step. The lights on the wall are dim, some no longer working, forcing us to walk in shadows for two floors. Halfway up, Aliz stops and looks at me.

"What did he say?"

I keep walking, brushing past her.

"Cassie, I can tell you're upset."

Does she know my real name? Is she also lying?

"He said you'd want to bite me." My voice is like ice. "The mark will make me *ask* for it."

"Even if you do, I won't."

I take a step back down, so our eyes are almost at level. My face is dangerously close to hers.

"I felt your fangs on my neck, Aliz," I say. "We both know what you wanted."

Her lips part. As red deepens her cheeks, she grabs my hand. "Yes," she says. "I wanted to bite you. But now I know the consequences. Trust me—"

A sound, halfway between a chuckle and a gasp, escapes my lips.

I can't trust my own fucking shadow.

I snatch my hand free and don't reply, climbing up the stairs faster than before.

"Whatever he said—" she starts, trying to keep up.

"Leave me alone," I snap. "We aren't friends."

This time she lets me leave. When I reach our room, I close the curtains around my bed tight, squeeze my eyes shut, and try to breathe.

What has Penny done?

chapter SIXTEEN

My cheeks feel raw as the wind lashes against them. A thick fog has replaced the rain, diluting the burnt colours of autumn. I walk down to the campus village. Despite now having human students, only a handful of places are open during the day, like the coffee shop Stephan and I walked by on our first day. I get a flat white to go, hoping a warm drink will calm my temper before I call her.

But when I hear her voice, my anger at her betrayal flares through my nerves. "You're up early, aren't you?" Penny asks.

"Are you working with Faust Nocth?"

My eyes sting. I put my tongue between my teeth to stop myself from gritting them and stare out at the Raven River, meandering across flat rocks, riddled with moss. The fog is even thicker across the river, hiding the woods.

Penny hasn't said anything yet.

I want to scream at her. But if I want the truth, I have to stay calm. She's not working with a vampire. She wouldn't.

"What did he tell you?" she asks. I dig my nails into my palms.

"That you were here, eight years ago."

"What else?"

"Why didn't you tell me?" I ask. She hasn't denied it yet. "Why am I here?"

"You already know why."

"Faust Nocth told me that whatever mission you gave me is just a cover. You probably don't even need *The Book of Blood and Roses,* do you?"

"I do, Rebecca. Regardless of what he tells you—"

"Have you explored the tunnels? Do you know where the library is?"

"You wouldn't be there if I knew," Penny says, her voice just as sharp as my own.

"Really?" I nearly spill my coffee. "Because the dean implied otherwise. Apparently, I'm going to be useful, did he tell you that, too?"

"Watch your tone," Penny says, and I bite back my fear. I've done everything she's asked me to. Always.

"Does Callisto know about this?" *Are you a mole?*

"No," she finally admits. I squeeze the coffee cup, curtailing my temper. "But Faust is useful. I didn't tell you because I was hoping you wouldn't interact. Why exactly—"

"And the fact that you were here?" I interrupt her. "You never thought it would be helpful to tell me that in advance?"

"You were given the information you needed." Her cold voice tells me to drop the subject. But I can't.

"Was I, really? You told me fuck all, Penny. Which other vampires do you work with?"

"Only him." Her voice softens, and I want to believe her. "Like I said, Faust is useful, that's all. He'll sometimes tip me off on certain vampires or events. But I'm the only hunter he trusts."

"And do you trust him?" A seagull lands on one of the flat rocks of the river, cocking its head as it stares at me.

"Of course not. And neither should you. Try to stay away from him."

"That would have been a lot easier if you'd told me from the start,"

I say, but my temper has begun to simmer down. At least she admitted it. Though I'm pretty certain she's still hiding something.

As am I.

I walk into Gustavsson's class, feeling my pulse against my ears. I look straight at him and wait for him to look back. I wait for his eyes to give it away, that Nocth told him what I am. But he's busy fighting with his record player, cursing at it while another student offers to help.

According to the dean, Gustavsson dealt with the Red Ribbons, but I can't visualise the scrawny vampire *dealing with* anyone. The stark shadows of the crypt-like classroom only make his features look gaunter. When he finally casts his gaze in my direction, it doesn't linger.

I try to pay attention to his lecture. But I can't stop thinking about Penny. I play our conversation over and over, trying as hard as I can to believe her.

Callisto—Penny—has been the only constant in my life these past four years. Maybe she's right. Getting information from someone as powerful as Faust Nocth must have its advantages. But he's an Astra. She said it herself, they're dangerous. Not *ordinary* vampires.

Whether Penny is telling the truth or not about my mission to find the book, I have no choice but to continue. And since I can't focus on the lecture, I scribble away in my notebook, trying to make sense of the map of tunnels. There's still so much missing.

"Cassie," Ife whispers beside me once the lecture ends.

"Yes?"

When I look up, students are already making their way out of the music hall. And at the door, a mop of white hair. "Your roommate is here," she says, shooting me an inquisitive glance.

I walk out and find Aliz slipping into a narrow stairwell. I follow and find her leaning on the wall, directly beneath a lamp. The staircase is made of steep slabs of granite, vanishing into the dark.

"I didn't know if you'd follow me," she says, as I step down the first two steps, into the dark and cold nook. She seems uncharacteristically awkward, and I remember her expression last night. I lean on the wall opposite hers, staying as far as the narrow staircase allows.

"I didn't mean to snap at you last night," I say, my voice painfully self-conscious.

Aliz stares at me, wide-eyed. And then, to my absolute horror, she smiles. A genuine, honest smile, the kind she's not shared with me before. Warmth spreads through my chest, breath momentarily caught in my throat. "So we *are* friends, then," she says, and I blink, getting my senses back in order.

"Of course not. But I was rude." I tug my scarf a little tighter, ignoring the itch. "Why are you here?"

Aliz glances out of the staircase, towards the tunnel outside the music hall. Professor Gustavsson is the last to leave, and when I peek out, he offers me a small wave before heading on his way, cello case almost as wide as his shoulders.

"I won't let you become my Familiar," she finally says, keeping her voice low. "We're going to find *The Book of Blood and Roses* before the full moon. I promise."

That warmth I tried to push from my chest is there again. I nod, trying to not let emotion show on my face.

"And what if I ask you to—"

"I won't bite you," she says before I can finish. "What happened in the bathroom was a mistake. I got carried away."

"I did, too," I say.

Aliz clears her throat. "All right, then," she says, stepping forward, offering me her hand. "Let's get to work."

ALIZ PROMISED WE'D find the library, but during our first trip to the tunnels, I already feel like tearing my hair out. "It's *this* way," she argues, pointing at a narrow hallway we walked down barely ten minutes ago.

I snap my black notebook open, the web of tunnels a little hard to make out. I shove it in her face, keeping one finger pressed over the tunnel she wants us to take. "It leads to a class. We were *in* that class."

"When did you get the time to draw all this?" she says, flicking through the pages. "It's a mess."

"Before class," I say, snatching it back. "And if it's such a mess, we should work separately." Before she can protest, I add: "We'll cover more ground that way, won't we?" I'm used to working alone. And plus, if I'm not walking down narrow hallways with her, I won't feel the urge to grab her hand, either.

MONDAY ARRIVES, MY seventh night with the Familiar's mark, and the different halls and cafés of Tynahine all seem to be hosting a party of some kind. The only quiet place, aside from my room, is Tynarrich's dining hall. My neck itches incessantly, and I dig my nails into it over the red scarf, swallowing breath after breath.

My stomach burns, and the Scotch pie in front of me seems terribly unappetizing, the mutton filling taking on a greyish hue as it spills over the porcelain plate. I've been able to keep it together so far. But beneath the surface, cracks are forming.

Julia walks into the dining hall, pulling me out of my stupor. Her long hair is tied up in a messy bun. There's a gauntness to her, the residue of death. I try to picture her when she was eighteen and human, just like me, with full cheeks and maybe her almost-white hair a shade darker. I do know that some Converts take after their sires.

"You've been busy," she says, sinking into an armchair at the other side of the fireplace. Flickering candles cover the mantelpiece, their wax creating a film over the scratched-up mahogany. As always, she has a sketch pad under her arm and wastes no time in opening it.

"Busier than I expected," I say. I'm unable to add humor to my voice. *I want to see Aliz.* This thought slips into my mind as if it belongs to someone else. And in a way, it does. It's the mark, twisting me, telling me this time in the company of another vampire is time poorly spent. "How's the . . ." I gesture at her sketch pad, unsure what exactly Julia does in class. She smells like paint and turpentine, but all I can see right now is paper and two pencils. "Art?"

She lets out a short laugh, a breath caught at the back of her throat. "I'm working on a set of murals," she says. "*Scenes of Adolescence*. I can show you it once it's done, if you ever feel like visiting Traquair Hall. *These* are just to keep my hands busy." She opens the sketchbook at a random page, revealing a crowded train cabin. "The Tube," she says, running her fingers across the shadowy silhouettes. "Last thing I saw with human eyes."

I stare down at the drawing. The windows of the train are completely black. Some parts of the cabin are drawn and shaded with near photo-realism. Others are completely abstract, as though the paper itself is glitching. Just as I'm about to ask her about that fateful day, and what made her decide to leave her humanity behind, Julia tenses, looking across the hall.

I follow her gaze and see Aliz's *friend*. The strange vampire I saw a few weeks back, with cuts on her hands. That encounter feels like months ago already.

Her hair is half up, half down, silken waves picking up the warm glow of the surrounding lamps. A tartan coat, pink and cream, just about covers her miniskirt. The vampire catches my gaze and smiles. On the surface I could mistake it for kindness or curiosity. But there's a coolness in her flawless features that makes me shiver.

"Who's that?" I ask, before turning back to look at Julia.

"Elia."

I falter, suddenly remembering the Red Ribbons' conspiracy. "Elia Tamarit?" I whisper, and Julia nods.

"You've heard of her?"

"I've seen her with Aliz a few times." Only after saying her name, I realise I should have said *Astra*, instead. But Julia doesn't seem to notice this new familiarity.

"I'd be careful around her," Julia whispers. "She's not like the rest of the students here."

"What do you mean?"

"There are rumors that she used to bring humans to campus, years ago. As *snacks*."

I swallow. A chill spreads across my arms, and I breathe in.

"Then again, I would tell you to be careful around Astra, but you seem to like her just fine."

"No, I don't," I say, far too quickly.

Julia doesn't dignify me with a response. She continues to work on a memory, occasionally biting her pencil. Her sharp canines are whiter than the rest of her teeth.

Aliz is in our room. I know it even before opening the door, because the tight itch in my neck starts to soften, as though the mark can feel her proximity. I steel myself, a slow breath, before unlocking the door.

"Cassie," she says, slamming a book shut the moment I step inside. "Fancy seeing you here." There's a black velvet blazer splayed over her coffin. She's more dressed up than usual, wearing a tailored white shirt and velvet waistcoat. Her white hair is combed back, damp.

"Are you going to the opera or something?" I ask.

"No," she says. She spins her chair so she's facing me. A chain hangs from her collar, lopsided. "Elia's hosting a soiree at her place. I'd bring you along, but it's invite-only."

"Have fun," I say, dropping my bag on my desk. I take off my glasses and sit down on my bed, trying to ignore the itch as it continues to tighten, burning my skin. I need her fingers on the mark again to soothe it. I catch her looking at me, and her gaze leaves me a moment later. Even if the soiree wasn't invite-only, I wouldn't be caught dead going to a vampire party. Not unless I was going to kill someone.

"Don't scratch it." Only when Aliz says it, do I realise that I've started digging my nails into my scarf. She crosses the room. "You're going to hurt yourself." She slides her free hand under my scarf, and my tense muscles loosen.

"I'm not," I argue, as she draws a circle over the moon. Goosebumps raise at her touch, and I keep my eyes shut, knowing that if I look at her, my mind will wander. "But thank you." I open my eyes, shocked by my own words.

Aliz grins, pinching my neck. "You're very welcome, Cassie." My false name sounds too good as it spills from her lips, melodic, almost. What would *Rebecca* sound like? My cheeks burn while the absurd thought cements itself in my brain. I want her to say my name. I want her to know everything about me, the fact that I'm not a rich kid like everyone else at Tynahine. I want her to ask where Wishaw is, ask about my parents. I want her sympathy. Every new thought is more pathetic than the last, and I can't bear to look her in the eyes.

Her phone buzzes, and she lets go, crossing the room to pick up.

"I'm on my way," Aliz says into her phone, rummaging under her desk for a pair of brogues. "I mean—" There's a slight pause, and she presses her lips together. She shoots me a quick glance and then looks away. "You do remember what happened the last time you spiked blood, don't you?" she asks. I can picture her, Elia, with her doll-like features and perfect hair, at the other end of the line. Aliz smiles at whatever the other vampire replies, and then whispers something in another language.

My chest tightens. The other girls are just playthings. But I have a feeling Elia means much more to her.

"See you tomorrow, Cassie," Aliz says, barely looking at me.

"Wait," I say, and she stops right at the edge of her coffin. I step towards her. *Don't go,* I think. "It's lopsided," I say and unclip the golden chain pinned to her collar, then fasten it again until it's hanging in a perfect curve. "There."

"Thanks," she says, and for some stupid reason, Aliz's gaze has fallen to my lips.

"What kind of party is it?" I ask, hoping to snap her back to her senses. "A vampire orgy?"

She makes a face. "We'll just be playing cards. Although the loser usually does end up naked."

I wish she hadn't said that, because now I can't help but imagine her taking off her clothes. "Sounds fun," I say, and Aliz grabs my hand, which was still mindlessly attached to her collar. I feel her digits searching for my pulse. And then, seemingly without thinking, she lifts my wrist to her nose.

I stiffen. I've seen this, experienced this, many times over. Countless vampires digging their noses into the crook of my neck or inhaling, like Aliz does now, from my wrist.

But when Aliz sniffs, her eyes remain black, and her expression is more one of curiosity than thirst.

"I'm glad you don't have a scent," she says, putting a hand on my head. "This would be much more difficult if you did." I think of Nocth's warning: *Stop taking the garlic.* I don't know what expression I make, but Aliz cups my cheeks, her face serious. "I mean it," she says, her voice gentle. "And not having a scent isn't a bad thing. It's actually—"

"Can we not talk about my blood?"

Aliz would never be able to look at me the same if she ever smelled my real blood. None of the vampires I've met so far would. They'd turn into every other creature I've hunted the last four years. "Sorry," she whispers, taking a step back.

"Enjoy the strip poker," I add. Aliz shakes her head.

"I will," she says, and despite my harsh tone, there's warmth in hers. A warmth I don't deserve. She offers me one last smile, and then leaves. I stare at the door, my heart pounding. I wish I had an excuse to hate her, but I know by now that it wasn't on purpose. Aliz wants to get rid of the Familiar's mark just as much as I do.

THE NIGHT SKY is heavy with rain, the first drizzle a threat of the downpour to come. I keep my hood up, raincoat zipped to my chin, and an umbrella fighting the wind. I can't stay in our room. I couldn't stop thinking about her, and the itch made its way back onto my skin mere minutes after she left. It's one of the mark's most frustrating symptoms.

I walk through the campus village, my steps carrying me across cobbled stones, past willows. Several vampires, dolled-up, are making their way down the main street, heading in the same direction. With invites, I assume, to Elia's party. Aliz will sleep with her tonight, won't she? Images rush through my head; Aliz's hand slipping under her dress, Elia begging to be bitten, and Aliz giving her what I can't have, sinking her fangs into her, drinking her immortal blood.

Music comes from a building across a park, right on the edge of the campus village. Columns fringe the curved walls, the flat roof decorated with sculptures of women holding roses. The door is painted raven black, and even through the rain, I see the blur of my reflection fixed upon it.

When I look up at the wide floor-to-ceiling windows between the columns, I find glass draped with heavy curtains, crimson and gold. And leaning against one of those windows, with her chestnut hair falling past her waist in flawless waves, is the object of my envy. Elia is in a champagne gown, silk fabric stopping just above her ankles, with a slit running up to her thigh. Her shoulders shake as she laughs at something someone, out of view, must have said. Aliz is in there, amongst the shadows of vampires dancing.

My hunting instincts tell me to dig. Infiltrate, as I always do, and uncover their depravity. Prove if the rumors about Elia's *snacks* are true.

Just as I consider it, Elia turns. Her eyes don't wander across the damp street. They fall on me instantly, as though she already knew I was standing here. I swallow hard, and a moment before I look away, she raises a half-empty wineglass, swirling the blood inside in some kind of silent toast.

I hold my umbrella tight and stalk away, heart hammering in my chest. What if she tells Aliz I was there? My eyes burn, my neck itches. She has what I can't have. What I should have never wanted in the first place.

A lonely bench beneath the shelter of a tree, overlooking the river, provides me a spot to clear my mind of her. It's damp, but I don't care. I keep my umbrella up, breathing out, as though every new breath will rid me of these twisted thoughts. I pull out my phone, gritting my teeth until my jaw hurts.

Penny hasn't called since our last conversation. I go over everything she said, trying once more to believe her. But every time I look at a hidden corner of Tynahine, I can almost see her shadow, haunting the cobbled streets. What if she once sat on this very bench, overlooking the river?

Just as I scroll through our sparse call log, her name lights up the screen, as though she was in the same position as me, staring at her phone and waiting for me to call, before finally deciding to make the first move.

The wind nearly tears my umbrella from my hand when I hear her voice in my ear.

"How are you getting on?" she asks. I swallow. There's caution in her words. Distance. As if she's waiting for another argument.

"Nothing new," I say, squeezing the umbrella's handle tight, looking at the black pane of the river. Its current is fast, splashing against the rocks that litter it. In the distance, through a forest on the other side of it, I see lights on in a building. *The hunting lodge?*

"All right," she says. Her voice is softer than usual. "I've been doing some digging into Inverness. Everything's hinting at a blood party. But not the ordinary kind."

"Did the Night Dean tell you this?" I say before I can bite the words back. There's a sigh on the other end of the line.

"Not this time. Callisto has its own sources." Her voice is calm. I squeeze my eyes shut, trying to rekindle my trust.

"And who are these sources?"

"That information is only available to Stake ranked hunters," she says, voice cool. "You should know that."

"But it wouldn't hurt you to tell me." I breathe out. She doesn't reply. "What did you mean by 'not the ordinary kind'?"

"There are no known vampire clubs in Inverness," she says. "Outside of Tynahine, of course. But I've found fifteen cases similar to what you encountered in Silverbirch. Not killing but tasting. They're finding profiles, unusual flavours. This sounds like something *formal*."

"Right."

"I wouldn't usually send you to something like this," she says. "You won't be going in alone, but once I know more—"

"I don't need help." I say this quickly, and for once it isn't my pride talking. I don't want another vampire hunter in Inverness. I don't want one anywhere near Tynahine.

I can't let anyone see my Familiar's mark.

"That's not up to you," Penny says. "I also need you to stop taking your allicin supplements."

The wind picks up, blowing my umbrella inside out. Rain dampens my scarf.

"What?" I ask, my chest sinking. Did Nocth tell her to say this? But just before I can ask, Penny continues:

"I don't have an exact date for the party yet, but you'll be posing as a victim. Even if you're not on the list, they won't turn away S-Type blood."

Shit.

I can't. Faust Nocth already told me to stop taking the supplements, but if I do, Aliz will ask to bite me. And I don't think I'll be able to resist. I'm still searching for what to reply when Penny says, "Be ready."

"I'm always ready," I reply, but the words ring empty.

WHEN I GET back to my room, I pull out the jar of garlic supplements. Without them, no one will look at me the same. Much less Aliz. *Not yet,* I think. The supplements take between ten to fifteen hours to leave the system. As long as Penny warns me a few days in advance, I'll have time to stop, and then resume as soon as the party is over.

Aliz is still at her soiree. I wonder who lost the card game. I try my best not to think of her, clearing my mind as I change into my nightgown. The Familiar's mark has continued to grow, now stretching its vines down past my waist. I grimace at the sight of the twisted lines. I scratch furiously and stop just before opening a wound.

I wonder if she still has her clothes on. My breathing shortens as I imagine her slowly unbuttoning her velvet waistcoat. I cover my eyes and breathe. I've never felt this. She's twisted my mind entirely.

A wave of humiliation does away with my arousal before it can fully form. Aliz doesn't want *me*. If I didn't have the mark, she wouldn't spare me a second glance.

I'm so used to being wanted by every vampire I set my eyes on, but it's always been because of my blood. I'm not able to seduce her with it, not when it's polluted with garlic. *I should stop taking it.* I dig my nails into my chest, frustration bubbling.

It begins to itch, more than before, so I squeeze my eyes, hoping I'll fall asleep before it becomes unbearable.

chapter SEVENTEEN

Four stone columns tower at the entrance of the maze. The ground is muddy. Twigs cut my bare feet. Each hedge is a monstrous creature fashioned from jagged branches. A large crow with crimson eyes walks across the top of a hedge.

The Familiar's mark is no longer just a drawing. Its vines have come to life and slowly tear through my white nightgown.

"Cassie?"

Aliz's voice is tinged with thirst.

The humid air clings to my neck, and I run.

I tear a branch from a hedge and fashion a makeshift cross. My hands tremble as I race deeper and deeper into the shadows.

I trip on a fallen branch, and I bite my tongue to keep myself from screaming. Just two hedges away I hear Aliz's ragged, desperate breathing. My vision blurs, and I keep running, each step faster than the beating of my heart, until the narrow passages open.

Between four crumbling statues is a rosebush. Each statue holds a moon, each moon in a different phase. The first quarter is gilded in gold. The roses are in full bloom, their petals like fresh blood. Their too-strong scent burns my nostrils.

And just as I become transfixed by the roses, I see her.

Our eyes meet. "Don't move," Aliz whispers. Her eyes flash a horrible crimson. She's trying to compel me. I feel her will wrestling with mine. For a second, I think it worked, because I don't move. But then she steps forward, and something snaps inside me.

I run. Past the statues and the rosebush, back into the hedges. Why is she doing this? She promised. And I believed her. I should have killed her when I had the chance. My lungs are empty, but I keep running. I take another turn, and crash into a dead end.

Then a hand reaches through the hedge, grabbing my upper arm. Before I can scream, she pulls me through the branches, their sharp edges cutting my skin. My cross falls, and Aliz pulls me tight against her chest.

And as soon as I feel her skin against mine, every ache, every wound, vanishes. My mind clears, leaving nothing but her.

"Aliz," I whisper. She presses her lips to my temple, tightening her grip around me. I cling to her, trying to get even closer. I don't know why I was running from her in the first place.

"You're okay now," she whispers, lips to my ear. One hand is on my waist, the other on my shoulder. My tears dry against my cheeks. "It's over, Cassie." She's close but not close enough.

Cold bites under my skin, and I kiss her collarbone, her neck. Aliz's breath hitches, and she runs her fingers through my hair. I've wanted her since the moment she first saw me, since I first heard her voice. "Can I bite you?" she asks. She tilts my chin up, and her eyes are an awful, terrifying crimson.

My lips tremble, and a single, deadly syllable slips through, so quiet the night almost swallows it whole.

She descends on me, burying her fangs into the crook of my neck. Pleasure burns through my veins, and I dig my nails into her shoulder blades, unable to breathe as her tongue runs over the wound.

It's only when she bites a second time, when she swallows enough to weaken my knees, that I remember what's flowing through my veins. Aliz makes a strangled sound, gripping me, pulling at my hair as though that will somehow open her rapidly closing airways. "Aliz—" I gasp, reaching for her as she falls, my blood spilling from her mouth. Her teeth are stained red, and she chokes on the floor.

Nocth told me to stop taking garlic. Penny did, too. I didn't listen. "I'm sorry," I cry, on my knees. I wrap my fingers tight around a wooden stake, the one I was too scared to bury in her chest when I last had the chance. With the same mechanical force I've used a thousand times before, I slam it right through her rib cage.

I sob as I wait for her to turn to smoke and dust. But instead, Aliz continues to choke, clawing at the ground. The crow from the maze's entrance descends on her, picking at her eyes. And as I fight with the bird, the mark on my neck starts to burn once again. Each thorned line stabs me, growing inwards, wrapping around my rotten heart.

Someone is shaking my shoulders, and when I wake, she's leaning over me, eyes wide with worry. "Cassie," she says, and I draw in a breath, reality slowly falling back into place. "It's all right."

"What—"

"You were dreaming," Aliz says, and this time, when her hand leaves my shoulder, lifting from the lines of the mark, that torturous pain doesn't sear through me. Just a dull itch. I force myself to take even breaths, blinking my tears away.

"You're all right?" I ask, and my voice feels like sandpaper against my throat.

"Yes," she says, and she sits next to me, breathing out. It was a dream. My throat dries as guilt creeps up my neck, so visceral I want to throw up. The sight of Aliz's asphyxiated features is already engraved into the back of my mind.

I let her bite me. Even after the dean's warnings about the garlic in my blood. Somehow when the tears start, I can't stop them. She places a careful hand on my head. And against my better judgment, with her hand still in my hair, and my eyes burning, I wrap my arms around her. She's alive. It was just a dream. "I'm sorry," I mumble.

"No." She hugs me back, her arms surprisingly warm. "Please don't say that." She smells faintly of mint and honey, another girl's perfume. "I tried to wake you when I got in, but I couldn't—you weren't waking. What happened? Did I—"

"You died," I say, and she stiffens.

"So that *was* my name that you were saying," she says. I stop breathing. I was saying her name? *Fuck.* "How did I die?"

"You bit me."

She pulls back, horrified. "I'm sorry," she says, as though it was her fault that the Aliz I dreamt of sank her fangs into my skin. "I won't do it. I promise." She rests her hands on my shoulders. "Even with a stake to my heart."

I shudder, guilt clawing up my chest like a wild animal. She hugs me again, and it's too comfortable. I wrap my arms around her, breathing her in, and despite telling myself over and over that it is wrong, that I shouldn't feel like this, it feels right. *It's just the mark,* I think, holding her tight.

chapter
EIGHTEEN

Aliz is sleeping in her coffin. I hear her turn, from time to time, restless inside her box. My stomach clenches, hunger and thirst telling me to get out of bed, but I'm too scared to move, too aware of what I've done.

Why did I *hug* her?

Why did I wrap my arms around a *vampire* and feel safe in her embrace? Why did I feel comfort when she, in turn, pulled me closer?

What am I doing?

It's as if my soul is slipping from my body. Four years of hard work being undone by a single vampire. But as much as I tell myself that the softness I feel for her isn't real, my thoughts don't matter. All that matters is the ache in my chest, reminding me over and over of what happened in the dream.

I killed her. And all because of the garlic in my blood. And even though it was just a dream, a part of me knows it might happen. The dean said she won't have to compel me, that I'll be the one to ask her to bite me. And if that happens, Aliz will die.

I HOLD UP the pill as I wait for my coffee to finish dripping. I know I'm going to make things worse if I stop taking the allicin. My blood will smell the way it did before. But Aliz's dying features are engraved in the back of my mind, far too vivid. I can't risk my freedom. I can't risk her life, either.

I toss the pill into the closest bin and toss with it the persona I've built over the last three weeks. Cassie, with her dull-smelling blood, will vanish as soon as the allicin leaves my system. I look at the pill jar, with a false label reading VITAMIX B12. There are countless red tablets inside. All of them deadly.

This is a terrible idea.

I almost toss the entire jar into the bin, but my last thread of common sense stops me.

At lunch, I'm distracted, my head buzzing. The Silverbirch vampires are hosting a blood party. A formal one. I've only been to a couple of *formal* parties before, but they always tend to be bloodier. And Penny is sending up another hunter. What if they see my mark?

I dig my nails into my palms, staring down at my still unfinished map.

"What are you drawing?" Julia asks, her voice pulling me out of my spiralling thoughts.

I slam my notebook shut. "Random sketches, that's all," I say, and across from me, Ife furrows her brows. I glance back at Julia, and she has a sketchbook open, as always. Once again, she's drawing a Tube station, crowded with faceless people. "How are your murals going?" I ask.

"Terribly," she says.

"Nonsense," Stephan butts in. "You have to show us them."

"When they're finished," Julia says, a hint of colour staining her pale cheeks.

Ife looks at me from across the table, and then back at Julia.

"Has Julia freaked you out with her paintings yet?" Ife asks, lowering her voice. Julia elbows her, affronted.

"What do you mean?"

"Do you still have the sketch of Snowy?" Ife asks, and Julia, whose neck is flushed a deep pink, reaches into her bag, drawing out an old and very thick sketchbook. She leafs through it, opening on a page with a black background, a white rabbit at the centre, and beady red eyes. I glance at the sketch, and then look at Ife, whose features have stilled.

I'm unsure why Julia is showing it to me until Ife says, "Julia drew this last year. This is Snowy, a bunny I had growing up. I accidentally killed it when I was ten, when I had no control of my thirst. Not the nicest memory." Her eyes seem heavier than usual as she stares at it wistfully. "Here's the strange thing, Cassie. I'd forgotten about Snowy. At some point I pushed the memory aside, wrapped it up and shoved it into some deep cupboard in the back of my brain. And then, last year, Julia showed me this sketch, and everything came back to me."

"Wow," I whisper and look up at Julia. The Convert vampire seems increasingly uncomfortable, and finally snaps her sketchbook shut. "But could that not be a coincidence?" I ask. "Looks like a pretty ordinary rabbit."

"No," Ife says. "It even has a black spot on its tail, just like Snowy did." Her expression remains melancholic. "I think of it as the end of innocence. You'd think that growing up in a vampire household, I'd have been aware of what I was. But that was the first time I realised I was truly..." She doesn't utter the last word, but I can see it in her eyes. *A monster.*

I stare at Julia again, waiting for her to explain. After a heavy sigh, she says: "I'm not very good at gifts, so I figured I could give Ife an illustration for her birthday. I had different ideas, but for some reason, this is the one that stood out. My drawings changed after I was converted. I always considered myself a creative person, but that creativity used to depend on what my eyes could see. Once I became a vampire, all my ideas became somewhat random, almost like intrusive thoughts."

"Oh," Ife says, swiftly moving from the topic of Julia's conversion.

"I almost forgot! The venue for this year's Halloween Ball has been announced. It'll be in the hunting lodge!"

"How will they hold a *ball* in a lodge?" I ask.

"The university calls it a lodge," Julia says. "I suppose 'hunting palace' doesn't have the same ring to it."

"Haven't you heard of it?" Ife asks me, mistaking my silence for confusion. "The Halloween Ball is a Tynahine staple."

I shake my head. The last thing I can think of right now are silly parties. Or *balls*.

"I was allowed to attend last year," Stephan says. "Even though I wasn't a student yet."

"This year is going to be perfect," Ife says. "Did you know we're going to have a blood moon on the thirty-first?"

"Blood moon?" I ask.

"It's a lunar eclipse. The full moon will look red. Like blood."

The full moon. Ever so slowly, the deadline creeps up on me. We've got less than three weeks to find the library. But hopefully, come this Halloween Ball, I will be free of the mark already.

My last Integration class finishes at seven, and I head back to my room. When I open the door, someone is sitting on the coffin.

Someone that is not Aliz.

My muscles tense as I recognise her.

Elia.

"What are you doing here?" I ask, leaving the door open, giving myself a way to escape.

She tilts her head, that same cool and unnerving smile I saw from her last night appearing on her lips. "Just waiting on Aliz," she says. "She was supposed to have been here already."

"You have a key to our room?" I ask, putting my bag down on my bed. Aliz never mentioned this. No one is supposed to be allowed in here. Then I see what's in her hands. A small glass jar, metal cap unscrewed. The label says they're vitamin supplements, but the contents are a vampire's cyanide. I stop breathing as she shakes a pill into her hands.

"What are you doing?" I ask.

"Oh, are these yours?" she asks, lifting the jar, scrutinizing it. Does she know what they are? How did she even find them? "Vampires can take supplements. And I happen to be running low on B12."

If she had rummaged through my case, if she had found my weapons, there is no way that she would be this calm. Her legs are crossed, a flowy white dress hitting the top of her tan boots. Her pink coat lies beside her, and she lifts the pill to her lips.

"Don't!" I shout, and she stops, blinking before the pill touches her tongue.

"Why?" she asks, tilting her head back, pinning me with her hooded eyes.

"That pill is—"

Before I can say it, she slips it into her mouth.

I rush to her, knocking the glass jar out of her hands, red pills scattering everywhere. But I'm too late. Her throat bobs as she swallows her death.

Elia leans down, face level with mine. She looks like she's about to say something, but then I hear Aliz outside, carefully pushing the still-open door.

"You're here!" Elia sings, looking at Aliz. I wait for Elia's body to react. For her to choke, the way Aliz did in my dream. Cough, collapse, die. But instead, Elia jumps down from the coffin, crushing my garlic supplements beneath the stiletto heels of her boots. She reaches for Aliz and kisses her as though I'm not in the room.

"Uh . . ." Aliz pulls back, looks at me, and then at the mess on the floor. "What's going on?"

"Your roommate got angry. Just because I wanted one of her vitamins!" The cool voice she was using with me moments ago has climbed up an octave, making her sound younger, childish, even. *How is she still alive?*

"What did I tell you about coming into my room?" Aliz says, irritated. I know I should be brushing the pills up now, but I can't wrap my head around Elia not dying. "Look what you've done," Aliz adds, crouching down. Just before she can start scooping the stray pills up, I shout:

"It's garlic!"

Aliz freezes. Her hands draw back instinctively, and she gawks at me, confused.

"*Garlic?*" Elia draws the word out.

Aliz, in turn, doesn't say anything, she simply stares down at the floor. At a semester's worth of garlic supplements.

It's over.

They've figured it out.

"Why would you bring garlic into a university full of vampires, Cassie Smith?" Elia asks. *How is she still breathing?* The look in Aliz's eyes doesn't go beyond confusion, but I know it will shift, any second now, to an accusation. And then what?

"To hide the scent of my blood." The truth slips from me like a silver dagger, falling from my sleeve before a kill. My words catch them both off guard, and Aliz's shock seems exacerbated.

Elia takes a step towards me, lowering her voice. "And why must you hide your scent?" she asks, close enough that I can smell the rosewater in her hair.

I swallow, taking a step back, hitting the desk. "It has a strong fragrance." The kind that will drive a vampire mad with thirst. "Type-S," I say.

Elia picks up the half empty jar from the floor, and I wring my hands together, heart pounding in my chest. They can both feel it. I can't lie to them. Elia touches my chin, and I tense. "What does your blood type have to do with you keeping poison in a room you share with a vampire?" she asks, her crystal-blue eyes turning a shade darker, leaning towards crimson.

"Back off," Aliz snaps, her voice sharper than I've ever heard before. "She's telling the truth," Aliz says, and then meets my gaze. "You've been taking these pills, right?"

"I have." Pins and needles run up my legs as I think of what else I can say, without revealing the truth. Because God knows what they'll do to me if they find out I'm a hunter. "I can get my blood tested if you don't believe me. I wasn't planning on poisoning you."

"I believe you. But you should pick these up," Aliz says, her voice cautious. "And you might need to dust them off a little before taking them."

I stare at Elia, still alive.

"What are you doing here?" Aliz finally asks Elia, as I get down on my knees between them, picking up the scattered pills.

"Just wanted to remind you of our date," Elia says.

"You could have texted," Aliz says, uncomfortable. I ignore the jealousy clouding my thoughts. Somehow this new emotion makes the mark's symptoms worse, as though I can feel each individual line, all the way from my neck down to my waist. I bite my lip as I try to stop myself from scratching at it.

"Pick me up tonight," Elia says, and just like that, she's gone. But she clearly wasn't here to see Aliz.

She was here to see *me*. And only now that it's over do I see how deliberate that was. Taking poison just to show me she's immune. Does she know I'm a hunter? I glance at my side of the room. Nothing aside from my garlic supplements is out of place. But if she knows I'm a hunter, why hasn't she told Aliz?

"Don't worry, I'll have Faust change the lock." Just as I start scratching my neck, Aliz crouches down next to me. She presses her hand to my skin, the itch vanishing. "I'd help you clean up, but, uh, I think I should be careful."

"Definitely."

"Do you really have Type-S blood?" she asks.

"I do," I say. Aliz's hand remains against my skin, but she doesn't hide her hurt expression now that Elia is gone. Last night she said she was glad I didn't have a strong scent, and I didn't correct her. "I'm sorry I didn't tell you," I say, the words awkward on my tongue. "I know I should have."

"I assumed you trusted me," she says, not looking me in the eye. She draws her hand away from my neck. "But I get it. I'm a vampire."

"My blood's caused me problems in the past," I say. "Do you

remember—" My voice trembles. *This is a bad idea,* I think, but I better prepare her. "Do you remember asking about my perfume?"

Aliz blinks, frowning. "Perfume?"

Of course she doesn't. Aliz hasn't obsessed over every conversation we've ever had the way I have. "The day I arrived," I whisper. "You said the room smelled nice."

Her lips part. Her gaze searches mine. "That was your blood?" she asks.

"That's what you initially thought, wasn't it?"

Aliz lifts my wrist to her nose, just as she did last night. "You don't smell like garlic."

"I know. The pills don't have a scent."

As she lowers my arm, something in her features changes. She stares at my wrist, grip tight. Her eyes are on the exact spot where the bite mark from Inverness was. When Aliz healed my neck, the bite vanished along with Jannet's wound. But she must have seen it again while I was naked, seen it enough to recognise it.

"You've been taking garlic since you first came here?" she asks. I know what she's thinking.

And I know I'm risking everything by saying this, but I need to gain her trust back. "A vampire bit me in Inverness," I say, voice low, hands shaking. *What am I doing?* Aliz's face, which till now had a frown, slackens, her eyes wide. "I saw him compelling a girl in a pub, and after I confronted him"—I turn my wrist—"he bit me."

Aliz doesn't say anything.

My breathing shortens. My eyes burn, lower lip trembling as I try to figure out how to explain this in a way that won't let her see me for what I truly am.

"Did he—" The next word seems too thick for her throat, and when she finally squeezes it out, it's in a whisper. "Did he die?"

I swallow hard and nod. The fact I've killed is a disgusting side of me I hoped she'd never see, but she'll understand, won't she? *He. Bit. Me.* It's not my fault.

"The garlic killed him?"

The room is far too quiet. The garlic *would* have killed him. Slowly.

First, his lungs would have shut off, and as the garlic spread, his body would have decomposed. But it didn't. I drove a stake through his chest.

Vampires can tell when we're lying. I nod again, and hope she believes me.

Aliz cups my cheek.

"I won't tell anyone," she whispers. "Just—" She rubs the spot where the bite mark used to be. "Promise me you'll never do anything so stupid again. You could have died."

I meet her gaze, stunned. Her eyes are not disgusted. Instead, there's nothing there but worry. The garlic pills are still scattered around us, like speckles of blood. "You really won't tell anyone?" I ask.

"I won't tell anyone about your . . . *involvement*," she says. "But I must tell Faust that a vampire was compelling people in Inverness. Rogue vampires seldom work alone."

I nod, my shoulders relaxing. Nocth already knows what I am, so even if Aliz tells him that I was attacked, he won't do anything. Plus, he's the one who told Penny about those vampires. I pick up the remaining garlic pills. I skipped the first one already. Soon it'll leave my system. But based on how calm she is, that hasn't happened yet.

"I also . . ." she starts, "I also had a dream."

"A dream?" The change of subject is like whiplash, but I'm grateful for it. At least until she keeps talking.

"You told me that I died in yours," she says. She gets up and sits on my bed, looking down at me as I scoop up the remaining garlic pills. Her white hair is a mess, a few loose strands falling over her brows. Her lips are slightly red. But the lipstick isn't hers. "That explains it," she says.

"What do you mean?" I ask.

She doesn't look me in the eye. I feel as though she's searching for words, afraid, as I am, to say the wrong thing. Then she walks over to her side of the room, searching her desk for a notebook. She hands it to me. "When I woke up, I wrote what happened in my dream, to make sure I didn't forget." She clears her throat. "Tell me if it's anything like yours."

I stare down at the page, dread settling in my stomach. Aliz's handwriting looks like something out of a calligraphy manual. But I can't exactly appreciate it as I take in what she's written.

So thirsty I felt my throat was on fire. Cassie was scared. Behind my sister's palace: maze, crows, statues, rosebush.

I tried to compel her but it didn't work. I caught her, she kissed me. I asked if I could bite her and her blood was like lava, my lungs were aflame, I couldn't breathe. I couldn't heal.

She staked me?

The notebook falls to the floor, and I feel nauseous as I take it in. My throat is dry. She's waiting for an answer, but when I look at her, I can tell that my expression alone has answered her question. "It's the same," I say. I touch the mark on my neck, digging my nails into it. "The dean said we would both experience symptoms. Maybe the dream—"

"You should also write yours down," she says. "If it happens again, I mean." She felt the stake. Does she know what I am? Just as I start to panic, Aliz crouches down next to me. "It was only a dream, Cassie," she says. Her hand cups my cheek, and just like last night, when I hugged her, it feels far too comfortable.

I swallow hard. "I know," I say.

Suddenly, a realisation hits me. "Does that maze exist?" I ask. Aliz frowns, nodding.

"It's by my sister's old palace. The hunting lodge, as Tynahine calls it," she says. Her hand drops from my cheek, my skin suddenly cold. That is where most students believe Aliz lives, so it shouldn't surprise me that it was her sister's.

"What if your sister's library is in the hunting lodge?"

"That would be easy and convenient," Aliz says. "But it's not there. I looked already."

"I want to look again," I say, handing her back her notebook. "We can go after class."

"I can't." Her voice is tight. I lean against her coffin, unsure what's going through her mind. "I can't be alone with you."

"We're alone right now," I say.

She stares at the floor. "I've spent the day thinking of nothing else but you," she whispers, and her words latch onto me, twisting my sanity. "I thought the feeling would subside if I saw you, but instead..." She stares at me, and my chest tightens as I guess what she's going to say next. As I recognise the thirst lurking in her eyes. "I want you even more."

My skin burns, waiting, each second spent apart from her like a thorn digging deeper and deeper. I want her, too. "Being apart might make it worse," I whisper, pushing her words away, not allowing myself to cling to them. She doesn't mean it. She doesn't feel that way. Not really. *She's a vampire,* I remind myself. As if I still care about that small technicality.

"Maybe." She looks at her polished shoes. "But I don't trust myself. You'll be safer if we're apart."

"I'm not scared of you."

She stares up at me, gaze hard. "You were scared in the dream."

Aliz was there for me when I woke up. She indulged me with an embrace, told me I was safe. Meanwhile, when Aliz woke from her own nightmare, she was alone. "I'll search alone, then," I say, my chest tight.

"Don't go to the hunting lodge," she says. "It's too far from campus. Anything could be lurking out there."

"Like what, a vampire?" I ask, and she shakes her head.

"Funny," she says, reaching over to pinch me. "Please, Cassie," she adds, her fingers lingering on my skin. I spot a stray garlic pill and put it into the jar, screwing the cap tight. "I'll take you there once I'm a bit less... *thirsty.*"

The word makes me jolt, and I take a step back from her. These are the symptoms Nocth told us about. "What makes you think your thirst will decrease?" I ask. "The dean said the symptoms would only get worse."

"There must be a few remedies for thirst in the library," she says, her cheeks gaining colour. "There has to be *something*. And once I've figured that out, we'll go to my sister's palace."

I can go, anyway. She can't stop me. But for some reason, I decide to listen to her. "I'll keep searching in the tunnels," I say, and Aliz nods, relieved. "But if I don't find anything in the next few days, I'm going to the palace, with or without you."

"I'll go to the Palau Collection, then," she says.

"And will you be picking up books or girls?"

"Jealous, are we?" she asks, cocking her head to the side.

"Unbearably so," I reply, which makes her smirk harden into a thin line. "We need to keep each other updated, so you should give me your number." I draw out my phone and hand it to her.

"You only had to ask, Cassie," she says, quickly typing it.

"I'm quite literally asking," I say. She makes another face, disappointed by my reaction.

Never in a million years did I expect to have an *Astra* in my list of contacts.

I don't waste time, getting ready to spend the next few hours down in the tunnels. "Good luck," she says, just as I'm about to open the door.

I turn to look at her. She's leaning on her coffin; a strand of her white hair has fallen over her brows. She brushes it away. *I want you,* she said just a minute ago. I know it's just the thirst speaking. I know it's not real. I know I shouldn't believe it. But I've never wanted to hear anything as much as that before.

"You, too," I say as I leave our room.

chapter
NINETEEN

I stare at Aliz's number. I've never been away from Penny this long, and I have a feeling she's monitoring all my devices. Even if she isn't, I can't risk it. I need a burner phone, and luckily enough, the campus village has a couple of charity shops, each with a collection of phones and SIM cards.

I head into one of Tynahine's many cafés, one filled by only humans, and send her my first text. *Hi, this is Cassie.* Then a moment later, I add, *Cassie Smith,* because I don't know how many other Cassies she might have on her phone.

> Hi, this is Aliz. Aliz Astra.

My lips betray me, twitching into a smile. I pinch my skin. *How old am I?* I order a flat white with three shots of espresso, and the student working behind the bar smiles, too. I wonder if he's seen me with Aliz.

It's already dark outside. When I open my chat with Aliz, I see her typing, but she doesn't send a message. So, I write to her instead.

> I'm searching the tunnels till midnight.
>
> You can search after class.

> Don't get lost
>
> Also, Faust says the med depart's library will have the best anti-thirst options for me

I want to see her. The itch from the mark has spread down, across all thorns and lines, and all I can do to soothe it is dig my nails into my skin, but not scratch, because that'll only make it worse. Once I've finished my coffee, I head into the underbelly of the campus, notebook in hand. As I walk along the Cat's Tail, I remember my first meeting with Elia. She had blood on her hands. Tiny little wounds that vanished shortly after.

Now I know she's immune to garlic. And may or may not know that I'm a vampire hunter.

My steps echo on the curved walls. The lamps perched on the stone become sparse, further and further apart, and after I've turned a dozen corners I realise I have no idea where I am. For all I know, I could be directly beneath Tynarrich Hall, or all the way out at the hunting lodge.

I feel panic climbing up my throat as the realisation hits me.

I'm lost.

But it's not just that. Something about these tunnels feels different. It's only when I turn a third time, noticing the perfect arch of the ceiling, that I realise the floor is completely flat.

The meandering staircases and dusty classrooms are missing, and when I pull out my notebook to scribble the names of the tunnels, I realise they don't have any. There are no scratches, no cracks. And most important, they don't have electric or gas lamps.

All they have are candles, in perfect alcoves, dotting the way. All of them are lit, but the wax doesn't seem to be melting, as though they're frozen in time.

I don't know what it is about this place that unsettles me, but my gut tells me something sinister happened down here, eons ago. Goosebumps cool the back of my neck, and I turn, trying to follow my makeshift map back to the Cat's Tail. But the more I walk, the less sense my map makes.

I pick up speed, ignoring my racing heart, until I turn and come face-to-face with a dead end. For a split second, I expect a hand to reach through the stone and grab me, just as Aliz did in our shared dream. I breathe out, forcing myself to remain calm. And that's when I see it, so light it's barely visible.

Vines with intricate leaves, roses and thorns. It's an engraving, but there's something so lifelike to it that I can't quite believe someone was able to craft it. I run my finger over the stone, and the dream haunts me again. I see the rosebush at the centre of the maze, flanked by four statues.

Another chill. The sensation that I'm being watched, even though there are no audible footsteps near me. *I should get out of here.*

Just as I think this, the engraving on the wall changes, thorned vines shifting into words:

A phiuthar ghràdhach.
Tha m' fhuil agad.
Ach tha thu fhathast nad chadal.

"What—"

The stone moved.

And I think my eyes may be tricking me, that perhaps it's a screen, but when I reach out to touch it, the words are solid.

I swallow hard and scribble it down, trying not to think of how this is possible. I don't know Gaelic, but I recognise it enough from the cursive words they put under the names of train stations. I'm only halfway through the engraving when the words disappear, twisting into vines again. "Wait," I protest, but the wall doesn't care.

I stand there for a minute, waiting for the impossible to happen again. But it doesn't. I peer down at my notebook, at the half-finished inscription and the new, oddly even lines of the last few tunnels, then start making my way back.

Twenty minutes later, I find myself standing right in front of the dead end again. A shiver runs through me. What if I can't get out?

Sweat dots my forehead. I've always assumed that if I died, it would be at a vampire's hands. Not lost in a maze. I keep walking, the ground still too flat. I wait to hear a student, or even an animal, anything that will tell me that I'm heading in the right direction.

Finally, the ground gains an incline. I find a staircase I haven't seen before and rush up it, terrified it might just vanish. When I reach the top, I sit back down, catching my breath. I open a translator on my phone, quickly typing the words.

Dear sister,
you have my blood,
but—

I clench my teeth, trying to remember what the last line was. I scribble this into my notebook, beneath the Gaelic, hoping it'll suddenly make sense. *What was that?*

The sound of footsteps draws me away from the notebook. I shove it into my satchel and turn to the tunnel behind me. The silhouette of a woman comes into view, barely illuminated by the scarce lamp, and as she approaches, she covers her mouth and nose. "Cassie?" Julia's voice is muffled as she looks around.

"Yeah, it's me," I say, and she coughs. "What is it?"

"Something smells weird."

I sniff the air. "I can't smell anything," I say, getting up. "What are you doing down here?"

Julia points at a sign on the wall, an arrow above the words *Traquair Hall*. "Just finished class," she says and takes a step back. Her pale blue eyes gain a sudden red tinge, but she blinks, and it disappears. "Is that your *blood*?" She pulls up the collar of her jumper until it covers her nose. A sharp pain pierces my chest for a second as I realise what this means.

The garlic has left my system. I swallow hard.

"Aye," I say.

"But your blood didn't have a scent before," she says, confused. She stays at a safe distance, and I nod.

"I was taking garlic supplements," I say. "It neutralises the smell." She still hasn't moved, tense. "But I had to stop."

"Why?" she asks, her voice tight. This isn't good. Vampires like Julia, treaties-abiding vampires, have never tasted human blood. They're used to the synthetic, fragrance-free stuff that keeps them healthy and full, but doesn't indulge their desires the way my blood would. But if she attacks me, I'm pretty sure I'll be able to knock her out without hurting her. Julia remains tense, slowly walking towards me.

"It was upsetting my stomach," I say.

She takes a deep breath, then lowers her jumper. "Sorry," she says, trying to calm her voice. "I was just a bit shocked. I don't mean to be rude."

I gawk at her, watching as she inhales slowly, as though she's trying to get used to my scent. "Maybe I should have warned you," I say.

"It's fine; it's not your fault your blood smells like this," she says, and I stare at her.

My throat tightens.

Type-S blood doesn't only smell good. It makes all those who smell it thirsty, and depending on the vampire, that thirst can become all-consuming. But despite the tension in her features, Julia's eyes are no longer red. She's controlling herself.

I follow her as she makes her way along the so-called shortcut. Julia is incredibly thin, her cheeks sunken. As years pass, she'll start to fill out, blood will rush to her cheeks, and she'll build muscle. But I've heard it can take a Convert vampire decades to regain their strength.

"With that kind of blood you're a target for blood parties," Julia says. I hide my reaction. Blood parties aren't exactly a secret, but they're certainly not something that most *civilised* vampires would openly admit knowing about.

"Have you ever been to one?"

"No," she says, and she steps further towards the wall, keeping her distance. She was probably quite pretty when she was alive. What if Julia was a blood party victim? And instead of getting drained at that party, she was sired? I've had a few vampires offer me immortality before I revealed I was a hunter. Perhaps they do keep their promises.

"Well, almost," she says, breaking the silence.

"Almost?"

"I almost went to one, back when I was human. But they turned me instead."

Her words are light, but I can feel all the broken pieces behind them. "You were turned against your will," I say, and Julia looks back at me. After a short pause, she nods.

"I'd rather not talk about it," she says.

"Of course," I say. Who is *they*? I understand her not wanting to talk about it, but now it's all I can think of. The sketch of the Tube colours my mind. She said that was the last thing she saw with *human* eyes.

I want to ask more. Four years ago, my parents were killed. Four years ago, Julia was sired. I've heard that a dozen vampires are created each year. I know I shouldn't search for a connection between these two events. But I can't help it. I need a thread to pull on, something to bring me closer to the truth.

We step out into a new tunnel, modern and far better illuminated. It's busy with vampires, some of whom I've spotted in class, and all of those who are close enough to pick up my scent come to a sudden halt. Their noses twitch, eyes flashing crimson, suddenly ensnared by thirst. "Fuck," Julia mutters under her breath, while I slowly feel for the toggle on my watch. I could run. And no matter how good my blood smells, they still can't bite me unless I agree. "Don't look anyone in the eyes," Julia says.

She puts an arm around my shoulders, pulling me closer. Even through her coat, she's absolutely freezing. The vampires around us stare far too intently, but Julia's arm is enough to keep our fellow students from stepping closer. "You need to get outside," she says. She removes her arm from my shoulders, grabbing my hand instead, and rushes up the nearest staircase. "I'm glad it was me you ran into," she adds.

"Me, too," I say, surprised by my own words.

We pass through another hallway, and I spot that familiar head of white hair in the distance, far enough for her to not pick up the scent of my blood.

Aliz looks towards us, her gaze falling to my hand, still clasped with Julia's. Even from afar, I see a myriad of emotions pass through her face. And perhaps I would have felt guilty if she didn't have an arm around Elia's shoulders. "We can't go that way," I say, and Julia stares, spotting Aliz.

When we were together this morning, the garlic hadn't left my system yet. Now there's no hiding the scent of my blood. But I'm not ready to see her expression change. Just because Julia has been able to somewhat control her reaction, doesn't mean Aliz will. Especially not with the mark's magnetic pull.

"I suppose the good thing about you smelling like *you* is that you no longer smell like her," Julia says under her breath.

"What do you mean, 'like her'?" I ask as she drags me further up, until we finally reach an exit. I stop, reveling in the cold air, while Julia takes a deep breath.

"I recognise her scent. And it's all over you. Like"—she shakes her head—"all the time. So, you don't have to lie to me," she says. "You're more than roommates, aren't you?"

I stop for a moment, pressing my lips together. *All over me?* Suddenly I remember her reaction the morning I found the mark. All along, that was because of Aliz's scent.

It's as though I already belong to her. Julia is right about one thing. We aren't *just* roommates. What happened in front of the bathroom mirror wasn't roommate behaviour.

"It's complicated," I manage.

Julia stops by a fir tree, tightening the laces of her shoes. The bark behind her is thick with moss. "All right. I don't know what Aliz is like, but her family is dangerous. If you get involved with the Astras—"

"I won't," I say. The wind howls through the canopy, momentarily revealing a pocket of the night sky.

"Especially"—she lowers her voice, as though she's scared the trees will hear us—"*him*." We keep walking, trekking up the slope of pine needles. She picks one up, rolling it between her fingers.

"Ares?" I say, and Julia winces.

They say a Convert's appearance changes, just slightly, to resemble the vampire who sired them. Their hair might lighten, or the colour of their eyes might shift, too. Julia's hair is a very light blond. Almost white.

"He's not your sire, is he?"

The windy night starts to drizzle, and Julia laughs.

"Imagine that," she says.

"Why are you scared of him, then?" I ask. Julia stops, despite the light rain, and looks back at the campus village, glowing gold through the woods.

"It's hard to explain. And you might not believe me."

"Try me," I say, and she laughs again. Then, her expression sobers, something akin to fear slipping into her eyes.

"I dreamt of him." She puts her hands in her pockets, then takes them out again. "I know it sounds silly."

For some reason, my mind crawls back to one of my first trips down into the tunnels, when I found the Red Ribbons' meeting room, full of dust-ridden frames, and a small portrait labelled: *Ada, Dreamwalker of Rome*. At the time I didn't know who she was. "Is Ares Astra a Dreamwalker?" I ask. Julia's eyes widen.

"I've never heard that word before," she says. "But I guess it's fitting."

"What happened?"

She hesitates, still looking at the campus. "The dreams were incredibly vivid. They felt... real, even after I woke up. He had questions." Her lower lip trembles, so she bites it, drawing blood. "I couldn't answer them." She plays with a button of her jacket, clasping and unclasping it. "At first, I thought it was just my overactive imagination. But I had seen him out by the river, behind the humanities building. He'd looked right at me, and that's when the dreams started." She shoves her hands in her pockets again. "The dreams stopped once he left Tynahine. But I was scared to fall asleep for months."

"Have you dreamt of him again since then?"

"No," she says, and as the drizzle grows heavier, we start walking again, quickly, towards Tynarrich. "And please don't tell your roommate about this."

"I won't," I promise.

"Does the dean know your blood smells like this?" she asks. "I find it hard to believe Tynahine would accept someone who might make its students . . ." She hesitates, unable to find the right words.

"Lose control?" I offer, and Julia opens her mouth, but doesn't say anything. "He knows," I say. But I don't tell her how, exactly, he found out.

"And Astra?" she asks, as Tynarrich's towering walls appear before us. "Does she know?"

"I told her earlier today," I say, looking down at my boots. "But I don't know how she's going to react." She gawks at me with a stare halfway between pity and bafflement. "I know," I whisper before she can add anything. "I should have told her ages ago. And you. And Ife. But—"

"No," Julia says. "It's all right."

"It's not." My voice thins. "This is what happens. I always wait until it's too late." Julia places a cool hand on my shoulder, and when I look up, I feel as though I have a pine needle stuck between my vocal cords.

"Has anyone ever—"

She doesn't have to finish the question. And for some reason, I feel like I could answer. I could be honest. I don't know why, but I've got a gut feeling that she'd understand what I've lost. More than Penny, more than anyone in Callisto.

Vampires brought her into this world of shadows against her will. So that's one thing we have in common.

chapter TWENTY

The dean's number is on Tynahine's intranet, next to a photograph from the nineteenth century, in black and white. Faust Nocth hasn't changed one bit, his face frozen at the age of thirty. He's the last person I want to rely on, but I have no choice.

"Dean's office," says a familiar baritone. I grit my teeth and breathe out.

"This is Cassie," I say.

"Ah, my favourite vampire hunter."

My nails dig into my palms. I don't want to ask for favours. But I can't think of what else to do.

"I need a new room."

"Is that so?" The humor hasn't left his voice yet. Which is somewhat unnerving.

"I've stopped taking my allicin supplements." I hear his chair creak. I can practically see him leaning back.

"Wonderful. But moving is a terrible idea, Rebecca."

"It's only temporary," I say, trying to keep my temper out of my voice. "I need a few days for Aliz to get used to my scent before we sleep in the same room. She's already showed an"—I swallow, trying to find the right word—"*interest* in biting me. And I know what effect my blood has on vampires."

"And have you expressed an interest in being bitten?"

"Just give me a new room," I snap. My cheeks burn as I remember the feeling of her fangs, so light and sharp against my skin.

There's a long sigh across the line. I think he's going to say *fine*. But instead, he says: "I may not know how to undo the contract, but I *do* know how your symptoms will worsen. A Blood Familiar is supposed to be at their master's side at all times. The further apart you are, the worse the symptoms will get."

I think of the soothing effect of Aliz's touch and realise he is right. "How do you know so much about this?"

"Because Blood Familiars used to be the norm," he says. "At least before the treaties. They were easier to control, and being blood bound also gave them superior abilities. They became more like their masters, able to heal faster, fight stronger, and age slower. There were a few cases of humans who regretted performing the contract, and tried to get out of it before it became permanent. Those who ran away would always go insane, Miss Charity."

"Don't say that name," I snap, looking at the door. My heart quickens, bile rising up my throat. "What do you mean, *insane*?"

"Some said they felt the mark's thorns digging into their skin. Others had nightmares so vivid they were afraid to fall asleep—and finally, those who left their soon-to-be masters would start hallucinating. But they could only run until the full moon. Then they'd all come crawling back as loyal servants."

"What am I supposed to do?" I ask, not letting my voice crack.

"Considering that the symptoms worsen if you are apart, you'll have to stay as close as you can."

He hangs up shortly after this. I stare across the room at the coffin, unable to shake off the dread weighing down my chest. I still have time to take another allicin pill. Reverse this. But as soon as I think it, the ending of my nightmare flashes in my mind, Aliz clawing at her neck, unable to breathe.

If I can't move rooms, at the very least I need to find something to keep me safe while I sleep.

Maybe it won't be so bad. Julia responded quite well, all things considered, to the scent of my blood. But I can't expect the same from Aliz. Even when my blood had no smell, she still craved it. We can't risk her being in that state again, especially when I don't know if I'll keep my own senses in check.

I glance at some of the books on Aliz's desk, amongst them is one of the grimoires I found in Kinsnet's archive, *Beiteag's Book of Spells*. When I was a kid, my dad and I watched *Hocus Pocus* every Halloween, and I remember one of the characters using salt to ward off the witches. So, I leaf through the book, searching for that word in particular, and a hundred pages in, I find it.

Saltward for All Creatures: Vampires, Wolves, Goblins, the Fae, and More.

I steal a saltshaker from the dining hall, and then set the book open on the ground, reading the instructions twice, to make sure I don't skip anything. The trick is to call whatever is inside the perimeter your *house,* because vampires would then require an invitation to step inside. And seemingly, according to the grimoire, so do wolves, goblins, the fae, and *more*. Whatever *more* is.

Carefully, I draw my barrier around the bed. I glance back down at the book and say "This is my house." I step back and gasp when a soft blue light emanates from the powder. I don't know how or why, but it might just work. "Wow," I say.

I inspect every inch of the line just to make sure there are no open spots that will nullify its effects. Then, once I've bitten my nails down to the quick, I unlock my new phone. Aliz hasn't texted me. It's nearing one A.M. Hopefully she won't come back until five. We'll only be in the same room for an hour.

I get into bed, close the curtains, and finally send a text.

I have to tell you something.

i'm listening

Aliz's reply is instant. She must have been holding her phone.

> I've stopped taking my garlic supplements.

I wait for her to reply. Instead, her display picture pops up on my screen, a picture of her with slightly longer hair and a pair of sunglasses resting on the tip of her nose as she stares at the camera. *Fuck, she's gorgeous.* The phone vibrates, and I answer the call, expecting to hear anger.

Instead, she says, "I know why you've stopped."

I sigh, lying back on my bed. "You do?"

"I don't think it's a good idea, Cassie," she says. "I mean—thanks for not wanting to kill me, but your blood, smelling the way it did before, was already hard to resist."

"The full moon is still three weeks away," I say, and she falls silent. "We don't know what's going to change. If I stay on the garlic, the mark will trick you into thinking my blood smells good, anyway." I look down at my nails, uneven now that I've started biting them again. "I can't risk you getting hurt."

"Faust said that if I bit you, we'd seal the contract. I can't risk you becoming my Familiar."

"I'm not going to," I say, swallowing hard. "I won't let you bite me. No matter what."

"What if I compel you?"

"You won't." If I tell her I'm immune, all her panic would disappear. But I would be giving myself away if I did that. "I trust you."

"I'll move to a different room," she says. "I can stay in my sister's house."

My throat tightens, and I tell her about the conversation I just had with Nocth. About the proximity we must keep.

"I've left an air freshener next to the door, so you can spray the room as soon as you walk in. Oh, and wear a mask. Did you find any remedies for your thirst?"

"One book said to drink as much blood as possible," she says. "So, that's what I'm doing. Have you had any luck in the tunnels?"

I tell her about the flat tunnels, and the Gaelic words which appeared upon the wall. With the phone still pressed to my ear, keeping it in place with my shoulder, I read the translation in my notebook. "'Dear sister, you have my blood.' The rest of the words vanished before I could write them."

"'Sister,'" Aliz mutters. "Do you think that message might be for me? If my sister's library was nearby, maybe—"

"But your sister died before you were born," I say.

"Right," she says, voice uneven. "I should check it out, anyway."

"Don't get lost," I say.

When she hangs up, I remain still, staring at the ceiling. Maybe it won't be that bad. Maybe the mark's pull is already stronger than my blood.

chapter TWENTY-ONE

The palace in the woods is in a terrible state. Overgrown wisteria and ivy cascade down columns, each pillar riddled with cracks, bursting with moss. And just as I did last night, I run.

I can feel her behind me. Stalking me, then melting into the shadows of the abandoned palace. I run down a wide hallway, the moonlight shining through stained glass and casting grotesque shadows on marble sculptures.

Aliz Astra is at the door, clinging to it, her crimson eyes piercing the midnight dark. A sound catches in my throat, midway between a sob and a gasp. The sharp vines have spread over my skin, moving, cutting through me.

My bare feet ache against the cold marble floor, and I stop beneath a painting of a woman, a vampire with snow-white hair falling in a straight curtain, down past her waist, with nothing more than a thin sheet of fabric covering her. And although she's a figure in a painting, frozen in oil and thick brushstrokes, her eyes snap towards mine. Her red lips part, biting through the canvas. Paint cracks and crumbles as she reaches through the frame.

She's covered in blood, and her eyes glow a horrifying electric blue. Every sense in my body tells me to flee. I hear Aliz, too, closer, telling me to wait, telling me she's thirsty. I run through a glass ballroom and smash the wall, sprinting straight into the hedge maze.

I snap a stick and make a cross. I cry, telling her to stay back. My feet bleed as I get tangled in thorns. A dead end, and her hand appears through the hedge, pulling me through. And just like last time, when I'm in her arms, the pain, the fear, the helplessness, all fade, leaving only her. Like last time, I kiss her neck, I dig my nails into her skin, wanting her more than anything.

Then her red eyes are on mine, gentle, deadly. But she doesn't bite me right away. She takes her time, kissing my neck, pushing me onto the ground, pulling up my nightgown. Her fingers run over my skin, and she knows exactly how to touch me. I pull her closer, and I say, Bite me, over and over, as she kisses down my torso. I feel her tongue, her fingers burying deep inside me. I moan, and again I beg for her fangs.

And she gives me what I ask for, fangs sinking into my inner thigh, curling her fingers up, and—

I WAKE. My eyes are wet with tears, my heart racing, skin burning.

The feeling of what just happened, everything, still buzzing under my skin. I bury my head beneath my pillow. Tears of frustration wet my cheeks, the unbearable shame at having dreamt of her like that tightening my throat.

My body burns in a way it hasn't since I became a vampire hunter.

I remain still for another moment. Is she already here? I search my bedsheets for my phone, but I can't find it. It must have fallen, I think. I reach a hand through the curtains, and when I pull one back, the fabric opens an inch.

I peek out and see her staring right back at me, eyes bright red.

I freeze, still holding the curtain. Her expression is completely blank. She's sitting eerily still, legs folded, right at the limit of the saltward. A faint blue light shimmers from the ward, preventing her from getting through.

I open the curtain an extra inch, and she breathes in, as though she's only now aware of the fact that I can see her, too.

"Go to bed," I say, my voice calm.

"I was waiting for you to wake up." If it wasn't for her red eyes, I would assume she was completely fine. But I recognise that expression. Thirst, the sort of thirst that takes over a vampire's mind completely, has frozen her features in place, like the stillness before a storm. I swallow hard.

"Why?" I ask. The desire that could have made me easy prey has left me entirely, my hunting instincts slowly kicking in.

I might just have to tell her the truth. Show her my weapons so she cowers in fear, hides in her coffin, and waits until the monster leaves her room. My chest aches. She's looking at me the way the vampires in blood parties look at me. She sees a meal, not a person.

"You were begging me to bite you," she says, her face calm. Her voice is alluring, trying to pull me in. "I just want to give you what you asked for."

"Very kind of you," I say. "But it's not happening." I look across the room. There's a face mask on the floor. She must have tried to withstand the scent. The air freshener lies on the ground, too, along with a can of deodorant. She must have opened the window, and if the wind had blown just a little harder, it could have scattered the salt. Based on what she just said, I was talking in my sleep again. The shame that already clings to me deepens, burning my neck. "Go back to your coffin."

"One sip," she pleads. Her red eyes are too bright. I've seen this happen to other vampires. Their minds twisted, thirst the only remaining sense, louder than reason. I wish I'd never seen her like this. But I knew this was a possibility.

I take a deep breath and focus.

It's not my fault that my blood smells the way it does. But her thirst isn't her fault, either.

I climb off the bed, and I'm not sure if it's the sudden movement or the deadly look that's hardened my features, but she snaps back into lucidity, her neutral expression twisting into panic. "Stay back!" she shouts. Her arms tremble, and I can see her fighting the thirst, not allowing it to take over again.

"No," I reply, stepping over the saltward. She keeps her eyes tightly shut, her breathing uneven. "You need to get used to this, Aliz."

"I can't," she says, cowering towards her coffin. The danger in her voice is gone. She's back to the Aliz I know. "You have to take the garlic, I can't—"

"Well, I can't risk it," I say, crouching down in front of her. "Look at me."

"I swear I won't bite you." Her voice is hoarse. "So please—"

"I know you won't."

I push her down, and unlike every single other physical interaction I've had with her, I don't hide my strength. Later, if she asks how I did this, I'll lie. I'll tell her that I wasn't that strong, that she was weak because she wanted me. For this to work, for us to survive what's left of the month, I need her to listen.

"You're not going to bite me," I say in a cold voice, the one I use on hunts, keeping her wrists pinned down. "And no matter how much I want it, I won't ask you for it. Understood?" My dreams may tell me otherwise. But this is reality. I won't allow myself to be weak.

She holds her breath, eyes squeezed shut. She's really trying.

"What if I accidentally cut myself?" I ask, leaning closer to her, and Aliz turns her head, tears dampening her white lashes. "What if I fall or get a nosebleed? You wanted my blood before you knew what it smelled like. You know that."

"But this is a hundred—a thousand times worse!" she cries, struggling against me to no avail.

"I know."

"No, you fucking don't," she says, straining still. "This is torture."

I swallow, her words searing through me. I should have known she'd react like this. I should have known she'd lose me under the scent of my blood. "Please," I find myself whispering, and she looks at me, confused. Her eyes widen as she takes in my expression.

"What is it?" she asks, sobering.

My eyes burn. "I need you to see me as a person," I say, keeping my voice from breaking. My words probably make no sense to her. "I need this from you, more than anyone, Aliz." Her eyes are still bright crimson. Slowly, I draw my hands back from her wrists. She doesn't lunge at me. Despite the Familiar's mark making her want me far more than she should, exacerbating her thirst, she stays in control.

"Of course you're a person," she says. She takes my hand, not to pull me down, not to trap me, but simply to squeeze it. Warmth and salt streak my cheeks. "I'm the monster here, not you," she says. "But what if I compel you?" Despite all her struggling, despite saying it's torture, Aliz has somehow managed to get her eyes back to their normal colour.

"I trust you," I say in a small voice. I sit up straight, my knees still at either side of her hips. She stares up at me, eyes wide. Shocked.

"You do?"

"Yes," I whisper. "We'll survive this, Aliz." I run a finger across her brow, and she doesn't try to bite it, taking short and shallow breaths. "Have you had your dinner yet?"

"I couldn't drink it," she whispers. "The blood—" She tugs her shirt up, covering her nose. "It tastes sour."

I shudder. That's not good.

But before I can panic, an idea forms in my mind. Not the sort of idea a vampire hunter should have. But right now, at this moment, Aliz matters more than my principles. If I tell her, she'll probably say no. "Why don't you sit at the window?" I ask her, and she nods slowly. She seems to be calming down. I would hug her, but I know it would make things worse. "I have to make a call."

Nocth answers immediately.

"Dean's office," he says, just as he did before.

"It's Cassie," I say, hoping he won't say my real name with Aliz in the room. "I need help. Aliz—"

"Did she bite you?"

Aliz climbs up onto her desk, finally sitting on the window ledge, and I leave the room, standing out in the hallway, wearing just my nightgown and slippers. "No," I say, and I can't tell if his sigh is one of disappointment or relief. "Do you care about Aliz's well-being?" I ask.

"Of course I do," he says. I look up at the vaulted ceiling, my heart thumping.

"Well, she needs blood."

Callisto will kill me.

But I can't think of what else will help her get through this.

"Human blood," I say.

chapter TWENTY-TWO

There's silence on the other end of the line. For a second, I think the dean's left the phone on his desk and forgotten about me. But then I hear him again.

"Bring her to my office."

He hangs up, and for a moment, I don't move, coming to terms with what I'm doing.

Aliz is still sitting on the windowsill, head leaning on the frame. I watch her shoulders rise and fall, gulping down as much of the damp night air as she can. I step back into our room and clear my throat. She turns, and her eyes are bloodshot.

"We need to go," I say.

"Where?" Her voice is thin, afraid.

"The dean's office." Worry freezes her features, but quickly, I add, "We're going to get you blood, Aliz."

I watch her as she climbs back down from the windowsill, stealing glances of me. Her face is paler than I've ever seen it before, and I could swear her cheeks have a sunken quality to them now.

I get dressed as quick as I can, pulling a jumper over my nightgown, and a pair of jeans beneath it. I cover the tangle of vines on my skin with my tartan scarf. We take the stairs, walking past portraits, keeping a safe distance between ourselves. I stare at the paintings, expecting to see one of the white-haired vampire from my dream. It was Ada Astra, wasn't it?

"Cassie, I'm sorry," Aliz says, once we're outside.

"Don't be." I fall into step beside her.

I grab onto her arm as we enter the steep pine grove. "Believe it or not, I actually want you to be all right." Aliz doesn't say anything, and my cheeks burn. What if I've said too much?

The wind whips at my hair, and I search for a hair tie. She steals it from me before I can use it, and I feel her fingers in my hair, pulling it into a ponytail. I force myself to focus on the wet ground, on the cushion of pine needles. The campus village seems miles away, as though we're alone in the middle of nowhere.

I start walking again, hoping the howling wind will hide my racing heart.

"If he asks to speak to you alone again, please say no," Aliz says, as we reach the humanities department. "I don't trust him. Faust was alive long before the treaties. He's tasted human blood, so who knows..."

It's me she shouldn't be trusting.

Soon we reach the humanities building, and when Nocth says, *Come in*, he's not alone. Marcus is standing next to the desk, paler than when I last saw him, and with gauze pressed to the crook of his arm.

"I imagined we were going to pillage a blood bank," I say, staring at the wineglass half filled with crimson.

"That would entail breaking the treaties, Miss Smith," Nocth replies, not looking at us. He's scribbling in a notebook. Only when we shut the door, his gaze snaps up towards me, eyes suddenly crimson with thirst. Aliz stands in front of me, and I don't have to see her face to know she's probably on the verge of hissing at him. "Don't look at me like that, Aliz," he says. "We're doing this for you."

The red leaves his gaze quickly, and he offers me a cold smile. "Before Marcus's blood goes cold, please."

"How is *this* not breaking the treaties?" Aliz asks.

Faust leans back in his chair, staring at her with disappointment. "Article fifty-three, section two," he says. "'The consensual consumption of fresh blood may take place for medical purposes when synthetic blood is not sufficient.'"

"But is your Familiar actually consenting?" I ask. I know I shouldn't be arguing when all I want is for Aliz to get better. But what if Marcus was once like me, with a will of his own? Marcus scoffs, placing the gauze in a dust bin and glaring at me.

"Of course I am," he snaps. "A paper contract does not involve any form of compulsion. Everything I do for my master, I do willingly."

"Sure," I mutter.

I walk to the desk, watching as red reappears in Faust's eyes. I wonder what he would have said about my blood if Aliz wasn't here. I pick up the wineglass, blood swirling inside, and hand it to Aliz. I expect her to gulp it down, but instead she eyes it warily. Then up at Marcus. "I don't know if I can."

"You do realise you're a vampire, right?" I whisper. "You're supposed to *like* drinking blood."

"I know," she says before pinching her nose. She tilts the glass back, a droplet slips past her lips, running down her chin. Her tense shoulders loosen, and she makes a sound that tells me Marcus's blood doesn't taste sour. She finishes the blood in a single gulp. Then she stands, completely frozen, looking at the empty glass. Her eyes are wide, cheeks flushed, as though she can't believe what she just drank. "That was incredible."

The lines on my body sting. I feel the thorns digging into me, telling me that I shouldn't let her drink someone else's blood. I breathe slowly, ignoring the pain.

"Thank you," she adds, looking at the dean's Familiar.

"Marcus has agreed to donate a liter over the next four days," Faust says. "Tomorrow we'll start dosing it with synthetic blood, though I suspect this problem might continue until Miss Smith accepts to become your Familiar."

I stare at him plainly, allowing myself a smile. "You know that won't be happening."

"How are you getting on with your search for the library?"

"We're getting closer," Aliz says. "Do you think I can turn into a bat now?" she asks, and the dean sighs.

"The hormone required for transformation is only released with a bite," I say, and Aliz gawks at me.

"How do you know that?"

"Because unlike you, I actually pay attention in class."

She narrows her eyes, as though she's thinking of a rebuttal, but instead she turns back to her cousin. "When can I come and pick up the rest of the blood?" she asks, glancing at Marcus again.

"I'll send it to you," Nocth says. He presses his fingers to his temple. "The sun will be rising soon. You better be on your way."

I take Aliz's wrist and draw her out of the office.

I could let go of her wrist, bony and cold between my fingers. But something stops me, as though the wind might steal her away from me if I let go. I shouldn't have these thoughts. I shouldn't want to be close to her, especially not after what happened tonight. But for some reason, her tears, her pain, the danger in her crimson eyes, only flames the temptation drawing me to her.

"I'm sorry," she whispers again, as pine needles crunch beneath my boots, and wind batters the forest. Tynarrich glows atop its hill. *Home.* Nowhere has felt like that to me in the last four years. I slip my fingers from her wrist down to her hand.

"I know," I say, and fix my eyes on her. Her disheveled hair falls over her brows, blown about by the gale. There's a spot of blood by her lips. I wipe it away, catching a glimpse of her fangs. "We're going to get through this."

"We will," she says. Her gaze is soft, warm. Safe.

chapter TWENTY-THREE

I sit on her coffin, scribbling into the black notebook in which we are supposed to record our dreams. The chase through that strange palace, the painting coming to life—all of it feels more like a memory than a dream.

After what Nocth told me, regarding proximity, I've decided to stick closer to her. So I study in our room, instead of the library, and so far, my neck has barely itched at all. I continue writing my description of last night's dream until I get to the end of it. I can't write any of what happened next.

Aliz's breathing changes, the sound muffled by the wooden lid of her coffin. Then a gasp.

I stay still, with my legs folded, and stare at the notebook. Then I feel her trying and failing to open the coffin. I jump down, stepping past the saltward, in case she's overcome by thirst again. The lid creaks open, and I find myself staring at her family's emblem, the moon surrounded by thorns.

I hear short breaths, and then her voice, thin:

"Cassie?"

"I'm here," I say, waiting for her to climb out and face me. "Are you all right?"

She doesn't reply, the only sounds coming from her are the breaths, deeper now. A minute later, she clears her throat, and says, "I think Marcus's blood worked." The lid of her coffin raises the rest of the way, and she gets out, more disheveled than she's ever let me see her before. Her white hair sticks up in every direction, and one vest strap has fallen off her shoulder.

"That's good, then," I say, playing with the notebook.

"Your blood still smells really good." She clears her throat, leaning on her coffin as she stares at me. "But Marcus's blood was different. I always thought synthetic blood was filling, but it has never hit like this. I feel"—she glances down at her hands—"strong."

"I'm glad," I say, looking up at her again.

Her eyes pause on the saltward. After everything that happened last night, she must have forgotten its presence, and now she seems confused. "What is that?"

"A barrier," I say. "I found instructions on how to make it in a grimoire."

"You're a witch now. Fun," she says, before heading into the bathroom.

After a few minutes, I hear the shower switching off, and Aliz peeks out the door, damp hair sticking to her forehead. We stare at each other. "Did you have another weird dream?" I ask.

Her lips part. Colour rises to her cheeks.

"I've already written mine down," I say, walking towards her. Her shirt is only half buttoned, and her damp hair smells like mint. I glance up at her and hand her the notebook. She opens it, flicking through to the last page I wrote in. She bites her lip as she reads, sharp fang almost piercing through her skin.

Her gaze pauses on mine, silence a beat too long. "Did you omit anything?"

"A few details," I whisper.

She walks past me, heading back to her coffin. She leans on it, scribbling into the notebook. Her face remains neutral, not a hint of embarrassment. She prepares her breakfast, mixing Marcus's blood with her usual synthetic liquid. I wait for her to drink, twisting my sleeves as she tastes it.

"Does it taste spoiled?" I ask as she gulps the crimson down. Then she tosses the notebook across the room.

"Not as nice as last night. But filling." She wipes her lips and stares at her notebook, now on my lap. "I wasn't as prudish as you."

I keep it clasped shut, cheeks burning. I can't make myself read it. "Did you see your sister climbing out of a painting?"

"Yeah. That was pretty terrifying," she says. Then she sighs. "Though I imagine for you, it must have been even scarier."

My curiosity gets the best of me, and I open the notebook. Even when she wrote in a rush, her handwriting is still perfect, lines thin and curled. "These dreams must mean something," I whisper. "Your sister's palace, the maze . . ." My eyes skim down to the bottom of the page, and I regret it instantly. I slam the notebook shut, glaring at her. "You could have spared me the details," I hiss, and Aliz feigns offense. She folds her arms.

"I'm just being thorough, Cassie. Our dreams are clues. What if we miss something?"

"And what part of 'I took off your nightgown' is a clue?"

"I don't know. Maybe there's a secret message in the fabric."

My skin burns. "We should only write what matters," I say, gritting my teeth. "I've got to get going. I have Integration."

"There are only humans in that class, right?" she asks, and I nod.

Aliz seems relieved, until I add: "But all my other classes are with vampires. Last time I checked, Tynahine was still a vampire university."

She looks around the room, and I see worry creasing her features. "You need to be careful. Tynahine is no longer safe for you."

"I'm always careful," I say. "And I'm stronger than you think." I expect her to argue. But instead, she just sighs.

I spend the hours between Integration and Gustavsson's class down in the maze. I'm better prepared this time. I've redrawn the messy map in my notebook onto a larger sheet of paper, which I keep folded. Several chunks are still missing, though I have an idea of what those might be. I find my way back to the flat labyrinth with the curved walls and candle alcoves. Unlike last time, I have more than my unfinished map. Chalk, and if that fails, a ball of wool.

As soon as I trace the first white line on the wall, it moves, turning into stone, sprouting leaves and hardening with thorns, before vanishing completely. "This is normal," I say in a small voice. I draw another line, and it happens again, my attempt at keeping track of my steps swallowed by the wall. And as soon as I drop the first inch of wool onto the stone slabs, it dissolves. So despite being so well prepared, I run back the way I came, breathing out as soon as I'm on the stairs and slopes of the more familiar tunnels.

When I look at my watch, it's already time for Gustavsson's class.

The odd cough interrupts his lecture on leitmotivs. Julia warned Ife in advance, but still, when I sit down beside her, her full lips part, a flash of crimson appearing in her eyes before she blinks it away. "Are you serious?" she whispers. "*This* is what you really smell like?"

I mutter a small apology, but just like Julia said last night, Ife whispers that it's not my fault. "I'll get used to it," she adds. "Can I tell my brother about you? He's a doctor, and I'm pretty sure he'd love to study your blood."

"I'm not sure if I want to become a lab rat," I whisper. "But thanks." She elbows me. I try to imagine her brother. Before meeting Ife, I wasn't aware that vampires could be *doctors*. That implies the existence of vampire hospitals, too.

During class, more and more of my fellow students turn to stare at me, and their thirst is familiar. I stare back, my gaze hard. Eventually, they all look away. No one reacts as badly as Aliz.

"Smith?" a voice calls. It takes me a moment to remember my false surname. I peer towards the end of the dimly lit classroom. Gustavsson's lecture is already over, students filing out, their eyes turning crimson as they walk past me. Ife is putting her things in her bag, but she stops to glance at the professor, then back at me.

"Will you come here a moment?"

I clasp the buckles of my satchel. "Head along without me," I whisper to Ife. She stares at me, uncertain, but nods and slips out from the bench. I wait until she's out of the class before I walk down the aisle. Gustavsson glances up at me. A glint of crimson flashes in his eyes. He blinks it away in an instant and clears his throat.

"Faust was not lying about your blood," he says.

My lips part. How much has the Night Dean told him about me? I clench my fists behind my back and remain calm. "He warned you?" I ask, cocking my head. The classroom is empty. Gustavsson doesn't have a Familiar here to protect him.

The record player is still crackling in the corner, and Gustavsson snuffs out the candle closest to him, just as the wax drips into a metal dish.

"The Red Ribbons' trial ended last night. They've all had their fangs removed." I press my lips together, hiding my shock. "Some will be going to jail—including the girls who ambushed you—and the rest have been fined."

He knows what I am, doesn't he?

"Why are you telling me this?" I whisper, keeping my hand close to my satchel's clasp.

"Because you did something incredibly dangerous," he says, voice as low as mine. "I may not have been at Tynahine long, but even I know that if you come upon a secret club of vampire supremacists, the most reasonable thing to do would be to run the other way."

"That's exactly what I did," I say defensively.

"But you still got hurt." He rests an arm on his desk. I could swear that he looks worried. "At least that is what Faust told me. It's a miracle Tynahine hasn't been shut by the Council yet."

"I suppose so," I say. The record stops playing, leaving the hall far too quiet. "Did you call me here to talk about the trial?"

Gustavsson grimaces at my sharp tone.

"Yes." He touches a narrow, black velvet box on his desk. "When Faust told me about your blood, I thought it would be wise to give you this." He pushes the box across the wood. "Though don't let me see its contents, if that's all right."

I frown and pick it up. Keeping it out of his line of sight, I unclasp it.

Inside is a silver cross, plush against a red cushion.

"These are forbidden," I say, clasping it shut again. It's practically identical to the first cross Penny gave me, back when I was shadowing her missions and wasn't allowed a gun or stake yet.

"I know," says Gustavsson, brushing his pale blond hair out of his eyes. "But with that sort of blood, you're better safe than sorry."

I stare at him. I'll never get used to vampires *worrying* about my blood, instead of wanting to drink it.

"You have quite a piercing gaze, Miss Smith." I glance away from him, feeling my face burn. I mumble a quiet apology and place the box he gifted me in my satchel. And for some reason, I feel a little safer than before.

LATER THAT NIGHT, as I sit in a class on vampires' influence during the French Revolution, nausea sweeps through me. It's so strong I barely feel the itch in my neck. Even with Gustavsson's cross in my bag, I feel as though I'm being hunted by something.

To make matters worse, Elia, who I'd not spotted in this class before, decides to sit down beside me, her silky brown hair brushing against my arm.

Elia may be immune to garlic, but she isn't immune to my blood. "You weren't exaggerating," she whispers, far too close. I tighten my fingers around my pen, fighting the urge to stab her. "I'd hate to break the treaties. But you might be worth it," she adds.

"Do you want to die?" I say, and her only reply is light laughter. My heart thuds. I knew what I was getting myself into.

I've asked Penny more than a dozen times why Type-S blood smells the way it does, and she doesn't know. It's something I could investigate here in Tynahine; I'm sure I'd find the answers. But I must find *The Book of Blood and Roses* first. I can't focus on what the lecturer is saying, her voice grating as she scribbles on the chalkboard.

My dream plays in the back of my mind, Aliz reaching through the hedge, pulling me into a tangle of thorns.

I feel her hands slipping under my nightgown. Her fangs burying into me while I welcome every new bite.

I leave class early. Vampires stare at me as I walk past them in the hallways. I rush outside, into the light rain.

I can't shake the feeling, even as I trek into the pine grove, away from the busy hallways, that I'm being watched. I press my hands over my ears, trying to stay calm. But I can see them. Hear them. Every vampire that's chased me. Every vampire I've killed.

Delicious, they say.

Fear is not an option. I knew damn well what I was getting myself into.

ALIZ TAKES A sip of blood, legs dangling over her coffin. The hours I spent in class, she spent down in the tunnels. "I found the flat tunnels," she says. She's mixed Marcus's blood with a higher amount of synthetic blood to make it last longer, and so far, this new cocktail proves to be working. "But the walls didn't speak to me."

"They didn't *speak*," I say, staring down at my map. "The words were written on the wall."

My neck itches, and as I rub the scarf over my skin, she jumps down from her coffin, striding across the room. The saltward around my bed is still there.

"If I touch the mark, the pain will go away, won't it?" she asks. Her eyes are black. She can't overpower me. "Will you let me through?" I don't want to risk it. For some reason, the thought of Aliz sitting on the bed with me seems like a terrible idea, so I get up, walking over to my desk, and sit there instead. She doesn't complain, placing one hand on the desk at my side, and slipping the other beneath the fabric of the scarf. She can feel my pulse quickening but doesn't say anything.

We're close. I stare at her collar, trying to keep my mind on track.

It would be so easy to look up, to fall under her spell. I glance at her grey waistcoat, my hands restless. I want to touch her. But I can't. "The Halloween Ball will be in the hunting lodge," I say, breaking the silence.

"Yes," Aliz whispers. I'm not sure if she's paying attention to what I'm saying. Her breaths are shallow, few and far between. Her thumb grazes the mark, rubbing my skin until she raises goosebumps. The hand on the desk inches towards my thigh, and before she takes that risk, I say:

"I thought this was torture." I study the cut of her clothes, each seam lining up perfectly with her lean frame. I've already kissed her neck in dreams. I know what she's done to me in hers.

"As you said," her voice is strained, "I need to get used to you."

Not that long ago, Aliz Astra was taunting me. And in my boiling rage I'd wanted to spill my blood, weaken her senses, have her at my mercy. Right now, as she cages me against my desk, leaning her head gently against mine, I know I should have never wished for such a thing. I thought I'd have power over her, just as I have with every other vampire. Instead, the only *power* I have, at least right now, is restraint.

"The hunting lodge," I say, peeling her fingers from my neck. I clear my throat, inching back on the desk. This gesture is a wall, cutting through the fine line we were walking seconds ago. Aliz stands straight, coming to her senses. "I want to go there. I know you said you've already looked, but—"

"Sure." She walks over to her coffin. I can't see her eyes. I wonder if they turned red. Maybe they still are. "How does tomorrow night sound?"

"It would probably be better if we could go during the day, but I understand that'll be hard for you," I say, jumping down from the desk. My legs feel numb, as though I'd been sitting there for hours instead of minutes.

"I'd rather not go up in flames, if that's all right."

She places a second cup of blood in the microwave, and when she looks at me, her eyes are a dark burgundy. I don't know what expression I make, but she averts her gaze immediately, turning to the microwave. She drinks her dinner in a couple of gulps, with a thirst I've never seen her display back when her synthetic blood wasn't laced with Marcus's.

THE FOLLOWING NIGHT, Aliz and I set out for the hunting lodge. We leave the campus village behind, heading to the stone bridge that leads to the woods. She's in a coat she stole from her father before leaving Hungary, and despite having to walk through mud, instead of wellies, she's wearing a pair of oxfords.

"Do you own anything that isn't a suit?" I ask, as the cobbles are replaced by large slabs of stone, and the lampposts that fringe the stone bridge grow brighter.

"I was only allowed to wear skirts and dresses growing up," she says. Her tone is light, but I can sense bitterness beneath the current. "So as soon as I got here, I chopped my hair and raided Faust's wardrobe. His clothes were too big, of course. But he soon gave me an allowance to get my own suits."

"Really?" I ask. I can't picture Nocth being anything other than an insufferable arsehole.

"He's always had a soft spot for me," she says.

"Right. What about jeans?" I ask. "Or tracksuits?"

"Life is too short to dress casually," she says, grinning at me.

"You are quite literally immortal," I point out. Aliz laughs, giving me a push as we make our way over the river. "Why are you letting the university host the Halloween Ball in your palace?"

"Elia is the one who organises it," she says. "I suppose it'll be a good thing if she cleans it up. It's been empty for five years."

"Was it your idea?"

"No. But Elia never asks for permission," Aliz says. "Like, a few years ago I had a crush on a French student, and Elia stole her from me before I even got a chance to get her number." She glances down at me, hesitant with what she's about to say next. "And even though neither of us like humans, if she thinks I'm interested in you, she'll pursue you as well."

Aliz clears her throat, and I take a careful breath. I know it's just the mark, but she's certainly shown *interest.*

"You've never slept with a human?" I ask.

"Of course not. I only fuck vampires," she says, as though it's the most obvious thing in the world. I swallow, ignoring the jealousy twisting inside me. Aliz puts her hand on my shoulder, and I make the mistake of looking up at her. Her gaze is far too magnetic. "What's wrong?" she asks, voice dropping to a whisper. "Want me to make an exception?"

I gawk at her, and Aliz's lips part, knowing she said something she shouldn't have.

"What—" I shove her hand away, my cheeks aflame. "What the fuck, Aliz?"

"I'm kidding," she says, letting out an awkward laugh. "That came out wrong," she adds, and I take a sharp breath, wishing I could carve the words back out of my eardrums. "Sometimes I don't have a filter."

"You don't say."

"What were we talking about?" Aliz's voice is thin. "Elia?"

My heart's beating too fast.

"Aye," I say with an aggravated sigh. "I never imagined you two would fight over girls. Aren't you an item?"

"Hell no," Aliz says, and I fixate on the soft sound of our steps on the damp fallen leaves, ignoring the pleasure that runs through me when I hear her say that. "When I first came to Tynahine, I was obsessed with her. I mean, you've seen her, haven't you?" I bite down my irritation, but nod, hoping she'll change the subject. "But Elia ignored me completely until I turned twenty. I kept sneaking into her parties. She was furious with me, told me she hated the Astras with a vengeance, and . . ."

"And?"

Aliz's cheeks darken, and she scratches the back of her neck. "The rest is a tale too explicit for your innocent ears, Cassie."

"Sure," I say. My chest stings. Aliz pursued her for three whole years. Elia was able to resist her. Meanwhile, I've known her for a month, and she's already undone every thread of common sense that used to run through my body.

"Anyway! Elia said from the beginning that she wasn't looking for a relationship. I was upset at first. But then I discovered that we could have much more fun without committing to each other."

"And did it ever cross your mind that you were at a university, where most people come to study?"

"What about you?" she asks, ignoring my jab. "You and that blond girl have something going on, don't you?"

"Julia?" I ask, shoving my cold hands into my pockets. The woods around us grow dense, and my eyes struggle to adapt to the new depth of darkness.

"Whatever her name is," Aliz says. "I saw you both holding hands. It was adorable."

An immature side of me wants to tell her that something *is* going on between us. I want her to think that I have options, and that she's not the only vampire I'm interested in. But I can't risk spreading a rumor that will affect Julia. Just as I think of a reply that will get under Aliz's skin, I trip on a fallen branch.

Aliz catches me, pulling me back against her chest. "Sorry," she says, her voice an inch softer. "I forgot that you can't see in the dark."

"Pesky human eyes," I reply. She laughs. I wish I could bottle the sound. She still has an arm around me, but instead of letting go, she links her elbow with mine, keeping me at her side.

"I don't want you to fall again," she says. The woods are quiet. No one can see us. But I feel like I'm doing something unspeakable by not moving away. "This doesn't bother you, does it?" she asks.

"What?"

"Being so close."

"I hate it," I say simply. Aliz laughs again, though this time there's a darkness to the sound. She leans down, suddenly too close.

"I know you're lying," she whispers against my ear. "Aren't you?"

"Sure I am," I hiss, tugging myself free. What's wrong with her tonight?

"C'mon," Aliz says, throwing an arm around my shoulders. "Don't be cross with me, Cassie."

"Stop annoying me, then," I say.

"Annoying? Me?" she says. I wait for her to keep going, but instead she slows, staring through the branches at something I can't see yet. I hear her swallow, all while the hand resting on my shoulder plays with the fabric of my coat, nervous. The path starts to clear, and the semblance of an old road splits the woods in half. In the distance, I hear the river, and straight ahead, looming through shadows, the decrepit palace I saw in my dreams.

"Home sweet home," Aliz says, unease in her voice.

"You scared?" I ask.

The path is even, and the starry sky lends just enough light to the dirt road for me to know I won't trip again. All the same, Aliz keeps her arm around me.

"I moved in here the night I arrived," Aliz says. "With two maids and a bodyguard. But even with them nearby, it was terrifying. I couldn't sleep. I kept hearing sounds in the attic. There are rumors that there's someone squatting up there, but even though I lived here for two years before moving to Tynarrich, I never saw them."

The windows, which in my dreams are always smashed in, are intact. The frizzled-up wisteria is somehow in full bloom, despite being months past its season. Perhaps, like the rest of the small palace, the vines are frozen in time, lilac petals turned to glass.

It doesn't feel real. How could I have dreamt of a place like this before seeing it? I stare up, taking in every detail that matches the palace that haunts us both at night. When I glance at Aliz, she's doing the same, a grimace hardening her jaw.

The one thing that's missing now, though, is the panic I feel at the start of our dreams. Aliz's eyes are black. I don't have to run from her. And she's not going to chase me.

"Is that why you moved to Tynarrich?" I ask, as we approach the front gate. "Because of a squatter in your attic?"

"It was a contributing factor," Aliz says. "I wanted to feel like an ordinary student. And nothing set me apart from my classmates like living in a place like this."

She gestures up at the towering stone façade, and I try to imagine her leaving Hungary behind and moving into this lonely and decrepit place. What exactly made her move here? "Where is the maze?" I ask.

"Across the river," she says, letting go of my shoulder. "But I don't want to go near it."

The palace's front garden is overgrown, tall bushes and weeds crawling over the path, blocking our way. Aliz draws out an old, oxidized key. The front doors groan as she pushes them open.

"Why not?" I ask. My voice echoes into the dark hall. Aliz ignores my question, searching the ground for something. A second later, a lantern lights up in her hands, an old fashioned one with a black frame encasing a candle. She holds it up, its golden glow illuminating dozens of sculptures and paintings lining the walls.

Something akin to vertigo stops me from moving as I stare along the hall. It's just like the one from my dreams. I can't wrap my head around it being a real place.

I follow Aliz into the hallway and stare up at the paintings.

Even in the dim light, I can make out her features, and I know it's her: Ada Astra is painted like Circe, amongst lions. She's in a deep burgundy gown, and her white hair is piled above her head in intricate curls, her lips ruby red. She's breathtaking and terrifying. The sort of vampire I'm glad I'll never cross paths with.

This time, though, none of the paintings come to life. Even so, I'm afraid to walk past them, in case the paint cracks and she reaches out, covered in blood.

"You know why," Aliz says, snapping my attention back to our conversation. "Every nightmare has the exact same ending," she whispers, low enough for her voice to not echo off the ceiling, chipped frescoes adorning the surface. There's a faint whiff of soot, a chimney that must have been burning a few days ago. "I always catch you."

She runs a hand down my back, and I swallow hard, playing with the wire frame of my glasses.

A grand staircase marks the end of the hall. Behind it is the crystal ballroom, stars and branches visible through the glass ceiling. "Do you know where your sister's bedroom is?" I ask.

"Upstairs," she says. We begin our ascent, marble stairs covered in dust. A large portrait of Ada Astra decorates the landing, this one displaying a more natural side of the old heir. She's in a flowy, Grecian inspired dress, and her white hair falls in soft waves to her hips. Her blue eyes follow me as I walk past her.

"She was pretty," I say. Aliz frowns at me.

"Like me?"

"You're..." I glance at her, attempting my best impression of indifference. I cup her cheek. "*Gorgeous.*" It's true, but I ensure sarcasm drips from my voice, as saccarine as I can muster. She bristles, pursing her lips.

"Cassie," she complains. "Don't be mean."

"Don't fish for compliments," I reply.

The walls of the first floor are identical to those on the ground floor, a variety of sculptures, marble and bronze with limbs reaching out to grab passersby. Behind them, though, instead of paintings are mirrors. I gawk at my reflection. I barely resemble myself, my dyed red hair with a brassiness in it that I'd not noticed before.

But worse are my features, flushed, glasses hiding eyes that are somehow... softer. Everything about me before reaching Tynahine, all my edges and sharp corners, are blunt now, curved. I'm a picture of health. What would Penny think if she saw me?

The lantern moves, floating away, and only then do I remember Aliz doesn't have a reflection. Just like last time, I can hear her, feel her, but she's missing. Instantly, I'm there, ten days ago, just after finding the mark crawling across my collarbones, her hand tugging my hair, her tongue running up my neck, fingers slipping beneath my shirt, pressing her knee between my legs.

"It's creepy," Aliz says. "Perhaps you should hold the lantern, so it doesn't look like you're being stalked by a ghost."

I take it from her, its weight enough to ground my thoughts. Just then, my old phone vibrates. I draw it out, Penny's face filling the screen. I decline the call as fast as I can and shove it back into my pocket.

"You could have answered," Aliz says.

"It's fine," I say. It vibrates again. I can practically see Penny, sitting in her office, irritation blooming across her features. I decline the call again and hold my phone close, out of sight as I open our chat. *Can't talk,* I type quickly.

"Your girlfriend?" Aliz asks.

"Why are you so obsessed with my love life?" I counter. My voice comes out too harsh, leaving no room for a lighthearted reply.

"I'm not," she says curtly. Luckily enough, Penny doesn't call again, though she doesn't reply to my text, either. I feel myself growing awkward, until Aliz says: "That's her room." Her voice changes, lowering with graveness. Double doors stand at the end of the mirrored hall, sculptures at either side holding long swords.

Somehow, Ada Astra's room is exactly what I was expecting. A grandiose chandelier hanging from the vaulted ceiling, crystals catching the lantern's glow. Unlike the rest of the house, this room is free of dust, as if someone has been taking care of it. The walls boast painted landscapes framed in gold.

There are swords perched on the wall, too, some with a gleaming sheen to them, iron or silver, while others are rusty needles that look like they'd crumble the moment you touch them.

At the centre of the room, on a stained-glass podium three steps high, is a coffin. It's a monstrous thing, as wide as my own bed, padded with red cushions. The white wood looks like porcelain, and engraved in gold is the same emblem that decorates Aliz's coffin. And my neck.

She stops beside me, staring at it. "What if someone's inside?" she whispers.

A cold draft slams the door shut. Aliz jumps at the sound, grabbing my shoulders and letting go just as fast. She hisses something under her breath. Then the palace is completely silent.

"Don't be ridiculous," I finally say. "This is your sister's coffin, isn't it?"

"Yeah," Aliz says.

"Can I open it?" I ask, making my way up the three steps.

"Go ahead," she says. Her arms are crossed, and she shifts uncomfortably, looking between me and the coffin.

I open it just an inch, and scream.

Aliz echoes my scream. She grabs a rusty sword off the wall and immediately drops it when she sees my expression. I shouldn't laugh, but I can't help it. "You really are a scaredy-cat," I say, opening the empty coffin all the way up.

"Thanks," she grumbles. I focus on the coffin. There's nothing inside but more white wood. Unlike Aliz's, there's no mattress or bedding. But on the inside of the lid are long and deep scratch marks.

"Okay, this is actually creepy," I whisper as I feel Aliz come to stand next to me.

"There's nothing in here," she says. "Can we go?"

"Did your sister have a study?" I ask. "Maybe we'll find something there."

Just then, my eyes pause on one painting right in the corner of the room that's different to the rest. The canvas has been slashed with an angry diagonal line. I lift the torn edge, until the vaguely familiar features come into view.

The woman in the painting looks like a soldier, her jet-black hair cut short just below her ears. She wields a silver sword, and on her neck, barely visible, is a black moon surrounded by thorns.

"My sister's Familiar," Aliz says behind me. "Legend says she was a bodyguard who was immune to compulsion. So in order to control her, Ada consulted with witches to find a curse that would bind them together." Aliz steps closer to the painting, taking in the mark on the Familiar's neck. "I wonder how much of that was true."

Pain twists through my mark. I'm in the exact same position. Immune to compulsion, but on the brink of losing the only defense I have. "What's her name?" I ask, a sinking feeling in my chest.

"Catherine Lovelace," Aliz says. My hands go cold.

No.

I think back to Penny's office and the silver sword that hangs there, that once belonged to the same woman in the painting. My eyes sting. Finding out that Callisto had once worked for the Astras was bad enough. But *this*?

Callisto's founder was also Ada Astra's Familiar.

I feel as though the floor is about to vanish beneath my feet. I storm away from the painting, swallowing my panic. My hands have gone numb, my throat too tight to utter a single word. I need to calm down.

It makes sense, I tell myself, digging my nails into my palms, trying to get the feeling in them back. If it was Callisto who killed Ada Astra, they did it to free Catherine from her contract. And if Penny ever finds out I'm in the same position, I know she won't hesitate to do the same to Aliz.

"We still have time," Aliz whispers, and I feel her at my side. "We'll break the contract. I promise."

I can't look at her. I walk to the window to try and calm down.

And when I look out into the night, I see it.

Stretching out in the shadows, past the river and the glass ballroom, is the maze. A shiver runs through me. It's a perfect circle, smaller than I thought. The hedges, just like in my dreams, are overgrown, some passages blocked entirely by their creeping branches. I set the lantern on the floor and stare out. At the centre of the maze stand four sculptures, each holding a moon. Just like in my dreams, the first quarter moon is gilded gold. The rosebush is not visible from here.

And as I stare at the outline of the maze and the pattern of hedges, something clicks in my mind. Aliz comes to stand next to me, tense as she takes in the site of our shared nightmares.

Without saying anything, I reach into my satchel, drawing out my notebook. In it is my map of the tunnels. The centre is still missing, but the same three tunnels, the curves I drew from memory, appear now near the entrance of the hedge maze.

"It's a map," I whisper.

"What?"

I'm not sure if it's intentional or not, but Aliz's breath is on my ear. Her low voice, which I could listen to all day, harnesses me, pulling me away from the maze and back indoors, into Ada Astra's bedroom. I can hear my own careful breaths, far too loud.

Aliz's fingers stop on the notebook, not prying it away from me, but tilting it enough that she can see it. Her fingers press against mine. We're too close. Close enough for the mark to burn my skin, not with an itch, but with another feeling entirely. A craving. It whispers to me of what I want.

Bite me.

I squeeze my eyes shut, trying to rid myself of the thought, but I can still feel her breath on my skin. The dreams I try to not think about come to life. Her fangs, my blood. I want her to consume me again. *No,* I tell myself.

"Am I too close?"

Each new beat of my heart is like a knock on a door, demanding to be let in from the rain. "No," I whisper, waiting for her to come even closer. Her other hand rests gently against the glass. I should run. But I want her so much that I tremble.

The hand on my notebook glides to my wrist, and the bound pages slip to the wooden floor. Aliz reaches down for it, shoulder brushing my thigh. She stays on her knees, staring out the window with a grimace. Then she glances up at me. Her eyes are black.

"No," Aliz says, as though she knows exactly what I'm thinking.

She stands up, and slowly, the urge leaves me. Shame stings my chest, and I breathe out, unable to look at her. The thought wasn't my own. And although I should be terrified by what crossed my mind, Aliz was able to control herself. Just as she promised.

I look through the window, slowly putting back the pieces of what I was thinking before she came to stand beside me.

"The maze," I say again, keeping my distance. "It looks like a map."

"A map?" Aliz's voice is soft. "To what?"

"I could be wrong," I say, pressing my hand to the glass, staring out into the night. "But I think it's a map to the library."

chapter TWENTY-FOUR

I take Penny's call the next morning sitting on the bench by the river. My eyes are bleary with sleep, the same torturous dream still echoing in my mind. The hunting lodge, the maze, Aliz's fangs. It's only nine o'clock, so the campus is empty. Most human students have by now adjusted their sleep schedules to match those of their vampire classmates. I stare up at the grey sky and the heavy clouds threatening rain.

"Why didn't you pick up yesterday?" she asks, voice sharp.

I swallow my irritation. "Believe it or not, I'm trying to find the fucking library," I say. "But I'm getting closer to it. I think I've finally figured out the map."

There's a heavy pause, and when Penny breaks it, her voice is surprisingly small. "You have?"

"I think so," I say. We will put my theory to the test tonight, and then hopefully, if it works, by tomorrow I will be free.

"That's good," she says. "On Monday night you're going into Inverness," she says. "The blood party is being held in the city centre."

I'd forgotten about the *party* already. I swallow hard. "Where?"

"Inverness Castle," she says. "You'll need a red dress and..." She hesitates. "You've stopped taking your supplements, haven't you?"

"Yes," I say.

"How did Aliz Astra react to your blood?"

I stare at the river, water reflecting the grey sky. "Have you asked the dean the same question?" I ask and hear an aggravated sigh across the line.

"No, Rebecca. I haven't."

"She's gotten used to it," I say, ignoring my mistrust. I don't want to talk about Aliz with her. I don't want to hear Penny say her name ever again. "I'm fine."

I spend the rest of the day working on the map. I sit at my desk, an empty cup of coffee at my side as I try to line up the tunnels I've drawn so far with the hedges of Ada Astra's maze. I have a picture on my phone, not the best quality, but it's clear enough. At one o'clock, the coffin in my room creaks open. Aliz crawls out in an unceremonious manner, practically falling as she fights with the lid of her coffin. She yawns into her elbow before glancing over at me.

"Tonight's the night," she says, looming behind me. Her sleep shirt is half open, with just a few buttons keeping it closed, and I try my best not to look at her. Her hands rest on my shoulders, kneading my skin through my jumper. "You're so tense," she adds. One more day of this. If I finish the map tonight, this torment, this hyperawareness of her, will finally be over.

But I don't finish the map.

As much as I try, twisting the page and trying to jam Ada Astra's hedges into the circle, there are still gaps that don't fit, and worst of all, with each new line, I find myself getting more and more tired, my exhaustion mixed with dread. Monday's mission will not be like my previous trip to Inverness. As the day goes by, Penny sends me more information.

My target is a vampire called Eugene Trellis. He is the organiser, roughly six hundred years old. Until now he has worked exclusively in Edinburgh, and this is his first foray into the Highlands. A note, between parentheses, says that he's seeking to turn Inverness into a new "vampiric destination." The party is a way for him to find investors for a club. So, it'll be a show of wealth.

And power.

My hand aches as I scratch lines onto paper, searching for the quickest way to the centre, as though it's no more than a puzzle, a mere diversion. Perhaps to Ada Astra it was.

"You can't miss another Integration class," Aliz tells me, just as I propose we continue our search. "How are we going to find the library if you get kicked out?" I can't help but laugh at this. Now that I know the dean wants me here, I doubt I'll get kicked out. But all the same, I go to class, listening to Clemence's lecture on sixteenth-century vampires and their impact on modern feminism.

All through the class, Aliz's name flickers across my phone's screen, random messages popping up in our shared chat. If Stephan sees them, he doesn't say anything, extremely focused on the lecture. *What does pizza taste like?* she asks, followed by, *What do you think would happen to a vampire if they went to the moon? Should I go to the moon?*

And all through her nonsense, I try to not smile, taking notes instead.

After dinner, Aliz and I head down into the tunnels. If I'm right about the maze, if it really is a map, tonight might be the end of our search. We'll find the library and *The Book of Blood and Roses,* and the Familiar's mark will finally vanish from my neck. The thought alone makes my heart race, but I try to stay calm. Aliz looks at the map, holding it carefully in front of her. In the middle of the chaos of the tunnels is the perfectly round labyrinth, with a red line tracing the quickest way to the centre.

She doesn't say anything, but based on how she looks at me, I can tell she's as hopeful as I am.

Students turn to stare at us as we walk past them, and I wonder what they imagine we're going to do down here. Slowly, the straight walls start to curve. The ground becomes flat.

We reach a tunnel with a wide opening and a staircase on one end that's been bricked up. "That must be the tunnel to my sister's place," says Aliz. "The hunting lodge used to be connected to the campus, but a century ago it got bricked up to stop students from going there." I swallow, thinking again of the ache of our proximity by her sister's window. Her breath on my neck.

"I think this is our way in," I say, indicating the two entrances separated by two Corinthian columns, with another two on either side. "If I drew it correctly, we should take the left one," I say.

"Of course you drew it correctly," Aliz says. "You're a genius."

I offer her a blank stare, biting my cheek to keep myself from smiling.

The first five tunnels perfectly match what I sketched, giving me a confidence boost. We're finally going to find it, despite Ada Astra's best efforts to keep it hidden.

Aliz starts to slow behind me, putting more distance between us, and I don't have to ask why; when I last stepped into this maze, even if I didn't know it was one at the time, the tunnels were just about wide enough for a single person. Now, if we walk side by side, our arms will be pressed together.

"Why are we stopping?" she asks, a slight strain in her voice. I don't turn, afraid I might find red eyes boring into mine.

"This wall wasn't meant to be here," I whisper, staring at my map beneath the glow of one of the labyrinth's candles. Aliz leans close enough to see the map, her arm pressing to mine.

"Did we take a wrong turn?" she asks. I glance up at her. Her eyes are black, reflecting the flickering glow of the lantern.

"No, but I must have missed a hedge." I hand her the map and draw out my phone, trying to make sense of the shadowy lines from the picture. "Maybe we should have turned left," I say, and as we do just that, we come upon another wall. It's longer, higher, and, unlike the rest, covered with elaborate stone engravings—the same design I saw last time. Roses and thorns. Aliz grabs my hand.

"It's moving!" She gasps with disbelief. Aliz's eyesight is better than mine, so it takes me a few seconds more to realise that she's right: The stone leaves on the rose's stem appear to flutter, and the petals open just a little wider.

"Maybe this is it," I say, not fully understanding what I'm looking at. She takes my hand, and we remain still, waiting for the stone to move faster, change, reveal a door. But nothing happens. "Or not," I add.

I attempt to draw a new path on the map, resting the paper on the wall, afraid the stone might start moving.

"I feel like you're not freaking out enough," Aliz says, staring at the engraving, whose stone leaves still flutter, as if blown by an invisible wind.

"Did your sister dabble in witchcraft?" I ask, and it wouldn't shock me if Ada did, considering what's in her magnum opus. But Aliz shrugs, whispering that at this point I know as much about Ada Astra as she does.

"If I'm right, we might actually be next to the centre of the maze," I say, staring at the solid wall. I wait for the Gaelic words to appear on it again, but they don't.

"The library is behind this wall?" Aliz asks, standing closer.

My gut tells me it is. But there's no door. And I doubt the dean will approve a request to knock down a wall that is most certainly enchanted.

"We need to get here," I say, pointing at another line on the map, the south point of the hexagon. It takes us nearly half an hour, running into walls I'd missed, before a distinctly floral scent reaches my nostrils. We pick up the pace, the endless walls coming to a sudden halt.

I expect to find a rosebush like the one in the maze.

Instead, we find an alcove decorated with the same intricately etched engravings as the last wall, surrounding an altar with stone vines.

Inside the alcove is a single rose and, behind it, a black candle.

"This must be it," Aliz says. I nod, still staring at the altar. "But there are two doors."

"You take the right, and I'll take the left," I say.

"Or"—she grabs my hand before I can step forward—"we can take one door at a time, so neither of us gets lost."

"Fine," I say. After a deep breath, I open the left door.

A gust of cold air carrying a faint, damp scent hits me in the face. But I can't make out a library. Even Aliz with her superior eyesight says there's nothing beyond the darkness. I tighten my grip on her fingers and without another word we step into the shadows.

The hand that was in mine vanishes. I whip my head around, but Aliz is gone. There are no candles in here, but slowly, my eyes adapt to the thick darkness.

"Aliz?" I call. My voice doesn't echo. I don't even hear myself. I just know I spoke. The brick walls are covered in moss and something that looks like kelp and barnacles. And strangely out of place, there's litter, plastic bottles and empty trays of fish suppers.

I can't see the end of the tunnel. The ground is vibrating, and just as I reach down to pick up a piece of plastic, I hear it. A roar, something colossal. I stare ahead, stupefied, expecting a monster.

Instead, it's a river.

A wall of clear water races towards me so fast I don't have time to reach the door before it crashes against me. My head hits the wooden door, and water shoots up my nostrils and into my sinuses. Instead of just dying or passing out as I should, I fight with the handle to open the door, my empty lungs burning.

And then, the voice:
A phiuthar ghràdhach,
tha m' fhuil agad.
Ach tha thu fhathast nad chadal.

I dig my nails into the door even as the current crushes me against it. Then the river is in my lungs, in my eyes, and in my ears, and everything fades, my scream caught in my throat.

When I open my eyes and cough, expecting to vomit a river, I see Aliz. She's on the ground, covering her head, her breath short.

We're back out in the hallway between the two doors and beneath the altar with the rose and the candle. And I'm as dry as a bone. "Aliz?" I croak, expecting to find my vocal cords shredded. But they're fine. I'm fine, somehow. I breathe out, clenching my fists to stop my hands from shaking.

"Did you see a river?" I ask, and she finally looks up, lowering her arms. She's gone a full shade paler, washed out, her lips purple.

"A river?" she croaks, staring at me. "No. It was—" I hear her clearing her throat. "It was dawn."

She looks at her arms. Her cheeks are damp, face frozen with panic. And I don't stop to think about common sense before I close the distance between us and pull her into my arms.

"It wasn't real," I whisper.

"It felt real," she says. Then she's breathing me in, her damp lashes brushing my neck, the sensation enough to make me forget about the river. But as much as I want to stay like this, running my fingers through her soft hair, I remember what I heard.

"'Dear sister, you have my blood, but . . .'" I start, recalling the translation in my notebook. "I heard a voice say that. But there was something else . . . 'chadal'?"

"My Gaelic is as good as yours," she says. "Which I'm assuming is not very good."

"But did you hear it, too?"

The voice we heard must have belonged to Ada, but Aliz won't admit it.

"I didn't hear anything," she says. "How are we going to get through?" she asks. I draw my hand away, inching back and putting air between us.

"We'll find a way."

But though I say that, I know that whatever is beyond the altar might be far more dangerous than the labyrinth.

chapter
TWENTY-FIVE

That night, I don't dream of the maze.
Instead, I relive one of my earliest, bloodiest missions.
The night I killed Cieri.

Cieri, an Italian vampire who had made a name for himself in London, had organised a party in one of his underground clubs. He had handpicked fifty human victims, all with interesting blood profiles. I let myself get captured, just as Penny instructed, and stood in handcuffs, as the other humans were brought out one by one onto a stage for the guests to take their pick of them.

Penny dressed me up the exact way I needed to be in order for Cieri to choose me. White dress, long blond hair. He had a type. She also gave me a needle to prick my skin before he inspected me. It was my first mission working alone—I'd been sent out into the shadows to prove my worth to Callisto.

All I wanted was to save the other humans, but instead, I was forced to look the other way as fangs tore through their flesh, their screams as loud as the music. I followed Cieri to his private booth. He ran his hands down my white dress, told me my blood was unlike anything he'd smelled before. He promised he would turn me into a vampire if I asked nicely.

Something possessed me then. Instead of staking him, finishing him fast the way I'd been told to, a twisted part of my mind told me to take my time. To give him a taste of his own medicine. See, if you let a vampire bleed out, it won't kill them. It will be excruciatingly painful, though, so I slashed his neck, his legs, I near enough carved his heart out of his chest. By the time I finally staked him, my dress was soaked through with his blood, coating me like a second skin. I threw up next to the dust left by his corpse, and wiped my mouth clean, tasting blood. I wouldn't get rid of the taste for days.

When I wake, I can still taste the blood. Stolen blood, from previous victims dragged into his clubs. I pull the covers over my head, trying to breathe. There are careful steps outside my bed, behind the saltward.

Bile burns my throat, and I cover my mouth. Penny told me to be more careful after that mission. She'd been disappointed. Disturbed, even, by the mess I'd made. She'd said: *Maybe you aren't ready*. When I was denied my first promotion a year after that mission, she brought up Cieri's death as one of the reasons, saying I'd acted more like a monster than a hunter, even though it never happened again.

"Cassie?"

I swallow the acid in my throat. I breathe. But I can still feel his blood caking my skin.

"Are you all right?"

I wipe away tears. I don't want her to see me like this. But the mark, now travelling down past my waist, stings, warning me that we've been apart for too long. Telling me it'll tear me to shreds if I don't get close to her again.

I open a gap in the curtains. Aliz stands behind the saltward. Her eyes are black. I am the only threat in our room. Concern furrows her brows, and I can't seem to move my lips, make a single sound, as I step over the ward.

Only when I've wrapped my arms around her, pressing myself to her until the ache in my neck returns to a dull itch, do I realise what will happen next.

Every night, every dream I've had, has echoed in Aliz's mind. Every image of awful delight letting her know—letting both of us know—what we can have if we just give in. But that false paradise is gone.

If our dreams are still connected, when she goes to sleep this morning, she will share my dream of Cieri, and see me as I really am.

A monster.

"What happened?" Her voice is small, her hand on the nape of my neck cool, gentle, familiar. I open my mouth. I have to tell her what I saw, what she'll experience once she goes to sleep, but my lips tremble, my throat seizes. I can't hide.

I can still feel the blood from my dream sticking to my skin and then spreading, sullying her as well.

"I'll write it down," I whisper. I stare at the blank page, then at what I wrote the previous night. The pen nearly slips from my finger as I try to find the words that will save me. Maybe Aliz's dream won't change. Maybe she'll still be in the maze.

My eyes sting, and I copy what I wrote the previous night.

THE MAP IS almost complete. Just one hallway left, with a question mark in the middle, and a hexagon hiding what I hope is Ada Astra's library.

Aliz and I experienced different illusions when we tried to cross the final hallway. I drowned, while she was consumed by sunlight. I heard a voice. She didn't. There must be a way through. I search for answers in Tynahine's most eclectic library, the Palau Collection. I wonder if the alchemist from which it borrowed its name is still alive. Maybe she'd have a few ideas on how to get through.

But as soon as I sit down with a book, my mind drifts towards something I can't ignore.

Has Aliz dreamt yet?

Has she seen my true colours?

Aliz is always there for me. But now I'm hiding in a library because I can't bear it. I chew on my lip till it bleeds, till my eyes sting. My head hurts, and I finally give up, running back to Tynarrich as my skin itches and burns.

I slot my key through the lock, expecting the worst. Aliz, knowing what I am, hating me the way any sensible vampire would.

And when I step in, when she turns to stare at me, I think it's all over. Her face is pale. Eyes red.

I can explain, I try to say. But I can't say anything. Aliz rubs her eyes.

"My dream was not the same as yours," she starts. Her voice trembles. "I don't—" She looks at her notebook, and her hand shakes as she reaches for it. "But I don't understand it."

The room is quiet but for the sound of the wind outside.

"It was more like a memory than a dream," Aliz whispers. "Something I'd forgotten." She rubs her head. Her voice is tight. "It was just before my seventeenth birthday. My father had a Council meeting, and someone . . ." Aliz stares right through me, as though she's still stuck in her dream. "Someone locked me in my room with no blood supply."

She touches her throat.

"And what happened next?" I ask. Aliz shakes her head.

"I woke up," she says. "With the feeling that something terrible was about to happen."

I should be relieved that we didn't share the same dream. But instead all I feel is the need to ease her fear. "It was just a dream," I say. I drop my bag next to my bed, and just like I did when I woke from my own nightmare, I get too close to her. I thread my fingers through her hair, some of it damp with sweat, and draw her close. She wraps her arms around my back, resting her head on my chest. She sighs and then looks up at me.

"It's suspicious," she whispers. Her hand plays with the fabric of my jumper, while her cheek rests against my left breast.

"What is?"

"You being so nice to me."

I frown at her, my glasses slipping down to my nose. "I'm always nice," I say. She looks away, sinking into me. She sighs again, but she doesn't sound as scared as she did moments ago. "But I don't like what's happening," I whisper, running my fingers through her hair. "Our dreams are no longer connected."

"Isn't that a good thing?" she asks.

"It just means things are getting more unpredictable," I say. "And I have a feeling they're only going to get worse."

Neither of us says anything after that. Aliz doesn't move her arms and instead holds me tight against her. So I stay as I am, too, trying to convince myself for the millionth time that I need this proximity only to appease the mark—and not to satisfy something far deeper inside me.

chapter
TWENTY-SIX

On Sunday, we attempt to find a different entrance into the maze, but once again, we end in front of the alcove and its two doors. And neither of us dares to step back into the nightmares conjured within. As the blood party looms over me, my nightmares remain the same: Every night I dream of infiltrating Cieri's party, and every night I fail to save any of his victims because I focused, instead, on killing him. Aliz, on the other hand, dreams her own strange nightmare, of being locked up in her room with no blood by an unfamiliar figure, growing thirstier and thirstier with each passing night.

When Monday finally arrives, I get ready to go to Inverness. Aliz walks into the room just as I finish zipping up my bag. There are a dozen weapons inside. Nocth told us we must stay together, and as much as I would rather remain here with her, I can't let a blood party take place and do *nothing*. "Where are you going?" she asks.

"To Inverness," I say. "I'm meeting a family friend." It's only half a lie. Penny is sending another hunter as backup, despite my insistence on not wanting help. But whoever this other hunter is, I can't let them see my mark, and I definitely can't let them anywhere near Aliz.

"But we're not meant to be apart," she says, coming to stand next to me. Her hand pauses upon mine, fingers cool as they press against my skin.

"As long as you don't fall asleep, you'll be fine." I can't be sure of anything anymore. "You have class, don't you?" She nods. "And I'm sure Elia will have organised a party of some sort."

"For once, she hasn't," Aliz says and sighs. I shouldn't be relieved that they won't be spending the night together. But I can't help it. "Just . . . be careful. Last time you were in Inverness you got bitten."

"I'll be fine," I say, glancing down at our hands, still linked. "And you'll be, too, as long as you don't go to sleep before I'm back."

Her fingers run over my knuckles. "Come back soon, then," she whispers.

This proximity is dangerous. "You're so needy," I say, trying to get under her skin. I look back up and freeze as she leans closer, nose almost touching mine. She tilts my chin up, and my breath catches in my throat.

"Needy?" She inches nearer, enough for me to feel her cool breath on my lips. "Me?"

I can't summon a reply. All I can manage is to swallow and reach for the front of her shirt. And that's exactly when she draws back, letting go and stretching her arms above her head. "See you when you get back, Cassie." I stare at the door long after she leaves, digging my nails into my palms.

THE FAMILIAR'S MARK starts itching as soon as I leave the room. I've covered it with tattoo concealer, which I reapply once I reach Inverness. I stop in a pub by the river with a blackboard advertising an open mic and get a can of Irn-Bru. Mismatched lamps hang from the ceiling, and potted plants, some dead, others barely alive, fringe the windows.

I don't know why I do it, but I unlock my burner phone and take a picture, capturing the lights, the colourful ceiling, and the sparkling river in the background, and send it to Aliz.

> we could get dinner here
>
> once the days are shorter.

She replies two minutes later.

> I would love that.
>
> We can celebrate the mark being gone.
>
> Reckon they sell blood?

I chuckle, staring at her profile picture. My neck itches more than usual. Nocth already told me being apart would worsen the symptoms.

Once the ice in my glass has melted, I glance out the window. The waning moon is reduced to a nail clipping in the firmament. The party doesn't start until midnight, but I need to get ready.

I head to the train station and freshen my makeup in the bathroom. I can't let anyone recognise me. A blond wig and no glasses should do the trick. I tighten my garter on my left thigh, Gustavsson's silver cross and three sheathed daggers strapped to it. My gun and a stake are inside a golden clutch bag. I leave the rest of my stuff in a locker.

The walk to the castle takes longer than it should thanks to my high heels. I've got a pair of rolled up ballerina flats in my clutch, but I can't put those on until my mission is done.

I reach the castle and hide behind a tree, waiting. Then I see them: humans in red suits and dresses. I can tell they've been compelled, based on how they drift towards the castle with glazed eyes. I know this is the vampires' method: They taste a particular human's blood, and if they like it, compel their victim to come to the blood party dressed in red. Like every other blood party, the vampires haven't discriminated on gender or body type—it's the taste of their blood that matters. I was worried that I wouldn't know where to go, but the humans walk towards the north tower, entering through a small metal door.

I do my best to ignore my budding fear, reminding myself I've done this a hundred times. I'm not the inexperienced girl I was when I first infiltrated Cieri's party.

I mimic the trance-like look on the other humans' faces and slowly walk up the slope towards the stone buildings that form Inverness Castle. Outside the door in the northern tower, I see a vampire security guard. His nostrils flare when he smells my blood.

He doesn't hesitate in opening the door.

I step through, and that familiar scent, metallic, sweet, smoky, slips into my nostrils.

The scent of a blood party.

VAMPIRES, ESPECIALLY THE converted, prefer the cold. Considering Converts must die before being brought back to life, their body temperature tends to remain several degrees lower than that of a human. The castle is freezing, and if I wasn't acting like I'd been compelled, I'd probably be rubbing my arms to warm up. Goosebumps cover my bare skin, and the silver cross Gustavsson gifted me with, strapped beneath my skirt, feels like a sheet of ice.

The castle was renovated recently, but the vampires have managed to make the space look ancient, with ornate velvet curtains shielding the windows. What if it's an auction, like in my dream? What if my nightmares have been preparing me for tonight? But as I look around, the humans aren't being led backstage. Instead of an auction, I suppose they're just planning for a rather democratic slaughter.

The humans are herded towards the front of the large hall by some invisible force. I'm guessing people have hosted wedding receptions in the castle. Proms, too. But soon the floor will be sticky with blood. I scan the sides, see curtains hiding private booths. But none of the humans are being dragged into the shadows just yet.

While the humans are all dressed in red, the vampires are wearing black, which will make us much easier to find.

I can't save the humans individually. I need to dismantle the whole party by finding Trellis and killing him, so this doesn't happen again. Kill him like I killed Cieri—but I don't want any of his victims to get hurt this time. I think back to the five vampires I saw in the warehouse. Was Trellis one of them? I keep my breathing even, hoping that if any of them see me, they don't recognise me.

I look around as surreptitiously as I can. I can't see the five vampires from the warehouse amongst the other vampiric guests. Then I feel someone behind me sniffing my neck. My knee-jerk reaction is to elbow them. But I won't. I have to act like I've been compelled. So I let the vampire, a tall woman with dark blond hair in a sparkling black cocktail dress, cup my chin and tilt my face towards hers.

"You'll be mine as soon as the chase starts," she says. *Chase.* There won't be an auction, because instead they want the humans to *run*—to scream, to beg for their lives. The vampire caresses my bare shoulder. "Or maybe I should steal you away now, before anyone else gets their hands on you." Her gaze wanders down my red dress.

Then I spot someone at the other corner of the hall.

She's wearing a midnight-black gown with a plunging neckline. Her distinctive chestnut hair, which she usually wears in loose waves, is tied up in an intricate bun, ringlets framing her face. She lifts a wineglass, filled with what I'm assuming isn't synthetic blood, to her lips, and even from this distance, even with my disguise on, when Elia meets my eyes, I know she recognises me. With blood staining her lips crimson, she raises her glass at me.

She doesn't show any sign of surprise. Almost as if she was expecting to see me here tonight. Almost as if she already knows what I am.

How did she know?

A horrible smile, the kind I've never seen her sport at the university, the smile of a monster, twists her features.

A shiver runs through me, but before I can take as much as a single step towards her, the band—a harpsichord and wind quartet—stops playing, silence falling as a man takes the stage. His lined face tells me he's too old to be Heritage. I look away for just a second, but when I look for Elia again, she's gone.

That fucking bitch.

I didn't want to kill anyone from Tynahine. But my grace doesn't extend to someone who attends a blood party. Is the other hunter here yet? I scan the premises, searching for someone who could fight alongside me.

"Well, this party has been a long time coming!" the old vampire on the stage says, and the crowd erupts into applause. I didn't see him at the Silverbirch. "But I believe we have a fabulous selection of the finest hearts for you to drink from tonight."

I maintain my dazed expression, not reacting to his words.

"We will give the snacks a ten-minute head start—the castle is large enough for the chase to be exciting. We do ask, just to ensure that cleanup is easy in the morning—" There's laughter, and I stiffen. It's not my first time hearing this, but you never get used to jokes about slaughtering humans. "—that once you've caught them, you compel them, and then bring the bodies back to the main hall so we can dispose of them efficiently."

Suddenly, he snaps his fingers, and the *snacks,* as he called them, wake from their trances. They look around, and then down at their matching red clothes, confused. "Welcome, friends!"

My neck starts itching, fear rising in my chest. I think of all my past missions. All the humans I couldn't save. I won't let anyone die tonight. I can't let it happen again.

"We're going to play a little game of hide-and-seek! You can hide wherever you want," the vampire says as the humans start to mutter, and one screams when she sees a pair of fangs. "Though I ask that you do not destroy castle property, or I'll be in trouble." He smiles down at the humans, and when his gaze sweeps quickly over mine, he doesn't recognise me as a threat. "You've got ten minutes to find your spot," he says. "And if you haven't been caught by sunrise, you will live."

That last word, *live,* changes the air in the room. The humans' compulsion seems to snap to an end, filling the hall with sounds of confusion. None of the humans appear to know where they are, or why they're wearing red. I spot a clock directly above him. It's only ten past midnight. The sun won't rise for at least another six hours. They're not planning on letting a single one of us survive the night.

"And your time starts"—he makes a flourishing gesture with his hand—"now!"

No one moves at first. Most of the humans are still trying to get their bearings. Some of them are smiling, sure that it must be some kind of joke. I see a middle-aged man talking to a vampire, trying to figure out what's happening, as if the vampire might actually help him. *Shit.*

I take a short breath. I studied the floor plans of the castle before coming here, but as I look around, I see only one exit, a hall leading deeper into the castle. I don't know what kind of traps will await us there. But I need to get the humans out.

There are just fifteen humans. It's more than half the number of humans that are usually at a blood party, but that means the vampires will be fighting much harder to get their hands on one. I clasp the first wrist I find, pulling a girl my age with me towards the opening. "Run!" I shout, and the word grabs the humans' attention, making them all turn towards us.

Most of the humans who escape blood parties end up having their memories erased, Callisto's vampire prisoners compelling them to forget. I know I won't be able to do that, but I need to get them out of here as fast as I can.

"And they're off!" I hear the host sing, followed by more applause.

"If you're wearing heels, take them off!" I shout, as they start to realise that this is real. When the first one slips her feet out of her red stilettos, the rest follow suit. One falls in the commotion, crying. The hallway comes to an end in front of a grand staircase. A security guard waits at the top, a walkie-talkie on his hip.

"Good luck," he says cheerfully. "You've still got eight minutes, so—" Before he can finish talking, I reach for the stake in my clutch and plunge it into his chest. He turns into a cloud of smoke. I scan the top of the staircase and the hallway for any other vampires, but for now, we're alone. I press a finger to my lips while the humans stare at the dust on the stairs. Some of them look like they're about to pass out, one presses a hand over his mouth to stop himself from screaming.

"You all want to live, don't you?" I ask, and a few of them nod, while others stare at the dust left by the vampire's corpse. "Well, you'll have to do as I say and stay quiet."

"Shouldn't we hide?" one asks as I scan the hall for security. "He said that—"

"You'll die," I whisper. "The only way to survive is by getting out of here."

"What's going on?" an old woman asks, her voice breaking. *Fuck.* I know that if this was my first contact with a vampire, I would be reacting like this, too. I also know that not all of them will be able to keep up with me. I pull out Gustavsson's silver cross, and search through their faces for the one who seems to be the most alert.

"Hold this," I say, handing it to a tall girl with brown curls. "If you see anyone behind us, hold it up. And don't look them in the eyes."

"What are they?" she asks.

"They're vampires," I say. Under normal circumstances they wouldn't believe me. "And they want to kill us. So, stay behind me."

We run. The next security guard, stationed at a corner, is more taken by the scent of my blood—and possibly that of the others—than she is by the weapon in my hand. So, before she spots it, I jump on her. This one realises what I am, but instead of fighting me, her eyes flash red, trying to compel me.

"Not happening," I say, before plunging my weapon into her. I miss the first time, staking her shoulder as she tries to run, her blood spraying me. But I don't miss again. One of the humans screams. "It's you or them!" I shout. There's blood on my face, but if my bloody face is the most terrifying thing they see tonight, then I'll have done my job.

At the end of the hallway is a rose window. And if there's a window, it means we've finally reached one of the exterior walls. "Do not look them in the eyes!" I remind them. I already know there will be more vampire guards here.

And there are: The victims can hide, but they're not allowed to escape. That would ruin the fun. At least a dozen vampires are all lined up by the windows, and my heart races. I've done this before. But there are too many vampires. Where the fuck is Penny's helper?

I search the features of the security guards, and to my utter shock, *Jannet* is amongst them. Stella is right behind her. *How?* Gustavsson told me they'd both been sent to jail and had their fangs pulled out. Did they escape?

Despite my initial shock, a thrill runs through me now that I see them. I've been waiting for this moment since they introduced themselves in the archive. It's their fault I've got the fucking Familiar's mark, after all. The makeup that's covering it is supposed to be resistant to sweat, but it's starting to melt, the beige joining the blood in ruining my dress.

"Oh, they've made it all the way here!" one of the security guards says. They're armed with batons. I suppose shooting us would be a waste of our blood. "You'd have had a better chance of living if you'd hidden, instead of trying to run."

"And you would have had a better chance of living if you'd kept your mouth shut," I say as I take the first shot. The silver bullet finds its way into his brain, and he collapses. I finish him off with a stake, granting him a far quicker death than he deserves. Then several things happen at once; just like in the warehouse outside Silverbirch, most of the vampires turn into bats. And when I try to grab one as it flies past, it escapes.

Just five vampires remain, amongst them Jannet and Stella. Jannet hasn't recognised me yet. I see her squeezing her eyes shut and realise that neither she nor Stella knows how to turn into bats. Instead of attacking me and risking being staked, one of the vampires turns to the humans, eyes glowing red. "Kill her!" she commands them.

I told the humans to close their eyes so they couldn't be compelled, but they didn't listen, and suddenly they lunge at me, a pair of hands gripping my neck. A fist collides with my face, and I guess this is why I'm usually not allowed to focus on saving victims until the organiser of the blood party is dead. A young guy picks up my silver gun, while another continues to strangle me. But the girl with the silver cross, who must have kept her eyes shut, starts pulling them off me, shouting at them, hoping to snap them out of their trances.

The lights in the hallway, in the entire castle, suddenly switch on. The ten minutes are up. The guests will be turning into bats and swarming through the castle any second now. I don't want to hurt the humans, but I can't waste time. I elbow one of them out of the way, get my gun back, and shoot the vampire that compelled them straight in the head, before driving a stake through her chest.

Screams ring out in the distance. Obviously not all the humans followed us. I wanted to save *everyone*. I reload my gun, blood boiling, and Jannet lunges at me. She's terrified, eyes bright red as she strangles out the word *die*. "You first," I say.

When I drive my stake through her, her smoke reaches my nostrils, burning my lungs. I don't feel the satisfaction I used to after killing a vampire. Instead, a sickly dark thing spreads across my bones, a reminder of what I really am. What would Aliz think if she saw me now?

I look up. Only Stella remains. She's shaking, her pale skin almost purple as she stares at the pile of dust that used to be Jannet. Then she looks at the humans, at the blood on my face. "I didn't want to hurt them," she starts, her voice breaking. "I never wanted to—"

A gunshot makes the walls tremble. My ears ring, and Stella's brains spill out of her now cracked skull. Down the hall stands a figure dressed in black, wearing a white mask with a black cross painted down the middle.

Penny had told me she would send another hunter.

"You took your time," I mutter, raising my stake to drive it through Stella's limp body.

"Don't," the other hunter says. "We're running low on prisoners. Once she heals, we can use her to train against compulsion."

Even with a mask muffling her voice, I recognise her. "I thought you were sending someone," I say. My hand, still holding the stake, trembles.

It's Penny.

Here, in Inverness.

A part of me, the part that's known her for four years, couldn't be happier to finally see her again. We've never been apart this long, and I didn't realise how much I missed her until now. But another part of me is terrified. The deadliest vampire hunter Callisto has ever produced is now only twenty minutes away from the new life I've built in Tynahine. If she sees the Familiar's mark, which I'm hoping is still concealed by makeup and blood, she won't think twice before killing Aliz.

My throat feels like sandpaper, and Penny reaches down to touch Stella's body. It will take weeks for her brain to unscramble, for her broken skull to seal shut again. "What are you doing here?" I ask, still in disbelief. I can't quite believe it's Penny. She takes off her mask, and my eyes sting as I take her in. Her sharp features are clean of makeup. She's as inexpressive as always, incapable of showing whether she missed me or not.

"Is Trellis dead?" she asks, ignoring my question. She turns Stella onto her side and writes something on the near-dead vampire's cheek.

"I'm on it," I say, catching my breath. "But we need to get the humans out first."

"You're here to kill Trellis, not rescue his victims."

"We can't leave them here," I say. "We're outnumbered."

Penny studies me for a long second. My neck burns, each individual line of the Familiar's mark itching as I wait for her to notice it. But after a sigh, she tears her green eyes from mine and looks at the humans behind us. "Eugene Trellis should be in the rooftop bar." Slowly, I stand back up. Penny fights with the window until it squeaks, giving way. "I'll deal with him."

"Wait," I argue before she goes. "Trellis is *my* target." Penny didn't see his smug face when he sentenced his victims to death.

"Then why are you wasting time at the other end of the castle?"

she snaps. Is saving lives *wasting time* to her? I ball my fists, but before I can argue, she nods. "Fine. But don't waste another second."

She's angry. But I'll deal with her anger later. And I know that she'll be able to get the humans to safety much quicker than I could. They seem to be in shock, unable to process what happened. I put my hand out in front of the girl holding Gustavsson's silver cross.

"If Callisto tries to recruit you, say no," I whisper, not letting Penny hear me.

As I run through the castle, something feels off. I don't come across a swarm of vampires searching for their prey. Just silence. Now that the lights are on, I can find my bearings. There's even a sign pointing towards the rooftop garden.

I keep waiting for an ambush. But then it hits me. The guests know a hunter is in the building. They'll be expecting the full force of Callisto. Everyone must have fled. I'll be lucky if Eugene Trellis is still around. Penny will kill me if he got away. I run, making sure my gun has bullets, and finally find a staircase leading to the roof.

Automatic doors slide open, and there he is: the same man who announced the rules of the game with such jubilation, now on his phone arguing with someone over the band. "This is the first blood party in Inverness in over two centuries, and the harpsichord was out of tune!" he hisses, before sensing my presence. "Oh, dinner's here," he says and hangs up. "How'd you get so much blood on you, darling?" he asks.

I expected it to be harder. But Trellis hasn't planted any traps, as some of my past victims did. And unlike his guards, he doesn't think of escaping. Nor does he put up much of a fight. I screw on the silencer and shoot him in the shoulder first. He screeches, the silver far more painful than the bullet wound itself.

The streets of Inverness are still lively, buildings well illuminated. When I look up at the moon, it resembles a hook, digging right into my soul, telling me that my time is running out.

"I'd give you a ten-minute head start, just like you gave us," I say, looming over him, blood dripping from my red dress. "But I have a feeling you wouldn't get far."

"Mortal scum," he hisses, eyes flashing red. "Don't you know who I am?"

"A terrible party planner," I say, pressing my lips into a smile. I pull out a stake, and just as I'm about to drive it through his chest, something smashes against my waist, a kick like a wrecking ball. My weapon falls from my hands, and I roll across the ground, as though gravity suddenly changed direction.

I groan, and when I look up, I see her standing eerily still next to Trellis and looking at me with indifference. Her bun has come undone, and her chestnut waves fall past her waist.

Elia's eyes glow red in the darkness, but she doesn't try to compel me.

Because she knows what I am.

chapter
TWENTY-SEVEN

Cold slips through my damp dress as the blood dries on my skin. Her red gaze flickers to my stake, just a metre away from me. I can reach it—my body aches as though I've broken a rib, but I can reach it, I have to. Just as my fingers crawl mere inches from the weapon, Elia kicks it aside, all the way to the other end of the roof.

No. I look up at her, expecting her to kick me next.

"I'm afraid I can't let you kill him, Rebecca," she says, and a chill runs through me.

"Thank you," Trellis says, the silver bullet still burning through his shoulder. "Now get this bloody—"

But then Elia does something bizarre. She crouches, the hem of her black gown brushing against the damp floor. And Trellis gawks at her, confused, while she draws out an old camera and snaps a photograph of him.

I still have my gun. Somehow, the pain in my chest seems to have faded, as though I imagined it. Whatever Elia is planning, I won't let her get away with it. I'll fucking kill Trellis, just as Penny ordered me to. I stagger to my feet, and Elia puts her camera away just as I aim my gun at Trellis again.

She tuts and slams me on the ground before I can pull the trigger, knocking the air out of my lungs. My face is pressed against the stone, and I feel her on top of me. She clasps my arms tight behind my back, and I let out a strangled sound as pain shoots through me.

She leans close, lips next to my ear. "Don't get in my way." She tightens her grip, and I get a whiff of her rosewater perfume. "You've done your job. Now let me do mine."

My arms feel as though they're about to break, but I blink, taking in those words. Her nails dig into my skin, and I can't move. I bite my tongue, trying to distract myself from the pain. "You'll behave now, won't you?" she asks as Trellis continues to moan, the stench of burnt flesh rising from his wound. "Hm?"

"Sure," I hiss.

"They'll be arriving in a minute," Elia says, letting go of me. I don't know where my gun is, but when I turn, I see that Trellis's expression has changed completely, pain morphing into horror. *Who* will be arriving in a minute?

"No," he says, and his wide eyes meet mine. "Kill me!" he shouts, scrambling to his feet, and falling as his wound worsens.

And then it clicks. There's only one organisation that a vampire like Trellis could fear as much as this.

"You work for the Council?" I ask, and Elia puts her hands on her hips, looking down at Trellis as though he's no more than a child. If it wasn't for the silver bullet in his shoulder, he could have transformed into a bat.

"I do some freelance work for them from time to time," she says. "Sort of like a vampire hunter, but with brain cells."

She glances at her phone, and I try to marry the image of this woman, a vampire who was able to overpower me completely, to the annoying girl who was sniffing me in class the other night. "I would leave, if I were you," she adds. "The Council is not too fond of Callisto. Your lot never abides by the rules. So, unless you want to join my friend Eugene in his cell, you should go."

She's right about the Council not liking Callisto. Every time they've tried to include us in their treaties and set some ground rules for our operations, we've said no. One of Callisto's most basic rules, which I now know Penny has broken, is to never cooperate with vampires. There's a light drizzle, and it's so cold it might at any moment turn to snow. "How do I know you're telling the truth?" I ask, rubbing my bare arms. I have to make sure that the humans got home safely. "How do I know you're not helping him escape?"

"Good point," she concedes. "I'm afraid you'll just have to trust me."

"And why would I do that?"

I hear the choppy rhythm of a helicopter, and then I see it in the distance, a white dot drawing closer to the castle. Trellis moans, trying to get up again. If Elia is helping him escape, he's certainly a good actor, because I've never seen anyone quite so terrified.

"You don't really have a choice." She cocks her head. "What would you get out of killing this man? Would it bring any of his victims back to life? Undo the trauma those mortals just went through?"

"I would stop him from organising something like this ever again," I hiss. She's right. I need to get out of here.

"Don't worry. Once the Council have interrogated him, they'll make him sunbathe." She puts her hands behind her back, grimacing. "You really should go."

Despite my instincts telling me to do the opposite, I turn back the way I came. The pain I felt in my arms, the sensation that they were about to break, has vanished. How? Dread settles in me as I walk down the staircase, searching for my way back to the main hall. Red velvet drapes decorate the innards of the castle. It's still too quiet. There were at least a hundred vampires in the hall before I ran, and somehow, I can't wrap my head around all of them vanishing like this.

When I finally reach the hall, with the bandstand and its separate booths, there are bodies everywhere—of vampires. That scream I heard, which I thought belonged to a human, could have been a vampire instead. And next to each unconscious vampire lies a broken wineglass. Did Elia spike their drinks? Though it isn't something I want to consider, Elia might be on my side. The thought makes my head ache. The world was so much easier to understand when hunters were good and vampires were evil.

"When I said you should go, I meant it," a voice says behind me. Elia crouches down next to one of the bodies. *How did she get here so quickly?* "They're taking Trellis away, but are coming back for this lot, so get out of here."

"Why didn't you kill them?" I ask.

"Because I've already killed enough," she says without looking up at me. "Plus, these bastards might know things. Things we'll never learn if we kill them now."

I hate that she's right.

"What's that on your neck?" she asks suddenly, her voice changing. Too late, I remember that the makeup hiding the mark must have faded, revealing the Astra crest and its thorny vines. The lines burn. And that's when I hear it. The sound of a gun being cocked.

I look up, seeing a narrow window and a gun peeking out of it. "Move!" I shout, and I throw myself on top of Elia just as the first gunshot booms. We tumble until we hit one of the unconscious vampires, and when I meet her blue eyes, they're wide. "There's another hunter," I say, looking back. Penny won't shoot *me*, will she? "Get out of here."

"Did you just save my life?" Elia asks, disbelief in her voice.

"Just hurry," I say. *What have I done?* I turn just in time to see Penny jumping down from the narrow window. She lands and aims her gun. Elia has vanished already, with a speed which I can't quite make sense of, but I'm glad she possesses. I stand, staring back at Penny, trying to keep my composure.

"What are you doing?" she asks.

I scratch my neck, trying to find an answer. I don't think there's anything I can say that would make sense to her. Handing over a vampire to the Council is not something that's ever been done before, at least not that I'm aware of. And as I stare at Penny, without moving, I realise I'm in deep shit. Deep enough for her to undo all the work I've done until now.

"She helped us," I say, keeping my voice steady.

One of the vampires next to her groans, waking from the effects of Elia's poison.

Penny responds by shooting him, the sound of her weapon like thunder.

"You've become soft," she says, reloading her weapon. "Weak."

"I haven't," I say, and I barely sound like myself when I add, "But my mission was to put an end to the party. The Council are on their way, so unless we leave—"

"Good. Then you'll stay here and fight them with me."

"We don't fight the Council," I say. We don't get on with the Council, but we're not supposed to attack them, either. "We don't kill treaties-abiding vampires, you told me that yourself." What if she kills me? What if I survived that fucking chase just to be killed by Penny, of all people? "But if you want to stay, I won't stop you."

"That was an *order,*" she says. My fear morphs into something else. "I thought you were stronger than this." Her disappointment crawls beneath my skin. "I thought I could trust you to be amongst them, and not—"

"Why should I trust *you*?" I ask. It's only now that I've seen her again that her betrayal—her omission about her days in Tynahine— spreads through my chest. "How many of my missions came from Nocth's intel?"

When I say his name, Penny—who's spent the last four years training me and showing me the ropes of this twisted world, who after my parents' deaths, became the only person I could consider family—raises her gun and fires.

I duck, and I am pretty certain she missed on purpose, because I'm still alive. "How dare you," she starts, voice cool. "After everything—"

I hear the sound of steps above, announcing the Council's fast approach, and Penny turns, reloading her weapon. There's no way we can fight the Council. Not just the two of us. "Penny!" I shout. "Let's go!"

"I'm disappointed in you." Her words sting more than a slap in the face.

I almost stay. The last four years of my life have prepped me to stay. But the mark on my neck stings, twisting into me, telling me I must go back to Tynahine—and back to Aliz.

And for some stupid fucking reason, I listen to it. I leave Penny behind.

I sprint into the freezing air, and my dress feels like cardboard, dried blood flaking off it. Penny will never forgive me for this. She'll kick me out of Callisto. She'll hunt me down to make an example of me. Panic rises in my chest as I slide down a grassy hill, onto the road, each new breath more painful than the last.

I've spent four years fighting to learn the truth about my family, and I've just thrown it all away. My throat catches, eyes stinging as I think of my parents, of their mangled bodies which I'd promised to avenge. Penny is not the only person I've disappointed tonight.

What have I done?

I try to swallow my pain, stop my hands from trembling. There's still time to run back. To be the hunter I promised Penny I could be.

A car honks, and a flash of pink comes to a sudden stop right next to me. The car is not just pink, it's hot pink, and it draws me out of my grief for a moment. "Little hunter." Elia leans out her window. Her hair is back up in a bun, and her black gown is hidden beneath a fluffy pink jumper. "Need a ride?"

I stare at her, then back at the castle. "I do, actually," I say, voice trembling. When I climb inside her car, I see her steering wheel is a gaudy amalgamation of pink fur and glitter. "This can't really be your car," I say, rubbing the tears from my eyes.

"If you don't like it, you can walk back to Tynahine," she says. I lean back as she pushes down on the pedal.

"I left a bag in the train station," I say. My throat feels like sandpaper. I can still see Penny aiming her gun at me.

Elia stops at the station, parking just beneath the statue of a Highlander with a seagull resting on his feather bonnet. I was planning on washing some of the blood off there, but she tells me I can take a shower back at her place. I try to stop my hands from shaking, but all I can see is Penny's back as she turned away from me when I was leaving her. What if the Council kills her?

What have I done?

I sit back down next to Elia, trying to keep it together. "So, you're a blonde," she says, as she speeds out on the main road of the city. "I *knew* it."

"My hair's black, actually," I say, removing my wig. For a moment I expect my old hair, my short black bob, to reappear. But instead, I reveal Cassie's auburn tresses, matted with sweat, still half pinned to my wig-cap. I shake my head, slowly letting my hair breathe, and Elia pulls a face. "What?" I say.

"You look better blond. You should dye it. I might even date you."

"Yeah, no thanks," I say. She sounds different. Less guarded. "Why didn't you tell me you knew what I was?"

"Because you would have tried to kill me," she says plainly. "I mean, you would have failed miserably. But I think Aliz wouldn't have been too happy if something happened to you."

"Sure," I say. I look at her again. I used to hate her guts. And yet I just ruined my relationship with Penny—with Callisto as a whole—for her. *What the fuck is wrong with me?* "How do you know my name?"

"Faust told me," she says. I clench my fists. "He also asked me to keep quiet, so don't make that face."

She pulls over on a quiet street. For a second, I wonder if she has a house out here, as well as her apartment on campus. But when she brakes, she doesn't move from her pink seat. "That thing on your neck. What is it?"

"A tattoo," I say, and she notices the lie, furrowing her perfectly sculpted brows.

"Here." She pulls out a makeup wipe and hands it to me. I sigh and wipe the remaining concealer from my neck, revealing the small moon. Elia stiffens when she sees it, her skin paling. "The Astra emblem," she says, voice low, before adding, "is that a *Familiar's* mark?"

"You know what it is?"

"Anyone older than the treaties can recognise one," she says. "Never had a Blood Familiar myself, but I studied all sorts of blood contracts back in the day." When exactly was *back in the day*? Based on what she just said, she must be older than the treaties. "In fact, if you visit my library, you'll find some of the papers I wrote on them."

"*Your* library?"

"The Palau Collection," she says, as if it's the most obvious thing in the world. She notices my confusion and elaborates. "A few centuries ago, my name was Elia Palau." My eyes widen, and she uses my confusion to reach out, pressing her cool fingers against the swirling lines of the Familiar's mark. Her touch doesn't have the same effect as Aliz's.

"You're Palau?"

"I just said that, yes," she says.

"*The* Palau? The alchemist?"

"Oh." She makes a face, pulling her hand away. "I only practised alchemy for two centuries. But enough about me, tell me about that mark. How long have you had it for?"

I'm still trying to wrap my head around Elia working for the Council. Finding out that she's also the university's old alchemist is just mind-boggling. *How old is she?* "Two weeks," I say. "We've got until the next full moon to get rid of it. The night of your Halloween Ball."

"And Aliz doesn't want to seal the contract?" she asks, pulling out another wipe to remove her own makeup. Why a vampire as beautiful as Elia would feel the need to wear makeup is beyond me.

"Of course not," I say, my chest tightening. "It was an accident."

Elia stares at me in silence, her eyes wide. "You really believe that?" she asks.

"What do you mean?"

"I can tell you're telling the truth," she says, blinking. "You *genuinely* believe you got a whole Familiar's mark—a blood contract that can only be performed during a full moon—by *accident*?"

"Aliz didn't do it on purpose," I say. Even if Elia wants to convince me otherwise, I know she didn't.

"How did you get it, then?" She kicks off her heels, crossing her legs. "She had to give you her blood, didn't she?"

"Two Red Ribbons tried to kill me."

"How thoughtful of them," she says, scrunching her nose. "Jannet and Stella?"

I nod. I don't like the way Elia is looking at me.

"So, in your mind, these two girls decided that the night of a full moon would be the best time to attack you?"

"If Aliz had really wanted to make me her Familiar, she would have sealed the contract already."

"And then you would know for sure she's doing it on purpose," Elia says. "Maybe she doesn't want you to know that."

"Why are you accusing her of this?" I say, my voice hitching. "Isn't she supposed to be your friend?"

"Of course she is," Elia says, and her gaze darkens. "But I'm not naïve. Aliz is still an Astra. And the Astras will manipulate you without you even knowing that you're under their spell—"

"She isn't like that!" I shout, my heart racing. I don't know why her words are getting to me, but I can't seem to stop myself. "You didn't see how she panicked after realising what this was. You haven't spent hours with her looking for her sister's library, you've got no—"

"Ada's library?" Elia asks. "So *that's* what you were doing down there."

"What?"

"There's a rose down at the library's entrance," Elia says, and I drop the makeup wipe, mouth agape. "It shows me if anyone ever gets too close." She fishes out a small pocket mirror, flicking it open. Inside, I see the reflection of the rose and the candle, and she lifts it up to her nose. "I *knew* it was you I saw down there the other day. I could smell your blood without even opening the mirror."

"How—"

"A witch made this for me back in my alchemy days," Elia says, handing me her mirror. I sniff it, just as she did, and I smell the rose, the candle wax, and the damp tunnel.

"You said this is the entrance to the library?" So, I was right. But knowing where it is and getting inside are two different things. "How do we get in?"

"Only I can go inside," she says lightly. "Ada could as well, but she's dead."

"You knew her?"

"Well . . ." Elia's expression softens, and she lowers her head. "We were lovers, on and off, for five centuries."

"How old are you?" I know this isn't the most important question right now, but I can't help myself.

"I thought you would have guessed after seeing I'm immune to garlic," she says. "But I was born in Hispania. Back when old Augustus was emperor."

"You—" I gawk at her, trying to process those words.

"Two thousand years, give or take a few decades."

"No."

"Yes," Elia says. "Born and raised in a small seaside town, in modern Catalonia. Got converted when I was twenty-three."

I don't say a word. *Two thousand.*

"Obviously my first name was not Elia. I've had several, depending on where I lived. First, I was Flora, and then when the Western Empire fell and my native Latin started to branch out, I switched to Clotilde. Then I was Elisenda, the most feared vampire in Barcelona." She smiles at the memory. "A few centuries later, when Ada and I crossed paths in Rome, she started calling me Elia, and it stuck."

"Your first language is *Latin*?" I say, unable to wrap my head around this. I knew, based on what Julia had told me, that Elia was old. But I don't think I've ever met a vampire this old. She's over a thousand years older than Tynahine itself.

"*Ita,*" she says with a smile, and I assume that means yes.

"Can you get me into the library?" I ask, suddenly remembering what we were talking about.

"The library?"

"Ada Astra's library," I say. She crosses her legs, considering my words for a moment.

"Definitely not," she finally says.

"The cure is in there," I say. "I can't become a Familiar."

"And I can't let a vampire hunter enter Ada's library. Forget it." Panic starts to climb up my chest, but Elia doesn't seem to care. "Aliz must be wondering where you're hiding," she says, changing the subject.

"Can't you find the cure for us, then?" I ask.

"You know, she hasn't slept with anyone in over a week." Elia ignores my question. "Aliz isn't a nymphomaniac by any means, but I did think it was interesting that her appetite for company took such a sudden dip." I try my hardest not to react to those words. Try to not read between the lines. "Don't tell her that I said this, of course. But even at our last party, at least while I was there, she was just moping about in a corner."

"Why haven't you told her what I am?" I ask. "Aren't you afraid I'll hurt her?"

"If Aliz is anything like Ada, or her father, she'll not be easy to kill," she says. "Even for a seasoned serial killer, such as yourself."

I breathe in, glaring at her. "Thanks."

"What else should I call you?" Elia asks, all warmth slipping from her voice. "How many people did you kill tonight?"

"It was self-defense."

"I'm not asking *why*," she says, rain pattering on the roof of her pink car. "How many?"

I lean further back into the leather seat, words dying in my mouth. It's the word *people* that sticks out. I've spent almost half a decade hating vampires with every fibre of my being. My hatred has given me purpose; it has been the only thing that's kept me going, but now, admitting that I've killed a vampire feels no different to admitting I've killed a human.

We reach Tynahine by driving through the same roads Marcus took when he first brought me here. He must have known what I was then, too. Before long we've arrived, and Elia parks her car and leads me through the campus village. Her house is huge, with modern décor, albeit with too much pink for my taste. The only hint of her real age is a few paintings and tapestries that look hundreds of years old.

She switches on the light, and I see her, radiant.

Two thousand years.

Roughly the same age as Aliz's father.

"I'm sure you've got plenty of questions," she says, fetching a towel out for me. "But we can talk tomorrow."

I look down at my phone. It's already three A.M., Aliz sent me a message just an hour ago:

> Get back safe

I feel unease in the pit of my stomach. There's no reason for me to worry. It's still early, she's probably in class. And yet I can't shake off the dread settling in my bones.

Suddenly, pain shoots across the lines of the mark, thorns tearing through my skin. I gasp, dropping both the towel and the phone. Each line feels like molten lava. Elia stares at me from across the room, blinking, and I breathe, trying to ignore the pain. Slowly, it softens again, turning back into an itch.

"What just happened?" Elia asks.

"I'm fine," I say, voice shaking, not quite believing my own words.

Dread continues to climb up my chest as I shower, rinsing blood from my skin with Elia's rose-scented shower gel. The mark itches incessantly, in a way I've only felt in my dreams before. What's going on? I change back into my old clothes and Elia grabs my bloodied red dress. "Let me wash this," she says, tossing it into a basket. "You did almost take a bullet for me, after all," she adds.

I want to see Aliz. Every time I think this, the itch in the Familiar's mark worsens. I rush through campus, leaving the stone village behind and running up the pine grove to Tynarrich. I stop next to a tree, catching my breath for a second. Something's wrong. I'm not sure what, but I can sense it.

Even when I enter the hall of residence, I can't seem to calm down. I tap my foot in the lift, wishing it would climb faster. The doors open on the ninth floor, and I run.

I slot the old key into the lock and breathe out. As soon as it opens, a strange smell hits my nostrils. The room is pitch black, and through the shadows, I see that the curtains on her side of the room have been torn down. I stand still, confused. The mark has stopped itching. My ears ring.

"Aliz?" I call, taking a step back. I look down, my feet stepping on something wet. I hit the light switch. The carpet has a black-and-white pattern. But here, next to her coffin, the white marks are bright red.

There's blood everywhere.

"Aliz?" I call again, my hands going numb.

Then I hear it. The shower is on, the door to the bathroom is half open. She hasn't replied, so I walk over, still not entirely sure what I'm seeing. The blood trail continues to the bathroom, and when I look inside, the white tiles are stained red.

She's sitting in the shower, her knees bent, cradling her head. Her white shirt, soaked through with blood, clings to her body like a second skin.

"What—"

As soon as she registers my presence, she growls. But she doesn't look up at me, her muscles taut as she crouches tighter, trying to make herself smaller. Just as I'm about to ask her what happened, she vomits. Blood spills from her mouth, straight into the drain.

When she finally looks at me, her cheeks are sunken and pale, and her eyes, her beautiful black eyes, are glowing bright red.

chapter
TWENTY-EIGHT

I step inside the bathroom. Her eyes continue to glow that monstrous red, but she doesn't try to compel me.

"Aliz?"

There's no reply at first, just a low growl, like that of a frightened animal on the verge of lashing out. I keep walking, and it's only when my hand stops on the outside of the shower screen that she finally speaks.

"Go away," she growls.

"What happened?"

"I didn't want to," she says in a small voice, hiding her face again, cradling her head. Even her fingers look thinner. It's as though she's shrinking. "I didn't—"

"It's all right," I whisper, stepping into the shower. My shirt gets wet before I can reach the tap, the water scalding hot. Aliz hisses again when the water stops, glaring up at me with those terrifying eyes. "What happened?"

As soon as I reach down, she pushes me away, crying, droplets of blood running down her chin. "She forced me to," she sobs.

"Who? Aliz—"

"Arla!"

She makes a retching sound, and I didn't think it was possible for her to lose more blood. It's only now that I realise how bad the situation is. I still don't know what's happening, but if she continues to lose blood—

I kneel outside the shower and search for the dean's number. "It's all right," I whisper, trying to soothe her without getting too close. I've never seen her like this. I rush out of the bathroom, almost slipping on my way to her fridge. There's only a quarter of a bottle of Marcus's blood left, but I try to stay calm, breathing as I fill one of her paper cups with the substance. I stick it in the microwave then finally find Nocth's number.

As I wait for him to pick up, I head back to the bathroom. She hasn't moved. Her arms are still around her knees, soaked through in the glass cage that is the shower.

"Dean's office?"

"Nocth?" I have to stay calm. "This is Cassie Smith."

"Oh. What a lovely surprise."

My chest is about to cave in. "Something is wrong with Aliz. She's—" I look around the bathroom, blood everywhere. "She's vomiting blood, crying, and—"

"Did she say the name *Arla*?" His voice has lost all humor.

"Yes," I say, and the microwave beeps. Aliz doesn't look up.

"Leave your door open. I'll be right there," he says. I rush over to the microwave, hoping that now, once she drinks, she'll feel better.

I walk back into the bathroom slowly, letting her hear my footsteps. "You must be cold there," I say, before crouching down in front of her. "Have this, Aliz."

She grabs the paper cup and throws it, almost hitting me with it. Blood splashes on the shower's glass wall. "I didn't want to," she mumbles, hiding her face. "She forced me—Arla forced me to kill her—"

Kill her?

"It's all right," I whisper. I reach out to touch her, and she slaps me away.

I head back out, my throat tight, and open the door. Nocth arrives just a few seconds later, in a suit similar to the one he was wearing the last time I saw him. He scans our bedroom quickly, taking in the puddles of blood, but doesn't say anything. His eyes pause on my saltward, and when he turns to look at me, for a second I could swear he looks disturbed. "She's in the bathroom, right?"

"Yes."

He walks into the white-tiled room, and Aliz doesn't react to his presence.

"Did your memories come back, Aliz?" he asks, and I follow him, lingering just outside the shower. He gets down on the ground, staining his suit trousers, and forces Aliz to look at him. "You remembered what happened?"

Aliz swallows hard, her nostrils flaring. "I didn't want to—"

"I know." Nocth brushes her soaking hair away from her brows and pulls out a vial of blood. Before Aliz can react or push it away, he tips her head back and pours it into her mouth. She makes a choking sound, but he covers her lips, forcing her to swallow. "Listen to me," he says, and from outside of the shower I see his eyes taking on a red glint. Can he compel other vampires? "You will remember what I say."

"Yes," she says in a trance.

"You did not undergo a coming-of-age ceremony," he says. "You never met Arla. You never met that human girl. You did not kill anyone."

His eyes continue to glow, and Aliz stares transfixed. She gives a small nod.

"You ran away from home because you fought with your parents."

Another nod.

"You have never tasted fresh blood."

And upon saying this, he leans forward, pressing his lips to her forehead. It's for just a second, enough to seal his words into her mind. A moment passes, and her muscles lose tone, her eyes shut, and she faints.

He holds her, his expression somber. It's only then that he realises I'm still there, watching.

"I think it'll be better if you wash her, instead of me," he says. "Put her into something dry and let her rest in your bed."

"All right," I say, my chest aching.

Nocth offers me a sad smile. "Come to my office once you've got her in bed. I'll send someone to clean the room." He's gone before I can ask him any questions, leaving Aliz, still unconscious, on the floor.

I get to work, grabbing a towel and a spare nightgown. She'll probably kill me for putting her in a dress, but I don't want to cross into her side of the room yet, not when there's so much blood. I peel her soaked clothes off her and shower her down, blood running off her skin. I expect her to wake, but she doesn't, her breathing shallow.

It's only when I wrap the towel around her and press my forehead against hers, that I feel my eyes burn, tears stinging. After a short breath, I carry her out, maneuver a nightgown over her head, and pull the covers up to her neck. "I'll be back soon," I whisper, and Aliz remains fast asleep.

NOCTH'S OFFICE IS exactly as it was last time I saw it, except the tapestry has changed, replaced by a baroque painting. It's a portrait of a shirtless man, with long black hair, holding up a candle, as if helping the viewer navigate the dark night.

"Caravaggio really captured my likeness, didn't he?" he asks, as he catches me looking at it.

"What was that?" I ask. I'm exhausted, more so now than when Elia drove me home. The adrenaline of seeing Aliz in that state and trying to stop her from expelling every last ounce of blood left in her veins has subsided. I'd almost forgotten about Penny, who I left stranded in the castle. What if the Council have captured her? Killed her?

Nocth sighs, tapping on his desk. His black hair, usually perfectly in place, has a few loose strands falling over his eyes. He brushes them back, and I see his sleeves are still damp from holding Aliz. "Has Aliz been having nightmares recently?"

"Yes," I whisper. Maybe I should have told him sooner.

"What of?"

"Being locked in a room without blood." I pause, looking down at my hands. "She said it was a memory, though she had forgotten it at some point."

He rubs his temples. "I told you to stay close to her. You being away clearly triggered her to fully remember what happened."

"Were you expecting me to sit back and let a blood party take place in Inverness?" I snap. "What exactly did she remember?"

"Her seventeenth birthday. Aliz thinks that she came to Tynahine because she didn't want to get married. Now, while that is partially true, the real reason is one that she forgot."

I swallow hard. "You erased her memories, right?"

"Yes," he says. "Well, I altered them. I replaced certain people, certain events. Her parents accepted these alterations. They also accepted her exile, so long as it meant she could be saved."

"Saved?"

"Just before Aliz turned seventeen, Ares's right-hand woman, Arla, forced Aliz to undergo an ancient coming-of-age ceremony. I won't go into detail, but one of the things she did was force Aliz to drain a human girl."

I stare. *Forced her.*

"Aliz didn't kill the girl, one of the other attendees did, but they still celebrated and congratulated her on that first draining."

"But—" My mouth is dry, and I'm glad there wasn't food at the blood party. "But the Astras abide by the treaties, don't they?" *They fucking wrote them.*

"Arla had worked for Ares for centuries. She was the only human he ever converted, and for the first millennia, she was fiercely loyal to him. But at some point in the last century, she joined a cult known as the Vassals. The Vassals are fervently against the treaties, and so when they got the opportunity to get close to the heir of the Astra family, they were certain they could bring her into the cult."

His jaw tenses.

"But instead of indoctrinating her, they broke her. I found Aliz seconds before she walked out into daylight." I gasp, unable to imagine Aliz, seventeen, ready to immolate herself. "I took her away from the family home, hoping that she would recover if she couldn't see the place where—" He clears his throat. "But she wouldn't drink blood. Not even the synthetic kind. She couldn't stomach it."

I listen, my throat tight.

"I waited three days. I thought that if I didn't insist too much, she would end up reaching for a cup. But every time she drank, she threw up again. And you know what happens to a vampire if they spend a week without blood."

"They become parched," I say. Monsters, limbs and necks elongated, faces completely disfigured.

"So, I altered her memories. My plan was to wait until she finished aging and then, slowly, try to help her come to terms with what happened." He lets out a heavy sigh. "But the mark must have dug deep into her subconscious to open that wound."

"Will she dream about it again?" I ask.

"It depends," he says. "Have you had any particularly traumatic dreams?"

"Yes," I say, remembering Cieri. "But I'm all right."

"You need to stay closer to her from now on," he says.

"We're already sharing a room," I say. He sighs.

"Maybe you ought to share a bed."

My skin burns at the thought. "But Aliz needs to sleep in a coffin," I argue.

"Two weeks sleeping outside one won't kill her," he says. "You want to stop the dreams, don't you?"

"Of course I do." Somehow, I can feel myself calming down the more I think about it.

"Put this in her blood." He leans across the desk, handing me a crimson vial. "It's a little more of my own, which should help to solidify the effects of the hypnosis."

I'll do anything to keep her from having a nightmare like that again. "Did you compel her?" I ask, and he raises a brow.

"I don't have my uncle's power," he says. "If I could compel her, I would erase the memory completely. Instead, I'm just blocking it."

"What do I say to her now?"

"Tell her that her sickness has returned," he says. "You called me, I helped. Aliz won't remember anything, but she'll know she threw up."

"All right." I hesitate.

"Was that a saltward that I saw next to your bed?" he asks in a low voice, as if he's afraid someone might hear us. I frown.

"I found instructions for one in a grimoire. I needed protection until she gets used to the scent of my blood." He simply stares at me. I can't make out what's behind his gaze. Then, I say: "I saw Penny."

I watch his expression carefully. In a way, it reflects Penny's when I said his name, though Nocth doesn't twist with rage. "In Inverness?" he says, caught off guard. "Why was she there?"

"Didn't you tell her about the blood party?" Nocth shakes his head. "She got rather angry when I mentioned your name."

"Oh, she detests me," he says, voice light. "And I can't blame her."

"Why?" I ask.

He leans back and looks at his watch. "You should go. Aliz will wake soon."

ALIZ IS AWAKE by the time I reach our room. She's formed an odd cocoon with my bedsheets, pressed against the wall with the pillow at her side.

Although I was only gone for half an hour, the room is spotless.

"Do you like my new coffin?" she asks, her voice muffled beneath the sheets.

"It's imaginative," I say, sitting down next to her. I peel the top of the sheet down just enough to see her eyes. They're red, but she doesn't have the same fear, the same panic, as before.

"Did my sickness come back?" she asks, and I nod. She still has a gaunt appearance, and I run my fingers across her cheekbones, unnaturally sharp. She pulls the top of the sheet back over her head. "Sorry. It must have been disgusting."

"It's all right," I say. "I was worried." An odd calm spreads through me now that I'm near her. "Why did you go to sleep early?"

"I didn't," she says, voice muffled beneath the duvet. "I came back to my room to grab a book, but I can't remember what happened next. Did I . . ." She peeks out of the bedsheets again, her eyelashes damp. "Did I hurt you?"

"No," I whisper. She lets out a sigh of relief and unravels the top of the sheets. "Are you thirsty?"

"Extremely," she says, swallowing hard. "I threw up, right?"

"Yeah. But it's all right. How long should I heat your blood for?"

"Forty-two seconds," she says. "At six hundred watts."

"Forty-two seconds," I repeat, and she offers me a small smile. New curtains separate our rooms, replacing the ones that she tore down. I text the dean, telling him to get her more of Marcus's blood, because all that's left now is the synthetic kind. I empty the vial of Nocth's blood into it, hoping she will be able to drink it. Forty-two seconds later, I carry the cup over, and she peels herself free of the covers.

She's so thirsty that at first, she doesn't notice what she's wearing. She downs the whole thing in ten seconds, and very slowly, her red eyes turn black. Her sunken cheeks fill out again, and my chin trembles, because I thought I was going to lose her.

"Are you all right?" I ask, and before I can help myself, I pull her close, wrapping my arms around her. Slowly, Aliz returns the embrace. I expect her to tease me, to say something funny. But instead, she simply sighs. When she sniffs my neck, I don't feel the usual fear. Not the pull towards her, either. Instead, all I can think of is what Nocth said. She was forced to drain someone.

"I'm going to get changed," I whisper. I clear my throat, and Aliz nods.

"I'll head over to my coffin, then."

"Actually, I think we should try to sleep together," I say. She gawks at me, tired eyes widening. "According to Nocth, the fact that we were so far apart is probably what triggered the return of your sickness." I speak as quickly as I can, trying to not let any hesitation slip into my voice. "Apparently sleeping in the same room isn't close enough. So, until the mark's gone, we'll have to stay even closer."

Aliz nods. "I like being close to you," she says. Her gaze, exhausted, is on my hand. I wish she wouldn't say things like that because I like it, too. I head into the bathroom to brush my teeth and get changed. Some of the vines of the Familiar's mark have started to spread down my arms. It's a miracle they've not travelled upwards, to my face, or hiding it would be more of a nightmare than it already is.

I glance at the shower. The white tiles are impeccable, as though not a single drop of blood ever splashed against them. I press my lips together and try to burn the image out of my mind.

If we're going to be sleeping in the same bed from now on, I should probably buy some proper pyjamas. When I tug at the curtains of my bed, I find Aliz holding up the fabric of her borrowed nightgown and staring at the lace trimming. "Sorry," I whisper. "I didn't have anything else. Do you want to change?"

"You saw me naked," she says. I lie down beside her, outside of the covers, and nod.

"You've seen me naked, too, so we're even."

"Fair enough," she whispers, sighing. "Thanks for taking care of me, Cassie."

"You would do the same for me," I say, brushing a strand of her snow-white hair away from her face. A thin, cool layer of sweat glistens on her skin. Instead of letting go of her, I keep my hand there, cupping her cheek.

"But I already did, and I basically ruined your life." The muscles of her face are tense, as though she's holding back tears.

"Well," I whisper, running a thumb over her brow, messing the short white hairs. "Turns out Elia knows how to get into the library."

"Elia?" Aliz says, gawking at me.

I nod. "The entrance is behind the rose nook. And she knows how to get past it."

"How—why does Elia know?"

"She saw my mark," I say.

"No, about the library," she stresses, blinking fast.

I stare at her. Elia must have kept her identity secret even from Aliz, because had Aliz known that she was Palau, she would have probably asked for Elia's help right away. "I think it'll be better if Elia explains," I say. "Tomorrow we'll ask her to take us there." Elia already said no to me. But surely she won't turn Aliz down, will she?

Suddenly, Aliz frees herself from her little cocoon and pulls me into her arms. "Oh, Cassie—" Her voice breaks, and she tightens her grip. "Thank *fuck*, I—" She sniffs, her chin resting on my head to ensure I can't see her tears. "I wouldn't be able to live with myself if the contract was sealed."

Slowly, I return her embrace. I'm not a vampire. I can't tell when someone is lying. But Elia is wrong. Ares and Ada may have manipulated those around them, but Aliz is not the same.

My nose is pressed to the crook of her neck, lips on her collarbone. Her skin should be cold, but it burns instead. Her sniffling quietens, and I squeeze her. I wish this moment, as horrid as its inception was, would last forever. She sighs, hugging me tight, and I wish it didn't feel so right. So natural.

I'm about to fall asleep when I hear her voice. "Oh, Cassie," she whispers, running her fingers through my hair.

"What is it?" I ask, looking up at her. "Is my blood—" She shakes her head.

"It still smells good, but the thirst isn't torture."

"What is it, then?" I ask. Her forehead touches mine, and for a moment, I think our lips, already close, are going to meet. Her white lashes brush against my own, and my breath hitches.

"I'll tell you tomorrow," she whispers. "We should sleep."

We're millimetres apart.

"Tomorrow," I echo, lowering my face, until it rests just above her chest. Aliz lets out a sigh. Slowly, she wraps an arm around me again, ensuring our skin is pressed together.

Please don't dream, I think, squeezing her hand.

chapter
TWENTY-NINE

Cieri doesn't haunt my dreams that night. When I wake, Aliz is still asleep, her chest rising and falling, one strap of my nightgown having slipped off her shoulder. Her collarbones are sharp, the curve of her small breasts shallow beneath the silk. I hide my face to yawn, and then look at hers. Her full lips are slightly parted.

Staring at her allows me to forget for a moment the fact that I have probably ruined my relationship with Penny. But then my skin prickles with dread, and I reach for my phone, beside my pillow. No missed calls, no messages. When I check to see when Penny was last online, all I see is nine P.M. *What have I done?* My throat stings, and before I can think too hard about how to approach this mess, I type:

> Where are you?

I receive no reply, but almost immediately, a single tick turns double and blue. Unless the Council have confiscated her phone, Penny is alive. Relief and unease mingle in my chest, and I exhale, trying to figure out what to do next.

Just as I put my phone back down, ready to get up, Aliz stirs, and still asleep, she grabs me, pulling me closer. A hand rubs my waist, and I swallow hard. Her legs tangle with mine, and I feel her nose on my neck, sniffing. "Aliz?" My voice comes out in a croak.

"Five more minutes," she mumbles, before pressing her lips to my neck.

"Aliz!" I hiss, pulling myself free from her grip, and she complains. When I turn to look at her, she's fast asleep. Meanwhile, the spot she just kissed feels like it's on the verge of catching fire. "Damn it," I whisper.

At this, her eyes finally open, and she yawns, looking around. "Did you have a dream?" she asks me, rubbing her eyes.

"No," I say. And considering Aliz isn't vomiting blood, I have a feeling she didn't, either.

"Same here," she says. "So, sticking together really does get rid of the symptoms."

"Seems like it," I say and swallow.

Now I just have to convince Elia to let us enter the library. Or have her bring us *The Book of Blood and Roses* instead. But as long as I'm a vampire hunter, I have a feeling she will not want to help me.

ELIA, I LEARN as we sit in Tynarrich's dining hall, hasn't been entirely forthcoming with Aliz.

"You knew..." Aliz runs her fingers through her hair, staring at Elia. She's wearing a fitted pink cardigan and a matching skirt. Her smile is not entirely appropriate for the situation. "You knew Ada?"

"I'm sorry I didn't tell you," Elia says, leaning back. "You're nothing like her, you know. And considering she's been dead for two hundred years—"

"What exactly was your relationship with her?" Aliz snaps.

Elia looks towards the window, branches knocking against it, and sighs. "We were on and off for half a millennium."

I feel Aliz's hand tense next to mine, and she leans forward, mouth open. "You were together?"

"Like I said, on and off."

"You lied to me," Aliz says.

"I didn't *lie*," Elia argues. "I simply kept some information to myself."

"So all the times we went into the Palau Collection, you never thought to mention, *Hey, this is my library*?"

"You never asked," Elia says. Her eyes meet mine, and there's an accusation hidden behind her gaze—and a camaraderie between liars. I swallow hard. I have to tell Aliz the truth about who I am. Tell her now. Because I'm not just concealing the truth, the way Elia did—Cassie Smith is a whole identity. And I know that if I was in her shoes, I wouldn't be able to forgive me.

"Can you take us to the library now?" Aliz asks, and my heart quickens.

"Ada's library is only open when the moon is in its first quarter," Elia says. I think of the maze, with the four statues. The crescent moon gilded gold. *Of course.* "Which is a week from now. But you'll need my help getting in," she says and fixes me with her gaze. A shiver runs through me.

"A week," Aliz whispers, before sighing.

I check my phone. Penny still hasn't replied. I send her another text. *Are you all right?* I need her to reply, but I'm also scared of what to say if she asks me any questions. I start typing *I'm sorry.* If she's still alive, if she got out of there, which knowing her, she probably did, I don't know how I'm going to repair this.

Stephan, Ife, and Julia walk into the dining hall, immediately spotting us over in the corner. They look for another table, but I wave them over. I know they're not particularly fond of Aliz and Elia, but there's not much I can do about that. Julia takes the spot on the sofa next to me, squeezing me against Aliz.

"You didn't come to lunch," Julia says. She's wearing mascara, staining her platinum lashes black.

Aliz lets go of my hand, and I'm about to grab hold of it again, when I feel it on the small of my back. I'm wearing a jumper, so it's not as though the contact is that direct, but I shiver when she runs it up my back. "Yeah," I say. "I slept in."

I look across the coffee table at Ife, sitting on Stephan's lap with a mug of blood at her lips. She sips it slowly, eyes gleaming. She's noticed our proximity. "It's not what you think," I say, and Aliz's hand draws away.

It's not just Ife who looks at me like that. Everyone seems to wait for me to say something, to admit that my relationship with Aliz is more than what it seems. But whatever it is they're imagining, it's certainly not that, as much as I wish it was.

I think of last night and Aliz saying, *I'll tell you tomorrow.*

Tell me what?

I LEAF THROUGH newspapers for any signs of the general public finding out about the blood party, but as always, the things that happen in the vampire world remain hidden, even when they're in plain sight. I risk calling Penny and hearing the call tone stretch out. She doesn't answer, and I realise I may have to start preparing for the very real possibility that she's going to try to kill me.

I'm not scared of vampires. But Penny? I've been fortunate enough until now to have never crossed her. *Just answer me,* I text, forming a column of ignored messages.

Shortly after one A.M., Aliz texts me.

> Meet me up on Tynarrich's roof?

I've never been to the roof before. My neck itches again, telling me that we've spent too long apart. I head up all nine floors and search for an extra door, leading to a stone staircase. Tynarrich's roof is flat, with two stone benches on either side, and a railing along the edge.

I wonder if Aliz has brought girls here before. And just as I think this, I hear her behind me. She steps out, coat buttoned up to her neck, a grey scarf hiding half her face. All my anxieties slip away when I see her, my chest warming. "Fancy seeing you here," she says. I want to step closer to her, be greedy. I turn away and look up at the night instead.

It's been years since I last saw a sky with stars as vivid as this one, the Milky Way hanging above us like a belt of silver paint. She comes to stand next to me, leaning on the bronze railing which has oxidised through the centuries to a pale turquoise. She tugs on her scarf, pulling it down so I can see her cautious smile. Her hair is the same colour as the stars, and I find myself reaching to brush a strand from her eyes.

"So, what is it?" I ask, not beating around the bush.

"What is what?"

"Why'd you ask me to come up here?" I wish I'd said it in a kinder way. Aliz shifts uncomfortably beside me, sticks one of her brogues through the bronze railing and then pulls it back out.

"I wanted to see you. Is there anything wrong with that?"

"No," I say. *I wanted to see you, too,* I almost add, but I manage to bite back the words. "I was just wondering why here."

"Oh!" Aliz pulls away from the railing and jumps onto a stone bench. "I suppose there are some things I'd rather not say in our room." She notices my confusion, and I notice the slight shade of red in her cheeks. "I'm a firm believer in the wind being able to wipe away words we shouldn't have said."

"It's not particularly windy." Which is odd, considering how high up we are. It's just damp and freezing. Aliz sits down, crossing her legs.

"Come here," she says, and I hesitate, just to make sure her words don't have the power to compel me yet. I take a short breath and walk over to the stone bench. There are names scratched onto it, dates, too, all the way back to the 1300s. And while I study the unfamiliar names, Aliz takes my hand, slowly slipping my glove off and pulling one finger free at a time.

When her skin touches mine, I lose track of my thoughts. Of what I'm doing here, and of what I asked her.

"Have you ever been in love?" she asks, and somehow the cold doesn't bother my bare hand as she keeps it linked with her own. I don't look at her. I can't.

"Yeah," I say, staring down at my boots. "It was a while ago. Vicki."

"Vicki?"

"We were classmates," I say. "She dumped me the day after prom. There was a band at the party, and apparently, I flirted with the bassist," I add. The memory doesn't sting. I barely remember it, anyway. Everything happened so fast. My parents died less than a month after prom, and Vicki sent me her condolences. I didn't reply.

"And after that?"

I shake my head. I know what I feel tonight. It's so painfully vivid I think my chest is going to burst, but I can't say it.

"What about now?" she asks.

I should have seen it coming. But I'm too stunned, only now realising where she was going with this. "What are you talking about?" I ask in disbelief. I get up, but Aliz grabs me, pulling me down onto her lap, arms tight around my waist. "Aliz—"

"It's a simple yes-or-no question," she says, her cheeks red, as though she regrets saying it, but can't take it back.

"What is wrong with you?" I hiss. "We've known each other for two weeks." Even as I say this, I feel my heart tightening, as though her hand has a fast grip on it. *Why did she have to ask that?*

"We've known each other for a month," Aliz argues.

"No," I say, gritting my teeth. "I've been keeping my distance, and now you're asking me about *love?*"

"I—"

"In a week we'll finally get into the library," I say, trying to keep my voice steady. "Don't ruin this."

She clasps my face, forcing me to look at her. My eyes sting, heart beating far too quickly. "I'm not *ruining* anything," she says, voice tight. "You can call it whatever you want. Fever, obsession. I just need to know if we're on the same page," she says. "This madness can't be mine alone."

She's close enough to kiss. If I inched forward, I'd have her. Slowly, her words sink in. I stop breathing, my anger momentarily fading as I realise what she's saying. Aliz takes a shallow breath, and the wind begins to pick up around us. "Cassie, please." Desperation tightens her voice. I don't make a sound, and she squeezes my hands. "You could say you don't love me," she says. "I'm a vampire. I'll be able to sense if you're lying."

"Aliz—"

"Please." Her voice is dry, just on the brink of breaking. I take a deep breath, and she remains still, waiting.

She's a vampire. My natural enemy. A creature I've hated blindly for four years. My heart thunders as I realise what I'm about to admit. In seven days these feelings will leave us both, and it would have been so much easier to keep these words to myself.

"I don't love you," I say. Aliz flinches.

The words, the truth hidden behind them, break every rule I've abided by these last four years. My feelings are suddenly as clear to me as the stars above us. I don't know how long I've known, but I'm no longer in denial about them. I wait for Aliz to say something, but she doesn't. Carefully, I place a hand behind her head, and feel her sigh against me.

"Thank you." She pulls back. Her cheeks are still flushed, and the cold has slipped under my coat. The wind is blowing but it hasn't carried my words away. They remain very firmly in place, the lie a seashell, the truth a pearl hidden within.

Aliz loves me. It's the most preposterous thing I've ever heard, and yet, at least for now, it's true. It's true, but not real. I know that. There is no way that she could fall in love with me. Just like the Familiar's mark can summon dreams, I'm certain it can summon these false feelings, too. Another trick to draw us closer and seal the contract.

"What'll happen when we get rid of the mark?" I ask.

"Maybe we can be friends," she says. "I know you didn't particularly like me before all this, but—"

"Friends sounds good," I say. I can't imagine myself without these feelings. I'd be like an empty vessel.

The silence that follows is louder than the wind, and just as I clear my throat, she clasps a gloved hand over my eyes, holding me in place. "Aliz?"

"Can I kiss you?" she asks. Her breath is cool against my skin. I inhale sharply, heart thudding.

"I thought you said we're just friends," I say. I can't see her, but I feel her warmth radiating on me.

"Just friends—once this is over." Her other hand snakes behind my back. "But for now—" I hear her swallowing. "You said you trusted me, right?"

"Yes," I say.

I wait for her to convince me further, and I think of ways in which I can ask her to do it without saying it outright.

But then her lips are on mine, cool and soft, and it's like being set alight. Her lips move slowly, cautiously, and although I'm sure she knows how much I want her, she pulls back. Her breathing quickens. "More," I whisper. I grab her collar, drawing her mouth to my own. We're still not close enough. Our teeth knock together, and she pushes me down. Before I can get used to the cold stone beneath me, her lips find mine again, hungrier this time, tongue trying to pry them open.

Her knee presses between my legs, and a gasp escapes me. Aliz's wet kiss moves down to my neck, her hand still a blindfold. "Let me see you," I say digging my nails into her coat. But Aliz pulls back.

"No," she says, breathless.

"Why not?"

Her hand finally pulls away from my eyes, and I blink, adjusting to the dim light. There's a faint red glow in her irises. Her breathing is still uneven, and she bites her lips. The fangs which should terrify me, which should be like a sudden shower of ice-cold water on my desire, are just another part of her that I love.

"It's too dangerous," she says.

"Maybe we should go, then." The words sting as I say them. I need more.

When she climbs off me, I take a deep breath. The freezing October air sinks through my coat.

We walk back inside, down the narrow staircase. Silence hangs between us. We just crossed every line and boundary we'd silently imposed. I can't imagine being able to sleep pressed against her after what just happened there. And worst of all is the dampness between my legs, cool and slick.

There's always been tension between us, but now the air is thick with it, about to snap. My skin burns beneath my jacket, the fabric far too warm. Our hallway is deserted, lamps casting a faint glow on the emerald ceiling. Without thinking, I take her hand, and Aliz glances at me. Her lips part, but she doesn't say a word.

Instead of going straight to our room, she tightens her grip on my hand and takes a right turn. She guides me towards the common room at the end of the hallway. Three velvet armchairs, green like the ceiling, form a little circle, while the surrounding bookshelves are bursting with volumes that I'm only now realising must all belong to Aliz, if she really had this hallway all to herself prior to my arrival. "Why are we here?" I ask, glancing out the window, shutters lifted to reveal a faint outline of the hills.

Aliz leans against a bookcase, across from me, while I rest on the back of an armchair. "We're here because I need to know what's going to happen next." She rubs her forehead. Her shoulders are tense.

I step closer, taking her hand again. I need to feel her against me. Every nerve in my body is like a match, about to catch. I run my hand from her shoulder down to her waist, the stiff wool of her coat rough against my fingers. Aliz takes a sharp breath but doesn't move. I want to tear every last item of clothing off her, feel every inch of her skin. "We'll go to our room," I say.

"I assumed as much," she says, voice cautious. "What I want to know is what'll happen when we cross that doorway." She swallows, and just like on the roof, there are nerves—or perhaps just impatience?—thickening her voice. "Are we going to act like nothing happened, sleep next to each other, without touching, or . . ." She lets go of my hand, reaching to trace a slow line up my neck, making me shiver before she clasps my chin, tipping me up to face her. Her eyes are still black. Safe.

"Or . . . ?" I ask, so low she wouldn't have heard me if not for her vampire senses.

She leans close enough for me to feel her breath on my lips. "Or make a terrible mistake?"

I'm not entirely sure which one of us closed the distance first, but suddenly we're kissing again. Her lips are slow, careful, as though she's doing this for the first time, trying to savour every second. I wrap my arms around her neck, nibbling her lower lip, pressing her harder against the bookcase.

"Define 'mistake,'" I whisper, trying to steady my voice.

Her gaze darkens, looking at me the way she did at the start, back when I felt she could see right through me.

"I want to fuck you," she says. My lips part with a gasp, but I can't find anything to say. My skin was already burning, but her words have set me ablaze.

"That would be a terrible mistake." I keep my lips close to hers. "But you should do it, anyway."

Aliz pushes herself off the bookcase, and me in the process, until she's pressing me against the back of the velvet armchair. In a matter of seconds, she unbuttons my coat, and her lips are on mine before I can say a word, hungrier than they were a moment ago. This kiss is rough, and my legs may have given way if not for her thigh, pressed between mine. I suppress a moan, trying to get my thoughts in order, before I manage to say:

"Here?" She kisses her way down my neck, hand on my waist, slipping beneath my jumper vest. "I thought we were going to our room!"

"No," she says, drawing back to whisper in my ear. "I said I'd *fuck* you in our room."

I swallow hard, anticipation building in me as her hand finds the hem of my skirt.

"What if someone hears us?"

"You'll just have to keep quiet," she says, lips curving into a crooked smile. But before her fingers reach me, Aliz pulls back, hesitating. "Are you sure you want this?"

"Yes," I say, practically interrupting her. "I do." I don't care if I sound desperate. But now her question echoes in the back of my head, drawing out another one that I've been trying to ignore. "But you . . ." I look at her, heart thudding. "You wouldn't want this if it wasn't for the mark."

Instantly, I wish I hadn't said it. Because Aliz inches back from me, brows furrowing. "I still have free will, Cassie."

"Yes," I say, and for some stupid reason, my eyes burn. "But think back to before I had the mark, Aliz. There's no way you—"

"I'm not going to regret this," she interrupts. "I don't care how I felt or what I thought back then. *Now* matters, too." Her voice softens, putting a sudden break on my spiralling. "And I will be very careful. I promise."

Aliz waits for me to nod, and then wraps her arms around me, pulling me close until my lips rest against her neck. I take a deep breath. "But you'll have to keep your eyes shut," she says, as her hands start to roam down my body again. "Can you do that for me?"

I want to see her. But I say yes all the same. I need her more than she can possibly imagine. More than she craves my blood. Her kisses are lighter this time, moving down to my neck. I have a jumper-vest on, over my shirt, and if I hadn't been wearing it, I'm pretty sure Aliz would have tried stripping me naked here in the common room.

"Are you sure no one will come?" I ask, and my breathing hitches when I feel her fingers, tracing a slow line across my underwear, but not touching where I need her to. I dig my nails into her neck, kissing her again, as though that'll somehow make her go faster.

"Oh, you most definitely will," she whispers. Finally, a finger traces down my centre, sending a jolt of pleasure all the way to my toes. I have to bite my lip just to keep my voice down. I cling to her, biting her neck while her finger traces a slow circle over my underwear. The warmth in my core grows, and "Fuck," I moan against her, her fingers pressing harder and faster.

A sound comes from the other end of the hallway. The lift doors open, and someone pushes out a trolley full of cleaning supplies.

"Shit," Aliz says. "I completely forgot about the cleaners."

"You've got to be joking," I say. She grabs my wrist, and we run from the common room. Aliz slots her key into our door and pulls me inside just as the cleaners turn around the corner.

Then she's fighting with my clothes, asking to cross the saltward before pushing me down onto the bed, and climbing on top of me. Just as she did up on the roof, Aliz covers my eyes with her hand again. I want to see her, but all I can focus on are her fingers, sinking beneath my underwear. "Fuck, you're so wet," she says, her touch slow, as though she's trying to memorise me.

I bite my tongue to keep myself from moaning. She pulls my underwear down my thighs, and as soon as she touches me in earnest, I find myself already ridiculously close. "Aliz—" I gasp, and she hooks one leg between mine, spreading them.

"After you come," she starts, rubbing harder, "will you let me fuck you?"

"Yes," I cry, and although she told me not to, I open my eyes for just a second. Her white hair is dishevelled, falling over half her face. She licks her lips, and the sight of her tongue gets me even closer.

"Eyes," Aliz says again, and she leans down. I feel her hot mouth on my neck, lips brushing the lines of the Familiar's mark. She continues to stroke me, each caress sending a new wave of pleasure through my nerves, until suddenly I can't take another touch. I gasp, body shuddering as ecstasy spreads to my toes.

She doesn't stop, quickening her pace as my climax stretches. "Fuck!" I cry, her lips still on my neck.

"That was the plan, yes," she mumbles, and suddenly I feel a finger sinking in. My walls are still contracting from the first orgasm when she slips in another, and before I can get my breath back, she starts to move them, hard and fast. "Want to come again?" she asks, voice against my ear, I don't have time to answer, her fingers curling up inside me until I see white.

As much as I try to say something coherent, all I manage is to cry her name. I pull hard on the bedsheets, arching my back, each nerve in my body responding to her touch. She slows the rhythm of her fingers, and I didn't realise my ears were ringing until I hear her soft breaths.

Her free hand draws a line across my face, caressing my brow. "Was that good?" she asks, voice husky. My mind is still in a haze.

"Fuck yes," I breathe out. I run my fingers through her soft hair, and Aliz still has too many clothes on. Just before I can climb on top of her, she stumbles up.

"I better have dinner." She clears her throat. "I'll be right back."

"I'll—uh—" I want to pull her back into my arms. I need more. "I'll get changed."

She left me with my shirt unbuttoned, my bra on, and my tights halfway down one leg. I pull on my nightgown, knowing full well that she'll be pulling it off me again in a few minutes. Then I watch her as she fights with the microwave, pacing as she waits for the blood to heat up. There's a faint red glimmer in her eyes.

She downs her portion of blood. Nocth's Familiar donated some more after her memories came back. Aliz's tense muscles start to relax, and she sighs, leaning on her false window. She said she'd be right back, but I already feel myself growing impatient.

I cross the saltward and run my hand over the smooth wood of her coffin. Her gaze burns into my skin. I look at her, and she's still holding the glass, but her attention is entirely mine. The false window behind her shows an aurora, shimmering green above the hills. "What is it?" she asks.

"The other night you said you didn't fuck humans," I say, leaning against her coffin. She puts her paper cup down and licks the last speck of blood from her lips. Then, in just a few strides, she's right in front of me, trapping me against her coffin. Despite all her worries of our eyes meeting, she tilts my chin and forces me to look at her.

"Say that again." Her voice is as dark as her eyes.

Just as I open my mouth, she tugs my hair, and a kiss, harder than all which have come before, knocks the air out of my lungs. The wood of her coffin digs into my back. Just as I find her tongue, she draws back an inch. Then, with her grip on my hips, she lifts me up onto the wooden coffin.

"Say that again, Cassie."

I need her to touch me. But if I can get under her skin in the process, even better. "You said you didn't fuck humans," I say. I try to kiss her again, draw her closer, but she ignores my attempts. Her fingers hook beneath the thin straps of my nightgown, pulling the fabric down, achingly slow, until my chest is bare. She stares brazenly, lips parting. Then she kisses the mark, before slowly following the lines down.

"What else did I say?" she asks, as her fingers brush over my nipples. I choke down a sound, while I try to close my legs. As a response, she pushes them open, keeping herself between them. Her tongue replaces her fingers, and I knock my head back, warmth tightening my nerves. "Answer me."

Aliz is still fully clothed, but when I try to undo the buttons of her shirt, she tuts, holding my wrists at my sides. "I don't fuck humans," she says. "But what else did I say, Cassie?" One hand moves to my thigh.

"You asked—" I start, a tremor in my voice. Her fingers inch closer, taunting me with their proximity. "If I wanted to be an exception."

"And do you?" she asks, lips on my neck, sending a shiver across the thorned lines. Her fingers finally brush over my folds, but far too light. "C'mon," she says, and I pull her up for a kiss, hoping she'll hurry already.

I grab her shoulder as her thumb presses against my clit. I bite her neck, and I finally get a small victory from her, a sound caught in her throat. She digs her blunt nails into my thigh.

"You've already fucked me," I say, trying to remain in control, not arch into her touch. Her free hand grabs a fistful of my hair and gives a light tug.

"But you need it again, don't you?" she asks, lips on mine. *God yes.*

If I wasn't so twisted by her, I may have clung to my pride. But Aliz is right. I need it again.

"Yes," I say, breathless.

She draws her fingers away, pulling back until our eyes are at level. "Beg for it."

Whatever expression I just made makes her laugh. "You—" I don't finish the insult I was trying to conjure. She kisses me again, but her fingers draw further away. In our shared dreams, Aliz was like a wild animal. Now, she's so in control it's killing me. I need her. I tug at the buttons of her shirt, biting my lip when I see the hardened tips of her nipples against her vest.

"Be nice, Cassie," she whispers, lips on my neck. Her tongue runs over the Familiar's mark, and pleasure spreads through each individual line, until I can think of only one thing. She kisses her way down my torso, following the mark's path. I arch my back, needing more. "I'm not asking for much." She grabs my right leg, hoisting it over her shoulder. "Beg." I feel her breath between my thighs, and I thread my fingers through her hair.

"Please."

Based on the cockiness in her voice, that flimsy cruelty, I was expecting she'd make me work for it. But instead, Aliz proves she's just as impatient as I am, moaning when she finally spreads my lips and runs her tongue over my entrance and up to my clit. I try to bite down a sound, tugging her hair as I struggle to remain upright. "Fuck!" I cry. She slides three fingers into me, not giving me a second to breathe before working them fast and hard.

At some point we make it back onto the bed, and "It's my turn," I say, running a hand down her back. I find the hem of her shirt and slip my fingers inside. "How can I repay you?" Her skin is smooth and warm, and although I want to touch her the way she just touched me, I wait.

"I guess you could proofread an essay I was supposed to hand in tonight," she says, sounding a tad more nervous than I was expecting. I draw my hand back out and look up at her. "How does that sound?"

"Or I could go down on you," I say, fixing her with my gaze. Aliz lets out a short breath, before clearing her throat.

"I'd love that. But . . ." She hesitates. "I don't think I'd be able to control myself." Her gaze drops to my neck, to the Familiar's mark which is so stark against my skin. "But thanks."

"Maybe once the mark is gone," I say.

"Right," Aliz replies.

Our legs are still tangled together, my hand is still rubbing her back, but we both tense as we realise what I just said. This won't happen again once the mark is gone.

Once Aliz's feelings fade, things will go back to normal.

The only reason I was able to admit that I loved her, that I told a lie, knowing she'd recognize the truth, was because she thinks it's because of the mark. But as much as I wish it wasn't true, I know that what I'm feeling right now didn't bloom into my chest through the thorny vines of our blood contract.

I cannot continue to delude myself, because I know now, as well as I know the weight of a dagger between my fingers, that I love her, and I also know this is ridiculous, but what about my life isn't? What second in the last four years has been anything but that?

My love for Aliz isn't a curse or an enchantment. It's as real as it can get.

But I'm glad that Aliz's isn't. Because she's right about one thing.

She can't love a human, and she most certainly can't love a vampire hunter.

chapter THIRTY

I feel her cool breath on the back of my neck. Slowly, my eyes flutter open, the room pitch black. Aliz has one arm around my waist, the other above my head. I breathe in, wondering if it's just a dream. But then she stirs, mumbling incoherently against the nape of my neck.

"Morning," I say, my voice coming out hoarse. Last night we got carried away. At least until the moon is in its first quarter, we can be together. Afterwards we'll revert to being nothing to each other. I press my hands over hers, and she hums.

"Morning, Cassie," she says, her lips touching my neck.

I sit up, yawning, and then stop cold as my muddled memories of last night take shape. I had sex with a vampire. *Willingly*. I expect to feel some kind of shame, guilt, anything at all to remind me that we've made a mistake, but it doesn't come.

"Are you going to class?" she asks, stretching her arms as she yawns.

"In an hour," I say, staring down at my phone, the screen far too bright. For the first time, I don't have to search for the library. Instead, I must convince Elia to let me enter it. As soon as I move to get up, Aliz draws me back into her arms. "At least let me brush my teeth," I say, as her mouth meets mine.

"You might try to run away," she complains but lets me go. I brush my teeth in a hurry, drinking water, before heading back out into the room. Aliz grabs me before I reach the bed, pulling me down and climbing on top of me, her lips hungry. I wrestle with her pyjamas. Even if she won't let me get her off, I still want to feel her bare skin pressed to mine.

Good thing that I'm not actually here for an education, I think, as she kisses her way down my chest. Every spot she touches is ablaze. "We should be careful," she says, her fingers slipping between my legs. "I really wish you were a vampire," she adds, finger prying inside me. I stare down at her.

"Why?" I ask, trying to keep my voice steady. I dig my nails into her back, drawing her closer.

"I'm used to being rough," she says, as pleasure rushes through me, and I struggle to keep myself from moaning. "I didn't even know I could be this gentle," she adds, keeping her touch light.

"You can be rough," I say, breathless, waiting for her to quicken her pace. Instead, Aliz draws her finger out, and I release a groan of frustration. She tuts, meeting my gaze.

"*No,* I can't," she says, voice sharp. "You're human. You're considerably weaker than me, Cassie."

"Then at least be a little less gentle," I say, before gritting my teeth. I can't believe she called me weak. But Aliz doesn't know what I am. Her lips part as she considers my request. Then her mouth meets mine, a careful kiss.

"I'll think about it," she whispers after a short pause. "And close your eyes." She resumes her gentle touch between my legs, her fingers damp with my arousal, and I moan against her, moving my hips to get more friction.

The sound of banging on the door draws us out of our stupor. I open my eyes, and Aliz jumps up, stumbling away from the bed and almost tearing my curtains down in the process. She looks at me, eyes wide, as though she's only now realising what we were doing. "Hide," she whispers, and I run into the bathroom, locking the door behind me.

"Well," a voice says at the door. *Elia.* "That was fast."

"What was fast?" Aliz still sounds a little out of breath.

"You sleeping with Cassie. I thought you'd hold out a—" She stops the moment I walk out of the bathroom, still wearing my nightgown. Her lips part as she looks at me, and a flash of hunger appears in her eyes, tinted by a faint red glow. "Can I have a bite, too?" she asks.

"Fuck off," Aliz says.

Elia stares at her then at me.

"I have to talk to Cassie," she says. *This is it.* What can I possibly offer Elia? My blood?

"When did you two get so close?" Aliz asks, sounding more than a little irritated.

"When you weren't watching," Elia says, throwing an arm around my shoulders, drawing me close. "We're girlfriends now."

"Piss off," I say, pushing her arm away.

"Next time you need to let me join the fun," Elia says. "Ada and I used to share humans, back before the treaties. We didn't kill or compel our girls, of course. In fact, I was an ethical vampire before it was cool."

"I *really* don't need to hear about what your sex life was like with my sister," Aliz says. She puts the light on and searches around the room for clothes. Elia's expression changes slightly when Aliz isn't looking at us, becoming cooler. Accusing me of something. Is she jealous? "And don't tell anyone about us," Aliz adds. "We got carried away, that's all."

Her words sting. "Yeah," I say, trying to sound as if I believe her.

THE WINDOWS IN Elia's house are shuttered, a dozen false ones showing the landscape through cameras. The narrow streets of the campus village are speckled with dappled shadows, for once free of rain. Elia stands by one of those false windows, not saying a word.

"I've thought about it," she says. "I don't want Aliz to be roped into this. Having a vampire hunter as a Familiar would be a living nightmare."

I sigh, relief flooding through me as I sit on her couch. "Thank you."

"But I also won't let a vampire hunter near a single secret of Ada's library," she adds. "Not a whisper. Not through me, not through Aliz, and certainly not through your own eyes."

"But—"

"So . . ." She ignores my interruption, walking towards me. Her chestnut hair sways, waves like silk. "Leave Callisto."

I stare at her. For a moment, I focus on the itch in my neck. It's the only thing that can keep me from laughing at what she just said. "Don't be ridiculous."

"Callisto is a genocidal cult," she says. "And while I'm sure you think you're different, you still report back to other members of your 'organisation,' don't you?" Her voice is dripping with acid, and I stare at her, tightening my fists. "So, leave."

"I can't," I say in a low voice. "I have to find out who killed my parents."

"How long have you been hunting for?" she asks.

"Four years," I say.

"Did vampires kill your parents?" she asks. I nod. "And you can't find their killer without Callisto's help?"

I stare at her. I don't have an answer.

I've already made such a huge mess with Penny, who *still* hasn't replied to a single one of my texts. She's continued to ignore my calls, sending me a very clear message. Her silence can only last so long. Sooner or later she'll have to forgive me.

But I can't imagine myself going back to my old life. I've only been here for a little over a month, and yet— "They'll kill me if I leave," I say, and it's only half an excuse. I know that hunters are not allowed to quit. We know too much about Callisto. Or so they say.

Elia sits down beside me. "You can stay here," she says. "And I'll help you find whoever killed your parents."

"I—"

"I'm not expecting you to answer right away. But that's my deal. Agree to leave Callisto, and I'll let you into the library."

I don't say another word, my insides trembling as I exit her apartment. I walk out into the fading daylight, where vampires can't reach me, and look down at my phone. There's no way that I can leave. And I still haven't heard from her.

Please just tell me you're alive

I can't betray Penny. Penny is the one who found me when everything was falling apart. She gave me a reason to live. A future to chase.

I stop next to a bench and stare up at the hills. Penny also made me a killer. A shell of whoever I used to be. And these last four weeks have changed me in ways I can't even begin to fathom.

But still I can't leave Callisto.

I can't leave Penny.

She's my family.

AMBROSE HALL IS busy, vampires walking past our table carrying trays stacked with blood, or the occasional human trying to balance bowls of soup as they run, looking for an empty table. A month has passed since classes started, but aside from Stephan and me, most humans seem to be keeping to themselves, watching vampires from afar.

I stare down at the unanswered texts, then at my call log. Maybe it's a good thing that Penny never replied. It'll make doing what Elia wants a lot easier.

But can I really betray Penny? She gave my life meaning after I lost everything. But that *meaning* no longer makes sense. I can't hate vampires the way she wants me to. Not anymore.

Julia is half asleep, deep shadows beneath her eyes. "Last night was my deadline," she says, resting her head on the table. "I got fifteen minutes of sleep, but finally finished them."

"Your murals?" I ask.

"*Scenes of Adolescence*," Ife says with a little flair. "Is Traquair Hall open to the public yet?"

"I suppose so?" Julia says, leaning up slightly to look at her friend. "Though I'd much rather my work not be perceived."

"But you're an artist," Stephan argues, and Julia forces herself to have a sip of blood.

"So I've heard."

Despite her protestations, when Ife asks to visit Traquair Hall and see Julia's murals, the blond vampire doesn't say no. I tag along, even though I can already feel myself growing restless without Aliz. We reach the staircase where I crossed paths with Julia, not far from the maze, and we make our way up into a red-brick building that stinks of paint and melted plastic.

Traquair Hall has a diaphanous nave, with studios on each side separated by glass walls. It reminds me a little of Ikea, if Ikea also sold abstract art that goes way over my head. "I'm at the very end," Julia says as we walk past installations and sculptures. Stephan stops every now and then, distracted by what he sees. The hall is surprisingly quiet. The finished projects won't be appraised until later tonight, so most artists are trying to get a few hours of sleep.

"Oh, Julia!" Ife exclaims as we reach the end of the hall. "These are amazing!"

Julia's murals cover every available inch of her studio, including the floor, as well as an added ceiling, much lower than the real one. "The floor is dry," she says, handing us plastic coverings for our shoes before we walk on it.

Each wall contains a different scene, bustling with people. On the left wall, the glass one, is a beach, sky filled with paragliders and hot-air balloons, while the sea and the sand are clustered with people, and one girl in particular, who looks quite a bit like Julia, is carrying a jellyfish.

The photorealistic style she keeps in her sketchbook is missing here, replaced by stylized figures. And there's something off about every person, either too tall or too short, their proportions not making sense, yet when squashed together in a crowd of vibrant brushstrokes, they work.

I look towards the opposite wall. This one is of a party, just as busy as the coastal scene. The stench of turpentine nips at my nostrils. The party looks like it's in a hotel, and as I stare at it, I realise it's familiar. It's the Radstone, where I had my prom. A light prickling sensation crawls across the back of my head.

There must be a thousand hotels with an identical interior.

But the longer I stare at the scene, the more familiar it gets.

Not just the hotel, but the *people:* The faces of my old classmates, slightly distorted by Julia's heavy brushstrokes, fill every inch of the mural as they pass around a smuggled bottle of vodka. And standing by the stage, with a mop of green hair and thick, cartoon tears falling down her cheeks, is my ex-girlfriend, Vicki.

Julia is explaining the beach scene to Stephan and Ife, telling them about a trip to Blackpool, and how that was the last time she ever got sunburnt. The sound of her voice fades, replaced by a shrill ringing. I'm in the painting, too. I'm right at the centre of the mural, looking up at the stage, holding out my hand to a scrawny man with pale blond hair. While everyone else has that slightly uncanny look to them, this man is immortalised with delicate lines, as though he's in a Renaissance painting.

"Huh," Ife says beside me, resting a hand on my shoulder. "That guy looks a little like Professor Gustavsson, doesn't he?"

She's pointing at the man on the stage. She doesn't recognise *me,* of course, because I'm facing away, but I'm in a sparkly green dress that I wore to match Vicki's hair, and I'd recognise it anywhere.

"Gustavsson?" I say, voice small. Ever so slowly, the painting starts to move, and I hear the music in the back of my head. A bad Arctic Monkeys cover. Blue and red lights on the ceiling, a disco ball casting glitter onto the petite dance floor.

"The bassist," Ife adds.

I hear Vicki's nasal voice in my ear, louder than the ringing. *Everyone saw you.*

An accusation of something I still can't remember.

Because prom was a blur, even though I didn't drink. I never understood why I forgot that night.

I focus on the painting as the ringing in my ears gets louder. Julia has painted the band with oversized fangs, blood dripping from their mouths. I vaguely remember our religion teacher telling us the band had offered him a discount if they could start playing after sunset. So prom had started late.

"Who's Gustavsson?" Julia asks, standing next to Ife, and suddenly that night, over four years ago, sharpens, things I'd forgotten come back to life.

Vicki and I kissing in the photo booth, feather boas around our necks. A classmate throwing up on her table after four shots. A teacher screaming at her. The bassist, who everyone thought was so hot, smiling at me from the stage. A long inhale as he sniffed my neck. Fear, unlike anything I'd felt before, running up my spine, when his red eyes bored into mine.

"That's one of our professors," Ife says. "Did he pose for this?"

"No one posed," Julia says. "This scene just came to me on our first day of class."

"It came to you? Like Snowy?" Ife asks, and Julia nods.

Julia said she could paint things people had forgotten. Memories hidden by trauma.

Bile burns the back of my throat, and I finally tear my eyes away from the grotesque painting, but I can't get it out of my head. The music, loud enough to hide screams. Gustavsson taking my hand, and then—

"Cassie?" Ife says, hands squeezing my shoulder. "You all right?"

No.

I nod, my mouth too dry to speak. It can't be him. It doesn't make sense. I want to smash the mural to pieces, but an old fear has started to wrap cold scales around my chest.

"And this one?" Stephan asks, staring up at the ceiling, the mural depicting a birthday party.

"I'm running late," I say, though I don't specify for what. I'm not sure if they replied, but I don't turn back, walking, and then running out of Traquair Hall, goosebumps crawling over my skin.

No.

I think of the silver cross he gave me. That feigned worry. The slight frown when he said my name, *Cassie,* because he knew it wasn't my real name.

It doesn't make sense. It couldn't be him.

I stumble down the stairs to the tunnel, vision blurring. I still can't remember most of prom, but enough, the parts he didn't compel me to forget, are suddenly crystal clear, awakened by Julia's painting. Why was he at my prom?

No—my life before my parents' deaths was normal. Human.

I press my nails to my eyelids, swallowing hard. I blink away tears, staring around the tunnel, as I hear Vicki's voice in my head and the thing she said the morning after prom, which had never made sense to me.

Everyone saw you kissing the bassist!

My blood boils, and the ringing in my ears finally stops.

I breathe. Panic replaced by fury.

What the fuck did he do to me?

chapter THIRTY-ONE

A part of me still thinks I'm wrong. Maybe the Familiar's mark is making me paranoid. Nocth did say it can drive people insane. But those memories, those flashes of that night, feel real. I wade down to the Cat's Tail, taking the third staircase leading to the music hall.

He's playing already, each note sharp like a cut, as if he's running his bow over my veins, the strings drawing blood. I steady my breathing. I open the back door to the hall. Ife raises her brows when she sees me. "You could have waited for me," she whispers. "Where did you run off to?"

"I felt a bit nauseous," I whisper back.

I think back to Julia's painting and compare it to my own memories. He had been wearing a plain white T-shirt and torn jeans. I watch him now as he puts his cello on its stand. His suit is perfectly cut, hair brushed back from his eyes.

His voice, as he delves into a lecture on one of his own experimental operas, has a suffocating quality to it now.

Does he remember me?

I think back to our first meeting. Him calling me to the front of the class, telling me his office was a safe place. Was he waiting for me to recognise him?

The lecture feels longer, each second dragging as both fear and expectation inch forward.

I didn't know vampires existed until Penny found me.

Had I been of sound mind, I may have not believed her. But when she offered me revenge, I travelled back down to London. I followed her into the deepest corner of the abandoned convent where she kept her prisoners. The first vampire I ever laid eyes on was a Convert, a woman with sunken cheeks and sharp fangs who Penny had kept alive just for me.

I always pictured that vampire, with her crimson eyes, her wild expression, as the first. As my gateway into this world. But she wasn't.

It was Gustavsson.

People around us start to get up, benches screeching as they head out of the music hall. Ife puts her laptop into her bag, a tight curl falling over her face.

"Cassie, can I have a word?" his voice calls. I play with my watch and nod.

"Again?" Ife asks.

"Don't worry," I say. If she says something else, I don't hear her, my ears ringing again. I push myself up. I have a gun and two rounds of bullets in my satchel. A stake, though I'd rather not use it today. If I want answers, I need him alive.

I try to remember. See it again. The hotel, the stage. But the night is still a blur. I try to bring Julia's painting to life in my head, but it remains static. I reach the front of the classroom, and his eyes lock with mine. The back of my head tingles.

"Cassie," he says, flashing me a perfect smile. "I read through your proposal. Ravel is interesting enough, but it would be a good idea for you to include a woman composer as well. You remember Campbell?"

My body feels heavy. Cold. My breathing is short. I need to focus.

He watches me far too intently, waiting for my reply. *Why was he at my prom?*

"I do," I finally say, straining to make my voice sound normal.

The last student exits the class, door slamming, leaving us alone in the dim room.

A dozen possibilities flash through my mind. Ways to make him talk.

Silence lingers between us, every question I have dying in my mouth. Gustavsson looks away from me and shakes his head.

"I wish you wouldn't look at me like that, Cassie," he whispers. His voice, deep, velvety, crawls beneath my skin. He steps down from his platform, coming closer. "I've tried ignoring those looks from you," he says in a hushed voice. "But it's becoming unbearable."

He's too close. I step back until I feel a table against my lower back, while he puts one arm at my side, inhaling my scent.

My hand trembles. An old fear freezes me in place and leaves me unable to look away from him.

"You're going to get me into so much trouble," he whispers. He looks like he's going to say more, *do* more, but suddenly he pulls away, glancing at the back entrance.

"Oh, Miss Astra," he says. "To what do I owe your visit?"

I'm still frozen, skin crawling, and I don't realise she's here until she's at the front of the class. It's my first time seeing her in this candlelit hall, her hair gold instead of white. Relief floods through me as soon as I realise I'm no longer alone with him. She's here.

"Get away from her," Aliz says. Gustavsson takes another step back, raising both hands. His lips break into a crooked grin, an expression I've never seen him wear at the university, but one I saw prom night. "Ever *look* at her again, and you'll regret it."

Her hand takes mine, and my panic, everything that froze me in place, vanishes as she drags me away from him.

"I wasn't aware the Astras were so friendly with humans." His voice echoes against the frescoes on the vaulted ceiling, and Aliz's eyes flash red.

"Don't talk about my family," she says.

Gustavsson is clasping his cello case, his smile cool now that it's directed at Aliz.

"You know, you look nothing like your sister," he says. Before Aliz can push out another word, he adds, "We are related, did you know that?"

"What?" Aliz asks, her voice still sharp. I breathe out, trying to keep up with the conversation.

"You and I. Almost three hundred years ago, your sister blessed me with eternal life." He looks down at his hands, turning them as though he's seeing them for the first time. "She fell madly in love with me, though her love was fickle."

Aliz looks stunned. I am, too. Her fingers are tight against mine, and I can't tell if she's furious or afraid.

I recall the story he told during his first lecture. A mysterious aristocrat heard him play, stalked him for a year, and gifted him with eternal life. The reason why Gustavsson knows what he does about *The Book of Blood and Roses,* then, is because he once lived with the woman who wrote it.

"We're not *related,*" she finally says. "My sister sired many vampires." This time, when she starts walking, Gustavsson doesn't say anything. Though I can still feel his gaze on the back of my neck as we leave.

She doesn't let go of my hand as we walk through the tunnel, taking the first turn we find, down into a darkened and quiet stairway. Then she pulls me into her arms.

"What made you come here?" I whisper, feeling safe against her chest.

Aliz hesitates. "It's strange," she says, not loosening her grip. "But somehow, I could sense that you were in danger." Her fingers stop on my neck, resting against the Familiar's mark. A shiver runs across my skin, welcoming her touch.

I look up, chest warming when her eyes meet mine. Then she's glancing down at my lips, leaning closer. I clear my throat, and though I don't want to, I pull back. "We should be careful," I whisper. "If anyone sees us like this, you could get in trouble."

"I like trouble," she says and lifts my hand to kiss my knuckles. She pulls me close, and my racing heart starts to calm as I breathe against her neck. My eyes sting, but I have to keep my emotions to myself. This isn't something I can explain to her.

We go back to Tynarrich, walking a few metres apart to avoid anyone noticing our proximity. Knowing she's near keeps my fear at bay.

But I can't shake off the sickening dread, crawling deeper in my skin, as Gustavsson's voice and his crooked smile linger in my mind.

LATER THAT EVENING, when Aliz goes to class, I head to Elia's place.

I send her a photo of Julia's mural, along with a link to Gustavsson's profile in Tynahine's intranet. Despite having an entire library on campus, half of Elia's house is filled with books.

"I'll have to check other sources," she finally says, her voice low and careful. "But based on what you've told me, he might be a Vassal." I tense when I hear that word. The Vassals are the murderous Convert cult Nocth told me about. The ones responsible for Aliz's *sickness*. Elia must have noticed the change in my expression, because she asks: "Aliz's memories haven't come back, have they?" she asks. I stare at her. How can Elia know about Aliz's missing memories? Somehow, I'm not surprised.

"They—they did. But Nocth was able to—"

"Put another bandage on them?" Elia's voice is sharp. "When will Faust realise that Aliz will never grow up if he keeps sheltering her like this?"

"You didn't see her," I say. "She was vomiting blood."

Elia's gaze softens. "There has to be another way," she says. "I refuse to believe amnesia is the only cure."

"Did you ever see Gustavsson before?" I ask, getting her back on topic. Elia looks at me then, brows creasing. "Before he reached Tynahine?"

"Should I have?" she asks.

"He claims that he was sired by Ada Astra." I expect to see her eyes widen with surprise, but instead Elia makes a face tinged with disgust.

"She loved making fledglings," she says. "Whenever our relationship was going through a rough patch, she'd disappear somewhere across Europe and bring back a newly turned vampire to make me jealous." She swallows, looking down. "I stopped caring after the sixteenth century, so I'm assuming, if what he said was true, that he must have been one of her later conquests." Elia stares at the printed picture. "When your sire dies, a piece of you dies with them. They can become vicious after that sort of loss. I know I did. So perhaps Ada's death is what made him join the Vassals."

I stare at her. I knew Elia was a Convert, yet at the same time, I can't imagine her ever being human.

"Why would a Vassal ever go to Wishaw?" I ask. She looks at me, not hiding her confusion. "That's my town," I elaborate, and Elia nods.

"Scouting. He may have gone on a tour of every prom in Britain."

"Scouting for—"

"Blood party victims," Elia says. "You said your parents were killed by vampires."

"Yes," I say.

"How long after your prom?"

I scratch my neck so hard that I accidentally open a wound. Elia's pupils dilate, and she bites her lip, hard. I wipe the blood from my neck, staring her down, waiting for her to pounce on me. But after a long breath, the thirst leaves her eyes. "They died a month later," I finally say. And as I say it, I can feel my insides twisting. Elia doesn't speak, letting my thoughts breathe.

It may have been a coincidence. Yet at the same time, it doesn't make sense. If Gustavsson was looking for blood party victims, why wasn't I taken to one? I should have been the one who died, but instead, it was my parents. And somehow, Callisto was waiting on the sidelines to recruit me.

I remember Penny standing next to my parents' corpses. Her red hair was in a neat bun, her pale skin stark against her black clothes.

I'd thought she was a police officer, though soon she told me that what had happened to my parents was a crime that no ordinary cop could solve.

I'd never questioned Callisto finding me, Callisto betting on me, deciding that this random eighteen-year-old would for some reason be a good hunter.

My blood smelling good was something they only found out later.

But what if they had already known? What if Gustavsson, the Vassals, gave them a heads-up? My chest aches. Surely they could have found someone better than me. An athlete, a soldier. The only thing I had going for me was my blood.

"You know, if Callisto was interested only in protecting humans from vampires, I would have nothing against your organisation, Rebecca," she says, taking my hand. Her nails are pastel pink. "I would even help them, just as I help the Council. And the Council is by no means perfect. But the Council is not in bed with the Vassals."

I don't look up at her. I wish her words were jarring. I wish they didn't make sense.

"Do you believe in coincidences?" she asks.

I don't. But all the same, I don't want to believe it. Callisto allied with the Vassals. "Why would they work with them?"

"Both Callisto and the Vassals want to destroy the Council," Elia says, looking up at the crystal chandelier hanging from her ceiling. "The Vassals want the world to go back to how things were before the treaties. Callisto wants to rid the earth of vampires. They have entirely different goals, so you wouldn't think they'd ever work together, but while the Council still exists, they might as well help each other out."

"All my missions have been to dismantle blood parties," I say. "I've never once targeted the Council."

"Of course *you* haven't," she says, resting her head on her arm, looking at me with her piercing blue eyes. "But Callisto has rankings, don't they? Crosses, Hymns, Silvers, and Stakes. I'm assuming you're just a Cross."

I look away from her. She's right. I've been a Cross for four years.

Penny was already a Stake when I met her. I know that the missions Stakes go on are *different*. "How do you know so much about Callisto?" I ask, trying to keep my mind from racing.

"I had the pleasure of meeting its founder," she says, acid dripping from her tongue. *Catherine Lovelace.* I have a million questions. But I get the sense Elia doesn't want to talk about her.

What if she's right about Callisto?

If Callisto really does work with the Vassals, if I was *scouted* for them by Gustavsson, then there's a chance Callisto may have arranged my parents' deaths, just to make sure I had a reason to join them. What if they've spent the last four years dangling the carrot of revenge in front of me to keep me fighting, when they were the culprit all along?

What if Penny lied to me?

"If you're right about Gustavsson, what should we do?" I ask. I'm happy to take him on myself. But when we were alone in his classroom, I froze. That might happen again.

"I need a band for my Halloween Ball," Elia says, picking up her phone. "And I believe he's part of a quartet. Ada's little palace has many hidden corners in which we can ask him questions."

I nod. I find my thoughts spiralling back to what she said before. Callisto, working with the Vassals.

"When did you figure out I was a vampire hunter?" I ask. "When you found the garlic in my room?"

"No," Elia scoffs. "I knew the moment I first saw you," she says. "Your eyes were full of the hatred only Callisto's hunters have." She puts a hand on my head. "But you've changed."

I take in a deep breath, and I look at her as I exhale.

"If they are behind my parents' deaths, I'll crush them," I say.

"Them?"

"Callisto," I say. "So, I can't quit. Not if I can destroy them from the inside."

"My conditions haven't changed," Elia says.

Whether or not Callisto is working with the Vassals, I still need to get into the library.

I need to convince Elia that she can trust me.

"My mission here was to steal *The Book of Blood and Roses*," I say. "From Ada's secret library."

"*The Book of Blood and Roses*?" Elia raises her brows, leaning back. "Why does Callisto want a book of remedies?" She pauses. "It makes sense for your current predicament, of course."

"Remedies?" I ask. "I thought it was a list of every vampiric weakness. A way to—"

"Cure vampirism?" Elia mutters. "She certainly tried. But those *weaknesses* you speak of are in the 'Blood' section of the book. The remedies are in 'Roses,' which takes up the bulk of her work."

That bizarre name finally makes sense.

"I suppose Callisto is interested in the 'Blood' part of the book, then," I say.

Elia stares at me and finally sighs. "All right, Rebecca. Once the moon's in its first quarter, I'll take you to the library. But if you go back on your word and work for them again, I will kill you."

"I thought you'd done enough killing already."

"There's always an exception," she says, grinning at me.

The week, which I'd assumed would feel like an eternity, staggers to a sudden end. The half-moon sits atop the hills, a faint glow through the thick clouds. I've stopped going to Gustavsson's class, afraid that if I see him again, I'll either freeze or kill him. Julia eyes me warily; ever since I ran from her painting, she's been distant, as though she knows the effect it had on me.

And even though I haven't gone to Gustavsson's class, I still can't stop replaying prom, over and over, in my head, until what I remember becomes a tattoo, and the missing memories a void, threatening to pull me in. My only respite is Aliz, who can twist every emotion, every anxiety, into longing.

"Are we really doing this *here*?" I ask. Aliz presses her lips to the black moon on my neck, bringing my every nerve to life. The fifth floor of Kinsnet Library is empty, but I can hear the low murmurs of my fellow students in the floors below. I swallow and look at the clock. Elia told us to meet her by the nook at midnight, in just two hours.

In two hours, the fire that's been kindling between us will be snuffed out. For her, at least.

"You don't want to?" she asks, doing up the buttons she just pulled loose. I swallow hard.

"I do." I pull her closer, into a tight hug, and Aliz kisses my head, squeezing my shoulders. *I just don't want it to be the last.* I know it would be stupid for me to say that. But the price of my freedom is not only leaving Callisto. It's also losing Aliz.

"We can go back to our room," she says. "I don't want you to think I'm an exhibitionist."

"You're worrying about that *now*?" I laugh, tugging her shirt out from her trousers, just to allow me to press my hand directly against her skin. "Do I have to remind you of the first time I saw you?"

"No," she says, cupping my chin, forcing me to meet her gaze. "But I bet you couldn't stop thinking about it," she says. "I remember how fast your heart was beating."

"Yeah, because I was scared," I say, running my hand higher, until I find the clasp of her bra. I tug on it, but don't undo it.

"And now?" she whispers, lips close to mine.

"Terrified," I say, digging my nails into her back.

"Liar," she says, and she slips her hand between my legs, her fingers already familiar with every inch of me. I grit my teeth, biting my lip to keep myself from moaning, all while Aliz presses me against the bookcase. "What's wrong?" she asks innocently, two fingers slipping inside me, soon joined by a third. I pull her hair, trying to wipe the smugness off her face, but she knows she's in full control.

She kisses my neck, and I feel it deeply, viscerally. My blood burns, craving to be tasted by her. And I'm not sure if she could read my mind, but Aliz is able to distract me by slipping a fourth finger inside, fucking me harder than she ever has before. Being, as I asked her, a little less gentle. I bite her neck to keep myself from crying out, and it's the sound of her moan that drives me over the edge, the world momentarily disappearing as pleasure sears through me.

I hold her tight, breathing heavily, and Aliz kisses my cheek. "I wish I could return the favour," I whisper, still pressing myself against her. "I wish I could get down on my knees for you," I say against her ear, and I feel her shiver, her breath hitching. She lets out a nervous laugh and shakes her head.

"I'd love that, but I'd lose control."

I'm filled with momentary bitterness as I think of another girl touching her in a way I can't, feeling Aliz's fangs piercing their skin in a way that I'll never be able to feel. "Maybe I could tie you up," I say. She sighs, and when our eyes meet, there's a slight red tinge to her irises. "And blindfold you," I add.

"When did you become so kinky?" she asks, and despite the fact she's just gotten me off, Aliz slips a hand back beneath my skirt. A few seconds later, she pulls out, making a face. "We've got company," she says. I remember hearing those exact same words from her lips when I first encountered her, right here, on the fifth floor of the library.

Aliz wraps my scarf around my neck, making sure that the mark isn't visible, before we walk out from behind the book aisles, trying to act normal. Julia stares right back at us, holding a couple of books. Her nose twitches, and I remember her saying that she could smell Aliz on me. I don't want to even think of what she picks up now.

"Studying?" I ask awkwardly. Julia looks at Aliz for a moment, her expression not exactly a picture of joy.

"Yeah," she says, "We've got an exam tomorrow, Astra."

"Ah, you're right," Aliz says. "Can't wait."

I don't know if I should apologise, but that would just make things more awkward. "I think she doesn't like me," Aliz whispers, once we're heading back down the staircase. "Which is a first."

"I wouldn't like you, either, if it wasn't for this pesky mark," I tease, and Aliz glares at me.

"Maybe she likes *you*," she says.

"Don't be silly," I say.

"What? You're cute. Your blood smells nice. But it's weird. I feel like I've seen her somewhere. And not in class."

"What do you mean?"

"She's familiar. I just can't put my finger on why."

I think of what Julia said about Aliz's dad visiting her in her dreams. Julia was only converted four years ago but possesses abilities other vampires do not. So maybe she was sired by an Astra. Aliz lets go of my hand when we reach the ground floor of the library, and only as we leave it, the place where I first saw her, do I realise that she'll quite possibly never touch me like that again.

THE NOOK IS in front of us, rose and candle filling the ancient rock with a red glow.

"Well, this is it," Elia says as she picks up the rose. She clasps the stem tight in her hand, piercing her skin with its thorns. She then holds her bleeding hand over the candle, allowing the flame to lick her wound. She must have done this a thousand times, because she barely even winces.

Aliz copies her, clasping her hand around the stem, and hisses as the thorns dig into her. And something truly bizarre happens this time, because as the rose drinks her blood, it grows new leaves, and the flower's petals part a little wider. Fast, before her wound heals, she holds it over the candle, allowing her blood to mingle with the flame. "Ouch," she says.

"You should stay back," I say when it's my turn. Aliz gives a short nod, stepping as far back as she can, pressing herself against the wall.

She pegs her nose and says, "I'm ready."

I take the rose, and its thorns feel like shards of glass. I crush it against my palm, stifling my reaction as the stem grows an inch longer, more leaves unfurling. Aliz clears her throat, and I hold my bleeding hand over the candle, skin scalding as it meets the flame. I bite my tongue to keep myself from crying out.

"Here," Elia says, and she clearly came prepared, because after taking the rose and candle, she hands me a damp wipe and a bunch of plasters. I set about tending to my wounds, before looking over at Aliz. She's extremely tense, her face twisted with pain. Her eyes have taken on a burgundy hue, and she looks away immediately. When I wipe the blood from my hands, I find the small wounds have already vanished. *What the fuck?* This is the second time that a wound has healed much faster than it should have. So maybe I've started to gain some of those physical abilities Nocth told me Blood Familiars possess.

"All right, ladies," Elia says, holding up both the rose and the candle. "Follow me."

I swallow hard. This is it. Freedom within my reach. Elia uses her elbow to open the left door, the darkness beckoning us in. Both Aliz and I hesitate, remembering the horrors of the hallway. "Hurry up," Elia says. When we step in, the door doesn't slam shut behind us. Aliz takes my hand, and only then do I realise mine had been shaking. I take a careful breath, waiting for the river to come crashing towards me, but instead, the hallway changes.

Stone vines, with intricate roses and sculptures on either side, bloom from the walls. The sculptures, I realise, are identical to those at the centre of the hedge maze, depicting the different phases of the moon. But here they're not missing any limbs. Lanterns with blue flames appear on the walls, illuminating them, and in the distance, a pair of colossal wooden doors cut through the stone. Elia materialises again, her steps louder than they were before.

Elia turns to look at us, gaze flickering down to our linked hands. "Ada compelled one of Scotland's best witches to protect this place."

"A witch!" Aliz exclaims.

"And then she drained her."

"Why?" I ask.

"Well." Elia's heels click on the floor. Her voice carries an echo to it now. "The witch in question was fond of sacrificing babies in order to maintain her youth. So, in a way, Ada did the world a favour."

"Huh," says Aliz, and I can tell she's forcing herself to sound calm. There are two wooden plinths at either side of the giant doors, decorated with the Astra crest, identical to what covers the upper half of my torso. Elia places the rose on one side, the candle on the other, and automatically, the doors creak open.

"You go in first," Aliz says, looking at Elia. "I have to talk to Cassie."

"Don't take too long," Elia says, winking at me before disappearing into the darkness beyond the doors.

As soon as we're alone, awkwardness cements itself between us. "This is it," I say, breaking the silence. Her hand is cold against mine.

"Thanks for putting up with me these last few weeks," she says, forcing a smile. "We'll still be friends, won't we?"

The pain in my chest tightens, and I cup her face, taking in the features that I've come to know as well as my own reflection. Her black eyes, fringed by white lashes. Her pale hair which marks her as the sole heir to the Astras. Her full lips that I could kiss for days on end. I run my thumb across them and convince myself that this pain is the summit. After this, forgetting her will only get easier.

"Friends," I whisper.

Her eyes search mine, and after a moment's hesitation, her lips are on mine, desperate, hungry. Her voice is caught in her throat when she pulls back. "I wish I could feel this way forever," she says, holding me closer. "Love you like this."

I shiver, feeling tears burning the corners of my eyes. "Maybe you can," I say, and Aliz tightens her grip on me.

"No," she replies, voice so low that I barely hear her, even with her lips against my ear. "If this was real, it would ruin your life. I would have to send you to the other end of the world, so our paths never cross. So he never finds you."

I may not have met her father, but even I know he wouldn't approve of our relationship.

"I'm not going anywhere," I say, pulling back an inch. She doesn't loosen her grip on me.

"Then I'll be the one to leave."

I grab a fistful of her hair, pulling until she winces. And with that pained expression, I draw her to me for one last kiss, doing all that I can to hold back tears, to not feel. This might be the end. I may never have her like this again. I'll become her human roommate, who she'll tease but never want. And damn it, I want her to want me, regardless of what I am.

She draws away, still cupping my cheek. "I love you," she says one last time.

Before Elia can ask what's taking us so long, we manage to put distance between us. Aliz goes first, pulling the door towards her and holding it open for me. I step through, using the split second I have without her attention to rub away tears before they fall. Before she notices them.

There's a short hallway, and at the edge of it, a balcony, flanked by a low, but very wide stairwell. Aliz stops beside me, her mouth open, eyes wide.

In my mind, ever since Penny first told me about it, I could only imagine the hidden library as small and narrow. Just a few bookcases with some form of protection to keep their forbidden contents from the wretched hands of people like me. And after seeing the hedge maze with the rosebush at its centre, I'd figured it had to be a fraction of the size of the labyrinth protecting it. But instead, as gas lamps slowly flicker on, I find a great hall that rivals the dimensions of Kinsnet.

"Is this real?" Aliz asks, stealing my words before I can utter them.

"Your sister lived for nine hundred years," Elia says from the bottom floor, sitting on a wooden table. "One collects a lot of books over the centuries."

We make it to the bottom, and I feel the hall growing cold. Aliz is still wonderstruck, looking up at the balconies circling the hall, with their countless bookcases. "And I thought the library at home was big," she says wistfully.

"I asked Father if we could build another wing to allow for more books, but he said no."

The voice, with its thick continental accent, echoes against the walls. We all look up, and she's on the second floor, legs dangling over the edge. Her white hair cascades down to her ankles, matted, full of knots. Her eyes glow bright blue.

"Hello, Ada," Elia calls.

chapter
THIRTY-TWO

Aliz stumbles back, face losing all colour as she takes in the sight of the sister she never met. Only Elia, who clearly comes here often, given the immaculate state of the library, doesn't seem surprised by her presence.

"I don't understand," I say, and my words echo back at me. Ada Astra's head snaps in my direction, her blue eyes seizing my gaze. Her whole body, I notice, glows with a faint blue shimmer. She vanishes into a cloud of blue smoke, reappearing right behind me.

"Dinner?" she asks, her incorporeal hands resting on my shoulders. Her touch is like frost against my skin. I stagger forward, trying to shake her off me.

"No, not dinner," Elia says, in a chiding voice.

"Ghost," Aliz chokes the word out by mistake, her voice shaking. And upon hearing her, her long-dead sister saunters towards her, causing Aliz to back away until she hits a statue. They're both the exact same height, but where Aliz's frame is boyish, Ada is all curves, an hourglass figure that is visible even beneath her tattered nightgown. She has sharp and angular features, a jaw and cheekbones that could cut glass, and sunken eyes with thick white lashes. And I'm not sure if she's as beautiful as she is terrifying.

"*Ghost?*" Ada echoes the word with an almost mocking tone. She steps closer to Aliz, cocking her head to one side. "I am the *heir* to the Astra *empire,* the most powerful vampire to have graced the earth, the Dreamwalker of Rome, the—"

"Ada, dear," Elia interrupts, her airy voice making the ghost turn. "How many times are you going to forget the fact that you are dead?"

"Oh." The truth of her predicament doesn't seem to faze the old heir too much; she suddenly looks down at her shimmering body and holds up her hands, seeing Aliz through them. "Who would think that bastard would dare to procreate again?" Ada asks, knowing, somehow, who Aliz is.

My knees are about to give way. My head spins, because only now do I realise that I've been holding my breath the entire time. When I inhale, I try to do it as quietly as possible, to keep her from noticing me again. A *ghost.* My stomach burns, and I am certain that I'm going to be sick—certain enough that I cover my mouth as I try to calm down.

Aliz's hands tremble, one hand gripping the bookcase behind her as she tries to believe what her eyes are seeing. Finally, she squeezes out the word: "Nővér?"

Ada Astra's expression shifts, softening just a little. The ghost's ethereal voice switches into another language, and Aliz nods her head. She still looks like she's about to faint, but slowly, she lets go of the bookcase behind her and focuses on her sister.

The pair speak for a minute, and Ada slowly turns to look at me as Aliz explains our situation. "Ah," Ada finally says, vanishing and reappearing straight in front of me, her face inches from mine, her dead spirit clinging to my skin like condensation. "Why *wouldn't* you want her as your Familiar, sister? She has the eyes of a soldier. When war comes, wouldn't you want her to fight for you? I know I would," says the dead heir, her blue eyes not losing their unnatural hue. Does she know I'm a hunter? Has Elia told her?

I think of Ada's own Familiar. Callisto's founder.

"I don't want a slave," Aliz hisses.

"Slave?" Ada turns from me, aghast. "Oh, but she would be so much more. A Familiar is a part of your soul. And you would be a part of hers. Being able to compel her with words alone simply makes the transition easier. After a few months, she will no longer distinguish between her will and yours."

"No," Aliz says, all the more disturbed by the prospect.

"Well, then," the ghost says with a sigh. "I presume you're looking for *The Book of Blood and Roses.*" She floats off, sinking through Elia, who coughs and tries to swat her away. "I won't stop you from looking. What is mine is yours, dear sister. And this simple librarian will assist you however you need her to." Ada's ghost makes her way to a green sofa, and when she lies upon it, half of her body sinks through the cushions, disappearing.

Elia sits beside her and looks up at Aliz and me. "Go," she says.

A ghost. I still can't quite believe it. "Your sister," I whisper, and Aliz still looks shaken. "Are you all right?" I ask her.

"Well, I used to think my father was exaggerating when he talked about her. But she really is unhinged. I don't know how Elia can bear to be around her."

"Me neither," I mutter.

We split up, Aliz heading to the top floor, while I start with the first.

Half of the titles are in Latin and Greek, a couple in Italian, and just a few in Hungarian. I trail my gaze along the spines, feeling my pulse in my ears as I skip all the *A*'s. *The Book of Blood and Roses.* I keep picturing a medieval sort of tome, with handwritten text and well ornamented paintings and vibrant miniatures. But perhaps the book will be tiny, instead. Unassuming.

And I'm caught up in my theories when at last I see it.

Book of Blood—A, Volume I.

It's incredibly thick, but the spine itself isn't too tall. Plain black leather, with the words embossed in gold. I don't touch it, not fully registering the title until I see the book next to it. *Book of Blood—A, Volume II.* I crouch down, not saying a word yet, until I realise that the three bookcases nearest to me all have that same title, *Book of Blood—A*.

Penny said *book,* singular. But this—I keep walking, feeling my throat tighten. How was I supposed to smuggle all of these out? I start running, following the order, until my frustration reaches a boiling point, and I grab one at random, just to get an idea of its weight.

As soon as I lift it from the shelf, the book crumbles.

I stumble back, hitting the wooden balcony, while the dust that seconds ago was a full book continues to scatter around me. I don't breathe, waiting for it to rewind. It must be an illusion, I think, my heart thudding.

"Fuck!" Aliz shouts from the top floor. I lean out, just in time to see her lean down. "It just vanished!" she shouts.

"Keep it down," the ghost of Ada Astra says. "You're in a library."

I rush back to the books before *B* and lift one off the shelf at random. The exact same thing happens, pages crumbling between my fingers. "What is going on?" I ask.

"Those books are as ghostly as I am," Ada cackles. And when the lights flicker, the endless shelves are suddenly empty, cobwebs replacing their pages.

No.

"Father had them all burnt. He did not like my research."

"But . . ." I start, looking down the balcony, a sudden wave of vertigo almost knocking me off my feet. "We need it."

"Silence," Ada says.

"Please." Aliz rushes down the spiralling stairs, her face pale. "Sister. We *need* that book. We have to undo the contract!"

"Well, that's easy enough," Ada says, sitting back up, smiling at her blood kin. "Fortunately for you, I once had to sever the tie with a would-be Familiar, and it was a simple matter."

I tighten my grip on the wooden balcony, trying my best to hide my reaction to that. Could she be referring to Catherine Lovelace? But why would she have her painted, if she *severed* her contract?

"Simple?" Aliz asks, disbelief colouring her voice. "You know the cure?"

"What do you think can undo a *blood* contract, *sister*?" The ghost utters the word *blood* mockingly. I wonder if this is what Ada Astra really was like, or if this sour-mouthed creature is just an amalgamation of her worst qualities.

"I don't know," Aliz says, her voice trembling. But I notice a change in her expression, something sobering.

Ada waves her ghostly hand, and a book appears before her, with the same spectral glow as her skin. The words *Book of Roses—F, Volume IX,* are written on the front. She flicks through it, stopping halfway. "'To undo a Familiar's blood contract, both the recipient and the vampire must drink the blood of an enemy, straight from an eternal fountain, beneath the light of a full moon.'"

"An eternal fountain?" I ask as Ada clasps the book shut, and it vanishes.

"A vampire's disembodied heart, free of ribs and skin!" she says. "If you both eat a heart beneath the light of a full moon, the Familiar's contract will be erased."

Elia sits unmoving on the green sofa, looking up at the now empty bookcases. Are they always like this when she comes? Empty? I can't understand why such a place, an empty library, would be so well protected.

Slowly, I let the *cure* fall into place. If I was the only person involved, it would be easy enough. I could hijack any blood party, find any scumbag, and grab their heart straight out of their chest.

But Aliz is not like me. I wait to hear her protest, ask for a different solution, but she's gone terribly quiet.

"You've found your answer," Elia says, the warmth with which she spoke minutes ago missing. She sounds much older for once, two thousand years slipping from her tongue.

"There is no *Book of Blood and Roses*?" I ask, just one last time. "No real library?"

"Oh, it's very real," says Ada Astra, appearing before me in a cloud of blue smoke. "But it's all in my head." She steps close, lowering until I feel her ice against my ear. Her voice drops to a whisper. "So you cannot ransack my collection, *Blood of Callisto*."

I don't react. Aliz's hand is on my wrist, tugging me upwards, towards the stone stairs we first descended. *Did she hear that?* I look back at the ghost, and she smiles at me, showing me her horrible fangs. Then at the library, at rows upon rows of empty bookshelves.

Elia runs up behind us, and before I can get my breath back, the wooden doors of Ada's secret library are slamming shut behind us. Elia takes the candle and the rose, and ever so slowly, as we walk along the wide hallway, the campus begins to shift back. Ancient engravings turn to simple bricks. The high ceiling lowers, and we pass through the doors. Then the nook is before us, dark until Elia positions the candle and the rose within. Aliz still hasn't said a word since her sister's instructions defined our joint fate. I seek out her gaze through the dimly lit tunnel, and she doesn't meet mine.

Now I know how to get rid of the mark. How to set myself free, before every word Aliz says becomes my will.

Killing, taking a vampire's life, is second nature for me.

But not for Aliz.

chapter
THIRTY-THREE

Aliz cannot kill.

She's innocent. She's never wavered in her resolve to get rid of the Familiar's mark, and that innate compassion of hers is the very reason why she can't take someone else's life.

She lies beside me, still and silent, and I run my fingers through her hair.

"We'll find a way," I whisper.

She clasps her hand over mine and closes her eyes.

TYNARRICH'S DINING HALL is quiet but for the violent rain battering the windows, shutters raised now that night has fallen. "You knew there was no library," I say once Elia shows her face.

"Where's Aliz?" she asks.

"Studying," I say. Staying apart from her is becoming more and more uncomfortable. The dull itch in my neck burns. I swear I can almost feel them, as though there are actual vines, actual thorns pressed to my skin. I scratch at the lines through my tartan scarf, and Elia pulls my hand down.

"When Ada was alive, she had the most vivid memory you could imagine. It went beyond photographic. She could remember the day we met in colourful detail. She could remember the scents, the fabric of my dress, and each insult I spat in her direction. Everything."

I stare at Elia, taking in the bitterness with which she speaks.

"She *is* the library. Even as a ghost, she knows each and every book she's ever read by heart. So I knew she would have the answers you were looking for. Consider it a miracle that she decided to tell you. She is fickle, even in death."

"How exactly did she become a ghost?" I ask. "Did she die in the library?" I've never seen a human ghost, never mind a vampire one.

"She died in Budapest," Elia says. "And I'm not entirely sure *how* her spirit managed to cling to our world. I found her ghost after her father burnt her books. She'd been dead for four years when Ares got through her labyrinth. Probably compelled a witch to show him the way. And when I came down to look at the wreck, she climbed out from the ashes, with no memory of her death or the bitch who killed her."

"Catherine," I say carefully, and Elia's jaw tightens.

She clearly doesn't want to talk about Callisto's founder, so she continues. "I'd left my alchemy days behind by then, but I figured Ada must have left traces of her soul in *The Book of Blood and Roses*. Whether this was intentional or not, I'm not sure. But she's been haunting her library ever since."

"Do you visit her every month?" I ask, and Elia offers me a sad smile.

"I would be a fool to do that," she says. "Break my heart, again and again? I feel as though my life has been a drawn-out epilogue since the day she died. And seeing her frozen in time is just salt in the wound, Rebecca."

"Be careful with my name," I say. "That day, when I first saw you in the tunnels, you'd come from the library, right?"

"My wounds don't heal as fast as Aliz's do," she admits. She then directs me back to the matter at hand. "If you're going to undo the contract, I think the Halloween Ball is the ideal place. A disguise, loud music—and that little palace has more hidden rooms than you would expect. Ada wasn't just hunting animals, you see."

I shiver, trying to get the ghost's face out of my head. What did Elia ever see in Ada? "Right." I look out the window, shutters open to reveal a foggy night.

"Come check it out tomorrow," she says, getting up. "And I'll try to get more dirt on your professor. If he is a Vassal, then he would be the best target for this so-called *eternal fountain*."

"No." I grit my teeth. "If he is a Vassal, he might know more about my parents' deaths than Callisto ever told me." I look across the quiet hall, ensuring no one heard us. Elia frowns at my words. I can't kill him until I know the truth. He might even be able to tell me, outright, if he was working for them—and if Penny knew I was going to be recruited before my parents died.

THERE MUST BE someone I can kill. I snap the pencil between my fingers, staring down at an essay I'm writing for Integration on the fall of the Old Council. Centuries ago, the bloodthirsty family heads were murdered one after the other by their heirs in a bizarre yet calculated massacre known as the Coup of the Heirs. Ares Astra only escaped being a victim of patricide because his daughter was set alight by his old bodyguards a year prior to the coup and fall of the Old Council.

I need to find someone. We're running out of time. But how do I convince Aliz to go along with this? She's not bloodthirsty like Ada. I can hear her behind me, shifting in front of the microwave as she heats up a cup of blood. We haven't kissed—we've barely even spoken since leaving the library.

The words on the page blur together, and just as I rummage through my drawers for a new pencil, my phone vibrates. Under ordinary she-hasn't-been-playing-dead-for-days circumstances, I would have declined the call and told her to call back later. Now, when I see Penny's face appear on my screen, I'm too taken aback to think. My fingers move on their own, and I squeeze out, "Penny?" holding the phone to my ear.

"Are you with the leech?"

I look over at Aliz, remembering that her senses are far greater than mine, and she's staring right back at me, eyes wide. She definitely heard that. Oh *fuck*.

I rush out of our room without saying a word and sit down on the top step of the staircase, under the gaze of a dozen ancient portraits. "You're alive?" I ask, my heart slowing. *Why haven't you answered my texts?*

"No thanks to you," she says. Strangely enough, Penny doesn't sound angry. In fact, Penny's tone is exactly as it was when she last called me, before sending me to the blood party in Inverness. I'm still trying to gather my thoughts when she asks: "Have you found the book?"

The book is a ghost. I almost say this aloud. But then I remember my promise to Elia.

"I haven't," I say, and the lie comes so easy, because I've spent the last month and a half doing nothing but lying. "But—how did you get out? Did you fight the Council?"

There's a pause. Something I could mistake for a sigh.

"No, Rebecca. I did not fight the Council."

I cross my legs, peering back along the hallway to ensure Aliz is not eavesdropping.

"But I'm glad to tell you that you have officially been ranked as a Stake of Callisto. Once you return to London, you'll receive your new uniform and quarters. Oh, and a raise, of course."

I'm still staring down the hallway, her words not fully hitting me. They make absolutely no sense.

"I'm—what?"

"Finding *The Book of Blood and Roses* is still an important mission, but I have not been entirely forthcoming with you, Rebecca."

"What do you mean?"

"Crosses, as you already know, work alone. You are expected to see vampires, *all* vampires, as your natural enemy." My eyes are locked on my boots, trying to figure out where this is going. "The main purpose of sending you to Tynahine was to see if you would be able to integrate—meaning work alongside them without losing sight of your mission. Sometimes—and I don't like it—we have to work with the Council. You proved to me in Inverness that you can distinguish between evil and—I don't like calling vampires *good*, so let's say, *tolerable* vampires."

I stare ahead, not blinking. Elia said Callisto is working with the Vassals. But what if she's wrong? Nocth had mentioned that if Callisto sent a hunter, it would be to oversee Integration. That my supposedly real mission would be a cover, and he was right. The only reason I'm here is to prove I could blend in.

"So, you're not angry with me?" I whisper. My head hurts. Penny sent me here as a *test*? Was she just acting when she tried to shoot me in Inverness?

"Quite the opposite. You went above and beyond what I expected of you," she says. "You uncovered the Red Ribbons *and* dismantled that party in Inverness."

"I . . ." For some reason, I don't buy it. Penny has never been impressed by *anyone* in the four years that I've known her. There's no way I'd ever be the subject of her admiration. I swallow hard and focus. "So I've finished? I can come home?"

"Not yet," she says. "I still want you to find *The Book of Blood and Roses*. And once you hand it over, I'll tell you who killed your parents."

There is no book. I almost say it. But Penny hangs up. Afterwards I feel as though I've just survived an earthquake. What the actual fuck was that?

A test?

Sometimes we work with the Council. I want to scream. I think of Elia, of Gustavsson and his secrets, but somehow, I can already feel myself being roped back in by Penny. She finally gave me the promotion I wanted. I'll finally learn what happened to my parents. Maybe

Elia is wrong about Gustavsson, maybe it's a coincidence. Penny wouldn't betray me. She wouldn't use me. And now she's finally realised my true worth.

Suddenly, I feel the thorns digging inwards, slicing through my skin. I choke, and when I press my hand to my skin, I'm sure I'll find it soaked with blood. But it's dry. The last time I felt this sort of pain was the night Aliz's memories returned.

When I get back to the room, I can barely breathe. But Aliz is all right. She closes the book she was reading and turns towards me. "I didn't mean to eavesdrop," she says as I close the door. "I can't control—" Her expression changes suddenly as she looks at me. "What's wrong?"

"The mark," I say through gritted teeth. She rushes towards me, pressing her hand against it, the scalding sensation slowly receding. I breathe out. "Thanks."

Aliz's hand trembles on my neck, and as soon as I place my own hand over hers, she asks:

"Who was that?"

I swallow hard, not letting go of her hand. What if I just tell her everything now? *No.* I can't.

"A family friend." Penny is family. My words aren't exactly a lie. All the same, I can't look Aliz in the eye as I say it. "I'm sorry you overheard that."

"Did she . . ." Aliz falters, and I already hear the strain in her voice. "Did she really call me a leech?"

I've used that word in my head. I've directed it silently at every vampire I've met here at Tynahine. Ife, Julia, Elia, Aliz. But now the word makes my skin crawl. "She's a bigot," I say. Aliz tilts my chin up, her expression hurt.

"Your family has worked with vampires for centuries," she says. "So, why would you associate yourself with someone like that?"

"How do you know my family works with vampires?" I ask, trying to worm my way out of her question.

Her cheeks gain a red tinge. "Because I googled you," she says. "You never tell me anything about yourself."

My breathing stills. I feel warmth draining from my face, and I look at her. Aliz draws out her phone, her face still tense as she opens a website. "'The Smiths have been longtime partners with the Macleod and Willow families, a partnership dating back to the eighteenth century.' That's on your parents' website. I know those are vampire families."

I try to find my voice, but there's a lump in my throat.

"Why should a family that's made their fortune thanks to vampires have the nerve to be bigoted towards us?"

"I'm not like them," I squeeze out, trying to ground myself.

"What *are* you like then, Cassie?" she says, her voice growing tight.

"I'm not like them," I insist, and as I reach for her, she steps back, face still flushed with anger. "I may have been like them before coming to Tynahine. I won't lie to you, but—"

"You are *always* lying!" she says sharply. Whatever expression I make forces a bitter laugh from her. "You think I can't tell? You lie to me all the time. Right from the moment we first spoke."

My eyes burn. All this time I'd thought I'd been careful. Aliz looks like she wants to say more—to say the words that will ruin everything between us.

"Tell me, do you think I'm a *leech*?"

Aliz doesn't raise her voice. Yet somehow, it's loud. It echoes in my head, the words *tell me* a lasso around my mind, digging deep into the space that's been shrivelled and burnt since I first became a vampire hunter. Pain sears across the Familiar's mark, thorns digging into me, and I say, "No."

My face is limp. I recognise this feeling. I thought I'd forgotten it, but it's as real as it was before I became immune to it.

"Then why don't you trust me?"

Her grip on my will has loosened, and I gawk at her, her black eyes without even a hint of red.

"What's wrong?" she asks.

"You just compelled me," I say. My legs crumple, but I don't let myself fall. I look away from her. Not meeting her eyes won't make any difference. I can feel it, her will mingling with mine. Strings tugging at my words, my thoughts, my movements.

"What?" Aliz is still furious, but when she takes in my expression, something shifts.

It's over.

We still had six days left, but somehow, something—I clasp my hands over my mouth and try to slow my breathing, try to stop myself from screaming. *No.* I didn't go through months of torture at Callisto training to bypass compulsion just for Aliz to be able to do it without even *looking* at me. "This can't be happening," I say.

"I didn't—"

"Try it," I say, my throat tight. "Give me an order."

She shakes her head, not looking me in the eye. But she must have felt it, too, a new power granted by the Familiar's mark, because she looks up at me again, expression resolute. The wind blows against the window.

"Twirl," Aliz says, and my body moves, tethered to her volition, spinning around.

I RUN.

I run because although she told me to twirl, she didn't tell me to stay, and as long as I'm not next to her, I'm still free. I don't care if it hurts. I can't let it happen again. I can't let Aliz compel me. No matter what.

I run till I'm past the pine grove, past Kinsnet Library, out in the uncharted field that stretches behind campus. I run to the river, to the bridge that leads to the hunting lodge. Its bricks are riddled with moss, slowly eroding under a few centuries of rain.

Someone is sitting on the wall, legs dangling over the edge. Her hair looks white beneath the dim glow of the half-moon. As I get closer, I see a sketchbook on her lap and a small watercolour palette resting beside her. Julia turns when she notices my presence and tenses. I've been meaning to ask her about her paintings. I know my reaction must have set off some alarms. I wanted to see if there are any sketches that might help me find out more about Gustavsson, or what I've forgotten. But after she ran into Aliz and me in the library, I have a feeling she might be a little less fond of me now.

I'm about to break the silence when I notice her gaze is glued to my neck.

I'm not wearing a polo neck or a scarf. I clasp my hand over the mark, but it's too late.

She's seen it.

"It's not what it looks like," I say. But it *is*.

"What is it?" Julia says, voice wavering.

Of course she doesn't recognise it. My stomach feels heavy. "A Familiar's mark," I say, and she stares at me, silence falling between us. I step closer, till I'm practically next to her. "I'm Aliz's Familiar," I say. For a long moment, minutes perhaps, Julia doesn't say anything.

"Familiar," she says. I dig my nails into the damp wall of the bridge. "You performed a blood contract?"

After a moment, looking into the black river that flows beneath us, I tell her. I'm not sure why, exactly, I can speak to her like this. Maybe because of that strange link in our pasts, which Julia doesn't even know of. But I lean on the wall next to her and tell her everything. "I'll be under her command until the day I die," I say, chest aching.

The damp, cold wind blows at the pages of her sketchbook.

"Immortality isn't as bad as you'd think," Julia finally says, putting down her paintbrush. "I thought my life was over when I was first sired. But the night is just as beautiful as the day when you have our eyes." After a moment, she hands me her sketchbook. The first page is an exact replica of what's in front of us, a sinuous river, moss-covered rocks dictating the water's path, and the Highlands rolling in the distance.

But the colours don't match what I see. The shadows that cloak my vision aren't present on the thick, still-damp pages. Night, captured here upon Julia's sketchbook, is a myriad of blues and violets, of sparkling water and vivid stars.

"Being a vampire has its perks," she says.

I don't know how, but looking at the painting calms me. Slowly, as I breathe, I'm able to focus on the present. "Why are you telling me this?"

"Because only humans can be Familiars," she says. "So if you want, I can sire you, Cassie."

I look up at her, and she's smiling. I've been so caught up in not missing the deadline, on breaking the contract before the full moon, that it hadn't occurred to me that there was another way. A far more obvious way.

Laughter bursts from me before I can stop it, and Julia gawks down at me, brows knotted. "What?"

I shake my head. "I can't," I say. "I'm glad you've made peace with what you are. And thanks for offering, but . . ." I shake my head. "But no thanks." She lets out a whistle-like sigh, before glancing down at me. I feel as though I've offended her. "I know you didn't have the choice," I add. "I'm sorry, Julia."

"Don't apologise," she says softly. She pats the space beside her on the damp wall. Adrenaline is still rushing through my veins. But there's something soothing about Julia. And *soothing* isn't a word I ever thought I'd associate with a vampire. "I don't hate what I am now, but the way I was converted certainly could have been better." I hoist myself up onto the stone ledge, moss between the old bricks. My boots feel heavy as they dangle above the snaking river. I turn to look at her, and she begins to flick through her sketchbook. "Do you want to know how it happened?" she asks.

"If you are comfortable sharing," I say in a small voice.

She presses her lips into a tight line. I have a feeling that, whatever her story is, she'll never be *comfortable* with it.

"Well, I should warn you that it's not a pretty tale," she starts, trying to force her voice into a casual tone. "It involves my death, after all. But most important, I still don't know why they did it."

"They?"

"The—" She hesitates, as though her tongue is stuck on the roof of her mouth. "A vampiric organisation. Not the Council," she clarifies. "I don't remember any names, just—" She flicks through the pages until she stops on a portrait of a woman. With thin layers of watercolour, she's painted a grey hood hiding the vampire's face. The portrait is so detailed that it seems like the woman might come to life at any moment. "She was the one who split us."

"*Split?*" I ask, zipping up the top of my jacket. The mark still itches, but I focus on Julia's voice.

"It was three weeks after graduation. I was eighteen," she starts, turning the pages of her sketchbook until she stops on the drawing of the Tube I saw a while back. "I was going to meet my parents in Trafalgar Square. But the train didn't stop. I honestly don't know how they did it, exactly.

"They hijacked the train. No one panicked. They must have compelled us to stay calm, though I don't remember that." A bitter smile breaks her stoic features. "The train finally stopped at an abandoned station, and the woman split us into two groups. On the right, the party food. Conventionally attractive or with good blood. The rest of us were on the left. I remember standing there for hours, waiting for the end. But here's the funny thing, Cassie. I can't remember my death."

"I'm sorry," I whisper. Julia takes a careful breath. She stares up at the sky. Her hair is almost as white as Aliz's.

"I woke up in a cage," she says. "Each new vampire had their own cage with silver bars. And I was so, *so* thirsty." She makes her way through the pages, finding another drawing. This one is of a large hall, with rows upon rows of cages. Some of them are broken. The silhouettes inside each cage are a blur, but only one, a girl in the cage closest to where Julia must have been, is drawn with photorealistic detail.

"They were starving us on purpose. Do you know what happens to a vampire if they don't drink blood?"

I nod. If a vampire goes seven days without drinking blood, they become *parched*. Slowly, I try to wrap my head around what Julia is telling me. The nightmare she went through. Then I think of my parents. Their deaths, at the hands of parched vampires.

Before I can jump to conclusions, she resumes her story. "The people in the cages around me began to transform, and although I don't remember her name"—she presses her finger beneath the caged woman in her sketch—"we promised each other that whoever turned first would try to get the other one out. She didn't tell me, but she'd spent four days without blood already, because three days after I woke up in there..."

Her pale eyes become bloodshot.

"She—transformed?" I whisper.

"She burst right through her cage," Julia says. "I'm not sure if you've ever seen a parched vampire. They're huge. But somehow, in her last moment of sanity, she—" Julia tightens her grip on her sketchbook. "She cracked the bars of my cage, not enough for the others to notice, but enough for me to..."

She lets me fill in the gaps of what happened next. "I was so thirsty, I couldn't think straight. Somehow, I made it to a hospital, and instinct led me to the morgue." Her shoulders tremble. "Before I could desecrate a corpse, Ife's brother found me."

She inhales deeply, closing her sketchbook with a thump. "And now you'll never look at me the same," she says in a small voice.

Instinctively, I grab her hand. "Don't say that." I feel my throat tighten. "None of what happened was your fault."

Julia bites down another pained smile, her pale lashes damp. "I couldn't save anyone. All those people—" I squeeze her hand. I want to tell her that I know how she feels. But I can't think of any words that fit the hole in Julia's chest. I can't find them for myself, either. Just revenge.

"The people who kidnapped you..." I tread carefully, waiting for her to change the subject. But she doesn't. "Did they have any emblems? Anything..." She opens the first page of her sketchbook, and there it is, an insignia on someone's uniform. A red *V*, with a silver sword cutting through it. Somehow, I know what it is. A shadowy vampire organisation that is not the Council is what Julia called them. *The Vassals.* She closes the book again, and I can hear my pulse in my ears. Both Aliz and Julia were victims of the Vassals.

And if Gustavsson is what I think he is, then my parents were also the Vassals' victims.

"Does the Council know that happened to you?" I ask, and Julia frowns as she thinks.

"They must. Ife's brother contacted them immediately. Though I can't remember them interviewing me."

"Ares Astra is the president of the Council," I say carefully, and Julia tenses. "Do you think his"—I hesitate, unsure of what to call them—"*visits* could have anything to do with how you were converted?"

"Maybe," she whispers. "But luckily enough, I haven't dreamt of him in three years." She closes her sketchbook, holding it tight. "Remember, if you don't want to be Astra's familiar, I'm happy to sire you. Though I might need instructions on how to do that."

"Thank you," I say. She smiles. And although Julia doesn't know it yet, I'm planning on avenging her, and all those humans she couldn't save, too.

BY THE TIME I reach the hunting lodge, everything that happened with Aliz has been summoned back into my mind. Elia sits by the entrance, and I stare up at the old palace in awe. She's already finished decorating the exterior, cobwebs and ghosts on the top half, pumpkins and scarecrows between each column. Red fairy lights dangle from the wisteria. "What do you think?" she asks.

"I'm her Familiar," I say. Elia's eyes flicker to my neck, and she cocks her head.

"No, you're not."

"But Aliz compelled me."

"With just her words?" she asks. I nod, weakness returning to my knees.

"Rebecca, you still have the thorned vines around the mark, don't you?"

"Yes?" I ask, and Elia takes my hand, soothing me.

"If the contract were to be sealed, only the moon and the first ring of thorns would remain on your neck. All these other lines represent your resistance to the contract. Obviously your body, and Aliz's powers, are going to try to make you seal the contract, so now it's letting her feel the power of what comes with having a Blood Familiar."

The pressure that had been building in my chest slowly starts to deflate. I sit down on the front steps and Elia crouches at my side. "It's not too late," she says, finger pausing on the mark. "You're still free, Rebecca."

"So, it's up to her now?" I ask.

Elia sighs, looking out at the woods. "Seems like it. But Aliz is stronger than you think. She cares for you, you know." I make a face. "Outside of whatever the mark makes her feel, she cares for you."

"Gustavsson," I say as I pick up one of the smaller pumpkins, knocking on it to check if it's real. "Has he agreed to play at the ball?"

"Yes," she says. "But he might run away if he knows we're on to him." Elia pauses, staring at me intently. "And we need him there. Whether you get him to talk or not, he's the only target for the ritual, Rebecca."

Elia gets up, dusting down her trousers. It's my first time seeing her in something other than a skirt or dress. She pushes one of the large doors open, revealing the interior of the palace, decorated much like the outside, with dried wreaths and pumpkins. The portraits of Ada Astra have all been removed and replaced by far more macabre paintings. A ghoulish old man devouring a child, face covered in blood. Ghostly figures marching across a hill. "I have contacts in the Prado," Elia says. "Can you even call it a Halloween party if you don't have Goya's *Pinturas negras* on display?"

"I can't say I'm familiar with them," I say. I don't know where the Prado is, either. But all the same, I'm transfixed by the canvases, a dozen candles reflecting off the glass keeping them safe. "By *contacts*, do you mean you compelled someone who works there?"

"I don't kiss and tell," she replies. I sigh and focus on an enormous canvas, four metres long. The thick brushstrokes make up a congregation of old women, their macabre expressions sending shivers down my spine. There's a large goat presiding over their meeting. The title, embossed into the frame, reads *El Aquelarre*.

"What does that mean?" I ask, pointing at the words.

"The coven," Elia says, lowering her voice.

The surrounding sculptures have also been replaced. Instead of nymphs or busts of old vampires, there are creatures with grotesque expressions carved in marble, with great horns or bat wings, and all of them holding little basins which on the night of the party, I assume will be filled with blood.

"What if we're wrong about Gustavsson?" Even as I ask this, I know we're not. "What if he's innocent?"

We bypass the grand staircase, which she's cut off with red rope, and walk straight into the crystal ballroom. She's adorned the crystal walls with twisted branches and fairy lights. She turns to look at me, her voice cooling before she says: "You've probably killed more than a few innocent vampires already, haven't you?"

"I only kill monsters," I say. There's a stage in the corner of the ballroom, and I stop to look up at it. My neck aches and itches as the mark tells me to return to my master. I ignore the pain. "I've never killed anyone who hasn't tried to kill me first."

"I suppose I'd be a hypocrite to hold your past against you," she says, taking my hand. Her soft grip is strangely comforting. "In my worst moments of thirst, I've taken lives that probably didn't deserve to be taken. Especially during my first year as a vampire."

I shiver at that, my prejudices bubbling up.

"I don't think Aliz will do the *ritual* with me," I say. I don't know what else to call Ada's cure. "She's not like us."

"I'll try to talk some sense into her," Elia says. She lets go of my hand and offers me a sad smile. As though she already knows it's a lost cause.

chapter THIRTY-FOUR

I don't get back to the room until after midnight. Aliz is sitting at her desk, going through some of the books we borrowed from the Palau Collection during the early days of the mark, back when neither of us knew Palau was, in fact, Elia. She seems surprised to see that I've returned, and in a way, I am, too. I didn't wait to see how she reacted to her compelling me.

My neck itches, and I try my best to ignore it. Our argument, unfinished, hangs in the air between us.

MY FRIENDS ARE at their usual table in the far corner of Ambrose Hall, playing cards. Stephan is drinking beer; the vampires, blood. I wait for them to bombard me with questions about my new life as a Familiar. But no such questions come.

I glance at Julia, her face serious as always as she picks up a card from the pile spread across the table. They're playing Go Fish, and as soon as I join, Ife steals my two queens. Julia hasn't told any of them about the Familiar's mark. She doesn't even look at my neck while we sit. I want to squeeze her arm and thank her, but I shouldn't.

"So, what are you all wearing to the ball?" I ask.

"Oh, it's a surprise," Ife says, picking a card.

"I wanted to go as a zombie cheerleader," Julia says, the choice slightly out of character. "But apparently that's not *formal* enough for Elia."

"And you, Cassie?" Stephan asks.

"Also a surprise," I say. I've not thought about it yet. My cards are absolutely crap, entirely mismatched. But then I ask Ife for her nines, and after gritting her teeth, she tosses three my way. I smile back at her, placing my first set upon the table. We play another three rounds before I hear them behind us.

Elia's arrival is heralded by the clicking of her stilettos upon the tiled floor. Then, a familiar pair of hands rests on my shoulders. My muscles loosen, the burning itch in my neck fades. I look up, and Aliz stares straight back down at me. Despite our proximity, she still feels miles away. Her gaze shifts across the table, and confusion creases her brows. I don't understand the expression until I see Julia, and the ice that she doesn't even try to conceal from her gaze.

"Invitations," Elia says, handing out little red envelopes while I feel tension growing between Aliz and Julia. But luckily enough, neither of them says anything.

OUR BEDROOM WINDOW is open, the night free of clouds. I catch a glimpse of the waxing moon. The ball is on Tuesday, and I feel more helpless now than I did when I first found the mark. I hear the door unlocking and quickly slip behind my bed's curtains. Aliz doesn't say a word when she steps inside.

You're always lying.

I know she suspects me. I'm not entirely sure what she suspects, but she hasn't looked at me the same since our fight. The pain in my chest is greater than the mark's sting. I don't want to be her Familiar, but I don't want to ruin her, either. She doesn't deserve this. Tugging at my bed's curtains, I look across the room. The black divider is pulled across, blocking her from view.

Things are worse now than when we first met. At least then, although we couldn't stand each other, I could still *see* her. And even though we still sleep side by side to avoid our nightmares coming back, that is the extent of our proximity. We don't speak. I swallow hard and make my way across the room, stopping just outside her curtains.

"Can we talk?" I ask.

"Sure." Her voice is nasal.

I lift one curtain and find Aliz staring down at me from her coffin. Her eyes are bloodshot.

"I probably shouldn't talk," she says. "I don't want it to happen again."

I take in her features. The urge to reach out and grab her hands burns through my veins. But I ignore it. "All right," I whisper.

I already know what I want to say. I know what I'll be giving up, but there is no alternative. Unless we magically find another cure before Tuesday night. "This might be a lot to ask from you," I start, trying to keep my voice composed. Sure of myself. "But if the mark becomes permanent"—I touch my neck, fingers trembling against my skin—"will you sire me?"

Aliz's eyes widen, and before I can make sense of her expression, she bends over, hiding her face. I hear a deep inhale before she says:

"You know, you've told me a lot of lies. But when you said you'd rather die than become a vampire, I knew you were telling the truth."

My chest stings.

"Only if we don't find another cure," I say.

I reach out to touch her knee. For a second I think she's going to push me away. Instead, she grabs my wrist and pulls me close, wrapping her arms around my shoulders.

"We'll fix it," I say, voice cracking. It could be worse. I could hate her. I could have more to lose. But if we're not able to perform the *cure,* I'd rather give up my mortality than my free will. And if anyone is going to turn me into the monster I've spent the last four years fighting, I want it to be her.

She pulls back slightly, brushing my cheek. Her eyes search mine, and I nod. In a matter of seconds I'm melting into her, her lips just as hungry as they were during our first kiss.

I climb up onto the coffin, pushing her down. The wood creaks as I undo the buttons of her waistcoat.

"Am I still not allowed to touch?" I ask. I tug the last pearly button of her shirt open. Beneath it, she's in a cotton vest, nipples hard against the fabric.

"I want you to," she says, breathless.

"But?"

She sits up suddenly, her shirt falling down her toned arms, while pushing me back in the process. "But I still don't trust myself," she whispers, hiking up my skirt. "You smell too good." She traces the contour of the mark with her fingers, a slow line from my neck down my torso, and although the thorns end just beneath the waist, Aliz continues, following her fingers with her lips, managing, in just a few minutes, to undo all my worries.

THE FULL MOON is hidden behind thick clouds right outside our window. Soon it will be at the same spot where it was when Aliz and I first performed the blood contract. Somehow, that night feels years away already.

While Aliz is showering, I strap on my weapons, just as I did when I went to Inverness. Three silver daggers to my thigh, but no cross this time. My stake, with my real name etched into the wood, I slot into a pocket that Elia has sewn into the white wings that go with my costume.

Its cut is not too dissimilar from that of the dresses I wear to blood parties. And considering what I'm going to do, perhaps it's appropriate. The fabric is pleated chiffon, with a layer of silk underneath it. I pull the dress on. It has long, off-the-shoulder sleeves, with a golden thread crisscrossed up the length of the fabric.

By the end of the night, if things go our way, it'll be dyed crimson with blood.

I'm struggling with the zip of the dress when the bathroom door creaks open. Aliz walks out, towel around her shoulders, wearing a white vest and a pair of black leather trousers. Her hair is still damp, sticking to her forehead.

"Could you give me a hand?" I ask, the zip stuck halfway up my back.

Aliz nods. I'm not used to her being so quiet. She's been communicating in texts, afraid of accidentally commanding me again. I only heard her voice in the middle of the night, when we got carried away, her lips on my neck, and her hand between my legs. She draws the zip all the way up and does a few buttons that I hadn't noticed were there.

"Thanks," I whisper while she reaches for her phone.

> What are you dressed as?

"Cupid," I say, putting on the wings. "Elia said she wore this same outfit eighty years ago."

Aliz's gaze stops on the spot where the Familiar's mark starts, well hidden beneath a coat of tattoo concealer. "What's *your* costume?"

I run my fingers along the leather waistband of her trousers. My dress may be eighty years old, but Elia has kept it impeccable. Aliz's trousers, on the other hand, look lived in, with tears hastily sewn shut here and there. She hesitates before she texts me again.

> It's a surprise.

Before I can complain about the vagueness of her answer, she asks if I want her to do my hair. "Sure," I say. I sit on my desk chair, and she slowly pleats my hair into a crown, leaving a few loose strands to frame my face. "Do I look decent?" I ask as she tilts my head.

"Like an angel," she whispers, momentarily forgetting her self-imposed silence.

"I suppose the wings help."

She kisses me, but I try to keep it chaste, pulling back before we can get carried away. I can't let her find the weapons strapped to my thigh.

I will tell her.

Regardless of what happens tonight, once midnight passes, whether I am free or the blood contract becomes permanent, I will tell her all that I've kept from her. Even if it costs me everything, even if she never looks at me again, I will not tell her another lie. At least once, I want to hear her say my real name.

> What are you thinking?

I stare at her text, then back at her, my throat dry. If I tell her the truth now, I will ruin everything. So, I say the one thing about myself that isn't a lie.

"I love you," I whisper.

chapter
THIRTY-FIVE

I cycle to the hunting lodge, bow bouncing between my wings as I cross the stone bridge. There are silver arrows stashed throughout the palace. It'll be fairly straightforward. Shoot Gustavsson in the head, and then beg Aliz to share his heart with me. Bile burns my throat, and I look up.

The moon looms full and bloated over the woods. It won't look red until midnight, during the eclipse. The wind nips my shoulders and the gaps in my flowy sleeves. Hopefully Elia has found a way to heat up the palace, or I may freeze to death before midnight strikes.

Elia has decorated the surrounding trees with the same crimson fairy lights as the rest of the house, and I recall that first dream of the maze, a crow with bright red eyes pecking Aliz's dying body.

The ball is already in full swing when I walk in, hallways crowded with vampires drinking from wineglasses. Just one misdemeanor will give me an excuse to kill.

To steal a heart.

The vampires around me turn to stare, and as I avoid their thirst-filled gazes, I realise I am somewhat underdressed. My skirt falls just above the knee. The surrounding vampires are in floor-length gowns covered in ruffles, lace, and crystals. Some look like avant-garde dresses straight off a runway, while others are period pieces from a myriad of countries and centuries. And all, regardless of their cut or style, are dripping with opulence.

Elia promised she'd convinced Gustavsson to play in a string quartet, and as I glance towards the end of the ballroom, I see him. My heart hammers in my chest. Even though he's one of four, I somehow hear his cello above the rest, the sound of it engraved in my ears. He doesn't glance in my direction.

Unease bubbles in my stomach. I soon spot Stephan and Ife amongst the dancing couples, the vampire laughing, throwing her head back while her human boyfriend whispers something in her ear. Stephan is dressed as a scarecrow, hay sticking out from a patchwork suit, a straw hat hiding his thick brown hair.

Ife is in an ethereal black gown with a bodice constructed entirely out of feathers, which elongate as they cascade down into the skirt. Silver details are sprinkled throughout, lines are painted around her eyes, creating swirling shimmers. Her hair is in braids, pinned atop her head with a little piece of hay sticking out, linking her costume to Stephan's.

I've never felt jealous of them until now, when I realise I'll never have what they have. Even if I miraculously get rid of the mark, even if Aliz decided that her feelings for me are real, we would never be able to act like they do. She wouldn't love me in public.

"How do I look?"

Beside me, in a nineteenth-century suit full of tears and loose threads, is Julia. Her skin is painted in a myriad of blues, greens, and purples. There are a few carefully placed lines cutting across her skin. Stitches, holding together the mismatched hues. And pulling it all together are two metal bolts, glued to her hair.

"Ghastly," I say. "Are you Frankenstein's monster?"

"The one and only," Julia says with a grin. "Want to dance?"

"I'm not very good," I warn her.

Julia laughs. "Me neither," she says.

Her cool hand feels brittle in my own, so light it could snap if I hold it tight. She glances around, trying to figure out the steps of the dance. "I think it's a waltz," I say, putting an arm around her waist and pulling her closer.

"I love waltzing," she says, stepping on me.

"My favourite dance," I reply, stumbling out of the way of a couple who clearly know what they're doing.

Stephan and Ife soon glide past us, too, and Ife calls out, "You're doing great, sweetie!"

"Thanks, Mum!" Julia shouts back. When she looks down at me, she's still smiling. And as I look at her, I decide that it won't be so bad. If Aliz sires me, at least I'll have vampire friends. And I'll be able to tell Julia everything. She'll understand, won't she?

The waltz comes to an end, and I feel a hand on my shoulder.

"Can I have this dance?"

Aliz's hair is combed away from her face, and at first, I have no idea what her all-black costume is supposed to be. For once, it's not a suit. Rather, it's an amalgamation of old leather and some other sturdy fabric, with a heavy cape falling past her waist.

"Sure," I say, and I send Julia an apologetic glance.

"Save me another one for later," Julia says before disappearing behind the other dancing couples.

"I don't know how to dance," I say, far more self-conscious of how I'm moving now that Aliz is in front of me.

Aliz raises a brow, giving me a *you don't say* look. Considering she's the heir to the Astra family, I shouldn't be surprised that Aliz is able to lead me so easily. We turn, and I feel something hard press to my thigh. I glance down and see a scabbard. I swallow and look up at her again.

"What exactly are you dressed as?"

"It's a little hard for me to text like this, Cassie," she says.

"Just tell me."

She twirls me, and when I'm facing her again, she says: "This is Catherine Lovelace's old uniform. So, I suppose you could say I'm dressed as a vampire hunter."

Aliz doesn't smile or laugh after saying this. For a horrible second, I think she's going to say it. *I know what you are.* But she doesn't. Her expression is somber for an entirely different reason.

"I've found someone," she whispers. "Well, Elia found him." Aliz's grip is tight on my waist. She glances towards the stage and then back down at me. "Gustavsson."

I struggle to keep my expression straight. If we kill Gustavsson before I get a chance to talk to him, I'll never know why he was at my prom. But there's too much at stake to worry about keeping him alive. I swallow hard and look over at our target. He's fixated on a few girls in the crowd, occasionally smiling at them. Is that what he did during my prom?

"Are you sure you want to do this, Aliz?" I ask.

Her expression softens, but the sadness remains there.

"Yes. I can't make you give up your mortality because of me. Because this *is* my fault. If I'd stopped to think for one fucking second before giving you my blood, I would have realised it was a bad idea. But I was so worried about you." The quick waltz is nearing its end, and Aliz's voice tightens. "I hadn't been able to think of anything but you, and suddenly"—she lets out a shaky breath—"you were dying. And I couldn't let that happen."

She presses her forehead to mine, and I breathe in carefully. The next dance starts. "How will we do it?" I ask in a low voice. I already have a plan bubbling in my head.

"Uh . . ." She glances over at him. "I could tell him I need to talk," she says.

"No," I whisper. I grit my teeth, feeling sick before I say it. "I'll lure him upstairs. He won't turn down my blood." Before Aliz can interrupt me, I add, "I won't let him drink. We just need to get him out of the crowd. You wait in your sister's room. I'll get him there."

Her hands shake as it becomes real. "It's dangerous."

"Of course it is," I say, and I reach up to cup her cheek. "But if you really want to do it, this is our best plan."

Despite being in a crowd, despite all the loose lips around us, Aliz ducks down and kisses me. A short and chaste kiss, but just as sweet. "Are you sure?" she asks.

"Yes," I say. "Do you know how to use that thing?" I ask, glancing down at the sword.

Aliz gives a brief nod. "I was a bit of a fencing prodigy as a child," she says. She takes a deep breath. "I just have to imagine I'm my father. Or sister. Or literally any other Astra to have walked the earth."

"I'll meet you up there at the end of the next dance," I say.

I still can't believe she's agreed to this. My hands tremble. If Gustavsson remembers me, and I have a feeling he does, he'll reveal my identity. Perhaps a part of it. He might say my name, and all of Aliz's questions will come tumbling out.

Hopefully those questions will be answered *after* we get rid of the mark.

I take a deep breath and reach back within myself until I'm the same vampire hunter I was before reaching Tynahine. When I could slip into a blood party and convince anyone I wanted to follow me off into a dark and dangerous place.

I start to cross the ballroom, and before I reach the stage, I bump into Elia, whose costume is a long muslin gown, Roman inspired. The sort of thing she probably wore in her youth, two thousand years ago. Her hair is half up and half down, silver threaded throughout it. She looks like a goddess, the little half-moon on her head telling me she's meant to be Diana.

"Good luck," she whispers. She was the one who was able to convince Aliz. I squeeze her hands, trying to find the words to thank her. Instead, I just nod and walk on.

The stage looms above me. The four musicians are in ruffled suits from the eighteenth century, with short trousers and knee-high stockings. Capes fall behind them, and their instruments are decorated with skulls and spiders. One of them has even put on a powdered wig.

Gustavsson is in the same getup, though his is a little less flamboyant. Instead of silver or green, his suit is black and white. And when his eyes meet mine, I know I've got him.

"Professor?" I call up. His fluid playing, which until now hadn't faltered at all, stutters, the scent of my blood turning his eyes crimson. I've done something a little risky, enough for all the vampires around me to turn and stare, too: I've made a small cut on my palm, which healed immediately, but left a film of blood.

"What is it, Cassie?" he asks. "Haven't seen you in class." His voice crawls under my skin, familiar. But I keep my face set in a mild picture of lust.

"I've been dying to see you," I say. "How long are you playing for?"

He looks at me, aghast. I press on.

"I want to continue our *conversation*."

"Won't Miss Astra mind?" he asks, glancing across the ballroom. I shake my head.

"She doesn't have to know."

He raises a brow and then looks at his fellow musicians. They stare at me, thirst staining their eyes red, but they don't stop playing. "I can escape at the end of this pavane," Gustavsson says. "One minute."

I glance up at the crystal ceiling, the moon hanging between the branches and red fairy lights. We're going to get rid of it. At the other end of the ballroom, I spot Elia drawing Julia into conversation, possibly to keep her from seeing me.

"Where shall we go?" asks Gustavsson. "There's a lovely maze out there."

He jumps down, leaving the quartet as a trio.

"Upstairs," I say. "I want to see the rest of the palace." I press my hand, with its drying blood, to his, and he inhales me a little deeper.

"Wherever you want, then, Cassie," he says. He grabs my wrist and pulls me through the crowd. I get déjà vu as I walk behind him, trying to keep up. My stomach burns.

Is this what happened on prom night? Did Vicki stand in a corner and watch as he dragged me, willingly, to another end of the hotel?

My throat tightens as I try to clear my mind of what might have happened. Of what he did that I no longer remember.

"It's closed off," he says, sounding disappointed when we reach the bottom of the grand staircase.

"Don't tell me you've never broken the rules," I chide, climbing over the red rope. He lets out a short laugh.

"See, I told you you were going to get me into trouble," he says.

"Isn't that what you want?" I ask, running up the marble stairs, past the portrait of Ada Astra, who watches as he chases after me. I laugh, speeding up, my heart thumping. I feel my pulse in my ears, nausea crawling up my chest.

I just need to get him into Ada Astra's room. Then we shut the door and kill him.

I spot a silver arrow behind one of the statues. Hopefully I won't have to use it. Hopefully Aliz hasn't forgotten her own skills and we'll get it over with quickly.

"I don't remember you being this fun last time, Rebecca!" he calls, just as I'm about to reach the end of the hall, where Aliz is hiding.

The sound of my name almost knocks me off my feet, and before I can even think of how to respond he grabs the back of my head, threading his fingers into the pleated crown, and slams me against one of the mirrors.

The pain blinds me for a second, and when I open my eyes, his hands are clasping my cheeks, and his eyes glow a vibrant red, boring into mine before he says: "Kill yourself."

"No!"

The scream comes from Ada Astra's room. Aliz runs out while I feel blood trickle down my face. She's not wielding her sword, instead she simply sprints towards us while Gustavsson stares back at her, amused.

"The useless heir," he says, before reaching forward and licking my face.

I can't use my stake. It would damage the heart. Instead, I lunge at him, knee between his legs. Just as he lets out a groan, he turns into a bat. I'm not allowing a repeat of Inverness, so before he can fly off, I reach for the silver arrow behind the statue. I ignore the pain in my head as I aim and release the arrow. He transforms back into his humanoid form, the arrow in his stomach.

I don't look at Aliz. I don't have time to see her expression—the slow realisation that I have lied to her about absolutely everything.

"Not a bad shot," Gustavsson says, his voice jarringly calm. Despite the fact that the silver will burn him, he wraps his hands around the arrow in his stomach, and pulls it out in one fluid motion, his hands sizzling. "But you should have aimed for my head."

He's wounded, but even so, before I can reach him, he again turns into a bat, disappearing down the staircase.

"No!" I shout.

I reach the arrow too late. When I pull back my bow, he's gone.

"Cassie?"

Adrenaline continues to pump through my veins, and I lower my weapon, turning.

Aliz stares at me, face drained of colour. "He compelled you to kill yourself," she says, voice tight.

"I'm fine," I say.

I look along the hallway, into the open door leading to Ada Astra's room. The open window is visible from here. And cut out against it, is a silhouette.

I recognise her even with a mask on. The woman who taught me how to survive in the shadows.

Penny lifts a weapon, a crossbow armed with a long stake, and fires.

chapter THIRTY-SIX

I push Aliz aside, the stake landing just an inch away from us. "Leave!" I shout, without looking at her.

Aliz stares up at me, eyes wide and confused. "What—"

"Run," I say, just as Penny's steps echo across the hallway, walking towards us, "Aliz, please—"

"What's the rush?"

Penny's rich voice, so familiar, fills the hallway. I stare at the crossbow in her hands, she arms it with another stake. *No.* "Go," I say again, but Aliz doesn't move, staring at Penny with a slack jaw. At the black uniform, the modern version of what Aliz is wearing. As soon as she's close enough, Aliz shields her eyes from the cross on Penny's white mask, hissing under her breath. "Aliz—"

"Don't worry, Rebecca, I'm not going to hurt her."

"Rebecca?" Aliz echoes.

I've been longing to hear her say my real name. But this is not how I wanted it to happen. My eyes burn. It's over.

It's okay, I tell myself. I just need to keep Penny distracted. Long enough for Aliz to run.

"What are you doing here?" I ask. I think back to our last call, when Penny said everything was fine.

"I won't hurt her, as long as you give me *The Book of Blood and Roses,*" she says slowly.

The mask doesn't come off. Carefully, I arrange my bow and arrow. I might not be able to defeat Penny in a fight, but I can keep her back long enough for Aliz to escape. "Go," I cry again.

"Who is Rebecca?" Aliz asks, staring at me. Her voice trembles. And Penny, behind her mask, laughs. It's a long drawn-out sound, which slips behind each statue, until it sounds as though they are laughing as well. Never, in four years, have I heard her laugh, so I can't imagine what her face looks like.

"I'm not the only one she's lied to, am I?" Penny says. "Poor little Miss Astra."

"Aliz, *go!*" I shout.

"I have a very simple proposition for you, Rebecca," Penny says, stopping two statues away from us. "Give me the book, and Astra lives."

"We don't have it," I choke out.

"Liar," Penny says. I was so busy looking at the crossbow that I didn't see her raise her left hand, a silver gun aiming straight at Aliz. Too late, I shove her aside. Aliz lets out a strangled sound, grasping at her waist, blood dripping to the white marble floor. "Our Father who art in Heaven," Penny starts, and Aliz hisses, covering her ears all while her torso burns, a silver bullet embedded inside her.

"Stop it!" I scream at Penny, and before I can think straight, I run at her, ready to plunge the arrow into her chest.

Penny laughs again and kicks me just as I reach her. The blow sends me flying against one of the sculptures, which falls between us, outstretched arm crumbling in two. I try to find Aliz, but before I see her, Penny is pulling me back up.

"Tell me where the book is, and she'll live." Penny slams my head against the mirror, and I feel the glass crack, my blood freezing cold when it reaches my neck. The hallway spins, and although the wound heals quickly, the pain in my head doesn't fade. "Tell me, and I'll make sure your own death is quick, Rebecca."

"My father burnt the library!" Aliz sounds far away. Her voice is still strained. Penny's grip slackens on me an inch.

"That's not possible," she says. "Faust told me you found it."

She takes off her mask, and I find Penny wearing an expression I've never seen before. Her eyes are wide and wild. For the first time since I met her, she's not an emotionless soldier.

"Why are you doing this?" I choke out.

Penny stares at me as if I'm a stranger. "Did you really think you could betray me and be rewarded for it?" she asks, hands around my neck, cutting off my breathing. "Give me my fucking book, you stupid, stupid girl."

She tightens her grip, and I see white. My eyes feel as though they're about to pop out of their sockets.

"I betrayed you?" I squeeze out, warm tears mingling the blood on my face. "I know I wasn't recruited by accident. I know—"

I don't know what Penny does next, but the room goes black. And with my last thread of consciousness, I hear Aliz's voice.

"The only thing in the library was my sister's ghost!"

I hit the ground, either because Penny let go, or because Aliz somehow got her off me.

I cough, trying my hardest to breathe. My ears ring, and when I look back up, the only person I see staring down at me is Aliz.

I look along the hallway, my heart racing, waiting to see Penny aiming her crossbow.

But she's gone.

Slowly, strength returns to my body, every internal wound knitting itself back together. I take careful breaths.

"I thought my sister was just trying to get under my skin," Aliz says, standing over me. The silver bullet which moments ago had been burning through her side has fallen to the floor. I can't make out her expression when I meet her dark gaze. "But you really did lie about your name."

"I can explain," I start, and Aliz's eyes widen in disbelief.

"I gave you so many chances to do so," she says, voice breaking. I move, ready to grab her, and she says, "Don't touch me!"

"Aliz!" I get up, trying to keep my mind in one piece. "Please—"

She runs from me, the way any ordinary vampire would run if they knew what I was. "Wait!" I shout.

"Don't follow me!" she snarls, and I feel those words, the power laced in them, stopping me in my tracks just above the staircase. She runs down, and I stay right there, staring at the portrait of Ada Astra. My eyes burn, and if I have a soul, it starts to crumble, falling apart while the lines hidden beneath a thick coat of makeup dig into my skin.

If I can't follow her, I'll find her, anyway. I run along the hallway, back to Ada Astra's bedroom. The window is still open, the way Penny must have come in. I wipe away tears, but it's no use. Aliz won't forgive me for this. Penny hates me. I've ruined everything.

I look out, and there, just outside the ballroom, is the maze.

Gustavsson stands at the entrance of it, arms folded, staring up at me with a wide grin, eyes glowing red.

Aliz will let our contract seal, and after midnight, her wishes will become my own. But if there's one thing I can still do, it's carve the truth out of that piece of shit.

I jump onto the roof of the ballroom, its thick glass damp. I don't look down to see if anyone has noticed me above them. I don't waste time, running across the sloping glass, not letting myself slide off the side. Just as I reach the edge, before I jump, Gustavsson vanishes into the maze.

chapter
THIRTY-SEVEN

In the dream, I was always the prey. Aliz was always the one hunting me.

Now everything is different. Everything is over. I snap a branch in two, making myself a cross. I stalk through the hedges, ire bubbling in my veins. *Don't follow me.* It's over. Even if I lose my free will tonight, Aliz will never look at me the same again. She'll never love me again.

I dig my nails into my palms. This is how I was back when I was training. When the wound of my parents' deaths was still fresh and open. And with every stake, every arrow meeting its target, Penny would say, *You're closer.* I rub tears away as I realise that I've wasted four years of my life.

And as soon as I got breathing room from Callisto, I started to feel whole again.

"You're so slow, Rebecca!" the vampire calls, three hedges ahead of me, and I speed up. I know the maze's path by heart already.

I reach him just as he arrives at the rosebush at the centre, sheltered by four statues. He stops, and I do, too, scared that the wrong move will send him flying off in bat form.

"I usually forget most of the girls I select," he says, inching behind the rosebush, leaning on one of the sculptures, missing its head. I take a careful step towards him but keep the makeshift cross down at my side. I have a stake tucked behind my costume wings. But I can't show him my cards yet. "Do you want to know why I remember you?"

"My blood tasted amazing?" I ask. The wind blows at the maze, the drying branches making a rattling sound. The moon's still high above us. If I were to carve out his heart and eat it alone, would that work?

"Oh, it still tastes good," he says. "Even better than when you were eighteen."

My chin trembles, and I try to get the image out of my head. That which I can't remember. Maybe my mind comes up with something far worse than the truth. Maybe all he did was a small cut. Maybe it was just a small taste. That's all Gustavsson did, wasn't it?

"No, Rebecca," he says, and his eerie grin softens, expression losing tension. "Usually, I don't get involved with what happens next, and while I wouldn't have known you were related, your father's blood smelled exactly like yours. Tasted even better."

The lines that cross my body burn, digging into me. For once I'm grateful for the pain, because without it, I would have lost my mind.

"Do you work with Callisto?" I say, blinking, trying to detach myself from his words.

"That's a rather loaded question," he says, snapping one of the roses from the bush and lifting it to his nose. I could swear that blood drips from the stem. "Sometimes they are running short on hunters, so we point them in the right direction. Most girls I pick are for parties," he says, inspecting the rose. "Though if I know Callisto is looking for people, I'll compel my girls to do a little more."

I dig my nails into my neck, breathing through the pain.

"You, for example. I made you run around the hotel three times. Run up the stairs, and even in high heels, you did an all right job. You showed potential. But the main test was when I compelled you to kill me. Some people are natural-born hunters, and as soon as I saw that look in your eye, I knew I'd found something special. We had such a wonderful time."

My fingers shake around my makeshift cross.

"And then you killed my parents?" Somehow, my voice is still steady enough, even though I feel as though every inch of me has cracked.

"It wasn't me," he says, lifting his hands up in a mock plea of innocence. The rose falls to the ground. "It was Callisto that ordered it. They had to give you a reason to join them, so they found one for you. I was just there to clean up the mess and have the leftovers. See, Rebecca, if you weren't about to die, I wouldn't tell you this. But I can see it in your eyes, you need closure, don't you?"

I give a small nod. *Die?* Does he really think he can kill me?

"The night your parents died was what we call the Feast of the Parched," he says. "The parched are quite easy to control, you just give them your blood and send them off to kill whoever you wish, without having to get your hands dirty. We kept fifty newly sired vampires in an old train station, deprived them of blood, and ever so slowly, they transformed. Then we set them free to ravage the city. The vampires who killed your parents had another five targets that night, so don't feel too special."

"Who is *we*?" I ask, as the massacre he described starts to come into focus. "The Vassals?"

"You've heard of us?" He cocks his head. "If only you'd completed your mission correctly, Rebecca," he chides, "you would have been made a Stake of Callisto, and who knows, we may have wound up working together."

At this, I finally snap, lunging forward. My blood boils as I knock him down, a scream caught in my throat. It was all my fault. If I hadn't caught his eye, if he hadn't smelled my blood, if I hadn't shown *potential,* my parents would still be alive. I land a punch in his face, and he laughs. Then I press my thumbs against his eyes, screaming at him, but before I push inwards, I feel the thorns of the Familiar's mark moving, shredding through my skin.

For a moment, I see white, the pain freezing every muscle in my body, telling me to seal the contract with Aliz. But Aliz is gone. And as I try to remember how to breathe, I feel him pushing me down.

"I seldom get to enjoy this," Gustavsson says, his grip on my arms gentle. "I've only led to the recruitment of a handful of hunters, but they all die before our paths cross again. So from the moment I saw you here"—he clasps my cheek, and I look up at him, taking in his crimson eyes—"I've been fantasizing about this moment. Every time you looked at me from the back of my classroom, I imagined how it would feel to snap your neck."

Slowly, the pain starts to recede. I wonder if midnight has passed already, if the mark is now permanent. Regardless, I feel my strength return to my muscles, and after a short breath, I throw my weight against him, flipping us over and digging my knee between his legs. He hisses, and I do what Penny did earlier, stringing together prayers to keep him down.

He covers his ears, all while I reach behind my back, through the feathers of my wings, where I know it's hiding, just in case. There's no point in keeping him alive. It's too late. I grip my stake, and just as I'm about to slam it into him, he stabs my arm. I miss, pain searing through me as I spot the open gash.

The wound heals a few seconds later, and, "That's interesting," Gustavsson says, as he gets on top of me again. "You became someone's Familiar? If I knew you were willing, I may have offered you the position myself," he says, grabbing the stake that missed his heart. "But alas, we're running out of time. The quartet are missing their cellist."

I stare at the moon as he plunges the stake through my torso, a guttural scream muffled as he clasps a hand over my mouth. I try to reach for the stake to pull it out, but I'm already losing feeling in my hands. The wound can't heal if the stake is still inside. My whole body feels like it's melting, my skin trying to lace itself back together but finding an obstacle.

Gustavsson ducks down, licking the side of the stake. My scream is bottled beneath his hand. "You know something, Rebecca," he says, his voice slowing. "When I moved their bodies into the car, your father was already dead. Yet somehow, your mother—and I'm sure you remember the state in which she was found—she was still breathing. I told her I was a police officer and to squeeze my hand if she could hear me."

Dread climbs through my chest, momentarily washing away the pain. *No.*

"She squeezed it, so then I told her what awaited you. 'Your daughter is going to spend the rest of her life avenging you,' I said. And I went into every detail of a hunter's training. 'They'll fry her brain,' I said, 'and they'll cut her off from her family,' I said as well. But I think what really killed her was when I told her what your missions would consist of. 'Your daughter will be the lowest of hunters. She'll be used as bait and will be dead after a few missions.' Oh, you should have seen her face."

My tears spill over my cheekbones.

I look up at the moon again, and that's when I see her behind him, a flash of white.

Her silver sword cuts through the back of his head, and Gustavsson lets out a growl, eyes wide. And before he can turn into a bat, Aliz plummets the sword down onto his neck, a clean slice through it, so that his head rolls into the rosebush, and his body falls limp beside my own.

If we left him, in a few hours, the strings between his severed neck would start to lace him together. His headless torso would pull itself towards its missing appendage, and after a few weeks, or sooner, depending on his strength, he'd regain consciousness. Such is the power of the undying.

"Forty seconds." Aliz's voice is trembling. Her eyes are bright red, and I know, without looking down, that my white dress is soaked in blood. She squeezes her eyes shut as she pulls the stake out of my stomach, and I let out a cry, unable to hold back tears. "It's all right," Aliz says. "I made it in time, I made it."

Before she explains what she means, I watch as she tears through Gustavsson's torso, cracking through his rib cage and grabbing his heart. It's smaller than I expected, still beating furiously. "Open your mouth," she says as she sinks her fangs into the organ, and blood drips straight onto my tongue. It burns the back of my throat. "Bite it," Aliz says, mouth covered in crimson. She swallows more, and as the wound on my chest starts to knit itself together, I sit up and bury my teeth into the heart's rubbery flesh.

Then the lines of the mark are tearing through me again. I try to stop drinking, pushing Aliz away as I feel them travelling up my torso, but she forces me, with a hand gripped behind my neck, to remain still. I swallow his blood and see my parents in the mortuary, their disfigured bodies the entryway into this awful world of monsters. Penny, beside them, offering me her condolences.

Penny, at the back of the church, telling me I can get my revenge. Handing me a train ticket to London, with the promise that I'll find out who did it once I'm *good enough*. Penny, sitting with me after my first mission, drying my tears, running her hand through my hair, promising me it'll get easier. *You'll get stronger.*

Then I see my parents again, out in the back garden, chatting about something I no longer remember, but with the sun, which so seldom shines in Scotland, washing their faces gold.

Aliz's arms are around me, her lips are on my head. She came back for me.

I hide my face in her chest. She squeezes me tight, kisses my hair again.

The itch on my neck vanishes.

She rubs my skin, and lets out an airy laugh, filled with disbelief. "It's gone!" she says. Aliz tilts my head up, and her eyes are bloodshot, but her irises are black. "We got rid of it, Cassie."

Her face falters, as though she remembers what adrenaline forced her to forget. "I wanted to tell you," I whisper.

"What's your name?" she asks, thumb running across my cheek. "Rebecca what?"

"Charity," I reply, before she bends down, pressing her lips to mine. The adrenaline, I think. Because now that the mark is gone, Aliz's feelings for me will disappear. That's what I think, at least, but as the kiss deepens, I forget about everything, drawing her as close to me as I can.

Only when I feel Gustavsson's stiff undead corpse beside me, do I stop, and Aliz looks at him. The cavity where his heart used to be has already begun to knit itself shut. "What do I do?" she whispers. I reach for the stake, covered still in my own blood, and hand it to her. Then I nod to the half-eaten heart on the ground next to us.

Her hands tremble before she slams it down into it, and in an instant, Sven Gustavsson's rotten existence turns into a cloud of smoke and dust.

epilogue

Dear Students,

On the 31st of October, during an unsanctioned event held in the hunting lodge, Professor Sven Gustavsson attacked a human student. The student suffered only minor injuries, but the Vampiric Council is conducting a thorough investigation into this issue. We take the safety of *all* our students, human or otherwise, extremely seriously, and will ensure that this remains an isolated blemish on this university's mission of coexistence.

If any of you had any inappropriate experiences with Professor Gustavsson, or any other member of faculty, please report it to campus security [here](). Those of you who were attending the Vampire Tradition in Music (U-34) will have a new professor by the end of November.

We apologise profusely for any distress this news may have caused.

Attentively,
Faust Nocth, Dean of Night and Humanities

"Come in," a voice calls from within the office, three full minutes after I knocked. Nocth has been swamped this past week, especially after a dozen humans demanded a refund of their tuition and left campus. I can't blame them for wanting to leave. The possibility of getting attacked by a professor was certainly not mentioned in the acceptance letter.

I walk in, the door creaking closed behind me. Faust Nocth glances up at me from his leather chair. He seems a little paler than usual, his black hair dishevelled. "I was waiting for you, Rebecca."

I stare him down. My nails hurt. A bizarre side effect of heartbreak, perhaps.

"Why have you been waiting for me?" I ask.

"I'd been hoping you'd have come by sooner, considering what happened at that little Halloween party."

I can picture Elia's face hearing someone call her Halloween Ball *little*. She might strangle Nocth for the offense. I blink at him, tilting my head to the side ever so slightly. "The only thing I did at the Halloween party was get rid of the Familiar's mark."

"And how did you do that?"

There's a stillness in his expression, as though a part of him doesn't want to know the answer. "By eating a vampire's heart. Wasn't particularly tasty, though."

"I see," he says. If he's disgusted by the mark's remedy, he doesn't show it. "You're free to leave Tynahine now, if you wish, Miss Charity. I'm certain Callisto will have a new mission for you already." I bite my lip. I haven't told anyone, except Elia, that I've left the hunters.

At least in my heart. Because now that I know they were behind my parents' murders, I can't walk away. I will hunt down every last *Stake* of Callisto, anyone who had a say in my recruitment. Penny included.

"What happened to me being *useful*?" I ask.

"You uncovered a Vassal," he says.

"Who *you* hired."

"I did," he concedes. "I first met Sven shortly before my cousin sired him. He was a different man back then."

"By different, you mean human."

"Yes, Rebecca." He sighs, leaning back in his chair before changing the subject. "You're free to study with us until the end of the semester. Penny did pay for four months of tuition, after all."

I shouldn't want to stay. Now that I finally have a target, a gateway to my revenge, I shouldn't hesitate. But I *am* hesitating. Elia, Julia, Ife, and Stephan are making me hesitate. I've never felt like I could grow roots anywhere, at least not in the last four years, and they've changed that. And if Aliz was still here, I wouldn't think twice.

She vanished on All Saints' Day, before I could apologise again or ask if that bloodstained kiss had been genuine. I texted her as soon as I realised she was gone. *I'm sorry. I can explain.* But she never replied, and whenever I look at our chat, she's always offline. I tried calling, too, and I let it ring for a whole minute, until I finally gave up.

"I'll stay," I whisper before I can fully think it through. Who knows where I'll get the money once the semester is up. But that's a problem for Future Rebecca. Then I think back to the email. To the little link to campus security. "Why don't you hire me?" I ask. "Who better to keep an eye on your vampires than a hunter?"

"If I were to hire you, Rebecca, I would have to reveal your identity," he says. "And then, how do you think my vampire students would feel about the fact that one of Callisto's murderers has been walking amongst them?"

I rest a palm on his desk, leaning closer. "I'm just a *Cross*-ranked hunter. Couldn't hurt a fly." I think about what he just said. Revealing my identity means admitting I lied to my friends. And once they know, they'll never look at me the same again. "But I suppose I'll stick to studying for now."

T‍YNARRICH'S DINING HALL is busy, but they've saved a seat for me. The sofa is old, warm leather ripped by a cat that used to hunt mice in the halls two decades ago. I plant myself next to Julia, while Ife and Stephan sit across from us.

On Julia's lap, as always, is her sketchbook. She's working on another landscape, and this time it's one I recognise. A forest with a footpath, bridges, old lampposts, and seagulls perched on branches. "Ness Islands?" I ask.

Her pencil stills, and she turns to stare at me.

"This is a real place?" she whispers. I look at the drawing a little closer.

"Aye," I say. "It's just twenty minutes from here." As I say this, I notice there's one island that's not entirely familiar. It's small, with a towering alder tree and a monolith just across from it. Before I can take a closer look, Julia turns to the next page, her face pale. I almost ask what's wrong, but I think I already know.

Just after the email about Gustavsson went out, Julia rushed into Traquair Hall to scrape Gustavsson's face, so perfectly captured by her paintbrush, off her mural.

Until now, if her drawings somehow managed to peer under the surface of someone close to her, like Ife with her rabbit, this *sight,* if it can be called that, was fascinating, even innocent. Gustavsson's appearance on her canvas, followed by his attack shortly after, has added a sinister layer to Julia's unusual skill. One she now appears to be terrified of.

Worse, perhaps, is the fact that all three of my friends saw me react to that mural in a way that did not make sense. And I still haven't told them why.

"It was you, wasn't it?" Ife whispers, after looking around the surrounding sofas, ensuring no one can hear her.

"*What* was me?" I ask.

"I saw you going into the Night Dean's office," Stephan says, scratching the back of his neck. "We're all convinced you're the one Gustavsson attacked."

"My mother works in the Council," Ife says, resting her hands on her lap. Her nails are decorated with daisies. "A few days ago, they had a hearing. Aliz Astra was there. She didn't say your name, but she did admit to killing Gustavsson to protect a human."

I swallow hard. The Council won't put her in jail for killing a Vassal, will they?

"She'll be fine," Julia says, recognising the muted panic in my expression.

"But why hasn't she come back?" I whisper, unable to keep the hurt out of my voice. And this is a question none of them have an answer for.

I KEEP WAKING in the middle of the night, certain I'll see her sitting on her coffin, slurping blood from a paper cup. But instead, I'm met with silence. So to escape this solitude, I start spending time at Elia's place.

"Your scent has changed," she says as she sits next to me, holding a glass of steaming blood.

"Really?" I'm pretty sure it hasn't *changed;* rather, it's gone back to how it used to smell before I had the Familiar's mark. But I watch her, waiting for her to reply.

She puts down her glass and lifts my wrist to her nose, inhaling slowly. "Petrichor," she finally says, after furrowing her brows. I've never heard anyone describe me like that before. And as I stare at her, feeling her proximity, my nails start to ache again.

There's pain in my stomach, too. A dark thing, lurking within me. Maybe I did some internal damage when I ate Gustavsson's heart. But I'm not sure if this is the sort of ailment I can visit a human doctor with.

"Has there been any sign of Penny?" I ask, trying to ignore the feeling.

As soon as my old mentor heard *The Book of Blood and Roses* was kept inside the memories of a ghost, she vanished. And I still don't know why she wanted it so frantically.

"No," Elia says. There's another question, one that I don't vocalise, but she answers, anyway. "And I haven't heard from Aliz, either."

We stay in a comfortable silence, and my eyes burn. The thorns may have left my skin, but now they've tightened around my chest, squeezing hard, digging into me every time I think of her.

Elia brushes a long strand of hair away from my face. "Your roots are coming in," she says.

The next morning, I take out my extensions in the on-campus hairdresser's, but keep the red hair. I'm not fully ready to let go of the girl Aliz fell in love with. Even if that love was never real in the first place.

She may be gone, she may have ignored my texts, but I can still feel her in the room. Her desk is a chaotic collection of unfinished essays and annotated books. I run my fingers over her cursive and picture her biting her pen. The false window glows with a crescent moon, partially hidden behind silver clouds.

I pull out my phone once I'm in bed. Aliz's profile picture hasn't changed. Her black sunglasses still rest on the tip of her nose as she stares, coyly, at the camera. She took that picture before meeting me. Back when I was a cold-blooded killer, and she had a dozen girls fighting for her attention.

The person I was before Aliz no longer exists.

Online

I stare at the word beneath her name. This is the first time she's been online in three weeks, but no reply comes my way. For a moment I imagine it. I imagine she calls me. Then I'd have her voice in my ear, and everything would be right again. Before reason can stop me, I start typing another message.

> I hope you're all right

I press my face into my pillow and lock my phone. It doesn't vibrate or light up. When I finally look at it again, she's left me on read.

THE ROOF OF Tynarrich Hall is windy. The moon is a perfect half crescent, ready to dip behind the black silhouette of the hills. I keep my hood up, jacket zipped above my neck. My breath turns into a pale cloud as I exhale. I've only been here for two months, yet I feel like a snake who's shed its skin and discovered an entirely different pattern forming underneath.

I don't know who this new version of myself will be yet. But I do know that I can't return to my old life. I glance down at my hands. I'm no longer just a weapon. There's more to me than my blood.

The wooden door to the roof creaks open, and I glance back from the railing. Every muscle in my body freezes when I see her standing there.

Aliz, who I haven't seen in three weeks, now stares back at me with wide eyes. The wind blows her white hair, and I wait for her to vanish, to reveal she's just a mirage. But she's real.

"So, this is where you've been hiding," she says, the wind muffling her words.

"Hiding?" is all I manage to say.

"You weren't in our room," she says. She takes a tentative step towards me. Then another. "I tried texting you back, but I couldn't find the words. When I got to our room, you were gone."

My eyes burn, and all I manage is to nod. She's here.

"I just got back an hour ago," she adds.

"Back?"

"From Hungary," she says. "Did Faust not tell you where I'd gone?" She pauses, and I see her cheeks redden. "You didn't notice I'd left?"

"I thought you didn't want to see me," I say. "You didn't reply to any of my texts."

"I just got my phone back today," she says. *She's here.*

"Right," I whisper. "How did the Council hearing go?" I ask. I need her to come closer.

"Better than I thought it would." She remains by the door, and I can't help but think she's just come here to say goodbye. She doesn't even owe me that much. She couldn't have possibly forgiven me yet.

"Did you see your parents?"

"Only my father's Familiar," she says. "Father was too busy, and my mother was indisposed."

Aliz finally walks across the roof and rests her hands on the railing, our arms almost touching. "I'm sorry," I say carefully. Her hands tighten on the rusting metal. "I wanted to tell you the truth. But I was a coward."

Aliz doesn't reply. Maybe she isn't ready for my apologies yet. But if she's only here to say goodbye, I must tell her. I think of what she asked me to say the last time we were up here, before our first kiss.

"I don't love you," I whisper.

It's the most honest lie I've ever told.

She doesn't say anything. The wind blows my hood down, red hair whipping my face.

"I know you said it was just the mark," I start, taking a careful breath. I have to say as much as I can before my mind gets in the way. "Okay, I'm sure the mark helped. And I know you don't feel the same. I'm not expecting you to forgive me, but you told me that the wind would carry away all the things we're not supposed to say." I bite my lip, digging my nails into my palms to keep my hands from shaking.

I feel her hand on my shoulder, gentle, and wait for her to say that it's too late. That the effects of the mark have worn off, and my lies washed away whatever feelings remained. Instead, her other hand nudges my chin up, her dark eyes glistening before she presses her lips to mine. "I don't love you, either," she whispers, between one kiss and the next. I don't move at first, unsure of what she's doing, of what's happening, before the kiss deepens.

"I can't tell if you're lying or not," I murmur, and she smiles against me, lips moving to my cheek.

"These three weeks have been hell. I didn't know I was capable of missing someone this much," she says, running her fingers through my hair. "Of loving someone this much. And it's so much clearer now, Rebecca."

I gasp at the sound of my own name. She pulls me into an embrace just as I feel my eyes burning, taking in her words. Her arms wrap around my back, and I squeeze her tight. Maybe it's a dream. Maybe I'll wake in the morning and it'll be over. But right now, it's real. She loves me—without a blood contract altering her thoughts.

"But I lied to you," I say, my voice small.

"I know," she whispers. "But Elia told me that you also saved her from a hunter. She told me everything. And I don't know what I would have done in your shoes." I wait for her to change her mind. My throat burns, and I tighten my grip on her.

We stay in this quiet embrace for minutes, not even a light drizzle pulling us apart. I sigh and look up at her. "Now what?" I ask.

"Do you want to be with me?"

I hesitate, just to tease her. "I guess I can put up with you a little while longer," I whisper as the wind blows, rustling her moonlit hair. I draw her closer, holding her tight.

I'll protect her.

I'll keep her safe. Safe from Callisto, safe from Penny, safe from the Vassals.

"That's very kind of you," she says, before our lips meet in another kiss, a kiss that cares not for the danger and consequences of what we're doing. A real kiss, an honest one, which promises many more to come.

The story will continue in

book two of the

CALLISTO CHRONICLES

acknowledgments

To my brilliant agent, Kiya Evans. Thank you for taking a chance on me and making my dreams come true. I couldn't be luckier to be on this journey with you (and Kris Jenner, of course). Here's to many more books.

The wonderful Ginger Clark, my agent across the pond, you've worked wonders. Team Mushens, and especially Liza Deblock and Alba Arnau (the best Catalan-London–based foreign-rights agent) for bringing my book to so many countries. To Txell from MB, *ets la millor*.

I couldn't be luckier to have not one but two fantastic editors. To Rebecca Hilsdon, from Penguin Michael Joseph, and Tricia Narwani, from Del Rey, thank you for your enthusiasm, for trusting me, for bringing out the best of this book. I feel as though the three of us are somehow telepathically connected, and I've grown so much as a writer since we started working together. And a special thank-you to Jorgie Bain at Michael Joseph and Ayesha Shibli at Del Rey.

My wonderful beta-readers: Thank you for going through the roughest versions of this book, in particular Kim and Paul. Kate,

Luce, and Yi-Jun, your feedback was invaluable, and the rest of the Scribes: our supreme leader Enty, Marnie, Caitlin, Lucy, Faith, Aly, Danni, Danny, Oli, Christina, and everyone else. Thank you. To my dear friends from Litopia, in particular Bev, for having read so many drafts of so many books, and to Kate, for your enthusiasm. To Pete, Johnny, Hannah, Jason, Rachel, PJ, Lyse, and everyone else who helped me shape my first pages into something decent. To l'Escola de Lletres of Tarragona, where I've learnt, and continue to learn, so much about this craft.

Toni, my earliest reader, my stage partner, thank you for putting up with me all these years, and for the notebook. Maria, who will be reading this in Spanish, I love you; you're the best friend anyone could have ever asked for. Thank you for the fountain pen. I'll use it wisely.

Mum, thank you for your unwavering belief in me. For letting me chase my dreams, however absurd. Dad, for telling everyone at the bar that your daughter is a writer, and to Juan for being a wonderful brother.

To my lovely Ade. Without you this book wouldn't exist. Thank you for your support all these years.

about the author

ANNIE SUMMERLEE lives in Spain with her partner, two cats, and a rescue dog. Her short stories have been featured in *404 Ink, Litro, So to Speak,* as well as other magazines and anthologies. She also writes in Catalan and Spanish.

about the type

  This book was set in Garamond, a typeface originally designed by the Parisian type cutter Claude Garamond (c. 1500–61). This version of Garamond was modeled on a 1592 specimen sheet from the Egenolff-Berner foundry, which was produced from types assumed to have been brought to Frankfurt by the punch cutter Jacques Sabon (c. 1520–80).

  Claude Garamond's distinguished romans and italics first appeared in *Opera Ciceronis* in 1543–44. The Garamond types are clear, open, and elegant.